PUSHKIN PRESS

'The Updike of his time... Zweig is a lucid writer,
and Bell renders his prose flawlessly'
New York Observer

'Stefan Zweig... was a talented writer and ultimately
another tragic victim of wartime despair. This rich
collection... confirms how good he could be'
Eileen Battersby, *Irish Times*

'An unjustly neglected literary master'
The Times

'Zweig is at once the literary heir of Chekhov, Conrad, and
Maupassant, with something of Schopenhauer's obser-
vational meditations on psychology thrown in'
Harvard Review

'The stories are as page-turning as they are subtle... Compelling'
Guardian

'Stefan Zweig's time of oblivion is over for good...
it's good to have him back'
Salman Rushdie, *The New York Times*

'He was capable of making the reader live other people's deepest experience—which is a moral education in itself. My advice
is that you should go out at once and buy his books'
Sunday Telegraph

'Zweig is the most adult of writers; civilised, urbane, but
never jaded or cynical; a realist who nonetheless believed
in the possibility—the necessity—of empathy'

Independent

'For far too long, our li
broken... it's tim

Los Angeles

'Zweig, prolific storyteller and embodiment of a vanished
Mitteleuropa, seems to be back, and in a big way'
The New York Times

'[During his lifetime] arguably the most widely read
and translated serious author in the world'
John Fowles

'One of the joys of recent years is the translation into English
of Stefan Zweig's stories. They have an astringency of outlook
and a mastery of scale that I find enormously enjoyable'
Edmund de Waal, author of *The Hare with Amber Eyes*

'The rediscovery of this extraordinary writer could well be on a par
with last year's refinding of the long-lost *Stoner*, by John Williams'
Simon Winchester, *Daily Telegraph*

'One of the masters of the short story'
Nicholas Lezard, *Guardian*

'Zweig belongs with those masters of the novella—
Maupassant, Turgenev, Chekhov'
Paul Bailey

STEFAN ZWEIG was born in 1881 in Vienna, into a wealthy Austrian-
Jewish family. He studied in Berlin and Vienna and was first known as a
poet and translator, then as a biographer. Zweig travelled widely, living in
Salzburg between the wars, and was an international bestseller with a string
of hugely popular works including *Letter from an Unknown Woman*, *Amok* and
Fear. In 1934, with the rise of Nazism, he moved to London, and later on
to Bath, taking British citizenship after the outbreak of the Second World
War. With the fall of France in 1940 Zweig left Britain for New York, before
settling in Brazil, where in 1942 he and his wife were found dead in an
apparent double suicide. Much of his work is available from Pushkin Press.

The Collected Novellas of STEFAN ZWEIG

Translated from the German
by Anthea Bell and Alexander Starritt

PUSHKIN PRESS

Pushkin Press
71–75 Shelton Street
London WC2H 9JQ

Original German texts © ATRIUM PRESS Ltd, London.

A Chess Story, Journey into the Past and *Confusion* used courtesy of New York Review Books in the USA and Canada, where *A Chess Story* is published by New York Review Books as *Chess Story*

Burning Secret first published in German as *Brennendes Geheimnis* in 1911
English translation © Anthea Bell 2008
First published by Pushkin Press in 2008

A Chess Story first published in German as *Schachnovelle* in 1943
English translation © Alexander Starritt 2013
First published by Pushkin Press in 2001
This translation first published in 2013

Fear first published in German as *Angst* in 1913
English translation © Anthea Bell 2010

The translation of this work was supported by a grant from the Goethe-Institut, which is funded by the German Ministry of Foreign Affairs.
First published by Pushkin Press in 2010

Confusion first published in German as *Verwirrung der Gefuehle* in 1927
English translation © Anthea Bell 2002
First published by Pushkin Press in 2002

Journey into the Past first published in German as *Widerstand der Wirklichkeit* in 1987
English translation © Anthea Bell 2009
First published by Pushkin Press in 2009

This edition first published by Pushkin Press in 2021

9 8 7 6 5 4 3 2

ISBN 13: 978-1-78227-707-1

All rights reserved. No part of this publication may be reproduced, stored in a retrieval system or transmitted in any form or by any means, electronic, mechanical, photocopying, recording or otherwise, without prior permission in writing from Pushkin Press

Set in 10.5 on 14 Monotype Baskerville by Tetragon, London
Proudly printed and bound in Great Britain by TJ International, Padstow, Cornwall on Munken Premium Cream 80gsm

www.pushkinpress.com

CONTENTS

BURNING SECRET

I

The Partner

T HE SHRILL WHISTLE of the locomotive sounded; the train had reached Semmering. For a moment the black carriages stood still in the silvery light of the heights up here, allowing a motley assortment of passengers to get out and others to board the train. Voices were raised in altercation, then the engine uttered its hoarse cry again and carried the black chain of carriages away, rattling, into the cavernous tunnel. Once again the pure, clear view of the landscape lay spread out, a backdrop swept clean by rain carried on a wet wind.

One of the new arrivals, a young man who drew admiring glances with his good clothes and the natural ease of his gait, was quick to get ahead of the others by taking a cab to his hotel. The horses clip-clopped uphill along the road at their leisure. Spring was in the air. Those white clouds that are seen only in May and June sailed past in the sky, a company clad all in white, still young and flighty themselves, playfully chasing over the blue firmament, hiding suddenly behind high mountains, embracing and separating again, sometimes crumpling up like handkerchiefs, sometimes fraying into shreds, and finally playing a practical joke on the mountains as they settled on their heads like white caps. Up here the wind too was restless as it shook the scanty trees, still wet with rain, so violently that they creaked slightly at the joints, while a thousand drops sprayed off them like sparks. And at times the cool scent of the snow seemed to drift down from the mountains, both sweet and sharp as you breathed it in. Everything in the air and on the earth was in movement, seething with impatience. Quietly snorting, the horses trotted on along the road, going downhill now, and the sound of their bells went far ahead of them.

The first thing the young man did on reaching the hotel was to look through the list of guests staying there. He was quickly disappointed. Why did I come? he began to ask himself restlessly. Staying up here in the mountains alone, without congenial companions, why, it's worse than being at the office. I'm obviously either too early or too late in the season. I'm always out of luck with my holidays; I never find anyone I know among the other guests. It would be nice if there were at least a few ladies; then a little light-hearted flirtation might help me to while away a week here agreeably enough.

The young man, a baron from a not particularly illustrious noble family in the Austrian civil service, where he was employed himself, had taken this little holiday without feeling any real need for one, mainly because all his colleagues were away for the spring break, and he didn't feel like making the office a present of his week off. Although he was not without inner resources, he was very gregarious by nature, which made him popular. He was welcome everywhere he went, and was well aware of his inability to tolerate solitude. He felt no inclination to be alone and avoided it as far as possible; he didn't really want to become any better acquainted with himself. He knew that, if he was to show his talents to best advantage, he needed to strike sparks off other people to fan the flames of warmth and exuberance in his heart. On his own he was frosty, no use to himself at all, like a match left lying in its box.

In downcast mood, he paced up and down the empty hotel lobby, now leafing casually through the newspapers, now picking out a waltz on the piano in the music-room, but he couldn't get the rhythm of it right. Finally he sat down, feeling dejected, looking at the darkness as it slowly fell and the grey vapours of the mist drifting out of the spruce trees. He wasted an idle, nervous hour in this way, and then took refuge in the dining-room.

Only a few tables were occupied, and he cast a fleeting glance over them. Still no luck! No one he really knew, only—he casually returned a greeting—a racehorse trainer here, a face he'd seen in the Ringstrasse there, that was all. No ladies, nothing to suggest the chance of even a fleeting adventure. He felt increasingly bad-tempered and impatient. He was the kind of young man whose handsome face has brought him plenty of success in the past and is now ever-ready for a new encounter, a fresh experience, always eager to set off into the unknown territory of a little adventure, never taken by surprise because he has worked out everything in advance and is waiting to see what happens, a man who will never overlook any erotic opportunity, whose first glance probes every woman's sensuality and explores it, without discriminating between his friend's wife and the parlour-maid who opens the door to him. Such men are described with a certain facile contempt as lady-killers, but the term has a nugget of truthful observation in it, for in fact all the passionate instincts of the chase are present in their ceaseless vigilance: the stalking of the prey, the excitement and mental cruelty of the kill. They are constantly on the alert, always ready and willing to follow the trail of an adventure to the very edge of the abyss. They are full of passion all the time, but it is the passion of a gambler rather than a lover, cold, calculating and dangerous. Some are so persistent that their whole lives, long after their youth is spent, are made an eternal adventure by this expectation. Each of their days is resolved into hundreds of small sensual experiences—a look exchanged in passing, a fleeting smile, knees

11

brushing together as a couple sit opposite each other—and the year, in its own turn, dissolves into hundreds of such days in which sensuous experience is the constantly flowing, nourishing, inspiring source of life.

Well, there were no partners for a game here; the hunter could see that at once. And there is no worse frustration for a player of games than to sit at the green baize table with his cards in his hand, conscious of his superior skill, waiting in vain for a partner. The Baron called for a newspaper. Gloomily, he ran his eye over the newsprint, but his thoughts were sluggish, stumbling clumsily after the words like a drunk.

Then he heard the rustle of a dress behind him, and a voice, slightly irritated and with an affected accent, saying, "*Mais tais-toi donc, Edgar!*" A silk gown whispered in passing his table, a tall, voluptuous figure moved by like a shadow, and behind that figure came a pale little boy in a black velvet suit, who looked at him curiously. The couple sat down at their reserved table opposite him, the child visibly trying hard to behave correctly, an effort apparently belied by the dark restlessness in his eyes. The lady, on whom alone the young Baron's attention was bent, was very *soignée*, dressed with obvious good taste, and what was more, she was a type he liked very much, one of those rather voluptuous Jewish women just before the age of over-maturity, and obviously passionate, but with enough experience to conceal her temperament behind a façade of elegant melancholy. At first he avoided looking into her eyes, and merely admired the beautifully traced line of their brows, a pure curve above a delicate nose that did in fact betray her race, but was so finely shaped that it made her profile keen and interesting. Her hair, like all the other feminine features of her generous body, was strikingly luxuriant, her beauty seemed to have become ostentatiously complacent in the self-assured certainty that she was widely admired. She gave her order in a very low voice, reproved the boy for playing with his fork—all of this with apparent indifference to the cautiously insinuating glances cast at her by the Baron, whom she did not seem to notice at all, although it was only his alert watchfulness that obliged her to exercise such careful control.

The Baron's gloomy face had suddenly brightened. Deep down, his nerves were at work invigorating it, smoothing out lines, tensing muscles, while he sat up very straight and a sparkle came into his eyes. He himself was not unlike those women who need the presence of a man if they are to exert their whole power. Only sensuous attraction could stimulate his energy to its full force. The huntsman in him scented prey. Challengingly, his eyes now sought to meet hers, which sometimes briefly returned his gaze with sparkling indecision as she looked past him, but never gave a clear, outright answer. He thought he also detected the trace of a smile beginning to play around her mouth now and then, but none of that was certain, and its very uncertainty aroused him. The one thing that did strike him as promising was her constant refusal to look him in the eye, betraying both resistance and self-consciousness, and then there was the curiously painstaking way she talked to her child, which was clearly meant for an onlooker. Her persistent façade of calm, he felt, meant in itself that she was beginning to feel troubled. He too was excited; the game had begun. He lingered over his dinner, kept his eyes on the woman almost constantly for half-an-hour, until he had traced every contour of her face, invisibly touching every part of her opulent body. Outside, oppressive darkness was falling, the forests sighed as if in childish alarm as huge rain clouds now reached grey hands out for them, darker and darker shadows made their way into the room, and its occupants seemed ever more closely drawn together by the silence. The mother's conversation with her child, he noticed, was becoming increasingly forced and artificial under the menace of that silence, and soon, he felt, it would dry up entirely. He decided to try testing the waters a little. He was the first to rise and, looking past her and at the landscape outside, went slowly to the door. Once there he quickly turned his head as if he had forgotten something—and caught her interested glance bent on him.

It attracted him. He waited in the lobby. She soon came out too, holding the boy's hand, leafed through the journals as she was passing and pointed out some pictures to the child. But when the Baron, as if by chance, came up to the table, apparently to choose a journal for himself but really to look more deeply into the moist brightness of her eyes, perhaps even strike up a conversation, she turned away, tapping her son lightly on the shoulder. *"Viens, Edgar! Au lit!"* She passed him coolly, skirts rustling. A little disappointed, the Baron watched her go. He had really expected to get to know her better this evening, and her brusque manner was a setback. But after all, her resistance was intriguing, and his very uncertainty inflamed his desire. In any case, he had found his partner, and the game could begin.

2

A Swift Friendship

W HEN THE BARON came into the lobby the next morning
he saw the son of his fair unknown engaged in earnest
conversation with the two lift-boys, showing them the illustrations
in a Wild West book by Karl May. His mama was not there;
she must still be busy dressing. Only now did the Baron really
look at the child. He was a shy, awkward, nervous boy of about
twelve with fidgety movements and dark, darting eyes. Like many
children of that age, he gave the impression of being alarmed,
as if he had just been abruptly woken from sleep and suddenly
put down in strange surroundings. His face was not unattractive,
but still unformed; the struggle between man and boy seemed
only just about to begin, and his features were not yet kneaded
into shape, no distinct lines had emerged, it was merely a face of
mingled pallor and uncertainty. In addition, he was at just that
awkward age when children never fit into their clothes properly,
sleeves and trousers hang loose around their thin arms and legs,
and vanity has not yet shown them the wisdom of making the
best of their appearance.

Wandering around down here in a state of indecision, the
boy made a pitiful impression. He was getting in everyone's
way. At one moment the receptionist, whom he seemed to be
bothering with all kinds of questions, pushed him aside; at the
next he was making a nuisance of himself at the hotel entrance.
Obviously he wasn't on friendly terms with anyone here. In his

childish need for chatter he was trying to ingratiate himself with the hotel staff, who talked to him if they happened to have time, but broke off the conversation at once when an adult appeared or there was real work to be done. Smiling and interested, the Baron watched the unfortunate boy looking curiously at everyone, although they all avoided him. Once he himself received one of those curious glances, but the boy's black eyes immediately veiled their alarmed gaze as soon as he caught them in the act of looking, and retreated behind lowered lids. This amused the Baron. The boy began to intrigue him, and he wondered if this child, who was obviously shy out of mere timidity, might not be a good go-between, offering the quickest way of access to his mother. It was worth trying, anyway. Unobtrusively, he followed the boy, who was loitering just outside the door again, caressing a white horse's pink nostrils in his childish need for affection, until yet again—he really did have back luck—the driver of the carriage told him rather brusquely to get out of the way. Now he was standing around once more, bored, his feelings hurt, with his vacant and rather sad gaze. The Baron spoke to him.

"Well, young man, and how do you like it here?" he began suddenly, taking care to keep his tone of voice as jovial as possible.

The boy went red as beetroot and looked up in alarm. He took the proffered hand almost fearfully, squirming with embarrassment. It was the first time a strange gentleman had ever struck up a conversation with him.

"It's very nice, thank you," he managed to stammer. The last two words were choked out rather than spoken.

"I'm surprised to hear that," said the Baron, laughing. "This is really a dull sort of place, particularly for a young man like you. What do you do with yourself all day?"

The boy was still too confused to answer quickly. Was it really possible that this elegant stranger wanted to talk, when no one else bothered about him? The idea made him both shy and proud. Making an effort, he pulled himself together.

"Oh, I read books, and we go for a lot of walks. And sometimes Mama and I go for a drive in the carriage. I'm supposed to be convalescing here, you see, I've been ill. So I have to sit in the sun a lot too, that's what the doctor said."

He uttered the last words with a fair degree of confidence. Children are always proud of an illness, knowing that danger makes them doubly important to the rest of their family.

"Yes, the sunlight's good for young men like you, it'll soon have you tanned and brown. All the same, you don't want to be sitting around all day. A young fellow like you should be going around in high spirits, kicking up a few larks. It looks to me as if you're too well-behaved—something of a bookworm, eh, with that big fat book under your arm? When I think what a young rascal I was at your age, coming home every evening with my trousers torn! You don't want to be *too* good, you know!"

Involuntarily, the child had to smile, and that did away with his fears. He would have liked to say something, but anything that occurred to him seemed too bold and confident in front of this amiable stranger who addressed him in such friendly tones. He had never been a forward boy, he was always rather diffident, and so his pleasure and shame now had him terribly bewildered. He longed to continue the conversation, but he couldn't think of anything to say. Fortunately the hotel's big, tawny St Bernard dog came along just then, sniffed them both, and was happy to be patted.

"Do you like dogs?" asked the Baron,

"Oh, yes, my grandmama has one at her villa in Baden, and when we're staying there he always spends all day with me. But that's just in summer, when we're visiting."

"We must have a couple of dozen dogs at home on our estate. I'll tell you what, if you're good while you're here I'll give you one of them. He's a brown dog with white ears, a young one. Would you like that?"

The child flushed red with delight. "Oh yes!" It burst out of him, warm and enthusiastic. Next moment, however, second thoughts set in. Now he sounded anxious and almost alarmed.

"But Mama would never let me. She says she won't have a dog at home because they make too much trouble."

The Baron smiled. At last the conversation had come around to Mama.

"Is your Mama so strict?"

The boy thought about it, looked up at him for a second as if wondering whether this strange gentleman was really to be trusted. He answered cautiously.

"No, Mama isn't strict. Just now she lets me do anything I like because I've been ill. Maybe she'll even let me have a dog."

"Shall I ask her?"

"Oh yes, please do," cried the boy happily. "Then I'm sure Mama will let me have him. What does he look like? You said white ears, didn't you? Can he fetch?"

"Yes, he can do all sorts of things." The Baron had to smile at the light he had kindled so quickly in the child's eyes. All of a sudden the boy's initial self-consciousness was gone, and he was bubbling over with the passionate enthusiasm that his timidity had held in check. It was an instant transformation: the shy, anxious child of a moment ago was now a cheerful boy. If only the mother were the same, the Baron couldn't help thinking, so passionate behind her show of diffidence! But the boy was already firing off questions at him.

"What's the dog's name?"

"Diamond."

"Diamond," the child said, crowing with delight. He was impelled to laugh and crow at every word that was spoken, intoxicated by the unexpected experience of having someone make friends with him. The Baron himself was surprised by his swift success, and decided to strike while the iron was hot. He invited the boy to go for a walk with him, and the poor child, starved of any convivial company for weeks, was enchanted by the idea. He chattered away, innocently providing all the information his new friend wanted and enticed out of him by means of small, apparently casual questions. Soon the Baron knew all about the family, more particularly that Edgar was the only son of a Viennese lawyer, obviously a member of the prosperous Jewish middle class. And through further skilful questioning he quickly discovered that the child's mother had expressed herself far from happy with their stay in Semmering, and had complained of the lack of congenial company. He even thought he could detect, from Edgar's evasive answer to the question of whether Mama was very fond of Papa, that all was not entirely well in that quarter. He was almost ashamed of the ease with which he elicited all these little family secrets from the unsuspecting boy, for Edgar, very proud to think that what he said could interest a grown-up, positively pressed his confidences on his new friend. His childish heart throbbed with pride to be seen publicly on such close terms of friendship with a grown man—for as they walked along the Baron had laid an arm around his shoulders—and gradually forgot his own childhood, talking as freely as he would to a boy of his own age. Edgar was very intelligent, as his conversation showed: rather precocious, like most sickly children who have spent a great deal of time with adults, and was clearly highly strung, inclined to be either fervently affectionate or hostile. He did not seem to adopt a moderate stance to anything, and spoke of everyone or everything either with enthusiasm or a dislike so violent that it distorted his face, making him look almost vicious and ugly. Something wild and erratic, perhaps as a result of the illness from which he had only just recovered, gave fanatical fire to what he said, and it seemed that his awkwardness was merely fear, suppressed with difficulty, of his own passionate nature.

The Baron easily won his confidence. Just half-an-hour, and he had that hot and restless heart in his hands. It is so extraordinarily easy to deceive children, unsuspecting creatures whose affections are so seldom sought. He had only to lose himself in the past, and childish talk came to him so naturally and easily that the boy himself soon thought of him as one of his own kind. After only a few minutes, any sense of distance between them was gone. Edgar was blissfully happy to have found a friend so suddenly in this isolated place, and what a friend! All his companions in Vienna were forgotten, the little boys with their reedy voices and artless chatter, those images had been swept away by this one hour in his life! His entire passionate enthusiasm was now devoted to his new, his great friend, and his heart swelled with pride when, as the Baron said goodbye, he suggested meeting again tomorrow morning. And then his new friend waved as he walked away, just like a brother. That moment was, perhaps, the best of Edgar's life. It is so very easy to deceive children.

The Baron smiled as the boy stormed away. He had found his go-between. Now, he knew, the child would pester his mother to the point of exhaustion with his stories, repeating every single word—and he remembered, complacently, how cleverly he had woven a few compliments intended for her into the conversation, always speaking of Edgar's "beautiful Mama". He was certain that the talkative boy wouldn't rest until he had brought his friend and his mother together. He didn't have to life a finger to decrease the distance between himself and the fair unknown, he could dream happily now as he looked at the landscape, for he knew that a pair of hot, childish hands was building him a bridge to her heart.

3

Trio

T HE PLAN, as it turned out an hour later, was excellent
and had succeeded down to the very last detail. When the
young Baron entered the dining-room, deliberately arriving a
little late, Edgar jumped up from his chair, greeted him eagerly
with a happy smile, and waved. At the same time he tugged his
mother's sleeve, speaking to her fast and excitedly, and unmistakably pointing to the Baron. Blushing and looking embarrassed,
she reproved him for his over-exuberant conduct, but she could
not avoid satisfying her son's demands by glancing at the Baron
once, which he instantly took as his chance to give her a respectful bow. He had made her acquaintance. She had to respond
to the bow, but from now on kept her head bent further over
her plate and was careful not to look his way again all through
dinner. Edgar, on the contrary, kept looking at him all the time,
and once even tried to call something over to the Baron's table, a
piece of bad manners for which his mother scolded him soundly.
When they had finished their meal Edgar was told it was time
for him to go to bed, and there was much whispering between
him and his Mama, the final outcome being that his ardent wish
to go over to the other table and pay his respects to his friend
was granted. The Baron said a few kind things that made the
child's eyes sparkle again, and talked to him for a few minutes.
But suddenly, with a skilful move of his own, he rose and went
over to the other table, congratulated his slightly embarrassed

fellow-guest on her clever and intelligent son, spoke warmly of the morning he had passed so pleasantly with him—Edgar was scarlet with pride and delight—and finally inquired after the boy's state of health in such detail and with so many questions that the mother was bound to answer him. And so, inevitably, they drifted into a conversation of some length, to which the boy listened happily and with a kind of awe. The Baron introduced himself, and thought that his resounding name had made a certain impression on the woman's vanity. At least, she was remarkably civil to him, although observing all decorum; she even left the table soon for the sake of the boy, as she apologetically added.

Edgar protested vigorously that he wasn't tired, he was ready to stay up all night. But his mother had already given the Baron her hand, which he kissed respectfully.

Edgar slept badly that night, full of a mixture of happiness and childish desperation. Something new had come into his existence today. For the first time he had become a part of adult life. Half-asleep, he forgot his own childhood state and felt that he too was suddenly grown up. Until now, brought up as a lonely and often sickly child, he had had few friends. There had been no one to satisfy his need for affection but his parents, who took little notice of him, and the servants. And the strength of a love is always misjudged if we evaluate it only by its immediate cause and not the stress that went before it, the dark and hollow space full of disappointment and loneliness that precedes all the great events in the heart's history. A great, unused capacity for emotion had been lying in wait, and now it raced with outstretched arms towards the first person who seemed to deserve it. Edgar lay in the dark, happy and bewildered, he wanted to laugh and couldn't help crying. For he loved this man as he had never loved a friend, or his father and mother, or even God. The whole immature passion of his early years now clung to the image of a man even whose name he had not known two hours ago.

But he was clever enough not to let the unexpected, unique nature of his new friendship distress him. What bewildered him so much was his sense of his own unworthiness, his insignificance. Am I good enough for him, he wondered, tormenting himself, a boy of twelve who still has to go to school and is sent to bed before anyone else in the evening? What can I mean to him, what can I give him? It was this painfully felt inability to find a means of showing his emotions that made him unhappy. Usually, when he decided that he liked another boy, the first thing he did was to share the few treasures in his desk with him, stamps and stones, the possessions of childhood, but all these things, which only yesterday had seemed full of importance and uncommonly attractive, now suddenly appeared to him devalued, foolish, contemptible. How could he offer such things to this new friend whom he dared not even call by his first name, how could he find a way, an opportunity to show his feelings? More and more, he felt how painful it was to be little, only half-grown, immature, a child of twelve, and he had never before hated childhood so violently, or longed so much to wake up a different person, the person he dreamed of being: tall and strong, a man, a grown-up like the others.

His first vivid dreams of that new world of adulthood wove their way into these troubled thoughts. Edgar fell asleep at last with a smile, but all the same, the memory of tomorrow's promise to meet his friend undermined his sleep. He woke with a start at seven, afraid of being late. He quickly dressed, went to his mother's room to say good morning—she was startled, since she usually had some difficulty in getting him out of bed—and ran downstairs before she could ask any questions. Then he hung about impatiently until nine and forgot to have any breakfast;

the only thing in his head was that he mustn't keep his friend waiting for their walk.

At nine-thirty the Baron came strolling nonchalantly up at last. Of course he had long since forgotten about the walk, but now that the boy eagerly went up to him he had to smile at such enthusiasm, and showed that he was ready to keep his promise. He took the boy's arm again and walked about in the lobby with the beaming child, although he gently but firmly declined to set out on their expedition together just yet. He seemed to be waiting for something, or at least so his eyes suggested as they kept going to the doors. Suddenly he stood up very straight. Edgar's Mama had come in, and went up to the two of them with a friendly expression, returning the Baron's greeting. She smiled and nodded when she heard about the planned walk, which Edgar had kept from her as something too precious to be told, but soon agreed to the Baron's invitation to her to join them. Edgar immediately looked sullen and bit his lip. What a nuisance that she had to come in just now! That walk had been for him alone, and if he had introduced his friend to his Mama it was only out of kindness, it didn't mean that he wanted to share him. Something like jealousy was already at work in him when he saw the Baron speaking to his mother in such a friendly way.

So then the three of them went out walking, and the child's dangerous sense of his own importance, his sudden significance, was reinforced by the obvious interest both the adults showed in him. Edgar was almost exclusively the subject of their conversation, in which his mother expressed a rather feigned concern for his pallor and highly-strung nerves, while the Baron, smiling, made light of these ideas and praised the pleasant manners of his new "friend", as he called him. This was Edgar's finest hour. He had rights that no one had ever allowed him in the course of his childhood before. He was permitted to join in the conversation without being immediately told to keep quiet, he was even allowed to express all kinds of bold wishes which had always met with a poor reception before. And it was not surprising that his deceptive feeling of being grown up himself grew and flourished. In his happy dreams, childhood was left behind, like a garment he had outgrown and thrown away.

At lunch the Baron accepted the invitation of Edgar's increasingly friendly mother and joined them at their table. They were now all together, not sitting opposite each other, acquaintances had become friends. The trio was in full swing, and the three voices of man, woman, and child chimed happily together.

4

Into the Attack

T HE IMPATIENT HUNTSMAN now felt that it was time to approach his prey. He did not like the informal, harmonious tone that they had adopted. It was all very well for the three of them to talk comfortably together, but talk, after all, was not his intention. And he knew that the element of companionship, a masquerade hiding his desire, kept delaying the erotic encounter between man and woman, depriving his words of their ardour and his attack of its fire. He did not want their conversation to make her forget his real aim, which, he felt sure, she had already understood.

It was very likely that he would not pursue his quarry in vain. She was at that crucial age when a woman begins to regret having stayed faithful to a husband she never really loved, when the glowing sunset colours of her beauty offer her one last, urgent choice between maternal and feminine love. At such a moment a life that seemed to have chosen its course long ago is questioned once again, for the last time the magic compass needle of the will hovers between final resignation and the hope of erotic experience. Then a woman is confronted with a dangerous decision: does she live her own life or live for her children? And the Baron, who had a keen eye for these things, thought he saw in her just that dangerous hesitation between the fire of life and self-sacrifice. She kept forgetting to bring her husband into the conversation. He obviously appeared to satisfy only her outer needs, not the snobbish ambitions aroused in her by an elegant way of life, and deep inside her she really knew very little about her child. A trace of boredom, appearing as veiled melancholy in her dark eyes, lay over her life and muted her sensuality. The Baron decided to move fast, but at the same time without any appearance of haste. On the contrary, he himself intended to be outwardly indifferent to this new friendship; he wanted her to court him, although in fact he was the suitor. He planned to display a certain arrogance, casting a strong light on the difference in social station between them, and he was intrigued by the idea of gaining possession of that beautiful, opulent, voluptuous body merely by means of exploiting that arrogance, outward appearances, a fine-sounding aristocratic name and cold manners.

The passionate game was already beginning to arouse him, so he forced himself to be cautious. He spent the afternoon in his room, pleasantly aware of being missed and wanted. However, his absence was not felt so much by her, his real target, as by the poor boy, to whom it was a torment. Edgar felt dreadfully lost and helpless, and kept waiting for his friend all afternoon with his own characteristic loyalty. Going out or doing something on his own would have seemed like an offence against their friendship. He wandered aimlessly around the hotel corridors, and the later it grew the fuller his heart brimmed with unhappiness. In his restless imagination he was already dreaming of an accident, or some injury that he had unwittingly inflicted, and he was close to tears of impatience and anxiety.

So when the Baron appeared at dinner that evening, he met with a joyous reception. Ignoring the admonishment of his mother and the surprise of the other guests, Edgar jumped up, ran to him and stormily flung his thin arms around the Baron's chest. "Where were you? Where have you been?" he cried, the

words tumbling out. "We've been looking for you everywhere."
His mother blushed at being involved in this unwelcome way,
and said rather sternly, "*Sois sage, Edgar. Assieds-toi!*" (She always
spoke French to him, although it was not a language that came
naturally to her, and she could easily find herself on shaky
ground in a conversation of any length.) Edgar obeyed, but
would not stop asking the Baron questions. "Don't forget," his
mother added, "that the Baron can do as he likes. Perhaps our
company bores him." This time she brought herself into it on
purpose, and the Baron was pleased to hear her fishing for a
compliment with that reproach to her son.

The huntsman in him was aroused. He was intoxicated,
excited to have found the right trail so quickly, to feel that the
game was close to his gun. His eyes gleamed, the blood flowed
easily through his veins, the words sprang from his lips with an
effervescence that he himself could not explain. He was, like
everyone of a strongly erotic disposition, twice as good, twice
as much himself when he knew that women liked him, just as
many actors find their most ardent vein when they sense that
they have cast their spell over the audience, the breathing mass of
spectators before them. He had always been a good story-teller,
able to conjure up vivid images, but today he excelled himself,
while now and then drinking a glass of the champagne that he
had ordered in honour of this new friendship. He told tales of
hunts in India in which he had taken part, as the guest of an
aristocratic and distinguished English friend, cleverly choosing
this subject as harmless although, on the other hand, he realized
that anything exotic and naturally beyond her reach excited
this woman. But the hearer whom he really enchanted with
his stories was Edgar, whose eyes were bright with enthusiasm.
He forgot to eat and gazed at the story-teller, drinking only the
words from his lips. He had never hoped to see someone in the

flesh who had known the amazing things he read about in his books: the big game hunts, the brown people, the Hindus, the terrible wheel of the juggernaut crushing thousands under its rim. Until now he had never stopped to think that such people really existed, he knew so little about those fairy-tale lands, and that moment lit a great fire in him for the first time. He couldn't take his eyes off his friend, he stared with bated breath at the hands that had killed a tiger and were now there before him. He hardly liked to ask a question, and when he did his voice was feverishly excited. His quick imagination kept conjuring up in his mind's eye the pictures that went with those stories, he saw his friend high up on an elephant with a purple cloth over it, brown men to right and left wearing gorgeous turbans, and then, suddenly, the tiger leaping out of the jungle, fangs bared, plunging its claws into the elephant's trunk. Now the Baron told an even more interesting tale of a cunning way to catch elephants, by getting old, tame beasts to lure the young, wild, high-spirited elephants into enclosures, and the child's eyes flashed. And then—Edgar felt as if a knife were suddenly coming down in front of him—Mama suddenly said, glancing at the time, "*Neuf heures! Au lit!*"

Edgar turned pale with horror. Being sent to bed is a terrible command to all children, because it means the most public possible humiliation in front of adults, the confession that they bear the stigma of childhood, of being small and having a child's need for sleep. But such shame was even more terrible at this fascinating moment, when it meant he must miss hearing such wonderful things.

"Just one more story, Mama, let me listen to one more, let me hear about the elephants!"

He was about to begin begging, but then he remembered his new dignity as a grown man. He ventured just one attempt, but his mother was remarkably strict today. "No, it's late already. You go up to bed. *Sois sage, Edgar.* I'll tell you all the Baron's stories afterwards."

Edgar hesitated. His mother usually accompanied him when he went to bed, but he wasn't going to beg in front of his friend. In his childish pride he tried salvaging this pathetic retreat by putting a gloss of free will on it.

"Well, Mama, then you must tell me everything! All about the elephants and everything else!"

"Yes, I will, my dear."

"And at once! Later this evening!"

"Yes, yes, but off you go to bed now. Off you go!" Edgar admired himself for succeeding in shaking hands with the Baron and his Mama without going red in the face, although the sob was already rising in his throat. The Baron ruffled his hair in a friendly manner, which brought a smile to Edgar's tense face. But then he had to reach the door in a hurry, or they would have seen big tears rolling down his cheeks.

5

The Elephants

H IS MOTHER STAYED downstairs sitting at the table with
the Baron for a while, but they were no longer discussing
elephants and hunts. Now that the boy had left them, a slightly
sultry note and a sudden touch of awkwardness entered their
conversation. Finally they went out into the lobby and sat down
in a corner. The Baron sparkled more brilliantly than ever, she
herself was a little merry after those few glasses of champagne,
and so the conversation quickly assumed a dangerous character.
The Baron could not really be called handsome, he was merely
young and looked very masculine with his brown, mobile,
boyish face and short hair, enchanting her with his lively and
almost over-familiar movements. By now she liked to see him
at close quarters, and no longer feared his glance. But gradually
a tone of audacity crept into what he was saying, bewildering
her slightly, rather as if he were reaching out for her body,
touching it and then letting go again. There was something
extraordinarily desirable about it all that sent the blood flying to
her cheeks. But then he laughed again, a light, unforced, boyish
laugh which gave all these little liberties the easy appearance
of childlike play. Sometimes she felt as if she ought to stop him
with a curt word of reproof, but as she was naturally flirtatious
she was only intrigued by those suggestive little remarks, and
waited for more of them. Enchanted by the daring game, she
ended up trying to emulate him. She cast him little fluttering

glances full of promise, was already offering herself in words and gestures, even allowed him to come closer. She sensed the proximity of his voice, she sometimes felt his breath warmly caressing her shoulders. Like all gamblers, they forgot the time and lost themselves so entirely in ardent conversation that only when the lights in the lobby were dimmed at midnight did they come to their senses with a start.

She immediately jumped up, obeying her first impulse of alarm, and suddenly realized how daringly far she had ventured to go. She was not unaccustomed to playing with fire, but now her excited instincts felt how close this game was to becoming serious. With a shudder, she realized that she did not feel entirely sure of herself, that something in her was beginning to slide away, moving alarmingly close to the whirlpool. Her head was full of a bewildering mixture of fear, wine, and risqué talk, and a muted, mindless anxiety came over her, the anxiety she had felt several times in her life before at such dangerous moments, although never before had it been so vertiginous and violent. "Good night, good night. We'll meet tomorrow morning," she said hastily, about to run away, not so much from him as from the danger of that moment and a new, strange uncertainty in herself. But the Baron took the hand she had offered in farewell and held it with gentle force, kissing it not just once in the correct way but four or five times, his quivering lips moving from her delicate fingertips to her wrist, and with a slight frisson she felt his rough moustache tickle the back of her hand. A kind of warm, oppressive sensation flew from her hand along her veins and through her whole body. Hot alarm flared up, hammering menacingly at her temples, her head was burning, and the fear, the pointless fear now ran right through her. She quickly withdrew her hand.

"Ah, stay a little longer," whispered the Baron. But she was already hurrying away, with awkward haste that made her fear and confusion very obvious. The excitement that her partner in conversation wanted to arouse filled her now, she felt that everything in her was topsy-turvy. She was driven by her ardent, cruel fear that the man behind her might pursue and catch her, but at the same time, even as she made her escape, she already felt some regret that he didn't. At that moment, what she had unconsciously been longing for over the years might have happened, the adventure that she voluptuously liked to imagine close, although so far she had always avoided it just in time: a real, dangerous relationship, not simply a light flirtation. But the Baron had too much pride to run after her and take advantage of the moment. He was certain of victory, and would not pounce on the woman now in a weak moment when she was tipsy; on the contrary, he played fair, and was excited only by the chase and the thought of her surrender to him in full awareness. She could not escape him. The burning venom, he could see, was already running through her veins.

At the top of the stairs she stopped, one hand pressed to her fluttering heart. She had to rest for a moment. Her nerves were giving way. A sigh burst from her breast, half in relief to have escaped a danger, half in regret, but it was all confused, and she felt the turmoil in her blood only as a slight dizziness. Eyes half-closed, she groped her way to her door as if she were drunk, and breathed again when she held the cool handle. Now at last she was safe!

Quietly, she opened the door of her room—and next moment shrank back in alarm. Something or other had moved inside it, right at the back of the room in the dark. Her overstrained nerves cried out, she was about to call for help, but then she heard a very sleepy voice inside the room saying quietly, "Is that you, Mama?"

"For God's sake, what are you doing here?" She hurried over to the divan where Edgar lay curled up in a ball, just waking from sleep. Her first thought was that the child must be ill or needed help.

But Edgar, still very drowsy, said in a slightly reproachful tone, "I waited so long for you, and then I went to sleep."

"But why?"

"Because of the elephants."

"What elephants?"

Only then did she understand. She had promised the child to tell him about them this very evening, all about the hunt and the adventures. And the boy had stolen into her room, naïve and childish as he was, waiting for her to come in perfect confidence, and had fallen asleep as he waited. His extravagant behaviour made her indignant—although it was really with herself that she felt angry. She heard a soft murmur of guilt and shame within her and wanted to shout it down. "Go back to bed, you naughty boy," she cried. Edgar stared at her in surprise. Why was she so angry with him when he'd done nothing wrong? But his surprise made the already agitated woman even angrier. "Go back to your room at once," she shouted—furiously, because she felt that she was being unjust. Edgar went without a word. He really was extremely tired, and was only vaguely aware, through the mists of sleep closing in, that his mother had not kept her promise, and wrong had been done to him in some way or other. But he did not rebel. Everything in him was muted by weariness, and then again, he was very angry with himself for going to sleep up here instead of staying awake. Just like a small child, he told himself indignantly before he fell asleep again.

For since yesterday he had hated his own condition of childhood.

6

Skirmishing

THE BARON had slept badly. It is always risky to go to bed after an adventure has been left unfinished; a restless night, full of sultry dreams, soon made him feel sorry he had not seized the moment after all. When he came down in the morning, still in a drowsy and discontented mood, the boy ran straight to him from some hiding place, gave him an enthusiastic hug, and began pestering him with countless questions. He was happy to have his great friend to himself for a minute or so again, not to have to share him with Mama. His friend was to tell stories to him, he insisted, just to him, not Mama any more, because in spite of her promise she hadn't passed on the tales of all those wonderful things. He besieged the displeased and startled Baron, who had some difficulty in hiding his ill humour, with a hundred childish demands. Moreover, he mingled these questions with earnest assurances of his love, blissfully happy to be alone again with the friend he had been looking for so long, whom he had expected since first thing in the morning.

The Baron replied brusquely. He was beginning to feel bored by the way the child was always lying in wait for him, by his silly questions and his unwanted passion in general. He was tired of going around with a twelve-year-old day in, day out, talking nonsense to him. All he wanted now was to strike while the iron was hot and get the mother alone, and here the child's unwelcome presence was a problem. For the first time he felt distaste for the affection he had incautiously aroused, because at the moment he saw no chance of shaking off his excessively devoted little friend.

All the same, the attempt must be made. He let the boy's eager talk wash over him unheeded until ten o'clock, the time when he had arranged to go out walking with the child's mother, throwing a word into the conversation now and then so as not to hurt Edgar's feelings, although at the same time he was leafing through the newspaper. At last, when the hands of the clock had almost reached the hour, he pretended to remember something all of a sudden, and asked Edgar to go over to the other hotel for a moment and ask them there whether his father Count Grundheim had arrived yet.

Suspecting nothing, the child was delighted to be able to do his friend a service at last and ran off at once, proud of his dignity as a messenger, racing along the road so stormily that people stared at him in surprise. He was anxious to show how nimble he could be when a message was entrusted to him. No, they told him at the other hotel, the Count had not arrived yet, and indeed at the moment wasn't even expected. He ran back with this message at the same rapid pace. But the Baron was not in the lobby any more. Edgar knocked at the door of his room—in vain! He looked in all the rooms, the music-room, the coffee-house, stormed excitedly away to find his Mama and ask if she knew anything, but she had gone out. The doorman, to whom he finally turned in desperation, told him, to his astonishment, that the two of them had left the hotel together a few minutes ago!

Edgar waited patiently. In his innocence he suspected nothing wrong. They couldn't stay out for more than a little while, he was sure, because the Baron wanted to know the answer to his message. However, time dragged on and on, hours passed, and uneasiness crept insidiously into his mind. Besides, since the day that seductive stranger had come into his guileless little life the child had been in a permanent state of tension, all on edge and confused. Every passion leaves its mark on the delicate organisms of children, as if making an impression on soft wax. Edgar's eyelids began to tremble nervously again; he was already looking paler. He waited and waited, patiently at first, then in a state of frantic agitation, and finally close to tears. But he still was not suspicious. His blind faith in his wonderful friend made him assume that there was a misunderstanding, and he was tormented by a secret fear that he might have misunderstood the Baron's message.

What seemed really strange, however, was that when they finally came back they were talking cheerfully, and showed no surprise. It was as if they hadn't particularly missed him. "We came back this way hoping to meet you, Edi," said the Baron, without even asking about the message. And when the child, horrified to think they might have been looking for him in vain, began assuring them that he had come straight back along the high street, and asked which way they would have gone instead, his Mama cut the conversation short. "Very well, that will do. Children ought not to talk so much."

Edgar flushed red with annoyance. This was her second mean, despicable attempt to belittle him. Why did she do it, why was she always trying to make him look like a child, when he was sure he wasn't one any more? Obviously she was envious of him for having such a friend, and was planning to get the Baron over to her side. Yes, and he was sure it was his mother who had intentionally taken the Baron the wrong way. But he wasn't going to let her treat him like that, as she'd soon see. He would defy her. And Edgar made up his mind not to say a word to her at their table in the dining-room; he wouldn't talk to anyone but his friend.

However, that turned out to be difficult. What he least expected happened: neither of them noticed his defiance. They didn't even seem to see Edgar himself, while yesterday he had been the central point of their threesome. They both talked over his head, joking and laughing together as if he had vanished under the table. The blood rose to his cheeks, there was a lump in his throat that choked him. With a shudder, he realized how terribly powerless he was. Was he to sit here and watch his mother take his friend away from him, the one person he loved, while he was unable to defend himself except by silence? He felt as if he must stand up and suddenly hammer on the table with both fists. Just to make them notice him. But he kept himself under control, merely laying his knife and fork down and not touching another morsel. However, they also ignored his stubborn refusal of food for a long time, and it wasn't until the next course came that his mother noticed and asked if he didn't feel well. It's so horrible, he thought, she always thinks the same thing, she asks if I don't feel well, nothing else matters to her. He answered briefly, saying he didn't want any more to eat, and she seemed satisfied with that. There was nothing, absolutely nothing he could do to attract attention. The Baron seemed to have forgotten him, or at least he never once spoke a word to him. His eyes burned worse and worse, spilled over, and he had to resort to the childish trick of raising his napkin quickly to his face before anyone could see the tears trickling down his cheeks, leaving salty moisture on his lips. He was glad when the meal was over.

During it his mother had suggested a carriage drive to the village of Maria-Schutz together. Biting his lower lip, Edgar had heard her. So she wasn't going to leave him alone with his friend for a single minute any more! However, his hatred was roused to fury only when she said to him, as they rose from table, "Edgar, you'll be forgetting all about your school work, you'd better stay in the hotel today and catch up with some of it!" Once again he clenched his little fist. She was always trying to humiliate him in front of his friend, reminding everyone in public that he was still a child, he had to go to school, he was merely tolerated in adult company. But this time her intentions were too transparent. He did not answer at all, but simply turned away.

"Oh dear, I've hurt your feelings again!" she said, smiling, and added, turning to the Baron, "Would it really be so bad for him to do an hour or so of work for once?"

And then—something froze rigid in the child's heart—the Baron, who called himself his friend, who had joked that he, Edgar, was too much of a bookworm, agreed with her. "Well, I'm sure an hour or two could do no harm."

Was it a conspiracy? Were they really both in league against him? Fury flared up in the child's eyes. "My Papa said I wasn't to do any school work while I was here. Papa wants me to get better here," he flung at them with all the pride of an invalid, desperately clutching at his father's authority. It came out like a threat. And the strangest part of it was that what he had said really did appear to discompose them both. His mother looked away and drummed her fingers nervously on the table. There was a painful silence. "Just as you say, Edi," replied the Baron at last, forcing a smile. "At least I don't have to take any examinations myself, I failed all mine long ago."

But Edgar did not smile at his joke, just scrutinized him with a longing but penetrating glance, as if trying to probe his soul. What was going on? Something had changed between them, and the child didn't know why. His eyes wandered restlessly, and in his heart a small, rapid hammer was at work, forging the first suspicion.

7

Burning Secret

WHAT'S CHANGED them so much, wondered the child, sitting opposite them in the carriage as they drove along, why aren't they the same to me as before? Why does Mama keep avoiding my eyes when I look at her? Why is he always trying to make jokes and clown about like that? They don't either of them talk to me the way they did yesterday and the day before, it's almost as if they had new faces. Mama has such red lips today, she must have painted them. I never saw her do that before. And he keeps frowning as if I'd hurt his feelings. But I haven't done anything to them, I haven't said a word that could annoy them, have I? No, I can't be the reason, because they're acting differently with each other too, they're not the same as before. It's as if they'd done something they don't like to talk about. They're not chattering away like yesterday, they're not laughing either, they're embarrassed, they're hiding something. They have a secret of some kind, and they don't want to share it with me. A secret, and I must find out what it is at any price. I know it must be the sort of thing that makes people send me out of the room, the sort of thing books are always going on about, and operas when men and women sing together with their arms spread wide, and hug and then push each other away. Somehow or other it must be the same as all that business about my French governess who behaved so badly with Papa, and then she was sent away. All those things are connected, I can feel that, it's just that I don't know how. Oh, I wish I knew the secret, I wish I understood it, I wish I had the key that opens all those doors, and I wasn't a child any more with people hiding things from me and pretending. I wish I didn't have to be deceived and put off with excuses. It's now or never! I'm going to get that terrible secret out of them. A line was dug into his brow, the slight twelve-year-old looked almost old as he sat there brooding, without sparing a glance for the landscape unfolding its resonant colours all around: the mountains in the pure green of the coniferous forests, the valleys still young with the fresh bloom of spring, which was late this year. All he saw was the couple opposite him on the back seat of the carriage, as if his intense glances, like a fishing-line, could bring the secret up from the gleaming depths of their eyes. Nothing whets the intelligence more than a passionate suspicion, nothing develops all the faculties of an immature mind more than a trail running away into the dark. Sometimes it is only a flimsy door that cuts children off from what we call the real world, and a chance gust of wind will blow it open for them.

Suddenly Edgar felt that the unknown, the great secret was closer than ever before, almost within reach, he felt it just before him—still locked away and unsolved, to be sure, but close, very close. That excited him and gave him a sudden, solemn gravity. For unconsciously he guessed that he was approaching the end of his childhood.

The couple opposite felt some kind of mute resistance before them, without guessing that it came from the boy. They felt constrained and inhibited as the three of them sat in the carriage together. The two eyes opposite them, with their dark and flickering glow, were an obstacle to both adults. They hardly dared to speak, hardly dared to look. They could not find the way back to their earlier light small-talk, they were already enmeshed too far in that tone of ardent intimacy, those dangerous words in which insidious lust trembles at secret touches. Their conversation kept coming up against lacunae, hesitations. It halted, tried to go on, but still stumbled again and again over the child's persistent silence.

That grim silence was particularly hard for his mother to bear. She cautiously looked at him sideways, and as the child compressed his lips she was suddenly startled to see, for the first time, a similarity to her husband when he was annoyed or angry. It was uncomfortable for her to be reminded of her husband just now, when she wanted to play a game with an adventure, a game of hide and seek. The child seemed to her like a ghost, a guardian of her conscience, doubly intolerable here in the cramped carriage, sitting just opposite with his watchful eyes glowing darkly beneath his pale forehead. Then Edgar suddenly looked up, just for a second. Both of them lowered their eyes again at once; she felt, for the first time in her life, that they were keeping watch on each other. Until now they had trusted one another blindly, but today something between the two of them, mother and child, was suddenly different. For the first time they began observing each other, separating their two lives, both already feeling a secret dislike that was still too new for them to dare to acknowledge it.

All three breathed a sigh of relief when the horses stopped outside the hotel. As an outing it had been a failure; they all felt that, but no one dared say so. Edgar jumped down first. His mother excused herself, saying that she had a headache, and quickly went upstairs. She felt tired and wanted to be alone. Edgar and the Baron were left behind. The Baron paid the driver of the carriage, looked at his watch, and walked towards the lobby, ignoring the boy. He went past Edgar, turning his elegant, slender back, walking with that slight, rhythmically springy gait that captivated the boy so much. Edgar had tried to imitate it yesterday. The Baron walked past him, he simply passed him by. Obviously he had forgotten the boy, leaving him there with the driver and the horses as if they had nothing to do with each other.

Something inside Edgar broke in two as he saw him pass like that—the man whom, in spite of everything, he still idolized. Desperation rose from his heart as the Baron passed by without a word, not even brushing him with his coat—and he wasn't aware of having done anything wrong. His laboriously maintained self-control gave way, the artificial burden of his new dignity slipped from his narrow shoulders, he was a child again, small and humble as he had been yesterday and for so long before that. It impelled him on against his will. With quick, unsteady steps he followed the Baron, stood in his way as he was about to go upstairs, and said in a strained voice, keeping back the tears only with difficulty:

"What have I done to you? You don't take any notice of me any more! Why are you always like that to me now? And Mama too! Why are you always trying to get rid of me? Am I in your way, or have I done something wrong, or what?"

The Baron gave a start of surprise. There was something in that voice that bewildered him and softened his heart. Pity for the innocent boy overcame him. "Oh, Edi, you're an idiot! I was in a bad mood today, that's all. And you're a good boy, I'm really fond of you." So saying he ruffled the boy's hair vigorously, but with his face half turned away to avoid seeing those large, moist, pleading, childish eyes. He was beginning to feel awkward about his play-acting. In fact he was already feeling ashamed of exploiting this child's love so ruthlessly, and that high little voice, shaken by suppressed sobs, physically hurt him.

"Upstairs you go now, Edi, we'll meet this evening and be friends again, you wait and see," he said in mollifying tones.

"But you won't let Mama send me straight up to bed, will you?"

"No, no, Edi, I won't," smiled the Baron. "So up you go now, I must dress for dinner."

Edgar went, happy for the moment. But soon the hammer in his mind started working away again. He had grown years older since yesterday; distrust, previously a stranger to him, had taken up residence in his childish breast.

He waited. This would be the test that decided it. They sat at the table together. Nine o'clock came, but still his mother did not send him to bed. He was beginning to feel uneasy. Why was she letting him stay up so long today, when she was usually so strict about it? Had the Baron told her what he wanted after all, had he given their conversation away? He was suddenly overcome by bitter regret for running round after him today with his heart so full of trust. At ten his mother suddenly rose from the table and wished the Baron goodnight. And strange to say, the Baron did not seem at all surprised by her early departure, or try to keep her there as he had before. The hammer in the child's breast was coming down harder and harder.

Now for the test. He too acted as if he suspected nothing, and followed his mother to the door without demur. But there he suddenly looked up, and sure enough, at that moment he caught her smiling at the Baron over his head. It was a glance of complicity, about a secret of some kind. So the Baron had indeed given him away. That was why she was going up early: he was to be lulled into a sense of security today so that he wouldn't be in their way again tomorrow.

"Swine," he muttered.

"What did you say?" asked his mother.

"Nothing," he said between his teeth. He had a secret of his own now. Its name was hatred, boundless hatred for both of them.

8

Silence

E DGAR WAS no longer restless. At last he was relishing a
pure, clear feeling: hatred and open animosity. Now that
he was certain he was in their way, being with them became a
cruelly complex pleasure. He gloated over the idea of disrupting
their plans, bringing all the concentrated force of his hostility
to bear on them at last. He showed his teeth to the Baron first.
When that gentleman came down in the morning and greeted
him in passing with a hearty, "Hello there, Edi!", Edgar stayed
where he was, sitting in an armchair, and just grunted a surly,
"Morning", without looking up.

"Is your Mama down yet?"

Edgar was looking at the newspaper. "I don't know."

The Baron was taken aback. What was this all of a sudden?

"Got out of bed on the wrong side today, Edi, did you?" A joke
always helped to smooth things over. But Edgar just cast him a
scornful, "No," and immersed himself in the newspaper once more.

"Silly boy," muttered the Baron to himself, shrugging his
shoulders, and he moved on. War had been declared.

Edgar was cool and courteous to his Mama too. He calmly
rebuffed a clumsy attempt to send him out to the tennis courts.
The faint, bitter smile on his curling lips showed that he was not
to be deceived any more.

"I'd rather go for a walk with you and the Baron, Mama," he
said with assumed friendliness, looking into her eyes. She obviously

found it an inconvenient response. She hesitated, and seemed to be searching for something to say. "Wait for me here," she told him at last, and went in to breakfast.

Edgar waited. But his suspicions were aroused. His alert instincts were busy detecting some secret and hostile meaning in everything the two adults said. Distrustful as he now was, he became remarkably perceptive in his conclusions. So instead of waiting in the lobby as directed by his mother, Edgar decided to position himself in the street, where he could keep watch not only on the main entrance but on all the other doors of the hotel. Something in him scented deception. But they weren't going to get away from him any more. Out in the street, he took cover behind a woodpile, a useful trick learned from his books about American Indians. And he merely smiled with satisfaction when, after about half-an-hour, he actually did see his mother coming out of a side door carrying a bouquet of beautiful roses, and followed by that traitor the Baron. They both seemed to be in high spirits. Were they breathing a sigh of relief to have escaped him? Now, they thought, they were alone with their secret! They were laughing as they talked, starting down the road to the woods.

The moment had come. Edgar emerged from behind the woodpile at a leisurely pace, as if he happened to be here by mere chance. Very, very casually he went towards them, giving himself time, plenty of time, to relish their surprise. They were both taken aback, and exchanged a strange look. The boy slowly approached them, pretending to take this meeting entirely for granted, but he never took his mocking gaze off them.

"Oh, so there you are, Edi. We were looking for you indoors," said his mother at last. What a bare-faced liar she is, thought the child, but his lips did not relax. They kept the secret of his hatred fenced in behind his teeth.

Then they all three stood there, undecided. Each was watching the others. "Oh, let's be off," said Edgar's mother, irritated but resigned, plucking at one of the beautiful roses. Once again he saw that slight fluttering of the nostrils that betrayed her anger. Edgar stopped as if all this were nothing to do with him, looked up at the sky, waited until they had begun walking, and then set off to follow them.

The Baron made one more attempt. "It's the tennis tournament today. Have you ever seen one of those?"

Edgar looked at him with scorn. He did not even reply, just pursed his lips as if he were about to whistle. That was all his answer. His animosity was showing itself.

His unwanted presence now weighed on the other two like a nightmare. They walked as convicts walk behind their jailer, with fists surreptitiously clenched. The child wasn't really doing anything, but with every passing minute he became more intolerable to them—he and his watchful gaze, wet as his eyes were with tears grimly suppressed, his resentful ill humour, the way he rejected all attempts at conciliation with a growl.

"Go on ahead," said his mother, suddenly angry, and made uneasy by his constant close attention. "Don't keep dancing about in front of my feet like that, it makes me nervous."

Edgar obeyed, but after every few steps he turned and stood there waiting for them if they had lagged behind, his gaze circling around them like Mephistopheles in the shape of the black dog, spinning a fiery web of hostility and entangling them hopelessly in it.

His malice and silence corroded their good humour like acid, his gaze soured their conversation. The Baron dared not utter another word of gallantry, he felt with annoyance that the woman was slipping away from him again, and the flames of passion that he had so laboriously fanned were cooling again in her fear of that irritating, horrible child. They kept trying to converse, and their exchanges kept dying away. In the end, they were all three marching along the path in silence, a silence unbroken except by the rustling whisper of the trees and their own dragging footsteps. The child had throttled any conversation.

By now all three felt irritation and animosity. The betrayed child was delighted to realize that the helpless anger of the adults was all directed against his own existence, which they had ignored. Eyes sparkling with derision, he now and then scanned the Baron's grim face. He saw that the man was muttering curses between his teeth, and had to exercise self-control himself to keep from spitting them out at him. At the same time, with diabolical pleasure, he observed his mother's rising anger, and saw that they were both longing for some reason to turn on him, send him away, or in general render him harmless. But he offered them no chance, he had worked on his hostility for hours and he wasn't going to show any weakness now.

"Let's go back," said his mother suddenly. She felt that she wouldn't be able to stand this much longer, she must do something, must at least scream under the torture.

"What a pity," said Edgar calmly. "It's so nice here."

They both realized that the child was mocking them, but they dared not say anything. In the space of two days the little tyrant had learned to control himself expertly. Not a muscle moved in his face to betray his irony. Without a word, they walked the long way back. Edgar's mother was still in an agitated state when the two of them were alone in her room. She threw her sunshade and gloves angrily down. Edgar saw at once that her nerves were on edge, her temper was demanding release, but as an outburst was just what he wanted, he stayed in the room on purpose to provoke it. She paced about, sat down, drumming her fingers on the table, and then leaped to her feet again. "What a sight you look, going around all dirty and untidy like that! In front of other people too, it's a shame. Aren't you ashamed of yourself, at your age?"

Without a word in answer, the boy went over to the mirror to comb his hair. His silence, his obstinate cold silence and the scornful smile playing round his lips infuriated her. She could have hit him. "Go to your room!" she cried. She couldn't bear his presence any more. Edgar smiled, and went.

How they were both trembling before him now, how afraid she and the Baron were, afraid of every hour they all spent together, fearing his pitilessly hard eyes! The more uncomfortable they felt, the more satisfaction and pleasure there was for him in staring, and the more challenging was his delight. Edgar was now tormenting the defenceless couple with all the cruelty natural to children, which is still almost animal in nature. The Baron was able to restrain his anger because he still hoped to trick the boy, and was thinking only of his own aims. But his mother kept losing control of herself. A chance to shout at him came almost as a relief. "Don't play with your fork," she snapped at him at table. "What a naughty boy you are, you don't deserve to be eating with grown-ups!" Edgar just kept smiling and smiling, his head slightly tilted to one side. He knew that she was snapping at him in desperation, and felt proud that she was exposing herself like that. His glance was perfectly calm now, like a doctor's. Once he might perhaps have been naughty in order to annoy her, but you learn a lot when you hate, and you learn it fast. Now he said nothing, he went on and on saying nothing, until the sheer pressure of his silence had her at screaming-point.

His mother could bear it no longer. When the adults rose from table and she saw that Edgar was about to follow them, still looking as if such devotion was only to be taken for granted, her resentment suddenly burst out. She abandoned all caution and spat out the truth. Tormented by his insidious presence, she reared and bucked like a horse tortured by flies. "Why do you keep following me around like a three-year-old toddler? I don't want you on my heels all the time. Children don't belong with adults, remember that! Go and do something on your own for an hour or so. Read a book, do anything you like, but leave me alone! You're making me nervous, slinking around like that with your horrible hangdog look."

At last he'd wrung an admission out of her! Edgar smiled, and she and the Baron now seemed embarrassed. She turned and was about to move away, angry with herself for showing the child her annoyance. But Edgar just said coolly, "Papa doesn't want me going around here all on my own. Papa made me promise to be careful, he wanted me to stay close to you."

He emphasized the word "Papa", having noticed already that it had a certain inhibiting effect on them both. So somehow or other his father too must be part of that burning secret. Papa must have some kind of secret power over the couple, something that he himself didn't know about, for even the mention of his name seemed to cause them alarm and discomfiture. Once again they did not reply. They had laid down their arms. His mother went ahead, the Baron with her. After them came Edgar, but not humbly like a servant, instead he was harsh, stern, implacable as a jailer. Invisibly, he clinked their chains—they were rattling those chains, but they couldn't break them. Hatred had steeled his childish power; he, who didn't know the secret, was stronger than the two whose hands were bound by it.

9

Liars

B UT TIME WAS RUNNING OUT. The Baron had only a
few days left, and he wanted to make the most of them.
Resistance to the angry child's obstinacy, they both felt, was
useless, so they resorted to the last and ignoble way out: flight,
just to get away from his tyranny for an hour or two.

"Take these letters to the post office, will you, and send them
by registered mail," Edgar's mother told him. They were both
standing in the hotel lobby while the Baron spoke to a cabby
outside.

Suspiciously, Edgar took the two letters. He had noticed a
servant delivering some kind of message to his mother earlier.
Were they hatching a plot against him after all?

He hesitated. "Where will I find you?"

"Here."

"Sure?"

"Yes."

"Mind you don't go away, though! You'll wait for me here in
the lobby until I get back, won't you?" In his awareness of having
the upper hand he spoke imperiously, as if giving his mother
orders. Much had changed since the day before yesterday.

Then he went out with the two letters. At the door he met
the Baron and spoke to him for the first time in two days. "I'm
just taking two letters to the post. My Mama will wait for me
here. Please don't leave before I come back."

The Baron brushed quickly past him. "No, no, we'll wait for you."

Edgar ran to the post office. He had to wait, because a gentleman in front of him had a dozen tedious questions. At last he was able to perform his errand, he ran straight back with the receipts—and arrived just in time to see his mother and the Baron driving away in the cab.

He was rigid with anger. He almost bent down to pick up a stone and throw it after them. So they'd got away from him after all, by means of a lie as mean as it was vile. He had known since yesterday that his mother told lies, but the idea that she could be shameless enough to break a downright promise destroyed the very last of his trust in her. He didn't understand anything at all about life, not now he knew that the words which he'd thought had reality behind them were just bright bubbles, swelling with air and then bursting, leaving nothing behind. What kind of terrible secret was it that drove grown-up people so far as to lie to him, a child, stealing away from him like thieves? In the books that he had read, people murdered and deceived each other to get their hands on money, or power, or kingdoms. But what was the reason here, what did those two want, why were they hiding from him, what were they trying to hide behind all their lies? He racked his brains. Dimly he felt that the secret was the bolt on the door of childhood, and once he had shot back the bolt and conquered the secret it would mean he was grown up, a man at long last. Oh, if he only knew the secret! But he couldn't think clearly any more. His burning, corrosive anger at knowing they had got away from him blurred the clarity of his vision.

He went out into the woods, and was just able to get safely into the shadows where no one would see him before bursting into storms of hot tears. "You liars, you cheats, traitors, rotters!" He had to shout the names he was calling them aloud or he would have choked. His rage and impatience, his anger, curiosity, helplessness, and the betrayal of the last few days, all repressed in his childish struggle to live up to his delusion of being an adult, now burst out and found relief in floods of weeping. It was the last fit of weeping in his childhood, the last and wildest, the last time he weakly gave himself up, like a girl, to the luxury of tears. In that hour of bafflement and rage he wept everything out of him: trust, love, belief, respect—his entire childhood.

It was a different boy who went back to the hotel. He was cool, he acted with deliberation. First he went to his room and carefully washed his face and eyes, so as not to give the pair of them the triumph of seeing his tearstains. Then he drew up his reckoning—and waited patiently, without any restlessness now.

The lobby was full when the carriage with the two runaways drew up outside. A few gentlemen were playing chess, others were reading the paper, the ladies were talking. The child had been sitting perfectly still among them, rather pale, darting glances here and there. Now, when his mother and the Baron came through the doorway, rather embarrassed to see him so suddenly, already about to stammer the excuse they had prepared in advance, he went up to them, perfectly calm and holding himself very upright, and said challengingly, "Baron, there's something I want to say to you."

The Baron was ill at ease. He felt as if he had been caught in some guilty act. "Yes, yes, later, in a moment!"

But Edgar raised his voice and said, loud and clear, so that everyone around could hear him, "I want to talk to you now. You have acted very badly. You lied to me. You knew my Mama was waiting for me, and you…"

"Edgar!" cried his mother, seeing all eyes turn her way, and she moved towards him.

But now, seeing that she was going to drown out what he said, the child suddenly raised his voice to a high pitch and almost screeched, "I'm going to tell you again in front of everyone. You told the most dreadful lies, it's mean, it's a horrid thing to do."

The Baron stood there looking pale, people stared, some of them smiled.

His mother took hold of the child, who was trembling with agitation. "Go up to your room at once, or I'll slap you here in front of all these people," she said hoarsely.

But Edgar had calmed down again. He was sorry he had sounded so passionate. He was not pleased with himself, for he had really meant to challenge the Baron in cool tones, but his rage had overcome his intentions. Calmly now, without haste, he turned to the stairs.

"Baron, please forgive his naughty behaviour. As you know, he's a nervous child," she stammered, cast into confusion by the slightly malicious glances of the people staring at them. She hated nothing in the world more than scandal, and she knew she must preserve her composure now. So instead of taking flight at once, she first went to the receptionist, asked about any letters and other indifferent matters, and then went upstairs as if nothing had happened. But she left in her wake soft whispering and suppressed laughter.

On her way, she slowed her pace. She had always felt helpless in a difficult situation, and was genuinely afraid of this confrontation. She couldn't deny that it was her own fault, and then again she was afraid of the look in the child's eyes, that new, strange, peculiar look that paralysed and unsettled her. In her fear she decided to try the soft approach. For in a struggle, she knew, this angry child would now be stronger than she was.

Softly she opened the door. There sat the boy, calm and collected. There was no fear in the eyes he raised to her, they did not even betray curiosity. He seemed very sure of himself.

"Edgar," she began in as maternal a tone as possible, "what on earth came over you? I was ashamed of you. How can anyone be so bad-mannered—how can a child in particular speak to an adult like that? You will apologize to the Baron at once."

Edgar looked out of the window. When he said, "No," he might have been talking to the trees.

His self-confidence was beginning to disturb her.

"Edgar, what's the matter with you? You're not yourself at all. I can't make you out. You've always been such a good, clever boy, anyone could talk to you. And suddenly you act as if the devil had got into you. What do you have against the Baron? You seemed to like him very much, and he's been so kind to you."

"Yes, because he wanted to get to know you."

She felt uneasy. "Nonsense! What are you thinking of? How can you imagine any such thing?"

But at that the child flared up.

"He's a liar, he's only pretending. He does it out of mean, horrid calculation. He wanted to get to know you, that's why he was nice to me and promised me a dog. I don't know what he promised you or why he's making up to you, but he wants something from you too, Mama, you can be sure he does. Otherwise he wouldn't be so friendly and polite. He's a bad man. He tells lies. Just look at him some time, you'll see how he's always pretending. I hate him, he's a miserable liar, he's no good…"

"Oh, Edgar, how can you say such a thing?" She was bewildered, and hardly knew what to say in reply. Something inside her said that the child was right.

"He's no good, and you won't make me think anything else. You must see it for yourself. Why is he afraid of me? Why does he keep out of my way? Because he knows I see through him, I know he's a bad man, I know what he's like!"

"How can you say such a thing, how can you say it?" Her brain seemed to have dried up, and only her bloodless lips kept stammering those phrases. Suddenly she began to feel terribly afraid, and did not know whether she feared the Baron or her child.

Edgar saw that his protestations had taken effect. He was tempted to go over to her side, to have a companion in the hatred and animosity he felt for the Baron. He went gently to his mother, hugged her, and his voice was emotional and cajoling

"Mama," he said, "you must have noticed that he doesn't have anything good in mind. He's made you quite different. You're the one who's changed, not me. He's turned you against me just so as to have you all to himself. I'm sure he'll let you down. I don't know what promise he's given you, I only know he won't keep it. You ought to beware of him. Anyone who tells lies to one person will tell lies to another too. He's a bad man, he's not to be trusted."

That voice, low and almost tearful, could have come from her own heart. Since yesterday she had had an uncomfortable feeling telling her the same, more and more urgently. But she was ashamed to admit that her own child was in the right. Like many people in such a situation, she extricated herself from the awkwardness of an overwhelming emotion by speaking roughly. She straightened her back.

"Children don't understand these things. You have no business meddling in them. You must behave better, and that's all there is to it."

Edgar's face froze again. "Just as you like," he said harshly. "I've warned you."

"So you refuse to apologize?"

"Yes."

They were standing close together, face to face. She felt that her authority was at stake.

"Then you will eat your meals up here. By yourself. And don't come down to our table again until you have apologized. I'll teach you good manners yet. You will not leave this room until I let you, is that understood?"

Edgar smiled. That sly smile seemed to have become a part of his lips. Privately, he was angry with himself. How foolish of him to have let his heart run away with him again, trying to warn her when she was a liar herself!

His mother walked out, skirts rustling, without looking at him again. She feared the cutting look in those eyes. She had felt uncomfortable with the child since sensing that he had his eyes wide open and was telling her exactly what she didn't want to know, didn't want to hear. It was terrible to her to find an inner voice, the voice of her own conscience, separated from herself and disguised as a child, going around masquerading as her own child, warning and deriding her. Until now her child had been a part of her life, an ornament, a toy, something dear and familiar, perhaps a nuisance now and then, but always going the same way as she did, keeping to the same rhythm as the current of her life. Today, for the first time, he was rebelling and defying her will. And now something like dislike would always be part of her memory of her son.

None the less, as she went down the stairs feeling rather weary, that childish voice spoke from her own heart. "You ought to beware of him." The warning would not be silenced. As she passed, she saw the glint of a mirror, and looked inquiringly into it, more and more closely, until the lips of her reflection opened in a slight smile and rounded as if to utter a dangerous word. She still heard the voice inside her, but she straightened her shoulders, as if shaking off all those invisible reservations, gave her reflection in the mirror a clear look, picked up her skirts and went downstairs with the determined mien of a gambler about to let her last gold coin roll over the gaming table, ringing as it went.

10

Tracks in the Moonlight

T HE WAITER WHO had brought Edgar supper in his room
closed the door. The lock clicked behind him. The child
jumped up, furious. It was obviously by his mother's orders that
he was being locked in like a wild animal. Dark thoughts made
their way out of him.

What's happening downstairs while I'm locked in here? What
are those two talking about now? Is the secret going to come
out at last, and I'll miss hearing it? Oh, that secret, I feel it all
the time, everywhere, when I'm with grown-ups, they close their
doors on it at night, they talk about it under their breath if I
unexpectedly come into the room, that great secret, it's been so
close to me for days now, right in front of me, and I still can't lay
hands on it! I've done all I can to find out about it! I've stolen
books out of Papa's desk drawer in the past and read them, and
there were all those strange things in them, except that I didn't
understand them. There must be a seal somewhere, and you just
have to break the seal to find out what the secret is, perhaps it's
in me or perhaps it's in other people. I asked the maid, I wanted
her to explain those bits in the books, but she only laughed at
me. It's horrible being a child, there's so much you want to know
but you're not allowed to ask anyone, you always look so silly in
front of grown-ups, as if you were stupid or useless. But I will
find out the secret, I will, I feel I'll soon know it. There's part
of it in my hands already, and I won't give up until I have it all!

He strained his ears to listen for anyone coming. A slight breeze was blowing through the trees outside, breaking the still reflection of moonlight among the branches into hundreds of swaying splinters.

They can't be planning anything good, or they wouldn't have thought up such miserable lies to keep me away. I'm sure they're laughing at me now, oh, I hate them, they're glad to be rid of me, but I'll have the last laugh. How stupid of me to let myself be shut up here and give them a moment's freedom, instead of sticking close and following all their movements. I know grown-ups are always careless, and they'll give themselves away. They always think we children are still little and we just go straight to sleep in the evenings, they forget that you can always pretend to be asleep and keep your ears open, you can make out you're stupid and be very clever all the same. When my aunt had that baby not so long ago they knew about it long before it came, it was only in front of me they acted all surprised, as if they hadn't guessed it was coming. But I knew about it too, because I'd heard them talking weeks before, in the evening when they thought I was asleep. And I'll surprise that horrible pair this time. Oh, if only I could see through doors and watch them while they think they're safe. Suppose I rang the bell now, would that be a good idea? Then the chambermaid would come and ask what I wanted. Or I could make a lot of noise, I could break some china, and then they'd open the door too. And I could slip out at that moment and go and eavesdrop. Or no—no, I don't want that. I don't want anyone to know how badly they treat me. I'm too proud for that. I'll pay them back tomorrow.

Downstairs a woman laughed. Edgar jumped; that could be his mother. It was all very well for her to laugh and make fun of him, he was just a helpless little boy to be locked in if he was in the way, thrown into a corner like a bundle of wet clothes.

Cautiously, he leaned out of the window. No, it wasn't her, it was some high-spirited girls teasing a young man.

Then, at that moment, he saw how close his window really was to the ground below. And almost before he knew it he was thinking of jumping out, now, when they thought they were secure, and going to eavesdrop on them. He felt quite feverish with delight at this decision. It was as if he held the great, the sparkling secret that was kept from children in his hands. Go on, out, out, said an urgent voice in him. It wasn't dangerous. There were no passers by below him, and he jumped. The gravel crunched slightly, but no one heard the faint sound.

During these last two days, stealing about and lying in wait had become his great pleasure in life. And he felt pleasure now, mingled with a slight frisson of alarm, as he tiptoed around the hotel, carefully avoiding the strong illumination of the lights. First, pressing his cheek cautiously to the pane, he looked through the dining-room window. Their usual table was empty. He went on spying in, moving from window to window. He dared not go into the hotel itself, for fear of unexpectedly meeting them somewhere in the corridors. They were nowhere to be seen. He was about to give up in despair when he saw two shadows in the doorway, and—he shrank back, ducking into the cover of darkness—his mother and her now inseparable companion came out. So he'd come at just the right moment. What were they talking about? He couldn't hear. They were speaking in low voices, and the wind was rustling in the trees. However, now he clearly heard a laugh, his mother's. It was a laugh that he had never heard from her before, a strangely high-pitched, nervous laugh, as if someone had tickled her. It was new and alarming to him. She was laughing, so it couldn't be anything dangerous they were hiding from him, nothing really huge and powerful. Edgar was slightly disappointed.

Why were they leaving the hotel, though? Where were they going by night, all by themselves? High above, the winds must be racing past on huge wings, for the sky, only a little while ago clear and moonlit, was dark now. Black scarves flung by invisible hands covered the moon from time to time, and then the night was so impenetrable that you could hardly see where you were going. Next moment, when the moon fought free, it was bright and clear again, and cool silver flowed over the landscape. This play of light and shade was mysterious, as intriguing as the game of revelation and concealment played by a woman. At this moment the landscape was stripping itself naked again. Edgar saw the two silhouettes on the other side of the path, or rather one silhouette, for they were as close as if some inner fear had merged them together. But where were the two of them going now? The pine trees were groaning in the wind, there was mysterious activity in the woods, as if the Wild Hunt were racing through them. I'll follow, thought Edgar, they can't hear my footsteps, not with all the noise the wind and the trees are making. And as the two figures went along the broad, well-lit road, he stayed in the undergrowth of the bank above it, hurrying quietly from tree to tree, from shadow to shadow. He followed them tenaciously and implacably, blessing the wind for drowning out his footsteps and then cursing it because it kept carrying the couple's words away from him. Just once, when he managed to catch their conversation, he felt sure he was about to discover the secret.

Down below him, the two of them walked along suspecting nothing. They felt happily alone in this wide, bewildering darkness, lost in their growing excitement. No premonition warned them that someone up among the dark bushes was following every step they took, two eyes were fixed on them with all the force of hatred and curiosity. Suddenly they stopped. Edgar immediately stopped as well, pressing close to a tree. He felt a thrill of anxiety. Suppose they turned now and reached the hotel ahead of him, suppose he couldn't get safely back to his room and his mother found it empty? Then all would be lost, they'd know he had been secretly watching them, and he could never hope to get that secret out of them. But they hesitated; there was obviously some difference of opinion. Luckily the moon was shining again, and he could see everything clearly. The Baron was pointing to a dark, narrow path going off to one side and down into the valley, where the moonlight did not fall in a broad stream as it did on the road here, but merely filtered through the undergrowth in droplets with a few direct rays of light. Why, Edgar wondered, does he want to go down there? His mother seemed to be saying no, but he, the Baron, was talking to her. Edgar could tell, from his gestures, how urgently he was pressing her to do something. The child felt afraid. What did the Baron want from his mother? Why was that bad man trying to drag her off into the darkness? Suddenly memories came to him from his books, which were the whole world to him, memories of murders and kidnappings, of dark crimes. Yes, that was it, the Baron wanted to murder her, and that was why he had kept Edgar away and lured her here on her own. Should he call for help? Cry murder? The words were already in his mouth, but his lips were dry and couldn't utter a sound. His nerves were on edge with agitation, he could hardly stand upright, he reached in his fright for something to cling to—and a twig cracked in his hands.

The couple turned in alarm and stared into the night. Edgar leaned against his tree in the dark, clutching it in his arms, his small body cowering in the shadows. All was deathly silent. But none the less, they seemed to have taken fright. "Let's turn back," he heard his mother say. She sounded anxious. The

Baron, obviously uneasy himself, agreed. The couple walked back slowly, keeping very close. Their self-consciousness was lucky for Edgar. Ducking low in the undergrowth, crawling on all fours, his hands grazed and bleeding, he reached the bend in the road to the woods, and from there he ran back to the hotel as fast as he could go. He arrived out of breath, and then raced up the stairs. Fortunately the key that had locked him in was still in the lock outside the door; he turned it, ran into his room and threw himself on the bed. He had to rest for a few minutes, his heart was beating as wildly as the resonant clapper of a bell.

Then he ventured to get up, leaned against the window and waited for them to come back. It was quite a long wait. They must have been walking very, very slowly. He peered out, cautiously, for the window frame was not in the shadows. Here they came at a leisurely pace, moonlight shining on their clothes. They looked like ghosts in the greenish light, and again a not unenjoyable thrill of horror went through him: was the man really a murderer, what terrible deed had he, Edgar, just prevented by his presence? He could see their features clearly, white as chalk. There was an ecstatic expression on his mother's face that he had never seen there before; the Baron's expression, on the other hand, was harsh and sullen. No doubt because his plans had been foiled.

They were very close now. Their figures did not move apart until just before they reached the hotel. Would they look up? No, neither of them glanced at the window. You've forgotten me, thought the boy with wild inner rage, with a sense of secret triumph, but I haven't forgotten you. I expect you think I'm asleep or I don't count for anything, but you'll soon find out how wrong you are. I'm going to watch every step you take until I've got the secret out of that horrible, nasty man. I'll wreck the plot you're hatching between you. I'm not asleep.

Slowly, the couple approached the door. And now, as they went in, one after another, the silhouettes came together again, and their shadow disappeared through the lighted doorway, a single black form. Then the forecourt of the hotel lay empty in the moonlight again, like a broad snowfield.

I I

The Attack

B REATHING HARD, Edgar stepped back from the window. He was shaken by horror. He had never in his life before been so close to anything so mysterious. The exciting world of his books, of adventures and suspense, that world of murder and betrayal had always, in his mind, existed on the same plane as fairy tales, close to the world of dreams, an unreal place and out of reach. But now, suddenly, he seemed to be in the middle of that terrifying world, and his whole being was shaken feverishly by such an unexpected encounter. Who *was* that man, the mysterious man who had suddenly come into their peaceful life? Was he really a murderer, always looking for out-of-the-way places, then dragging his mother off into the dark? Something dreadful seemed about to happen. He didn't know what to do. In the morning, he decided, he would either write to his father or send him a telegram. But might not the dreadful thing happen now, this very evening? His mother wasn't in her room yet, she was still with that strange and hateful man.

There was a narrow space between the inner door of his room and the outer door, which was not visible at first sight and which moved at a mere touch. The space was no larger than the inside of a wardrobe. He squeezed into that hand's breadth of darkness to listen for her footsteps in the corridor. He had made up his mind that he wasn't going to leave her alone for a moment. Now, at midnight, the corridor was empty, dimly illuminated only by a single light.

At last—those minutes seemed to him to go on for ever—he heard careful steps coming upstairs. He listened hard. The steps were not fast, like those of someone on the way to her room, but hesitant, dragging, very slow, as if she were climbing an infinitely steep and difficult path. There was whispering from time to time, and then silence. Edgar was trembling with agitation. Was it both of them, after all, was he still with her? The whispering was too far away. But the footsteps, although still hesitant, were coming closer and closer. Now he suddenly heard the hated voice of the Baron saying something in a low, hoarse voice, something he couldn't make out, and then his mother's voice, quickly contradicting him. "No, not tonight! No."

Edgar trembled. They were coming closer, and he heard everything now. Every step towards him, soft as it was, went painfully to his heart. And that voice, how ugly it sounded to him, the avid, insistent, horrible voice of the man he hated.

"Oh, don't be so cruel. You looked so beautiful this evening."

Then the other voice again. "No, I mustn't, I can't, oh, let me go."

There's so much fear in his mother's voice that the child takes fright. What does he want her to do now? Why is she frightened? They have come closer and closer, they must be right outside his door now. He stands just behind it, trembling and invisible, a hand's breadth away, protected only by the thin partition of the outer door. The voices were almost breathing in his ear.

"Come on, Mathilde, come on!" He hears his mother groan again, more faintly this time, her resistance waning. But what's all this? They have gone on in the dark. His mother hasn't gone into her room, she's passed it! Where is he taking her? Why doesn't she say any more? Has he stuffed a gag into her mouth, is he holding her by the throat and choking her? These ideas make him frantic. He pushes the door a tiny way open, his hand trembling. Now he can see them both in the dark corridor. The Baron has put his arm around his mother's waist and is leading her quietly away. She seems docile now. The Baron stops outside his own door. He's going to drag her off, thinks the horrified child, he's going to do something terrible.

With a wild movement he closes the door of his room and rushes out, following them. His mother screams as something suddenly comes racing out of the darkness towards them, she appears to have fainted away, her companion has difficulty in keeping her upright. And at that moment the Baron feels a small and not very strong fist in his face, driving his lip against his teeth, and something clawing like a cat at his body. He lets go of the alarmed woman, who quickly makes her escape, and strikes back blindly with his own fist before he realizes who it is he's fending off.

The child knows that he is weaker than his opponent, but he does not give in. At last, at last the moment has come, the moment he has wanted for so long, when he can let off steam, discharging all his betrayed love and pent-up hate. He hammers blindly at the man with his little fists, lips tightly compressed in feverish, mindless fury. The Baron himself has now recognized him, he too feels furious with this secret spy who has been embittering his life for the last few days and spoiling his game; he strikes back hard at anything he can hit. Edgar groans but does not let go or call for help. They wrestle silently and grimly for a minute in the midnight corridor. Gradually the Baron becomes aware of the ridiculous aspect of this scuffle with a boy of twelve, and takes firm hold of Edgar to fling him off. But the child, feeling his muscles lose their force and knowing that next moment he will be defeated, the loser in the fight, snaps furiously at that strong, firm hand trying to grab him by the nape of his neck. He bites. Involuntarily, his opponent utters a muted scream and lets go. The child uses that split second to take refuge in his room and bolt the door.

The midnight conflict has lasted only about a minute. No one to right or left has heard it. All is still, everything seems to be drowned in sleep. The Baron mops his bleeding hand with his handkerchief and peers anxiously into the darkness. No one was listening. Only in the ceiling does a last, restless light flicker—as if, it seems to him, with derision.

I2

The Storm

W AS IT A DREAM, a dangerous nightmare? So Edgar
wondered next morning as he woke from a sleep full of
anxious confusion with his hair tousled. His head was tormented
by a dull thudding, his joints by a stiff, wooden feeling, and now,
when he looked down at himself, he was startled to realize that
he was still fully dressed. He jumped up, staggered over to the
mirror, and shrank back from his own pale, distorted face. A red
weal was swelling on his forehead. With difficulty, he pulled his
thoughts together and now, in alarm, remembered everything,
the fight in the dark out in the corridor, his retreat to his room,
and how then, trembling feverishly, he threw himself on his bed
in his day clothes, ready for flight. He must have fallen asleep
there, plunging into a dark, overcast slumber and bad dreams in
which it all came back to him again, only in a different and yet
more terrible form, with the wet smell of fresh blood flowing.

Downstairs, footsteps were crunching over the gravel. Voices
flew up like invisible birds, and the sun shone, reaching far into
the room. It must be late in the morning, but when he looked at
his watch in alarm the hands pointed to midnight. In his agitation
yesterday he had forgotten to wind it up. And this uncertainty,
the sense that he was left dangling somewhere in time, disturbed
him and was reinforced by the fact that he didn't know what had
really happened. He quickly tidied himself and went downstairs,
uneasiness and a faintly guilty feeling in his heart.

His Mama was sitting alone at their usual table in the breakfast-room. Edgar breathed a sigh of relief to see that his enemy wasn't there, that he wouldn't have to look at the hated face into which he had angrily driven his fist yesterday. And yet he still felt very uncertain as he approached the table.

"Good morning," he said.

His mother did not reply. She did not even look up, but stared at the landscape in the distance, her eyes curiously fixed. She looked very pale, there were slight rings round her eyes, and that give-away fluttering of her nostrils showed that she was upset. Edgar bit his lip. This silence confused him. He really didn't know whether he had hurt the Baron badly yesterday, and indeed whether she even knew about their fight in the dark. His uncertainty plagued him. But her face remained so frozen that he didn't even try to look at her, for fear her eyes, now lowered, might suddenly come to life behind their heavy lids and fix on him. He kept very still, not daring to make a sound, he very carefully picked up his cup and put it down again, looking surreptitiously at his mother's fingers as they nervously played with a spoon. They were curved into claws, as if betraying her secret fury. He sat like that for a quarter-of-an-hour with the oppressive feeling of waiting for something that didn't happen. Not a word, not a single word came to his rescue. And now that his mother rose to her feet, still without taking any notice of his presence, he didn't know what to do: should he stay sitting here at the table or follow her? Finally he too rose to his feet and meekly followed. She was still industriously ignoring him, and he kept feeling how ridiculous it was to be slinking after her like this. He took smaller and smaller steps, so as to lag further and further behind. Still without noticing him, she went into her room. When Edgar finally arrived, he faced a closed door.

What had happened? He didn't know what to make of it.

Yesterday's sense of confidence had left him. Had he been in the wrong after all the night before when he mounted his attack? And were they preparing a punishment or some new humiliation for him? Something had to happen, he felt sure of it, something terrible must happen very soon. The sultry atmosphere of a coming thunderstorm stood between them, the electrical tension of two charged poles that must be released in a flash of lightning. And he carried this burden of premonition around with him for four lonely hours, from room to room, until his slender, childish neck was bowed under its invisible weight, and he approached their table at lunch, his demeanour humble this time.

"Good day," he tried again. He had to break this silence, this terrible threat hanging over him like a black cloud.

Once again his mother did not reply, once again she just looked past him. And with new fear, Edgar now felt that he was facing such a considered, concentrated anger as he had never yet known in his life. So far their quarrels had been furious outbursts more to do with the nerves than the feelings, quickly passing over and settled with a conciliatory smile. But this time, he felt, he had aroused wild emotions in the uttermost depths of his mother's nature, and he shrank from the violence he had incautiously conjured up. He could hardly swallow a morsel. Something dry was rising in his throat and threatening to choke him. His mother seemed to notice none of this. Only now, as she got to her feet, did she turn back as if casually, saying, "Come upstairs, Edgar, I have to talk to you."

It did not sound threatening, only so icily cold that Edgar shuddered at the words. He felt as if an iron chain had suddenly been laid around his neck. His defiance was crushed. In silence, like a beaten dog, he followed her up to her room.

She prolonged the agony by preserving her own silence for several minutes. Minutes during which he heard the clock

72

striking, a child laughing, and his own heart hammering away in his breast. But she must be feeling very unsure of herself too, because she didn't look at him now while she spoke to him, turning her back instead.

"I don't want to say any more about your behaviour yesterday. It was outrageous, and I am ashamed to think of it. You have only yourself to blame for the consequences. All I will say to you now is, that's the last time you'll be allowed in adult company on your own. I have just written to your Papa to say that you must either have a tutor or be sent to a boarding-school. I am not going to plague myself with you any more."

Edgar stood there with his head bent. He sensed that this was only a prelude, a threat, and waited uneasily for the nub of the matter.

"You will now apologize immediately to the Baron." Edgar flinched, but she was not to be interrupted. "The Baron left today, and you will write him a letter. I will dictate it to you."

Edgar made another movement, but his mother was firm.

"And no arguing. Here is paper and ink. Sit down."

Edgar looked up. Her eyes were hard with her inflexible decision. He had never seen his mother like this before, so rigid and composed. Fear came over him. He sat down, picked up the pen, but bent his face low over the table.

"The date at the top. Have you written that? Leave an empty line before the salutation. Yes, like that. Dear Baron, add the surname and a comma. Leave another line. I have just heard, to my great regret—do you have that down?—to my great regret that you have already left Semmering—Semmering with a double 'm'—and so I must write you a letter to do what I intended to do in person, that is—write a little faster, you're not practising calligraphy!—that is to apologize for my behaviour yesterday. As my Mama will have told you, I am still convalescing from a serious illness, and I suffer from my nerves. I often see things in the wrong light, and then next moment I am sorry…"

The back bent over the table straightened up. Edgar turned, roused to defiance again.

"I'm not writing that, it isn't true!"

"Edgar!"

There was a threat in her voice.

"It's not true. I didn't do anything I ought to feel sorry for. I've done nothing wrong. I don't need to apologize. I only came when you called for help!"

Her lips were bloodless, her nostrils distended.

"I called for help? You're out of your mind!"

Edgar lost his temper. With a sudden movement, he jumped up.

"Yes, you did call for help! Out in the corridor last night, when he took hold of you. Let me go, that's what you said, let me go. Loud enough for me to hear it in my room."

"You're lying, I was never out in the corridor here with the Baron. He only escorted me as far as the stairs."

Edgar's heart missed a beat at this bare-faced lie. His voice failed him. He just looked at her, the pupils of his eyes glazed.

"You… you weren't in the corridor? And he… he didn't take hold of you? He wasn't dragging you along with him?"

She laughed. A cold, dry laugh. "You dreamed it."

That was too much for the child. By now he knew that grown-ups told lies, made bold excuses, spoke falsehoods that would slip through the finest net, served up cunning double meanings. But this cold, brazen denial, face to face, enraged him.

"And did I dream getting this mark on my forehead?"

"How should I know who you were fighting? But I'm not entering into any arguments with you, you'll do as you are told, and that's that!"

She was very pale, and was exerting the last of her strength to preserve her composure.

In Edgar, however, something now collapsed, some last flickering flame of trust. He couldn't grasp the fact that the truth could simply be trodden underfoot, extinguished like a burning match. Everything in him contracted, became cold and sharp, and he said viciously, wildly, "Oh, so I was dreaming, was I? About all that in the passage, and this mark? And how you two went for a walk in the moonlight last night, and he wanted to take you down that path, did I dream that too? Do you think you can shut me up in my room like a baby? I'm not as stupid as you think. I know what I know."

He stared boldly into her face, and that broke her strength: the sight of her own child's face right in front of her, distorted with hatred. Her anger burst out wildly.

"Go on with it, you'll go on writing at once. Or else…"

"Or else?…" His voice was insolent and challenging now.

"Or else I'll smack you as if you *were* a baby."

Edgar came a step closer. He only laughed mockingly.

Her hand slapped his face. Edgar cried out. And like a drowning man flailing out with his hands, nothing but a hollow roaring in his ears, red flickering light before his eyes, he struck back blindly with his fists. He felt himself hitting something soft, now he was hitting her face, he heard a scream…

That scream brought him back to his senses. Suddenly he saw himself, and was aware of the monstrous thing he had done, hitting his mother. Fear overcame him, shame and horror, a frantic need to get away from here, sink into the ground, be away, gone, not to have her looking at him any more. He rushed to the door and raced downstairs, through the hotel and along the road, he had to get away, right away, as if a slavering pack of hounds were on his heels.

13

First Insight

FURTHER ALONG THE ROAD he stopped. He had to hold on to a tree, his limbs were trembling so much in fear and emotional upheaval, his breathing was so laboured as it broke out of his overstressed chest. His horror at his own actions had been chasing him, and now it caught him by the throat and shook him as if he had a fever. What was he to do now? Where could he go? For here, in the middle of the woods so close to the hotel where he was staying, only fifteen minutes' walk away, he was overcome by a sense of desolation. Everything seemed different, more hostile, more dreadful now that he was alone with no one to help him. The trees that had rustled in such a friendly way around him yesterday suddenly looked dense and dark as a threat. And how much stranger and more unfamiliar must all that lay ahead of him be! This isolation, alone against the great, unknown world, made the child dizzy. No, he couldn't bear it yet, he couldn't yet bear to be on his own. But where could he go? He was afraid of his father, who was short-tempered, forbidding, and would send him straight back here. He wasn't going back, though, he'd sooner go on into the dangerous, alien atmosphere of the unknown. He felt as if he could never look at his mother's face again without remembering that he had hit it with his fist.

Then he thought of his grandmother, that kind, good old lady, who had spoiled him since he was tiny, had always protected him when he was threatened by discipline or injustice at home. He would hide with her in Baden until the first storm of fury had passed over, he'd write his parents a letter from there saying he was sorry. At this moment he was so humiliated by the mere thought of being all alone in the world, inexperienced as he was, that he cursed his pride—the stupid pride that a stranger had aroused in him with a lie. He wanted nothing but to be the child he had been before, obedient, patient, without the arrogance that, he now felt, had been so ridiculously exaggerated.

But how was he to get to Baden? How could he travel all that distance? He quickly reached into the little leather purse that he always carried with him. Thank goodness, the shiny new golden twenty-crown piece that he had been given for his birthday was still there. He had never been able to bring himself to spend it, but almost every day he had looked to make sure it was there, feasting his eyes on it, feeling rich, and then always affectionately and gratefully polishing up the coin with his handkerchief until it shone like a little sun. But—the sudden thought alarmed him—would it be enough? He had so often travelled by train without even thinking that you had to pay, or wondering how much or how little it cost. A crown or a hundred crowns? For the first time he felt that certain facts of life had never occurred to him, that all the many things around him, things he had held in his hands and played with, were somehow imbued with a value of their own, a particular significance. Only an hour ago he had thought he knew everything; now he felt he had passed a thousand secrets and problems by without a thought, and he was ashamed that his poor amount of knowledge stumbled over the first hurdle he encountered in life. He grew more and more desperate, he took smaller and smaller steps on his faltering way down to the station. He had so often dreamed of flight, of storming out into life, becoming an emperor or a king, a soldier or a poet, and now he looked diffidently at the bright little station building and could think of nothing but whether or not the twenty crowns would be enough to get him to his grandmother's house. The shining tracks stretched on into the countryside, the station was empty and deserted. Shyly, Edgar went into the ticket office and asked at the window in a whisper, so that no one else could hear him, how much a ticket to Baden cost? A surprised face looked out from behind the dark partition, two eyes smiled at the timid child from behind a pair of glasses.

"A full fare?"

"Yes," stammered Edgar, but without any pride, rather in alarm in case it cost too much.

"Six crowns."

"I'd like one, please!"

Relieved, he pushed the shiny, much-loved coin over to the window, change clinked as it was pushed back to him, and all of a sudden Edgar felt wonderfully rich again. He had in his hand the brown piece of cardboard that promised freedom now, and the muted music of silver rang in his pocket.

The train would arrive in twenty minutes' time, so the timetable told him. Edgar withdrew into a corner. A few people were standing idle on the platform, not thinking about him, but the anxious child felt as if they were all looking at him and no one else, wondering why a child was travelling on his own, as if his flight and his crimes were written on his forehead. He heaved a sigh of relief when at last he heard the train's first whistle in the distance, and then the roar as it thundered in. The train that was to take him out into the world. As he boarded it, he saw that he had a third-class ticket. He had travelled only by first class before, and once again he felt that something had changed, that there were differences which had escaped his notice in the past. A few Italian labourers with hard hands and rough voices, carrying spades and shovels, sat opposite him and looked into space with dull eyes. They must obviously have been hard at work on the road, because some of them were tired and fell asleep in the clattering train, leaning back against the hard, dirty wood with their mouths open. They had been working to earn money, thought Edgar, but he could not imagine how much it was. All the same, he felt once more that money was something you didn't always have, something that had to be gained by some means or other. For the first time, he now realized that he took an atmosphere of comfort for granted, he was used to it, while to right and left of his existence there gaped abysses on which his eyes had never looked, going deep into the darkness. All of a sudden he understood that there were professions, there was purpose, that secrets clustered close around his life, near enough to touch, and yet they had gone ignored. Edgar learned a great deal from that single hour when he was all alone, he began to see through the windows of this cramped railway compartment and out into the open air. And quietly, in his dim apprehensions, something began to flower; it was not happiness yet, but a sense of amazement at the variety of life. He had fled out of fear and cowardice, he understood that now, but for the first time he had acted independently, had experienced something of the reality that had previously eluded him. For the first time, perhaps, he himself had become a secret to his mother and his father, just as the world had been a secret to him until now. He looked out of the window with new eyes. And he felt as if, for the first time, he was seeing reality, as if a veil had fallen away from what he saw and now showed him everything, the essence of its intentions, the secret nerve centre of its activity. Houses flew past as if blown away by the wind, and he found himself thinking of the people who lived in them, were they rich or poor, were they happy or unhappy, did they have his own longing to know everything, and were there perhaps children in there who, like himself, had only played games so far? The railwaymen standing by the tracks, waving their flags, seemed to him for the first time not, as before, just dolls and inanimate toys, placed there by indifferent chance; he understood that it was their fate, their own struggle with life. The wheels went round faster and faster, the rounded curves of the track now allowed the train to go down into the valley, the mountains looked gentler and more distant all the time, and then they reached the plain. He looked back once, to the place where they were still blue and full of shadows, distant and unattainable, and he felt as if his own childhood lay there, back in the place where the mountains slowly dissolved into the hazy sky.

14

Darkness and Confusion

B UT THEN IN BADEN, when the train stopped and Edgar
found himself alone on the platform where the lights had
just come on and the signals glowed red and green in the distance,
sudden fear of the falling night mingled with this vivid sight.
By day he had still felt safe, since there were people all around
him and he could rest, sitting on a bench, or looking into shop
windows. But how would he be able to bear it when the people
had gone home, they all had beds and could look forward to some
conversation and then a good night's sleep, while he would have
to wander round on his own with his guilty conscience, lonely in
a strange place? Oh, if only he could have a roof over his head,
and soon too, instead of standing around a minute longer in the
open air! That was his one clear thought.

He quickly walked along the familiar street, looking neither
to right nor left, until at last he reached the villa where his
grandmother lived. It was well situated on a broad road, but not
where all eyes could see it, hidden behind the ivy and climbing
plants of a well-tended garden, bright behind a cloud of green,
an old-fashioned, comfortable white house. Edgar peered through
the gratings like a stranger. Nothing moved in there, the windows
were closed, obviously they were all in the garden at the back with
guests. He was just putting his hand on the cool latch of the gate
when something strange suddenly happened; all at once what he
had thought for the last two hours would be so easy and natural

appeared impossible. How could he go in, how could he say good evening to them, how could he bear and answer all the questions? How could he stand up to the first glance when he had to confess that he had secretly run away from his mother? And how could he possibly explain the enormity of what he had done when he himself didn't understand it now? A door opened inside the house. Instantly, he was overcome by a foolish fear that someone might come out, and he ran on without any idea where he was going.

He stopped when he came to the grounds of the spa buildings, because he saw that it was dark there and he didn't expect to meet anyone. Perhaps he could sit down in the grounds and at last, at long last think calmly, rest, and get his mind in order. He timidly went in. A couple of lanterns were lighted at the entrance, giving a ghostly, watery gleam of translucent green to the young leaves. Further on, however, when he had to go down the slope, everything lay like one great black and seething mass in the bewildering darkness of an early spring night. Edgar slipped shyly past a couple of people who sat talking or reading here in the light of the lanterns; he wanted to be alone. But he could not rest even in the shadowy darkness of the unlit paths. Everything there was full of a soft rustling and murmuring that shunned the light, and was mingled with the sound of the wind breathing through the leaves that bent to it, the crunch of distant footsteps, or the whispering of low voices in what were somehow sensual, sighing tones, a soft moan of fear, sounds that might come from human beings and animals and the restless slumbers of Nature all at once. There was dangerous unrest in the air here, covert, hidden, alarmingly mysterious, something moving underground in the woods that might be just to do with the spring season, but it alarmed the distraught child strangely.

He huddled on a bench in this deep darkness and tried to think what to tell them in the house. But all his ideas slipped away before he could seize and hold them, and against his own will all he could do was listen, listen to the muted tones and strange voices of the dark. How terrible this darkness was, how bewildering and yet mysteriously beautiful! Was the sound made by animals, or people, or just the spectral hand of the wind weaving all that rustling and cracking, all that humming and those enticing calls together? He listened. It was the wind stirring the trees restlessly but—and now he saw it clearly—people too, couples arm-in-arm, coming up from the well-lit town and enlivening the darkness with their mysterious presence. What did they want? He couldn't understand. They were not talking to each other, for he heard no voices, only footsteps crunching restlessly on the gravel, and here and there, in the clearing before him, he saw their figures move fleetingly past like shadows, but always as closely entwined as he had seen his mother and the Baron yesterday evening. So the secret, that great, shining, fateful secret was here too. He heard steps coming closer and closer now, and then a low laugh. Fear that the people who were coming might find him here overcame him, and he huddled even further back into the dark. But the couple now groping their way along the path through that impenetrable darkness did not see him. They went past, still entwined, Edgar breathed again. However, then their footsteps suddenly stopped right in front of his bench. They pressed their faces together. Edgar couldn't see anything clearly, he just heard a moan come from the woman's mouth, the man stammered hot, crazed words, and some sense of warm anticipation pierced his fears with a frisson of pleasure. They stayed like that for a moment, then the gravel crunched underfoot again as they walked on. The sound of their footsteps soon died away in the dark.

Edgar shuddered. The blood was pulsing back into his veins again, hotter and more turbulent than before. Suddenly he was unbearably lonely in this bewildering darkness, and he felt a strong, primeval need for a friendly voice, an embrace, a bright room, people whom he loved. It was as if the whole baffling darkness of this confusing night had sunk into him and was wrenching him apart.

He jumped up. He must get home, home, be at home somewhere in a lighted room, whatever it was like, in some kind of human relationship. What could happen to him, after all? If they beat him and scolded him, he wasn't afraid of anything now, not since he had felt that darkness and the fear of being alone.

His need drove him on, although he was hardly aware of it, and suddenly he was outside the villa again with his hand on the cool latch of the gate. He saw the window shining with light through all the green leaves now, saw in his mind's eye the familiar room and the people there behind every bright pane. Its very closeness made him happy, that first, reassuring sense of being near people who, he knew, loved him. And if he hesitated now it was only to heighten the pleasure of anticipation.

Then a voice behind him, startled and shrill, cried, "Edgar! Here's Edgar!"

His grandmother's maid had seen him. She hurried out to him and took his hand. The door inside was flung open, a dog jumped up at him, barking, they came out of the house with lights, he heard voices, cries of delight and alarm, a happy tumult of shouting and approaching footsteps, figures that he recognized now. First came his grandmother with her arms stretched out to him, and behind her—he thought he must be dreaming—was his mother. Red-eyed with crying, trembling and intimidated, he himself stood in the middle of this warm outburst of overwhelming emotions, not sure what to do or what to say, and not sure what he felt either. Was it fear or happiness?

15

The Last Dream

A LL WAS EXPLAINED: they had been looking for him here,
they'd been expecting him for some time. His mother,
terrified despite her anger by the frantic way the distressed child
had rushed off, had made sure that a search was mounted for
him in Semmering. Everything had been in terrible turmoil, the
most alarming assumptions were rife, when a gentleman came to
say that he had seen the child in the ticket office of the railway
station at about three in the afternoon. They soon found out at
the station that Edgar had bought a ticket to Baden, and without
hesitation his mother immediately set off after him. Ahead of
her she sent telegrams to Baden and to his father in Vienna,
causing much emotion, and for the last two hours everything
possible had been done to find the fugitive.

Now they had captured him, but without using force. In quiet
triumph, he was led indoors, but strangely enough he felt that
none of the harsh words they spoke touched him, because he saw
joy and love in their eyes. And even that pretence, that appearance
of anger lasted only a moment. Then his grandmother hugged
him again, in tears, no one mentioned his wrong-doing any
more, and he felt he was surrounded by wonderful loving care.
The maid took his jacket off and brought him a warmer one, his
grandmother asked if he was hungry, was there anything else
he wanted, they questioned him and fussed around him with
affectionate anxiety, and when they saw how self-conscious he

felt they desisted. He felt, with pleasure, the sensation that he had despised but missed of being a child, and he was ashamed at his rebellion of the last few days, wanting to be rid of all this, to exchange it for the deceptive pleasure of his own isolation.

The telephone rang in the next room. He heard his mother's voice, caught a few words: "Edgar... back... yes, he came here... the last train," and wondered why she hadn't flown at him angrily, had just looked at him with that strangely subdued expression. His repentance grew wilder and more extravagant, and he would have liked to escape the solicitude of his grandmother and his aunt to go into the next room and ask her to forgive him, telling her very humbly, entirely of his own accord, that he wanted to be a child again and obedient. But when he quietly stood up, his grandmother asked, slightly alarmed, "Oh, where are you going?"

He stood there ashamed. They were already afraid if he so much as moved. He had frightened them all, and now they feared he would run away again. How could they understand that no one was sorrier for his flight than he was?

The table was laid, and they brought him a hastily assembled supper. His grandmother sat with him, never taking her eyes off him. She and his aunt and the maid enclosed him in a quiet circle, and he felt strangely soothed by this warmth. All that troubled him was that his mother didn't come into the room. If she could only know how sorry he was, she would surely have come in.

Then a carriage rattled up outside, and stopped in front of the house. The others were so startled that it made Edgar, too, uneasy. His grandmother went out. Loud voices flew this way and that through the darkness, and suddenly he knew that his father had arrived. Timidly, Edgar realized that he was alone in the room again now, and even that moment of isolation troubled him. His father was stern, was the only person he really feared. Edgar listened to the voices outside; his father seemed to be upset, he spoke in a loud and irritated voice. The voices of his grandmother and his mother chimed in, striking a soothing note, they obviously wanted to mollify him. But his father's voice remained hard, firm as the footsteps now approaching, coming closer and closer, they were in the next room, they were just outside the door that was now thrown open.

His father was very tall. And Edgar felt unspeakably small before him as he came in, nerves on edge and apparently really angry.

"What on earth were you thinking of, you little wretch, running away? How could you frighten your mother like that?"

His voice was angry, and his hands were working frantically. Stepping quietly, Edgar's mother had entered the room behind him. Her face was in shadow.

Edgar did not reply. He felt he ought to justify himself, but how could he say he had been deceived and beaten? Would his father understand?

"Well, don't you have a tongue in your head? What happened? You can tell me! Was there something you didn't like? You must have had a reason for running away! Did someone harm you in any way?" Edgar hesitated. The memory of it made him angry again, and he was about to voice his accusations. Then he saw—and it made his heart stand still—his mother make a strange movement behind his father's back. A movement that he didn't understand at first. But now that he looked at her there was a plea in her eyes. Very, very gently she raised her finger to her lips in the sign that requests silence.

At that, the child felt something warm, an enormous, wild delight spread through his entire body. He understood that she was giving him the secret to keep, that the fate of another human being lay on his small, childish lips. And wild, jubilant pride filled him to think that she trusted him, he was overcome by a readiness to make the sacrifice, he was willing to exaggerate his own guilt in order to show how much of a man he was. He pulled himself together.

"No, no… there wasn't any reason. Mama was very kind to me, but I was naughty, I behaved badly… and then… then I ran away because I was scared."

His father looked at him, taken aback. He had expected anything but this confession. He was disarmed, his anger gone.

"Oh, well, if you're sorry, then very well. I won't say any more about it today. I expect you'll think harder another time, won't you? Don't let such a thing ever happen again."

He stopped and looked at the boy, and now he sounded milder.

"How pale you look! But I think you've grown taller. I hope you won't play such childish pranks any more. After all, you're not a little boy now, you're old enough to see reason!"

All this time Edgar was looking at his mother. He though he saw something sparkling in her eyes. Or was it just the reflection of the light? No, it was a moist, clear light, and there was a smile around her mouth thanking him. He was sent to bed now, but he didn't mind being left alone. He had so much to think of, so much that was vivid and full of promise. All the pain of the last few days vanished in the powerful sensation of this first real experience; he felt happy in the mysterious anticipation of future events. Outside, the trees rustled under cover of dark night, but he was not afraid any more. He had lost all his impatience with life now that he knew how full of promise it was. He felt as if, for the first time, he had seen it as it was, no longer enveloped in the thousand lies of childhood, but naked in its own dangerous beauty. He had never thought that days could be so full of alternating pain and pleasure, and he liked the idea that many such days lay ahead of him, that a whole life was waiting to reveal its secret to him. A first premonition of the rich variety of life had come to him; for the first time he thought he had understood the nature of human beings—they needed each other even when they appeared hostile, and it was very sweet to be loved by them. He was unable to think of anything or anyone with hatred, he did not regret anything, and found a new sense of gratitude even to the Baron, the seducer, his bitterest enemy, because he had opened the door to this world of his first true emotions to him.

All this was very sweet and pleasant to think of in the dark, mingling a little with images from dreams, and he was almost asleep already. But he thought the door suddenly opened and someone came in. He did not quite believe it, though, he was too drowsy to open his eyes. Then he sensed a soft face breathing close to his, caressing his own with mild warmth, and knew it was his mother kissing him and stroking his hair. He felt the kisses and her tears, gently responding to the caress, and took it only as reconciliation, as gratitude for his silence. Only later, many years later, did he recognize those silent tears as a vow from a woman past her youth that from now on she would belong only to him, her child. It was a renunciation of adventure, a farewell to all her own desires. He did not know that she was also grateful to him for rescuing her from an adventure that would have led nowhere, and that with her embrace she was handing on to him, like a legacy, the bitter-sweet burden of love for his future life. The child of that time understood none of this, but he felt that it was very delightful to be loved so much, and that through this love he was already drawn into the great secret of the world.

When she drew back her hand from him, her lips left his, and her quiet figure went away, skirts rustling, a warmth was left behind, breathing softly over his lips. And he sensed a sweet longing to feel such soft lips many times again, and be so tenderly embraced, but this mysterious anticipation of the secret he longed to know was already clouded by the shadows of sleep. Once again all the images of the last few hours passed vividly through his mind, once again the book of his youth opened enticingly. Then the child fell asleep and began to dream the deeper dream of his own life.

A CHESS STORY

THE LARGE STEAMSHIP leaving New York for Buenos Aires at midnight was caught up in the usual bustle and commotion of the hour before sailing. Visitors from shore pressed past one another to take leave of their friends, telegraph boys in skew-whiff caps shot names through the lounges, cases and flowers were brought and inquisitive children ran up and down flights of stairs while the orchestra played imperturbably on deck. I was standing in conversation with a friend on the promenade deck, slightly apart from this turmoil, when flashbulbs popped starkly two or three times beside us—it seemed that a few reporters had managed to hastily interview and photograph some celebrity just before our departure. My friend looked across and smiled. "You have an odd fish on board with you there, that's Czentovic." And since I must have looked fairly baffled in response to this news, he explained by adding, "Mirko Czentovic, the world chess champion. He's worked over the whole USA with his tournaments and now he's off to conquests new in Argentina."

As a matter of fact I did now remember this young world champion and even some details of his meteoric career; my friend, a more attentive reader of the newspapers than I am, was able to expand on them with a whole series of anecdotes. Around a year previously, Czentovic had put himself on a level with the most established old masters of the art of chess—Alekhine, Capablanca, Tartakower, Lasker, Bogolyubov—at a single stroke; not since the appearance of the seven-year-old wunderkind Reshevsky at the 1922 New York Masters had the irruption of an unknown into the hallowed guild aroused such a general furore. For in no way was such dazzling success indicated by Czentovic's intellectual capabilities. It soon trickled out that in his private life this chess champion was incapable of writing so much as one sentence correctly in any language and, in the angry taunt of one of his disgruntled colleagues, "his education in every field was uniformly nil." The son of a dirt-poor boatman on the middle Danube whose tiny coracle was run over one night by a grain freighter, the then twelve-year-old was taken in out of pity after the death of his father by the priest of their remote hamlet, and the good pastor did his best to make up with extra help at home all that the dull, uncommunicative, thick-skulled child was unable to learn in the village school.

But his efforts were in vain. Even after the alphabet had been explained to him a hundred times, in each lesson Mirko would again stare at every letter in renewed ignorance; his lumbering brain lacked the power to retain even so simple a concept. When supposedly doing mental arithmetic, he still at fourteen had to employ his fingers to help, and reading a book or newspaper still amounted to an especial strain for the already adolescent boy. Yet Mirko could not in any way be called recalcitrant or unwilling. He obediently did what he was asked, fetched water, chopped wood, helped in the fields, tidied the kitchen and reliably carried out, albeit with an infuriating slowness, whatever task he was assigned. What, however, dismayed the good priest most about the intractable lad was his utter apathy. He did nothing without being specifically prompted, never asked a question, did not play with other boys and didn't of himself seek out any occupation that wasn't expressly decreed; as soon as Mirko had completed his household chores, he sat around stolidly in one room wearing the vacant expression that sheep wear in a meadow, taking not even the slightest interest in what happened around him. In the evenings, when the priest drew on his long-stemmed farmer's pipe and played his habitual three games of chess with the sergeant of the local gendarmes, the flaxen-haired adolescent slumped mutely beside them and stared, apparently sleepy and indifferent, at the chequered board.

One winter evening, while the two partners were engrossed in their nightly contest, they heard the tinkling bells of a sleigh on the village street approaching fast and ever faster. A farmer, his cap dusted with snow, tramped in hastily, his old mother lay dying, would the pastor please hurry to administer the last rites in time. The priest unhesitatingly followed him out. The gendarme sergeant, who hadn't yet emptied his glass of beer, lit himself one more pipe for the road and was just preparing to pull on his heavy boots when he noticed that Mirko's gaze was fixed unswervingly on the chessboard and its unfinished game.

"Well, do you want to take over?" he joshed, quite sure that the somnolent boy wouldn't understand how to move any of the pieces across the board. The lad stared at him diffidently, then nodded and took the pastor's seat. After fourteen moves, the gendarme sergeant had been beaten and also forced to admit that no inadvertently careless move of his own could be blamed for the defeat. The second game ended no differently.

"Balaam's ass!" the priest cried in astonishment after his return, and explained to the less biblically versed gendarme sergeant that a similar miracle had occurred two thousand years previously, when a dumb creature had suddenly spoken the language of wisdom. Despite the lateness of the hour, the priest couldn't resist challenging his semi-literate attendant to a duel. Mirko beat him, too, with ease. His play was dogged, slow, unshakeable; his broad forehead, once lowered, never lifted from the board. But he played with incontestable certainty; over the following days, neither the gendarme sergeant nor the priest was able to win so much as one game against him. The pastor, than whom no one was in a better position to judge his pupil's backwardness, now became curious in earnest as to how far this remarkable and one-sided talent would withstand a sterner test. After he had had Mirko's bristly straw-blond hair cut by the village barber, to make him tolerably presentable, he took him in his sleigh to the small town nearby, where he knew a café on the main square with a club of chess enthusiasts whose play experience had taught him he could not equal. The club's members were more than a little amazed when the pastor pushed a straw-blond, red-cheeked, fifteen-year-old lad in an inwards-turned sheepskin and high, heavy work boots into the coffee house, where the abashed boy stood in a corner shyly looking at the floor until he was called over to one of the tables. In the first game Mirko was beaten, because he had never seen the so-called Sicilian opening at the good pastor's house. In the second, he held their best player to a draw. From the third and fourth onward he beat them all, one after the other.

Now, it's very seldom that exciting events take place in a small provincial town on the middle Danube; for the collected notables, this rustic champion's debut was an immediate sensation. It was unanimously decided that the juvenile savant absolutely must stay in town until the following day, to allow them to call together the other members of the club and, above all, to notify old Graf Simczic, a chess fanatic, at his castle. The pastor, who now looked on his ward with an entirely new sense of pride, but whose joy in the discovery wouldn't, after all, lead him to neglect his duty of conducting Sunday Mass, consented to leave Mirko behind for a further trial. Young Czentovic was lodged in the hotel at the chess club's expense and that evening saw his first ever water closet. On the following, Sunday, afternoon, the chess room was packed. Mirko, sitting almost motionless for four hours at the board and without saying a word or even once looking up, defeated each player after the last. Eventually, a simultaneous match was suggested. It took some time before they could make the uneducated boy understand that in simultaneous games he was to take on the various players by himself. But once Mirko had grasped this practice, he soon settled to the task and walked slowly in his heavy, creaking shoes from table to table, ultimately winning seven out of eight.

Fervent discussions now ensued. Although this champion didn't strictly belong to the town, the crowd's local pride was nonetheless vigorously ignited. Perhaps the little town, whose presence on the map hardly anyone had yet noticed, would finally and for the first time gain the honour of sending a famous man out into the world. An agent named Koller, who otherwise provided chanteuses and cabaret singers for the garrison stage, offered—if a year's grant would be provided—to have the young man professionally trained in the art of chess by a distinguished little master he knew in Vienna. Graf Simczic, who in sixty years of daily chess play had never encountered such an extraordinary opponent, signed the contract at once. This was the first day in the astounding career of the boatman's son.

After six months, Mirko had mastered various secrets of chess technique, albeit with a peculiar limitation that was later much noted and mocked in professional circles. Czentovic never managed to play a game of chess from memory or, to use the technical term: blind. He entirely lacked the ability to relocate the battlefield to the unbounded space of the imagination. He always had to have the black and white board with the sixty-four squares and the thirty-two pieces tangibly in front of him; even during the period of his global fame he carried a folding pocket chessboard around with him so that, when he wanted to reconstruct a great match or solve a problem for himself, he could have the positions physically before his eyes. This in itself nugatory defect revealed a lack of conceptual ability and was as intensely discussed in those narrow circles as it would have been among musicians if an outstanding virtuoso or conductor had shown himself unable to play or conduct without the score open in front of him. But this strange idiosyncrasy in no way hindered Mirko's stupendous ascent. At seventeen he had already won a dozen chess prizes, at eighteen he captured the Hungarian championship and finally, at twenty, the championship of the world. The most audacious grandmasters, all of them immeasurably superior in intellectual force, in vision and in daring, each succumbed to his cold and tenacious logic just as Napoleon did to the cumbersome Kutuzov or Hannibal to Fabius Cunctator, of whom Livy reports that in his childhood he too demonstrated unmistakable signs of phlegm and imbecility. So it happened that the illustrious pantheon of chess masters, in whose ranks are united the most varied types of intellectual pre-eminence—philosophers, mathematicians; perceptive, ingenious or often creative minds—was breached for the first time by a total stranger to the life of the mind, a blunt, tongue-tied country bumpkin from whom not even the most artful journalists could wring a single publishable phrase. What Czentovic denied the newspapers in well-turned sentences, however, he soon abundantly compensated for with anecdotes about his person. The moment he stood up from the chessboard, where he was a master without parallel, he was hopelessly transformed into a grotesque and almost comical figure; despite his smart black suit, his pompous cravat with its rather flashy pearl pin and his effortfully manicured fingers, in his bearing and manners he remained the same limited farm boy who'd swept the pastor's kitchen in the village. In his maladroit and almost shamelessly crude way, and to the amusement and fury of his colleagues, he, in his petty and often even vulgar greed, tried to extract whatever money could be extracted from his talent and fame. He would travel to any town, staying always in the cheapest hotels, he would play in the most miserable club where his fee was guaranteed, he allowed himself to be depicted on soap adverts and even, ignoring the ridicule of his competitors, who knew very well that he was incapable of writing three sentences back to back, sold his name for a *Philosophy of Chess*, which had in reality been written for the enterprising publisher by a diminutive Galician student. Like every truly dogged character, he lacked any sense of the ridiculous; since his victory in the world championship, he considered himself the most important man in the world, and the knowledge that all these erudite, intellectual and splendid speakers and writers had been defeated by him on their own field—and, above all, the more palpable fact that he earned more than they did—transformed his initial lack of confidence into a cold and insolently unconcealed pride.

"But how could so rapid an ascent *not* turn such an empty head?" concluded my friend, who had just been recounting some examples of Czentovic's childish arrogance. "How can a twenty-one-year-old clodhopper from the Banat not come a bit unglued if he suddenly earns more in a week by pushing some pieces around a board than his entire village back home does with a whole year's log-chopping and bitter grunt work? And then, isn't it also terribly easy to consider yourself a great man if you aren't hobbled by the slightest inkling that a Rembrandt, a Beethoven, a Dante or a Napoleon ever lived? This boy knows only one thing in his walled-in brain: that he hasn't lost a game of chess for months; and since he doesn't even suspect that there's anything other than chess and money that's valuable on this earth of ours, he has every reason to find himself impressive."

These stories of my friend's didn't fail to arouse a particular interest of mine. Throughout my life, every type of monomaniac infatuated with a single idea has exerted a certain draw on me, because the more a person restricts himself, the closer, conversely, he approaches to the infinite; it is these apparently sequestered people who, like termites, build their particular obsessions into the most extraordinary and unique abbreviations of the world outside. So I made no secret of my intention to use the twelve-day voyage to Rio to take this exceptional specimen of a one-dimensional mind closer under my microscope.

But: "You won't have much luck," my friend warned. "As far as I know, no one's yet managed to get even the least psychological material out of Czentovic. Behind all those abyssal limitations of his that sly peasant has enough cunning not to expose his weaknesses, something he avoids by the simple expedient of not entering into any conversation that isn't with the modest country-men of his whom he meets in the small guest houses he stays in. If he smells out an educated person, he creeps back into his shell; that way no one can ever claim to have heard him say anything stupid or to have plumbed the supposedly bottomless depths of his ignorance." And indeed my friend proved to be right. Over the first few days of the voyage, I saw it would be completely impossible to get close to Czentovic unless by some gross intrusion, which, after all, is not my style. He did sometimes pace across the promenade deck, but always with his hands clasped behind his back in the proudly withdrawn bearing familiar to us from that well-known painting of Napoleon; he also completed his peripatetic deck circuit so hastily and abruptly that I would have had to trot after him to be able to introduce myself. And in the lounges, the bar, the smoking room, he never showed himself; as the steward confidentially explained, he spent most of the day in his cabin, practising or recapitulating chess matches on an enormous board.

After three days, it began to irritate me that his obdurate defensive tactics were outmanoeuvring my desire to approach him. I had never in my life had the opportunity to make the personal acquaintance of a chess master and the more effort I now made to imagine the type, the more inconceivable seemed a mind that revolved for a whole lifetime in a space of sixty-four black and white squares. From my own experience, I knew well the mysterious attraction of the "royal game", this singularity among the pastimes men have invented, which steps magnificently out from under the tyranny of chance to award its laurels only to the intellect or, rather, to a particular form of intellectual ability. But aren't we guilty of being insultingly disparaging if we refer to chess as a game? Is it not also a science, an art, poised between one and the other like Muhammad's coffin between heaven and earth, a unique synthesis of all opposites; ancient and yet always new, mechanical in its structure yet animated only by the imagination, limited to a geometrically petrified space yet unlimited in its permutations, always developing yet ever sterile, a logic with no result, a mathematics without calculations, an art without works, an architecture without materials, which has nevertheless proved more lasting in its forms and history than *any* works or books, the only game that belongs in every era and among every people, of which no one knows what god brought it to earth to kill boredom, sharpen the wits and tauten the spirit? Where is its beginning and where its end? Any child can learn its laws, any bungler can try himself on its field; and yet on this unchangeably narrow square is bred a particular species of master, unlike any others, people with an aptitude ordained solely for chess, specific geniuses in whom vision, patience and technique interact in as delicately determined a combination as in mathematicians, poets or musicians, but just at other levels and with other interconnections. In an earlier era of physiological enthusiasm, a scientist like Gall might have dissected the brain of one of these masters to discover whether there was a special coil in a chess genius's grey matter, a kind of chess muscle or chess cortex that would be more intensively developed than in other skulls. And how fascinated would those physiognomists have been by a case like Czentovic's, where a specific genius seemed to have been encased in total intellectual inertia like a thin thread of gold in a hundredweight of dumb rock. In principle I had always understood that such a singular, such an ingenious game must call forth its own specific matadors; but how hard, how impossible even, to imagine the life of a mentally unincapacitated person whose world reduces itself to the cramped monotony of black and white, one who seeks his life's triumphs in the mere to and fro, back and forth of thirty-two figures, a person to whom a new opening in which he moves forward a knight instead of a pawn signifies the great feat that will secure his niggardly corner of immortality in the recesses of some chess book—a person, an intellectual person who, without going insane and for ten, twenty, thirty, forty years, directs his mind's full analytic force time and again onto the laughable task of backing a wooden king into the angle of a wooden board!

And now, for the first time, one of these phenomena, one of these peculiar geniuses or enigmatic fools, was very close by, six cabins away on the same ship, and I, unfortunate that I am, for whom intellectual curiosity has always mutated into a kind of fixation, found myself unable to approach him. I began to cook up the most absurd stratagems: for example, to tickle his vanity by requesting a pretend interview for an important newspaper, or trapping him by his greed and inviting him to a lucrative tournament in Scotland. But I finally remembered that the hunter's most trusted method of luring the capercaillie consists of mimicking its mating cry; how could I capture the attention of a chess master more certainly than by playing chess myself?

Now, I've never been a serious chess player, for the simple reason that I've only ever set out the pieces frivolously and for my own enjoyment; if I sit for an hour at the board, it is in no way to exert myself, but quite the opposite, to relax out of mental tension. I "play" chess in the truest sense of the word, while the others, the real chess players, "business" it, to introduce a dubious new verb into the language. But for chess, like love, one needs a partner and I didn't at that point know whether there were more chess fanciers than the two of us on board. To tempt them from their caves, I laid a primitive trap in the smoking room, in that I and my wife, who is an even weaker player, ostentatiously arranged ourselves on opposite sides of a chessboard. We hadn't even made six moves when someone passing stopped; then another man requested permission to watch and, eventually, there also appeared the partner I had been hoping for, one who challenged me to a game. His name was McConnor and he was a Scottish mining engineer I heard had made a vast fortune drilling oil in California. In appearance he was stocky, with a powerful, hard and almost square-sided jaw, strong teeth and a replete complexion whose pronounced redness could probably be attributed at least in part to generous consumption of whisky. His conspicuously broad, almost athletically vehement shoulders also unfortunately made themselves felt in the character of his play, as this Mr McConnor belonged to that type of egotistical high achiever who takes a defeat in even the most inconsequential game as an aspersion on his personal sense of self. Accustomed to barrelling his way heedlessly through life and spoilt by the fact of his success, this solidly built self-made man was so unshakeably convinced of his own superiority that he saw any opposition as unbecomingly insubordinate and even borderline insulting.

Upon losing the first game, he became sullen and began to declare dictatorially that this could have occurred only through a moment of inattention; for his failure in the third, he blamed the noise in the adjoining room; and never was he willing to lose a game without immediately demanding a rematch. At first, this arrogant obstinacy amused me; after a while, I endured it as an unavoidable side effect of what I really intended: to tempt the world champion to our table.

It succeeded after three days and then only in part. Whether Czentovic had seen us through the porthole from the promenade deck or whether it was coincidence that he honoured the smoking room with his presence—in any case, as soon as he saw us laymen practising his art, he instinctively took a step closer and from that measured distance cast an appraising glance at our board. McConnor was just making a move. And just this one move seemed sufficient for Czentovic to realize how little it would merit his masterly interest to follow our dilettantish efforts. In the same self-explanatory manner that one of us, when offered a bad detective novel in a bookshop, puts it aside without even flicking through, he walked away from our table and left the smoking room. "Weighed and found wanting," I thought, irked a little by that cool, contemptuous glance, and in order to somehow vent my disgruntlement I said to McConnor:

"Your move doesn't seem to have delighted the master."

"What master?"

I explained to him that the gentleman who had just passed and looked disparagingly at our game was the chess master Czentovic. Well, I added, we would both survive and not have our hearts broken by his illustrious disdain; not every cat can get the cream. But to my surprise, my casual information had a wholly unexpected effect on McConnor. He got excited at once, forgetting all about our match, and his ambition began to thud almost audibly. He'd had no idea Czentovic was on board and Czentovic absolutely had to play against him. He'd never played against a grandmaster except once in a simultaneous match with forty others; even that had been tremendously exciting and he'd come extremely close to winning. Did I know the chess master personally? I didn't. Wouldn't I like to introduce myself to him and ask him to join us? I declined, on the grounds that I'd heard Czentovic wasn't particularly open to making new acquaintances. Besides, what allure could it have for a world champion to go a round with us third-rate amateurs?

Well, it would have been better not to talk about third-rate amateurs to so arrogant a man as McConnor. He leant back in irritation and brusquely declared that for his part he could not believe Czentovic would decline a civil invitation from a gentleman; he would see to it himself. At his request I gave him a brief physical description of the grandmaster and then he was already storming off onto the promenade deck after Czentovic, indifferently abandoning our poor match in his unrestrained impatience. Again I felt that, once the owner of those broad shoulders had thrown himself into something, he could not be stopped.

I waited eagerly. After ten minutes McConnor came back, not very cheerfully, I thought.

"Well?" I asked him.

"You were right," he answered, a little huffily. "Not a very pleasant man. I introduced myself, explained who I was. He didn't even shake my hand. I tried to tell him how proud and honoured all of us on board would be if he played a simultaneous match against us. But the man was damned stiff about it; he was sorry, he said, but he had contractual obligations to his agent expressly forbidding him to play without a fee at any point on his tour. His minimum he said was 250 dollars a game."

I laughed. "That's something I'd never have imagined, that pushing wooden figures around a board could be so lucrative a profession. I hope you took your leave just as politely."

But McConnor stayed completely serious. "The match is scheduled for tomorrow afternoon at three o'clock. Here in the smoking room. I hope we won't roll over too easily."

"What? You promised him the 250 dollars?" I exclaimed, totally shocked.

"Why not? *C'est son métier.* If I had a toothache and there happened to be a dentist on board, I wouldn't demand that he pull my tooth for nothing. The man's quite right to make the fee hefty; the real experts in every field are also always the best businessmen. And as for me: the clearer a deal, the better. I'd rather pay hard cash than have Mr Czentovic go easy on me and then have to thank him for it at the end. After all, I've lost more in an evening at our club than 250 dollars and that wasn't playing against world champions. There's no shame in it for a 'third-rate amateur' to be knocked over by Czentovic."

It amused me to see how deeply I had wounded McConnor's *amour propre* with the innocent little phrase "third-rate amateurs". But since he was willing to pay for our expensive sport, I could hold nothing against his misplaced arrogance, as it was finally going to lead me into acquaintance with the object of my curiosity. We hastily informed the four or five other gentlemen who'd outed themselves as chess players about the forthcoming event and, so as to be disturbed as little as possible by people passing by, reserved not only our table but also the neighbouring ones for the imminent match.

On the following day, our little group gathered at the appointed time. The middle seat opposite the master was naturally assigned to McConnor, who discharged his nervousness by lighting one heavy cigar after another and again and again looking impatiently at the clock. But the world champion—after hearing my friend's stories I had been expecting something like this—kept us waiting a further ten minutes to heighten the effect of his eventual entrance. Without introducing himself—"You know who I am and who you are doesn't interest me," this rudeness seemed to suggest—and with an arid professionalism, he began the practical arrangements. Since a simultaneous match was impossible on the ship due to a lack of boards, he suggested that we all play against him together. After each move he would go to another table at the end of the room so as not to disturb our discussions. Once we had made our countermove, and since, regrettably, there was no table bell to hand, we would tap a spoon against a glass. He suggested a maximum thinking time of ten minutes, unless we had other preferences. We naturally assented like shy schoolboys to each of his suggestions. The choice of pawns allotted Czentovic black; he countered our first move still standing and then went straight across to the spot he'd suggested, where he leafed casually through an illustrated magazine.

There's little sense in reporting on the match. Of course it ended the way it was bound to end, with our total defeat, which came after only twenty-four moves. That a grandmaster could knock over half a dozen mediocre or sub-mediocre players with ease was not surprising in itself; all that actually irritated us was the arrogant way Czentovic let us feel how easily he was dispatching us. Each time, he cast only an apparently cursory glance at the board, looking past us as indifferently as if we, too, were inanimate wood, and this insolent manner couldn't but remind us of the way you, without really looking, toss a scrap of food to a mangy dog. With a little delicacy he could, I thought, have alerted us to our mistakes or encouraged us with a friendly word. But even after the end of the match, this dispassionate chess automaton didn't utter so much as another word after saying "mate", but waited unmoving by the table to see if we wanted another match. I had already stood up, helpless as one always is against unashamed rudeness, to indicate by a gesture that, with the completion of this dollar transaction, the pleasure of our acquaintanceship had, for me at least, come to an end, when, to my anger, McConnor raised his hoarsened voice to say, "Rematch!"

I was shocked by the provocation in his tone; in that moment, McConnor resembled a boxer about to start thumping more than he did a civil gentleman. Whether it was the unpleasant treatment that Czentovic had meted out to us or just his pathologically touchy arrogance—McConnor's appearance had changed almost out of recognition. His face had gone red right up to the hairline, his nostrils were flared wide by the pressure within, he was sweating visibly and, below his tight-pursed lips, a furrow cut down his pugnaciously extended chin. It disturbed me to recognize in his expression a flickering of the uncontrolled passion that otherwise seizes people at the roulette table, when they have doubled their bet for the sixth or seventh time and the right colour still hasn't come. In that instant I knew that this fanatically arrogant man would play and play and play against Czentovic, betting the same or doubles each time, even if it cost him his whole fortune, until he had eventually won just one match against him. If Czentovic could sit it out, he'd found a gold mine in McConnor from which he'd be able to shovel a few thousand dollars by the time we reached Buenos Aires.

Czentovic was unmoved. "Of course," he answered. "The gentlemen now play black."

The second match altered nothing, other than that the addition of some curious fellow passengers made our circle both larger and more vivacious. McConnor stared as fixedly at the board as if wanting to magnetize the figures with his will to win; I felt he would have happily sacrificed 1,000 dollars for a joyous cry of "mate" against his cold-blooded opponent. Strange to say, some of his grim excitement seeped unnoticed into the rest of us. Each individual move was discussed more heatedly than the last; each time, one of us would hold the others back at the last moment before we could agree to give the signal for Czentovic to return to our table. Inch by inch we reached the thirty-seventh move and, to our own surprise, a position had developed that seemed strikingly advantageous, in that we had succeeded in moving our c-pawn forward onto the penultimate square, c_2; we needed only to push it forward onto c_1 to gain a second queen. We were by no means comfortable with this all-too-obvious opportunity; we unanimously suspected that the advantage we seemed to have achieved must have been intentionally placed there as bait by Czentovic, whose overview of the situation was naturally far further-sighted than ours. But despite intense communal searching and deliberating, we were unable to put our finger on the feint. Eventually, almost having run out of thinking time, we decided to risk the move. McConnor had already touched the pawn to push it forward onto the last square when he was grabbed roughly by the arm and someone whispered, quiet and fierce, "For God's sake, don't!"

We all turned around. A man of perhaps forty-five, whose sharp, narrow face I had already noticed on the promenade deck due to its almost chalk-like pallor, had joined us in these last few minutes when all our attention had been directed at the problem on the board. Feeling our scrutiny on him, he hastily added:

"If you promote up to a queen now, he'll take her right away with the bishop c_1; then you'll take the bishop with your knight. But in the meantime he'll move his passed pawn onto d_7, threatening your rook, and even if you put him in check with your knight, you'll lose and be finished off in nine or ten moves. It's almost the same position that Alekhine initiated against Bogolyubov at Pistyan in 1922."

McConnor dropped his hand from the piece in astonishment and stared in as much wonder as the rest of us at this man who had come as unexpectedly to our aid as an angel from heaven. Someone who could calculate a checkmate nine moves in advance must be a specialist of the first order, perhaps even a championship rival who was travelling to the same tournament; and in his sudden appearance and intervention there was something almost bordering on the supernatural. McConnor was first to compose himself.

"What would you advise?" he whispered agitatedly.

"Don't advance right away, escape, evade instead! First move your king off the row that's under threat, from G8 to H7. He'll then probably switch his attack to the other flank. But you can parry that with rook C8–C4; that'll cost him two tempi, a pawn and, with that, the upper hand. Then it'll be one passed pawn against another and, if you hold your defence together, you can still force a draw. That's as much as you can get out of it."

We were astonished again. The precision no less than the speed of his calculations was somehow bewildering; it was as if he were reading the moves from a printed book. Nonetheless, the unimagined opportunity his intervention gave us, to perhaps hold the world champion to a draw, worked on us like an enchantment. We moved aside as one to allow him a clearer view of the board. McConnor asked again:

"So, king G8 to H7?"

"Absolutely! Evasion first!"

McConnor obeyed, and we tapped the glass. Czentovic walked back to our table with his wonted nonchalant tread and assessed our countermove with only the quickest of glances. Then he moved his kingside pawn H2–H4, just as our unknown helper had predicted. And already the latter was whispering excitedly:

"Rook forward, rook forward, c8 to c4, then he'll have to cover his pawn before anything else. But that won't help him a bit! You'll ignore the pawn and strike with your knight, D3–E5, and with that you'll have re-established the equilibrium. Put all the pressure forward, attack instead of defend."

We didn't understand what he meant. To us his words might as well have been in Chinese. But now that he was under the man's spell, McConnor moved as commanded without a second thought. We again tapped the glass to call Czentovic back. For the first time, he didn't decide at once, but stared intently at the board. His brows knitted involuntarily together. Then he made precisely the move that the stranger had predicted, and turned to go. But before he walked away, something new and unanticipated occurred. Czentovic lifted his gaze and scrutinized our ranks; he evidently wanted to find out who was suddenly offering him such vigorous resistance.

From that moment on, our excitement expanded boundlessly. We had been playing without any serious hope, but now the thought of breaking Czentovic's cold pride drove hot blood rushing through all our pulses. Our new friend had ordained the next move and we were ready—my fingers shook as I tapped the spoon against the glass—to call Czentovic back. And now came our first triumph. Czentovic, who till then had only ever played standing up, hesitated, hesitated, and finally sat down. He sat slowly and ponderously; but in so doing his previous condescension to us was physically abolished. We had forced him to put himself on the same level as us, at least spatially. He thought for a long while, his eyes lowered unmovingly onto the board, his pupils hardly visible under his dark eyelids, and the strain of thought gradually opened his mouth, lending his round face a strikingly simple cast. Czentovic thought for several minutes, then made his move and stood up. And already our friend was whispering:

"He's playing for time. Good thinking! But don't go along with it! Force the exchange, exchange at all costs, then we can hold him to a draw and no god will be able to help him!"

McConnor obeyed. There began in the next moves between the two of them—the rest of us had long since sunk to the role of extras—a back and forth we found incomprehensible. After perhaps seven more moves, Czentovic looked up after long consideration and said: "A draw."

For a moment there was total quiet. You could suddenly hear the rushing of the waves and the radio jazzing away in the salon, you could hear every step on the promenade deck and the faint, fine swishing of the breeze coming through the frames of the portholes. None of us breathed, it had come too fast and we were all still almost shocked by this improbable event, that in a match already half lost this unknown had bent the world champion to his will. McConnor tilted back and the breath he'd been holding was audibly expelled from his lips in a satisfied "Ah!" For my part, I watched Czentovic. During the final moves he had already seemed to me to be growing paler. But he knew how to keep himself together. He maintained his apparently unconcerned posture and, while pushing the figures from the board with a steady hand, asked in only the most equanimous manner:

"Would the gentlemen like a third match?"

He asked the question merely practically, merely as business. But the strange thing was: he hadn't looked at McConnor, but had flicked a sharp glance directly at our rescuer. Like a horse recognizing a new, a better rider by his firmer seat, he must in our final moves have recognized his real, his actual opponent.

We instinctively followed his glance and looked in expectation at the stranger. But before he could collect himself, let alone reply, McConnor had already triumphantly shouted to him:

"Of course! And this time you have to play against him yourself! You versus Czentovic!"

But now something unforeseen happened. The stranger, who, oddly enough, was still staring in concentration at the empty board, gave a start when he felt everyone's gaze turned on him and heard himself addressed so enthusiastically. His expression became confused.

"Out of the question, gentlemen," he stammered, visibly disconcerted. "That is, under no circumstances... I don't even come into consideration... I haven't, it's been twenty, no, twenty-five years since I sat at a chessboard... and only now do I see how inappropriately I've behaved in interfering uninvited in your game... Please excuse my forwardness... I don't wish to bother you any further." And before we had recovered from our surprise, he had already retreated and left the room.

"But this is impossible!" roared the temperamental McConnor, thudding his fist on the table. "What's completely out of the question is that that man hasn't played chess in twenty-five years! He was calculating every move, every counter, five or six moves ahead. Nobody can do that just off the top of his head. It's out of the question—isn't it?"

McConnor had unintentionally addressed Czentovic with this last remark. But the world champion remained as cool as ever.

"That's not something I can judge. But the gentleman's play certainly was interesting and quite unusual; that was why I let him have that chance." Standing up nonchalantly, he added in his businesslike manner:

"If the gentleman or gentlemen would like another match tomorrow, I will be at your disposal after three o'clock."

We couldn't suppress a silent smirk. Each of us knew that Czentovic hadn't been generously giving our unknown helper a chance and that this remark was nothing other than a naive pretext to mask his own failure. Our desire to see such unswerving pride humiliated grew all the stronger. We peaceful, languid ship-dwellers had all been overcome by a wild, grasping belligerence; we were fascinated, provoked, by the idea that the grandmaster's laurels might be wrested from him on our very own ship here in the middle of the ocean, news that would be flashed by telegraph across the world. Moreover, there was the lure of the mysterious in our unexpected rescuer's intervening right in the critical instant, as well as the contrast between his almost timorous modesty and the unshakeable self-confidence of the professional. Who was this unknown? Had chance brought a hitherto undiscovered chess genius to light? Or was a famous master, for some unfathomable reason, keeping his name concealed? We debated all these possibilities with the greatest enthusiasm and even our most daring hypotheses weren't daring enough to reconcile the stranger's enigmatic timidity and surprising protestations with his unmistakable expertise. In one respect, however, we were all in agreement: on no account to forgo the spectacle of a renewed contest. We resolved to try everything to have our helper play a match against Czentovic on the following day, with McConnor promising to underwrite the material gamble. Since we knew from questioning the steward that the stranger was an Austrian, I, as his countryman, was allocated the task of presenting our request.

It wasn't long before I found the man who had fled so hastily. He was reclining in a deckchair on the promenade deck, reading. Before approaching, I used the opportunity to examine him. The sharply chiselled head rested on the pillow with an air of light fatigue; again I was struck by the pallor of his relatively young face, whose temples were framed by blindingly white hair; I don't know why, but I had the feeling that this man must have aged very suddenly. Hardly had I gone closer, when he stood politely and introduced himself with a name I knew as that of a distinguished old Austrian family. I recalled that a man of that name had been a member of Schubert's most intimate circle and that one of the old Kaiser's personal physicians had come from the same family. When I relayed our plea that he take up Czentovic's challenge, Dr B was visibly baffled. It turned out he had had no idea it was a grandmaster, and the most successful of them all at that, against whom he'd acquitted himself so well. For some reason, this seemed to make a particular impression on him, and he asked time and again whether I was quite certain that his opponent really had been a recognized grandmaster. I soon realized that this made my task easier and thought it merely prudent, sensing his delicacy, not to mention that the material cost of a possible defeat would be charged to McConnor's wallet. After long hesitation, Dr B eventually agreed to the match, but not without having explicitly asked me to repeat a warning to the others, that they ought not to place exaggerated hope in his ability.

"Because," he added with a far-away smile, "I truly don't know whether I'm capable of playing a game of chess by all the rules. Please believe that it wasn't false modesty when I said I haven't touched a chess piece since my schooldays, that is, in more than twenty years. And even then I was just another average player without any especial talent."

He said this so ingenuously it was impossible to doubt he was sincere. And yet I couldn't resist giving voice to my amazement at how precisely he had been able to remember each strategic combination invented by those various masters; he must have thoroughly concerned himself at least with the theory of chess. Dr B again smiled in that curiously dreamy way.

"Thoroughly concerned myself!—God knows, that's the truth, that I've thoroughly concerned myself with chess. But that was under very specific, indeed quite unique circumstances. It's a slightly complicated story, but could serve as a small addendum to the great and marvellous times we live in. If you have half an hour…"

He had gestured to the deckchair next to his. I gladly accepted his invitation. There was no one else nearby. Dr B took off his reading glasses, laid them aside and began:

"You were kind enough to mention that you, being Viennese, recognized my family's name. But I suspect you will hardly have heard of the legal practice that I ran first with my father and then subsequently alone, because we took on no cases the newspapers would report and avoided new clients as a matter of principle. In truth, we weren't a proper legal office any more, but confined our activities to advising and managing the assets of the larger monasteries, to whom my father, as a previous member of the clerical party, was very close. Moreover—now that the monarchy belongs to the past, I suppose it can all be talked about—we were entrusted with managing the funds belonging to some members of the imperial family. These connections to the court and the clergy—an uncle of mine was a personal physician of the Kaiser's, another was abbot of Seitenstetten—already reached back over two generations; all we had to do was maintain them, and it was a quiet, I might even say noiseless, task that this inherited trust assigned us, actually requiring no more than the strictest discretion and dependability, two qualities that my late father possessed in the highest degree; his vigilance was such that he succeeded, in the years both of inflation and of revolution, in maintaining his clients' considerable estates. Then, when Hitler took the reins in Germany and began his raids on the property of the Church and the monasteries, various negotiations and transactions from the other side of the border (intended to rescue at least portable property from confiscation) also went through our hands; and both of us knew more about certain secret political dealings of the Curia and the imperial house than the public will ever find out. But it was precisely the inconspicuousness of our firm—we didn't even keep a plaque on the door—and the care we took ostensibly to avoid all monarchist circles, that offered the safest protection against unwanted inquiry. In fact, in all those years, no ministry anywhere in Austria ever suspected that the imperial house's secret couriers were collecting or delivering their most important messages in our unprepossessing, fourth-floor office.

"Now, the National Socialists, for their part, even before they armed their troops against the world, had begun to muster just as disciplined and dangerous an army in all their neighbours' countries: the legion of the aggrieved, the frustrated, the resentful. In every ministry, in every business they had lodged their so-called 'cells'; at every turn, right up to the cabinets of Dollfuss and Schuschnigg, they had embedded their spies and listeners. Even in our nondescript practice, as I discovered, unfortunately, only too late, they had placed their man. He was no more than a miserable and talentless clerk whom I had employed on a priest's recommendation solely in order to give the firm the outward appearance of a normal business; in reality, we used him for nothing more than innocent messages, let him attend to the telephone and file the documents, that is, only those documents that were quite harmless and inconsequential. He was never allowed to open the post, I typed all important letters myself without making copies, I took any essential files home with me and moved all secret discussions without exception to either the order's priory or my uncle's consulting room. Thanks to these precautions, our informer got to see nothing of our real business; but through some unlucky coincidence, the vain, ambitious boy must have noticed that we mistrusted him and that all manner of interesting things were going on behind his back. Perhaps one of the couriers had in my absence carelessly referred to 'His Majesty' instead of, as agreed, to 'Baron Fern'; or the wretch must have opened our letters without permission—in any case, before I could even begin to suspect him, he had had Munich or Berlin assign him the task of keeping us under surveillance. Only much later, when I'd already long since been imprisoned, did I remember that the initial laxity in his work had in the last months been transformed into sudden eagerness and that he had often offered almost pushily to take my correspondence to the post. So, I can't absolve myself of a certain unwariness, but then, haven't even the highest diplomats and generals been taken unawares by the Hitlerites? How long and how lovingly the Gestapo had directed their attention onto me I learnt on the same evening that Schuschnigg announced his resignation and a day before Hitler marched into Vienna, when I was arrested by the SS. Luckily, I had managed to burn the most important papers as soon as I heard Schuschnigg's farewell speech on the radio and—literally in the last moments before the thugs smashed down my door—had sent the indispensable paperwork, for the assets the monasteries and the two archdukes had deposited abroad, to my uncle, in a laundry basket carried by my reliable old housekeeper."

Dr B interrupted himself to light a cigar. In this unsteady light I spotted a nervous twitch around the right corner of his mouth which I had noticed before and which, as I could see, returned every few minutes. It was only a fleeting movement, hardly more than a hint, but it made his whole face strangely restive.

"Now you probably think that I'm going to tell you about one of those concentration camps to which everyone who stayed true to our old Austria was sent, about the humiliations, the ordeals, the tortures I suffered there. But nothing of the kind occurred. I was put in a different category. I wasn't driven off to join those unfortunate souls on whom long-held resentments were taken out with physical and mental degradation, but assigned to the other, very small group, of those from whom the National Socialists hoped to extort either money or important information. In itself, my modest person was wholly uninteresting to the Gestapo. But they must have found out that we were the straw men, the administrators and confidants of their bitterest enemies, and what they hoped to gain from me was incriminating material: material against the monasteries, whom they wanted to prove had moved their assets fraudulently, as well as material against the imperial family and all those who had self-sacrificingly taken a stand for the monarchy. They suspected—and in truth, not without reason—that a significant proportion of the funds that had passed through our hands was still hidden out of reach of their greed; so they brought me in on the first day of their regime to apply their tried and tested methods to forcing these secrets out of me. The people in my category, from whom money or important material was to be extracted, were not deported to concentration camps, but kept back for special treatment. You will perhaps remember that our Chancellor and, for example, Baron Rothschild, from whose relatives they hoped to coerce millions, were not kept behind the barbed wire of a prison camp, but were given what appeared to be preferential treatment and conveyed to a hotel, the Hotel Metropole, which was also the Gestapo headquarters, where each was given a room of his own. This distinction was also bestowed on such an unremarkable personage as myself.

"A room to yourself in a hotel—that actually sounds very humane, doesn't it? But you can take it from me that what was intended for us 'dignitaries', by not cramming us twenty to an icy barracks, but housing us in well-heated rooms of our own, was not a more humane, but only a more sophisticated interrogation technique. The pressure with which they wanted to force the required material out of us was more subtle than raw beatings or bodily torture: that is, the strictest conceivable isolation. They did nothing to us—just placed us in total nothingness, because there is famously nothing that exerts more strain on the human spirit than nothingness itself. By locking each of us alone into a complete vacuum, into a room that was hermetically isolated from the world outside, they intended to induce—rather than from without, with beatings and cold—a pressure that would eventually open our mouths from within. At first glance, the room I'd been allocated seemed not at all uncomfortable. It had a door, a bed, an armchair, a washbasin, a barred window. But the door stayed locked day and night; on the table there was no book, no newspaper, no sheet of paper, no pencil; the window stared at a firewall; all around me and even on my person, they had constructed a total void. Every possession had been taken away: my watch, so that I couldn't follow the time, my pencil, so that I couldn't write, my penknife, so that I couldn't open my veins; even the tiny numbness of a cigarette was denied me. Never, other than the warder, who was prohibited from answering a single question or speaking a single word, did I see a human face, never did I hear a human voice; eyes, ears, all my senses were starved of nourishment from morning to night and from night to morning; you were left with yourself, irrecoverably alone with your body and four or five mute objects, table, bed, window, washbasin; you lived like a diver under a bell in the dark ocean of that silence, like a diver who guesses that the cord to the world above has torn free and that he will never be hauled back up out of the noiseless deep. There was nothing to do, nothing to hear, nothing to see, everywhere and always there was nothing around you, a complete timeless and spaceless void. You walked up and down, and your thoughts went up and down with you, up and down, again and again. But even thoughts, as insubstantial as they seem, need some basis, or they begin to rotate and revolve around themselves; they, too, cannot endure a nothing. You waited from morning to evening, and nothing happened. You waited some more, and more. Nothing happened. You waited, waited, waited, you thought, thought, thought till your temples hurt. Nothing happened. You remained alone. Alone. Alone.

"That lasted fourteen days, which I lived outside time, outside the world. If a war had broken out, I would not have known. My world consisted only of table, door, bed, washbasin, armchair, window and wall, and I stared always at the same paper on the same wall; every line in its zigzag pattern was carved into the innermost fold of my brain as if with an iron sickle, so often did I stare at it. Then, finally, they began the interrogations. You were abruptly fetched without really knowing whether it was day or night. You were called and led through corridors, not knowing why; then you waited, not knowing where, and found yourself suddenly standing in front of a table with a few uniformed people sitting around it. On the table was a sheaf of paper: files whose contents you couldn't know, and then began the questions, the real ones and the fake, the clear and the guileful, the trick questions and the cover questions, and while you answered, anonymous, malicious fingers leafed through the papers whose contents you couldn't know, and anonymous, malicious fingers wrote something in a log, and what they wrote you couldn't know either. But the most dreadful aspect of these interrogations was that I could never estimate nor appraise what the Gestapo's people already knew about the proceedings in my office and what they would first have to get out of me. As I mentioned before, I had sent the truly incriminating papers to my uncle at the eleventh hour, in the hands of my housekeeper. But had he received them? Had he not received them? And how much had that clerk given away? How many letters had they intercepted, how much might some inept priest in one of the German monasteries we represented already have been bullied into revealing? And they asked and asked. Which bonds I had bought for which monastery, with which banks I had corresponded, whether I knew a Mr Such-and-such or not, whether I had received letters from Switzerland, or from Steenookerzeel? And since I could never work out how much they had already discovered, my every answer entailed a monstrous responsibility. If I admitted something they didn't already know, I might be unnecessarily sending someone to the gallows. But if I denied too much, I condemned myself instead.

"The interrogation, however, wasn't even the worst of it. The worst was being returned to my nothingness afterwards, to the same room with the same table, the same washbasin, the same wallpaper. Hardly was I alone, but I tried to reconstruct the cleverest answers I could have given and what I would have to say next time to divert the suspicion that I had perhaps just called down with an unconsidered remark. I thought, I reviewed, I examined, I inspected each of my answers down to each and every word I'd said to the interrogators, I tried to weigh up what they would have written down though I knew I would never work out nor discover what that was. But these thoughts, once set in motion in that empty space, would not stop circling in my head, always starting again anew, in new combinations, and carrying on into my sleep; after every interrogation by the Gestapo, my own thoughts just as mercilessly took over the work of question-ing and delving and tormenting, and were perhaps even worse, because at least those other interrogations ended after an hour, while these ones never did, thanks to the artful torture of this loneliness. And around me always only the table, the cupboard, the bed, the wallpaper, the window, and no distraction, no book, no newspaper, no unknown face, no pencil to note something down, no matches to play with, nothing, nothing, nothing. Only now did I recognize how devilishly shrewd, how psychologically murderous this hotel room system really was. In a concentration camp you might have had to cart stones till your hands bled and your feet froze off in your shoes, you would have lain packed together with two dozen others in the cold and the stink. But you would have seen faces, you would have had a field, a hand-cart, a tree, a star, something, anything to stare at, while here everything was always the same around you, always the same, the same appalling sameness. Here there was nothing to deflect me from my thoughts, from my delusions, from my pathological recapitulation. And precisely that was what they intended—I was to gag and gag on my thoughts till they choked me and I had no choice but finally to spit them out, to speak, speak out about whatever they asked, and finally give up the men and the material they wanted. Gradually, I began to feel my nerves slackening under the strain of this terrible void and, conscious of the danger, I tightened them to breaking point, trying to find or contrive some kind of distraction. To occupy myself I tried to recite and reconstruct everything that I had ever learnt by heart, the national anthem and the nursery rhymes of my childhood, my schoolboy Homer, paragraphs from the civil law code. Then I tried mental arithmetic, adding arbitrary numbers, dividing them again, but in the void my mind was losing its ability to hold the numbers fast. I couldn't concentrate on anything. Again and again, the same thought flickered up: what do they know? What did I say yesterday, what must I say next time?

"This actually indescribable state of affairs lasted four months. Now—four months, that's easily jotted down: less than a dozen letters. It's off the tongue in an instant: four months—two syllables.

The lips articulate them in a quarter of a second: four months! But no one can recount, can measure, can communicate, not to anyone else, not to himself, how long a time in a spaceless, timeless place really lasts, and to no one can you explain how it corrodes and consumes you, this nothing and nothing and nothing around you, this always-the-same-table-and-bed-and-washbasin-and-wallpaper, and always this silence, always the same warder who pushes in the food without looking, always the same thoughts circling around in the void until you start to go mad. Various small signs made me worriedly conscious that my brain was becoming muddled. At first I had been internally lucid in the interrogations, what I had said had been calm and composed; the doubled thinking of what I should say and what I shouldn't had still been manageable. Now I could articulate even the simplest sentences only as a stammer, because while I spoke I stared hypnotized at the pen running its report across the paper, as if I wanted to chase my own thoughts. I felt my strength waning, I felt myself inching ever closer to the moment when I, to save myself, would tell them everything I knew and perhaps even more than that, when I, to escape this choking nothingness, would give up a dozen people and their secrets without even gaining myself more than a moment of rest. One evening it had come to that: when the warder happened to bring me my food in that moment of asphyxiation, I suddenly shouted after him: 'Take me to be questioned! I want to make a declaration! I want to declare everything! I want to tell them where the papers are, where the money is! I'll tell them anything they want, anything!' Fortunately he didn't hear me. Perhaps he didn't want to.

"In this hour of extreme need, something happened that I couldn't have anticipated, offering rescue, rescue at least for a little while. It was at the end of July, a dark, overcast, rainy day:

I remember that detail quite precisely, because the rain pattered against the windows in the corridor through which I was led to the interrogation. I had to wait in the interrogators' anteroom. You always had to wait before being interrogated: even this waiting was part of their technique. First they shredded your nerves by calling you, by suddenly collecting you from the cell in the middle of the night, and then, when you had prepared yourself to be interrogated, had tensed your mind and will to resist, they let you wait, pointless-pointedly, for an hour, two hours, three hours before the interrogation, to tire the body and cloud the mind. And they let me wait particularly long on that Wednesday, the 27th of July, a good two hours standing and waiting in the anteroom; I remember that date, too, so precisely because in that anteroom where I—naturally, not being allowed to sit down—had to prop myself up on my legs for two hours, there hung a calendar; and I don't have to tell you how in my hunger for anything printed, anything written, I stared and stared at that one number, those few words—27th July—hanging on the wall; I ate them right into my brain. And then I waited again and waited and stared at the door, when would it finally open?, thinking about what the inquisitors would ask me this time and knowing regardless that they would ask me something quite different from whatever I prepared myself for. But despite all that, this pain of waiting and standing was also a boon, a relief, because this was still a different room from my own, a little larger, with two windows instead of one, and without the bed and without the washbasin and without that particular crack in the windowsill that I had already examined a million times over. The door was differently painted, a different armchair stood against the wall alongside, to the left, a cabinet with files and a wardrobe with hangers, from which three or four military overcoats, my torturers' overcoats, were hanging. I had something new, something different to look at, finally and for once something different for my famished eyes, and they greedily sucked in every detail. I observed every fold of those overcoats; I noticed, for example, a droplet dangling from one of the wet collars, and as ludicrous as it may sound, I waited in absurd agitation to see whether this droplet would finally purl down along the fold or be able to hold out a little longer against gravity's pull and continue to cling on—yes, I stared and stared for minutes, holding my breath, at this droplet, as though it were my life that was dangling there. Then, once it had finally rolled away, I recounted the buttons on the coats, eight on one, eight on the second, ten on the third, then I again compared the lapels; my eyes caressed, toyed with, grasped at all of these ridiculous, meaningless trifles with a hunger beyond my power to describe it. Suddenly, my gaze caught something. I had discovered that the side pocket of one of the overcoats was bulging slightly outward. I took a step closer and believed I recognized in the bulge's right-angled shape what it was this swollen pocket was holding: a book! My knees began to shake: a BOOK! In four months I hadn't held a book in my hand, and even just the thought of a book in which I would see words rowed up against one another, lines, sides and pages, the thought of a book, in which other, new, unknown, diverting thoughts could be read, pursued and taken into the brain, intoxicated and yet somehow also stunned me. My eyes stared hypnotized at the little protrusion the book formed inside the pocket, they blazed at that unremarkable pocket as if wanting to burn a hole in the fabric. I was soon unable to contain my greed; I edged involuntarily closer. Just the thought of even touching a book through the coat material made the nerves in my fingers glow down to their tips. Almost without knowing it, I pressed myself closer still. Luckily, the guard was paying no attention to what must have been peculiar behaviour; perhaps it seemed natural to him that, after standing upright for two hours, a person would want to lean a little against the wall. Eventually, I was standing almost beside the overcoat. I had intentionally placed my hands behind my back so that they could reach for the coat inconspicuously. I touched the fabric and then through it did indeed feel something right-angled, something that was supple and crinkled quietly when I creased it—a book! A book! And like a shot the thought went through me: steal it! You might succeed and then you can hide it in your cell and read, read, read; read again at last! The thought, hardly had it struck, worked on me like strong poison; my ears began to thump and my heart began to hammer, my hands went ice-cold and stopped moving. But after this first moment of stupefaction, I quietly and craftily slid myself even nearer to the overcoats; with my hands still hidden behind my back and my gaze always fixed on the guard, I pushed the book higher and higher up out of the pocket. And then: a grab, a light, careful sliding and suddenly the small, not very substantial book was there in my hand. Only now was I afraid of what I had done. But there was no going back. What to do with it? I shoved the slim volume down behind me and into my trousers to where my belt gripped it, and from there bit by bit across to my hip, so that while walking I could hold it in place, military-style, at the trouser seam. Now for the first test. I stepped away from the wardrobe, one pace, two paces, three paces. It worked. I could hold the book steady as I walked by keeping my hand pressed hard against my belt.

"Then came the interrogation. It demanded more effort from me than ever before because, while I was answering, all my strength was concentrated not on what I said but above all on unobtrusively clutching the book. Luckily, the interrogation ended quickly on that occasion and I carried the book safely into my room—I won't hold you up with all the details, though it did once slip dangerously from my trouser in the middle of the corridor and I had to simulate a vicious coughing fit so as to bend over and push it securely back up under my belt. But what a moment it was as I stepped with it back into my torture chamber, alone at last and yet alone no longer!

"Now you probably assume that I gripped, scrutinized, read the book through right then. Not at all! I first wanted to savour the foretaste of having a book with me, to artificially prolong the wonderful and soothing pleasure of dreaming about what sort of book I would most like my booty to be: very densely printed, first of all, containing many, many letters, many, many very thin pages, so that I could read it all the longer. And I wished it would be a work I would find intellectually demanding, nothing flat, nothing light, but something that I could learn, learn verbatim, some poetry, or best of all—what a hubristic dream!—some Goethe or Homer. But it wasn't long before I could no longer restrain my hunger, my greed to know. Stretched out on the bed so that the warder wouldn't see if he happened to come in, I, trembling, pulled the volume out from under my belt.

"The first glance was a disappointment and even a kind of bitter anger: this book I had carried off at such hideous risk, that I had saved up with such incandescent expectation, was no more than a chess almanac, a collection of 150 matches between grandmasters. Had I not been barred and bolted in, I would in my initial rage have hurled the book through an open window, because what was I supposed to do, what could I do with this rubbish? As a schoolboy I had, like most others, now and then, out of boredom, tried my hand at chess. But what could I even begin to do with this theoretical stuff? Chess can't be played without a partner, let alone without pieces, without a board. Despondent, I leafed through the pages in case I might yet find something to read, an introduction or perhaps some instructions; I found nothing but the naked, square diagrams of each match, with, underneath them, an initially incomprehensible notation, A2–A3, KTF1–G3 and so on. This all seemed an algebra to which I had no key. Only after some time did I decode that the letters A, B, C, stood for the columns, the numbers 1 to 8 for the rows, and that they recorded the current position of each chess piece; the purely graphic symbols then at least began to have a kind of language. Perhaps, I thought, I could construct a kind of chessboard in my cell and then try to play through these matches; it seemed like a sign from above that my bedcover was patterned in broad check. Properly folded, one end could be laid out to leave sixty-four squares together. I concealed the book under the mattress and ripped out the first page. Then, from small crumbs I saved from my bread, I began to make what were of course laughably crude reproductions of the various chess figures, king, queen, and so on; after endless effort, I could finally begin to reconstruct on my bedcover the position depicted in the book. When, however, I tried to play the match, everything went utterly wrong with my ridiculous crumb figures, half of which I had darkened with dust so as to tell them apart. In those first days, I confused myself unremittingly; five times, ten times, twenty times I had to restart this one match from the top. But who on earth had as much unused and useless time at his disposal as I, the slave of nothingness; who else had such limitless greed and patience at his command? After six days I could play the match faultlessly to its conclusion, after a further eight days I no longer needed to have the crumbs on the bedcover to visualize the position in the book, and after eight days more the chequered bedcover, too, became dispensable; the book's previously abstract symbols, the A1, A2, C7, C8, automatically transformed themselves behind my forehead into visual, three-dimensional configurations. The shift had happened wholesale: I had projected the chessboard and its pieces into my interior and could see the current position in the formulae just as a practised musician can hear all the orchestra's voices and harmonies merely by looking at the score. After fourteen more days I was able to effortlessly play any match in the book from memory—or, to use the technical term: blind. Only then did I begin to understand what an immeasurable blessing my bold theft had secured me. For all at once I had an activity—senseless, pointless, you may say, but nonetheless one that nullified the nothing around me; in those 150 tournament matches I possessed a wonderful weapon against the crushing monotony of my place and time. To pace the relish of my new occupation, I rigidly divided up my every day: two matches in the morning, two matches in the afternoon and a quick run-through in the evening. Thus my day, which had previously been as formless as dough, was filled, and I was occupied, without even becoming tired, because the game of chess has the marvellous advantage that bending all your energies onto its restricted field doesn't, even with the greatest mental effort, slacken the brain, but instead hones it in agility and vigour. Little by little, after I had just been playing mechanically through the games, there awoke in me an artistic, a pleasurable appreciation of the game. I learnt to understand its finesse, its tricks and stings in attack and defence, I grasped the technique of forethought, of calculation, of riposte, and soon recognized the personal touch of each grandmaster as surely as you know the author of some verse from only a few of its lines; what had begun merely as a means of passing the time now became enjoyment, and the figures of the great chess strategists—Alekhine, Lasker, Bogolyubov, Tartakower—stepped as beloved comrades into my loneliness. Every day, my dumb cell was enlivened by unending variety and it was precisely the routine of practising that gave my thinking back its shattered certainty:

I felt my brain reinvigorated and even, as it were, freshly whetted by the constant mental discipline. That my thinking was again becoming clear and concise was proved when I was interrogated; I had unknowingly trained myself on the chessboard to defend against false threats and concealed manoeuvres; I gave no more ground in the interrogations from then on and it even seemed to me that the Gestapo were slowly beginning to regard me with a certain respect. Perhaps they were watching all the others go to pieces and asking themselves from what secret reserves I was drawing the strength for such steadfast resistance.

"This happy time, in which I systematically played through that book's 150 matches day in, day out, lasted around two and a half or three months. I then unexpectedly came to a dead stop. Suddenly I was again confronted with nothingness. Once I had played through each match twenty or thirty times, it lost the allure of novelty, of surprise; its animating, stimulating power was exhausted. What sense was there in repeating over and again these matches whose every move I already knew by heart? Hardly had I begun the opening, but the whole sequence automatically concatenated itself in my head; there were no more surprises, no thrills, no problems. To occupy myself further, to generate the exertions and diversions that had become indispensable, what I would have needed was another book with other games. Since this was completely impossible, there was only one way ahead on this strange, crazed course: instead of playing the old matches I would have to invent new ones. I would have to attempt to compete with, or rather, against myself.

"I don't know to what extent you've thought about the mental situation in this game of games. But even a moment's consideration must make clear that in chess, a game of pure thought, unaffected by chance, wanting to play against yourself is a logical absurdity. What chess's attraction fundamentally rests on is, after all, that its strategies are developed in two separate brains, that, in this war of the intellect, black does not know white's stratagems and seeks constantly to guess and disrupt them while white, for his part, tries to outstrip or parry the secret intentions of black. If black and white consisted of one and the same person, it would create a paradoxical situation in which one and the same brain would have to know and yet not know something; that is, when playing as white, it would have to forget on command what it had wanted and intended a moment before as black. This kind of doubled thinking actually presupposes a total division of consciousness, an arbitrary fading in and out of brain functions as if on some mechanical apparatus; wanting to play chess against yourself is as much of a paradox as jumping over your own shadow. Now, to be brief, this impossibility, this absurdity is what I in my desperation attempted over the following months. I had no other choice than this lunacy if I wasn't to lapse into either unmitigated insanity or a total mental atrophy. I was forced by the terrible position I was in at least to attempt this division into a black self and a white self, just so as not to be smothered by the awful nothingness all around me."

Dr B leant back in his deckchair and closed his eyes for a moment, as if trying to suppress a disturbing memory. The strange twitch he was unable to control again ran around the left corner of his mouth. He sat up a little higher in his chair.

"So—I hope that what I've explained up to this point has been fairly intelligible. But I'm not at all sure that I can give you as clear an idea of what followed. This new occupation placed such limitless strain on my mind that it was impossible to exert any control over myself while it was going on. I've already mentioned that in my opinion it is nonsensical per se to want to play chess against yourself; but even that absurdity might have had some small chance of succeeding on a real chessboard, because the chessboard's own physical reality would have allowed a certain distancing, a material externalization. In front of a real chessboard with real pieces, you can pause to think things over, you can place yourself purely bodily first on one side of the table, then on the other, and survey the situation now from black's perspective, now from white's. But when compelled, as I was, to project these struggles against myself, or, if you prefer, with myself, into my own interior, I had to keep the current position on all sixty-four squares fixed in my mind, and not just the configuration at any given point, but I also had to imagine both sides' possible future moves and indeed—I know how ridiculous all this sounds—calculate them twice or thrice, no, six, eight, twelve times over for each of my selves, always four or five moves ahead for both black and white. Forgive me for asking you to think this lunacy through, but while playing this game in the abstract space of my imagination, I had to calculate four or five moves ahead as white and then do the same as black—that is, deduce all possible situations arising from the match's development with two brains, the black brain and the white. But this splitting of my self wasn't even the most dangerous aspect of this abstruse experiment; devising matches myself made me lose the ground beneath my feet. When I had merely been playing through the tournament matches, as I had practised in the previous weeks, my efforts had after all been nothing more than reproductions, straight recapitulations of given subject matter, and as such no more of a strain than if I had learnt poems by heart or memorized paragraphs of law—a disciplined activity and excellent mental exercise as a result. The two matches that I rehearsed in the morning, the two in the afternoon, had constituted a definite workload that I could complete without the slightest discomposure; they substituted for a normal occupation and, moreover, if I lost my way or didn't know how to proceed in one of the matches, I still had a physical handhold on the book. That was why this activity had been so healing and, above all, so calming for my tattered nerves, because playing other people's matches didn't bring myself into play; which of black or white was victorious didn't matter to me, it was Alekhine and Bogolyubov who were fighting over the victor's laurels, and I myself, my mind, my spirit, enjoyed it simply as a spectator, a connoisseur of the back and forth and the beauty of their games. From that moment on, when I began to try to play against myself, it was myself I began unknowingly to challenge. Each of my selves, my black self and my white self, had to compete against the other, and each for its part was seized by an ambition, an impatience, to win and to conquer; as my black self, I could hardly wait to see what my white self would do. Each of my selves crowed triumphantly when the other made a mistake, and yet cursed itself for its own clumsiness.

"This all sounds like folly, and indeed, this kind of artificial schizophrenia, this splitting of consciousness with an admixture of dangerous excitement, would be unthinkable for a normal person in a normal state of mind. But don't forget that I had been violently torn away from any normality, I was a captive, innocent but imprisoned, expertly tormented by loneliness for months on end, a person who had long wanted something on which to vent his accumulated rage. And since I had nothing other than this senseless game against myself, it was into this game that I hurled my rage, my lust for vengeance. Something in me wanted to be proved right and there was nothing for me to struggle against but this other self within me; so as I played I worked myself up into manic over-animation. Initially I had still thought calmly, deliberately, I had taken breaks between one match and the next, to recuperate from the exertion; but my inflamed nerves soon stopped allowing me that pause. Hardly

had my white self made a move, but my black self pushed feverishly forward; hardly was one match finished when I was already
challenging myself to the next, because each time one would
be defeated by the other and demand his revenge. Never will
I be able even to estimate how many matches I played against
myself in those last months, deranged and insatiable in the
cell—perhaps a thousand, perhaps more. It was an obsession
against which I had no defence; from early till late I thought of
nothing but bishop and pawn and rook and king and A and B
and C and check and castle, all I was and all I felt drove me to
the chequered square. The pleasure had become a lust, the lust
become a compulsion, a mania, a frenetic rage, pervading not
only my hours of waking but soon also those of sleep. I could
think only in chess, only in chess movements, chess problems; I
would wake with a damp forehead and realize that I must have
continued playing unconsciously as I slept, and if I dreamt of
people, it was only in the movements of the bishop, the rook,
in the to and fro of the knight. Even when I was called to be
interrogated, I could no longer keep a grip on my responsibilities;
I suspect that I talked very confusedly in those last interrogations and my questioners would sometimes look at each other
in incomprehension. But in truth, while they questioned and
reported, I, in my disastrous desire, was just waiting to be led
back to my cell to continue my game, my frenzied game against
myself, onward into another match and another and another.
Every interruption became a nuisance; even the quarter of an
hour in which the warder tidied my prison cell, the two minutes
in which he brought me my food were agony for my fevered
impatience; sometimes the dish with my food was still standing
untouched at evening; in playing I was forgetting to eat. My
only physical sensation was a terrible thirst; it must have been
the fever of this constant thinking and playing; I would drain

a bottle in two long draughts and harass the warder for more, and in the next moment again feel my tongue dried out in my mouth. Eventually, my agitation while I played—and I did nothing else from morning to night—escalated to such a degree that I was no longer able to sit still for so much as a moment; I paced uninterruptedly up and down while I thought the matches through, paced ever faster and faster and faster up and down, up and down, and ever more heatedly as the match came to its conclusion; the craving to win, to subjugate, to defeat myself, was transformed into a kind of rage, and I trembled with constant impatience, because there was always one self in me for whom the other was too slow. Each drove the other on; as laughable as it may sound, I began to berate myself—with 'come on, come on!' or 'faster, faster!'—whenever one of the selves in me wasn't quick enough in his riposte to the other. It is now, of course, quite clear to me that the condition I was then in was a pathological type of mental over-exertion, for which I can find no other name than one so far unknown to medicine: chess poisoning. In the end, this monomaniacal obsession began to attack not just my brain but my body as well. I became ever thinner, I slept restless and disturbed, every time I awoke I needed an especial effort to force my leaden eyelids open; sometimes I was so weak that when I held a glass of water I struggled to bring it to my mouth, so badly did my fingers tremble; but as soon as the game had begun I was overcome by a savage strength: I paced up and down with my fists clenched, and as if through a red mist I sometimes heard my own voice, hoarse and malignant, shouting 'check' or 'mate' at itself.

"How this gruesome, this indescribable condition reached its crisis is something I myself am unable to relate. All I know about it is that one morning I woke up and it was a different waking than usual. My body was somehow detached from me,

I was resting cosy and comfortable. A thick, good tiredness, such as I hadn't known for months, lay on my eyelids, lay so warmly and amiably that at first I couldn't even bring myself to open them. For many minutes I lay awake and savoured this muted heaviness, this lying leisurely still with deliciously torpid senses. Then it seemed that I heard voices behind me, the voices of living people, and you can't imagine my elation, because for so many months, for almost a year, I had heard no other words than those dropping hard, sharp and malicious from my interrogators' bench. 'You're dreaming,' I said to myself. 'You're dreaming. Whatever you do, don't open your eyes! Let it last, this dream, or you'll see that damned cell around you again, the chair and the washbasin and the table and the wallpaper with the infinitely repeated pattern. This is a dream—keep dreaming!'

"But curiosity won the upper hand. Slowly and cautiously I opened my eyes. To a marvel: this was a different room in which I found myself, a room wider, more spacious than my hotel cell. An unbarred window let in unhindered daylight and a view of trees, green trees waving in the breeze, instead of my blank firewall; white and smooth shone the walls, high and white the ceiling rose above me—really, I was lying in a new, an unfamiliar bed, and truly, it was no dream; there were quiet human voices whispering behind me. I must have given a start of surprise, because I heard a footstep approaching. A woman with a graceful gait came closer, a woman with a white cap over her hair, a carer, a nurse. A shudder of delight ran through me: I hadn't seen a woman in a year. I stared at the lovely apparition and my stare must have been wild and ecstatic, because she hushed me at once with 'Easy! Nice and easy!' I heard only that it was a voice—was this not a person who was speaking? Did the world really still contain a person who wasn't interrogating, wasn't tormenting me? And more than that—an unfathomable wonder—it was a soft, warm, an almost tender woman's voice. I stared hungrily at her mouth, because in that infernal year I had ceased to believe that any person could speak kindly to another. She smiled at me—yes, she smiled, there were still people who could smile kindly—then placed her finger to her lips in admonition and went quietly on. But I could not obey her order. I hadn't yet sated my eyes on that miracle. I tried to haul myself upright in bed, to see her, to see this wonder of a human being who was kind. But as I tried to pull myself up by the edge of the bed, I found I couldn't. Where my right hand had been, my fingers and wrist, I felt something foreign, a big, thick, white dressing, apparently a voluminous bandage. I stared in confusion at this white, thick, foreign thing on my hand, then slowly I began to grasp where I was and to think about what might have happened to me. I must have been injured, either that or I had injured my hand myself. I was in a hospital.

"The doctor came at midday, a friendly older man. He recognized my family's name and mentioned my uncle, the Kaiser's personal physician, with so much respect that I immediately had the feeling he meant me well. He then posed all kinds of questions and one in particular that astounded me—whether I was a mathematician or perhaps a chemist. I said no.

"'Remarkable,' he mumbled. 'In your fever you kept crying out peculiar formulae—c_3, c_4. We had no idea what it was.'

"I asked what had happened to me and he gave me an odd smile.

"'Nothing serious. An acute irritation of the nerves,' and, after he had cautiously looked around, added quietly: 'And a wholly understandable one at that. Since the 13th of March, isn't that right?'

"I nodded.

"'It's no surprise with those methods,' he mumbled. 'You aren't the first. But don't worry.'

"From the reassuring way he whispered this to me and from the benevolence of his expression I knew that I was in safe hands.

"Two days later, the good doctor explained quite candidly what had happened. The warder had heard me screaming aloud in my cell and had at first believed that someone had broken in and that I was fighting with him. But no sooner had he shown himself at the door than I had flung myself at him, shrieking wild phrases that sounded something like, 'Make your move, you wretch, you coward!', then tried to grab him by the throat and finally attacked him so savagely he'd had to call for help. As they then dragged me off in this rabid state to undergo a medical examination, I'd suddenly torn myself free and dashed towards the window in the corridor, smashing in the pane and so slicing open my hand—this is the scar here, still deep. I had passed the first few nights in hospital in a kind of mental fever, but now he considered me to be wholly lucid again. 'Naturally,' he added in an undertone, 'that's something I won't be mentioning to the gentlemen in charge, otherwise they'll take you back there. You can count on me, I'll do what I can.'

"What this helpful doctor told my tormentors is beyond my knowledge. But in any case he achieved what he had wanted to: my release. Perhaps he declared me mentally unsound, or perhaps I had already become unimportant to the Gestapo since Hitler had occupied the Sudetenland and so considered the case of Austria to be closed. All I had to do was sign a promise to leave our homeland within fourteen days, and those fourteen days were so filled with all the thousand formalities that are now required of the erstwhile world citizen before he can travel abroad—military papers, police, tax, passport, visa, health certificate—that I had no time to think much about what had been. It seems that there are mysterious regulating forces operating in our brains, which automatically exclude anything that could disrupt or endanger the mind, because whenever I wanted to think back to my time in the cell, it was as if the lights went out in my brain; only after weeks and weeks, actually only here on this ship, did I first find the courage to recall what had happened.

"And now you will understand why I behaved so improperly and—I presume—so incomprehensibly towards your friends. I just happened to be strolling through the smoking room when I saw them sitting at the chessboard; I was rooted to the floor in dismay and amazement. I had completely forgotten that chess could be played at a real chessboard with real pieces, and that two different people sit bodily opposite each other to play it. I honestly needed a few minutes to remind myself that what those players were doing was at heart the same game that I in my helplessness had attempted against myself for all those months. The formulae I'd relied on in my grim exercises had after all only been substitutes, symbolic of these very pieces; my surprise that these pieces' movement across the board was the same as what my imagination had projected in my head was similar to what an astronomer must feel when, having used complicated methods to calculate the position of a new planet on paper, he actually sees it in the heavens as a white, clear star. I stared at the board as if magnetized and saw my diagrams, my knight, rook, king, queen and pawn as real pieces cut from wood; to understand the situation in the match I first had to retransform it back from my world of abstract notation into that of movable figures. I became curious to watch this real game between two opponents. That was when the embarrassing event occurred that I, forgetting all good manners, interfered in your game. But that false move of your friend's struck me like a knife in the heart. It was an act of pure instinct, holding him back, an impulsive movement, the way you unthinkingly grab a child you see lean over a railing. Only subsequently did I realize what a coarse impropriety I had committed by being so forward."

I hurried to reassure Dr B how pleased we all were that this coincidence had allowed us to meet him, and explain that all he had confided in me would only double my interest in watching him in the improvised tournament tomorrow. Dr B made a nervous gesture.

"No, please don't expect too much. It's to be no more than a test... a test of whether... whether I'm at all capable of playing a normal game of chess, on a real chessboard with actual pieces and a living opponent... because I now doubt more than ever that those hundreds and perhaps thousands of games I played really were proper chess matches and not merely a kind of dream chess, a fever chess, a fevered game in which intermediate steps were elided as they are in dreams. You cannot, I hope, seriously think that I would arrogate to myself the ability to go round for round with a grandmaster, let alone the world champion. What interests and intrigues me is just a posthumous curiosity to find out whether everything in the cell was still chess or had already crossed into madness, whether I was close before or already over that dangerous precipice—just that, no more."

We heard the gong calling us to dinner from the end of the ship. Dr B had reported all this to me far more comprehensively than I condense it here and we must have talked for almost two hours. I gave him my heartfelt thanks and said goodbye. But I hadn't even crossed the deck when he came after me and, visibly anxious and even stuttering slightly, added:

"One more thing! Would you please tell the other gentlemen in advance, so that I don't seem impolite afterwards: I'll only play a single match... it's to be no more than drawing a line

under an old account—a final settling-up and not a new start…
I wouldn't want to slip for a second time into the frenetic obsession that I now think of with horror… and for that matter…
for that matter, the doctor warned me at the time… explicitly
warned me. Anyone who has once lapsed into a mania is always
in danger, and having once been poisoned by chess, albeit that
I'm now cured, it would be better not to go anywhere near a
chessboard… So you understand—only this one trial for my
own sake and then: no more."

Punctually at the agreed time, three o'clock the following
day, we gathered in the smoking room. Our circle had been
enlarged by two more lovers of the royal game, two ship's
officers who had begged a break from their duties to watch the
tournament. Nor did Czentovic make us wait for him as he had
on the previous day and, once the colours had been assigned,
this remarkable match, between our *homo obscurissimus* and the
famed world champion, began. I am sorry it was played only
for us ignorant spectators and that its progress is as lost to the
annals of chess as Beethoven's piano improvisations are to
music. We did all try on the following afternoon to reconstruct
the game from memory, but in vain; we had probably paid too
much attention to the game's players and not to how it unfolded,
because the mental contrast between their two natures became
ever more physically apparent as the match went on. Czentovic,
the professional, remained as motionless as a block, his eyes
lowered sternly and staring at the board; thinking seemed for
him to be an almost muscular effort, forcing all his organs to
extremes of concentration. Dr B's demeanour, on the other
hand, was easy and unselfconscious. As a real dilettante, in the
loveliest sense of the word, for whom the pleasure in the game
is the game itself, the "*diletto*", he remained relaxed, he chatted
and explained in the initial intervals, lit a cigarette with a steady

hand and, when it was his turn, only ever looked at the board for a minute. Each time, it seemed his opponent's move had long been anticipated.

The obligatory opening moves were made quite quickly. Only at the seventh or eighth did something like a definite pattern begin to develop. Czentovic extended his thinking time; that was how we knew the struggle for supremacy was starting to bite. But to give truth her due, the gradual development of the positions, as in any real tournament match, was something of a disappointment to us laymen. The more the pieces wove each other into extraordinary configurations, the more impenetrable the actual state of play became to us. We were unable to make out what either opponent intended, nor which of the two presently held the advantage. We discerned that individual pieces were pushed forward like levers to break open the enemy front, but—since these exceptional players based each decision on permutations several moves ahead—we were unable to grasp the strategic intention behind this back and forth. A stultifying fatigue also set in, thanks to Czentovic's endless pauses, which were also beginning to visibly irritate our friend. I watched perturbed as he started to twitch ever more restlessly around his chair the longer the match went on, now nervously lighting one cigarette after another, now clutching his pencil to make a note, then ordering another mineral water, which he gulped down glass by glass; it was obvious that he thought a hundred times faster than Czentovic. Each time the latter, after seemingly unending deliberation, decided to push a figure forward with his heavy fist, our friend smiled like someone seeing the occurrence of something long expected, and made his riposte. His quick-working brain must have calculated all his opponent's options in advance. The longer Czentovic's decisions were delayed, the greater grew his impatience and, as he waited, an irritable, almost hostile expression hovered around his lips. But Czentovic would not let himself be hurried. He pondered stolid and silent, pausing all the longer the more the field denuded itself of figures. At the forty-second move, after a good three-quarters of an hour, we were all sitting tired and almost uncaring at the tournament table. One of the ship's officers had already left and someone else had begun to read a book, only looking up for an instant after every new development. But with a move of Czentovic's, the unexpected suddenly occurred. As soon as Dr B saw Czentovic touch his knight, he crouched like a cat before it springs. His whole body began to shake and hardly had Czentovic moved the knight when he pushed his queen sharply forward and triumphantly declared, "So, finished!", then leant back, crossed his arms over his chest and looked challengingly at Czentovic. A new light glowed in his eyes.

We all simultaneously bent forward over the board to understand the move that had been so exultantly announced. At first glance, no direct threat was visible. Our friend's declaration must then refer to a development that the short-range thinking of us amateurs wasn't yet able to discern. Czentovic was the only one among us whom this provocative announcement hadn't moved; he sat as still as if he had utterly failed to hear that insulting "Finished!" Nothing happened. Since we had all drawn in our breaths, we heard the ticking of the watch that had been put on the table to time the moves. Three minutes passed, seven minutes, eight minutes—Czentovic didn't stir, but to me it seemed his thick nostrils flared even wider with internal effort. Our friend appeared to find this mute waiting as unendurable as we did. He stood up with a jerk and began to pace up and down in the smoking room, first slowly, then faster and faster. Everyone watched him a little startled, but no one was more concerned than I was, because I noticed that, despite how intensely he paced up and down, he was always pacing out the same amount of space; it was as if he were colliding with an invisible barrier in the middle of the room that forced him to turn back. With a shudder I realized that in this up and down he must be involuntarily reproducing the dimensions of his former cell; this was how he must have stalked up and down, like an animal locked in a cage, in the months of his imprisonment; this was how he must have twisted his hands, hunched his shoulders; this and only this was how he must have paced back and forth all those thousands of times, the red light of madness in his fixed yet fevered gaze. But he still seemed to be thinking clearly, because from time to time he would turn impatiently to the table to see whether Czentovic had decided what to do. It went on for nine minutes, ten minutes. Then there finally happened what none of us had predicted. Czentovic slowly lifted his heavy hand, which had until then rested unmoving on the table. Rapt, we all watched for his decision. But Czentovic didn't make a move; instead, with a firm sweep of the back of his hand, he slowly pushed all the pieces from the board. It took us a moment to understand: Czentovic had given up. He had capitulated so as not to be reduced to checkmate in front of us. The improbable had taken place, the world champion, the victor of innumerable tournaments, had struck his colours before an unknown, a man who in twenty or twenty-five years hadn't touched a chessboard. Our friend, the inconnu, the debutant, had defeated the world's finest chess player in a fair fight.

Hardly noticing what we were doing, we had all been moved to stand up one by one. Each of us had the feeling that he must say or do something to express our delight and amazement. The only one who remained unmoving was Czentovic. Only after a measured pause did he lift his head and gaze stonily at our friend.

"Another game?" he asked.

"Of course," answered Dr B, with an enthusiasm that worried me, and even before I could remind him of his resolution to leave it at one match, he sat down and began to set up the pieces with fervid haste. He grabbed at them so violently that twice a pawn fell to the floor from his trembling fingers; the pained unease I felt at his unnatural excitement mutated into a kind of fear. An evident agitation had permeated the previously calm and quiet man; the twitch ran ever more often around his mouth and his body shook as if rattled by fever.

"Don't!" I whispered to him. "Not now! Leave it for today! It's too much for you."

"Too much! Ha!" He laughed loud and maliciously. "I could have finished twenty matches in the time it's taken for this dawdle! All that's too much for me is not letting this pace put me to sleep! Now! Come on, make a start!"

The way he said this to Czentovic was heated, almost aggressive. Czentovic looked at him calmly and deliberately, but there was now something of the clenched fist in his stony gaze. There was now something new between the two players, a dangerous tension, an ardent hate. They were no longer two partners wanting to test each other's ability in play, they were two enemies who had sworn the other's destruction. Czentovic hesitated a long time before making his first move and I had the distinct feeling that this long hesitation was intentional. It seemed that he, practised as he was in gamesmanship, had realized that he could use his slowness to tire and irritate his opponent. So he took no less than four minutes to make the most conventional, the simplest of all openings, pushing the king's pawn the customary two squares forward. Our friend immediately came out to meet him with his own king's pawn, but again Czentovic paused for an endless, almost unbearable length of time; it was like when a lightning bolt crashes violently to earth and you wait, heart thudding, for the thunder, which won't and still won't come. He thought quietly, slowly, that is—I was ever more certain—spitefully slowly; but it did leave me abundant time to observe Dr B. He had just drained his third glass of water and I remembered him describing his feverish thirst in the cell. All the symptoms of aberrant excitement were plainly evident on him; I saw his brow dampen and the scar on his hand redden and seem to become sharper than before. But he was still in control at that point. Only at the fourth move, when Czentovic again pondered interminably, did he lose his composure and snarl:

"Would you please just make your move!"

Czentovic looked up coolly. "As far as I'm aware, we agreed a period of ten minutes. I do not, as a matter of principle, play with less."

Dr B bit his lip; I noticed that the soles of his feet were tapping the floor under the table ever more restlessly and was myself made ever more nervous by my looming premonition that there was something unhinged working its way out of him. In fact a second incident occurred at the eighth move. He had been waiting with ever less restraint and soon could no longer keep the tension contained; he fidgeted back and forth and unwittingly began to drum his fingers on the table. Czentovic again lifted his heavy rustic head.

"Would you be so good as not to drum your fingers? It's distracting. I can't play like this."

"Ha!" Dr B gave a short laugh. "That much is clear."

Czentovic's forehead reddened. "What's that supposed to mean?" he asked, strident and hostile.

Dr B again gave a short and malicious laugh. "Nothing. Only that your nervousness is palpable."

Czentovic was silent and bowed his head. Only after seven minutes did he make his next move and the match dragged on at that deathly tempo. Czentovic seemed almost to turn to stone; in the end, he took the maximum agreed time before each and every move, while our friend's behaviour became stranger from one interval to the next. It was as if he were no longer paying attention to the match, but had diverted his thoughts onto something quite else. He stopped his rapid pacing and stayed sitting on his seat. Gazing into space with a vacant and almost crazed expression, he mumbled incomprehensible words to himself; he was either losing himself in the match's endless permutations, or—this was what I suspected—working out entirely other matches, and each time that Czentovic finally moved we had to draw him back out of his mental absence. He then needed a few minutes to reorient himself in the position; I was ever more convinced by the suspicion that Czentovic and the rest of us had long been forgotten in this cold madness of his that could suddenly erupt into violence. And indeed, at the nineteenth move the crisis broke. Hardly had Czentovic moved his piece when Dr B, without even really looking at the board, pushed his bishop three squares forward and shouted so loudly that we all jumped:

"Check! The king's in check!"

We all immediately looked at the board, expecting some extraordinary manoeuvre. But none of us expected what happened a moment later. Czentovic raised his head very, very slowly and—he had never done this till now—looked around our circle from one to another. He appeared to be enjoying something enormously, and a satisfied and distinctly mocking smile spread across his lips. Only once he had savoured this incomprehensible triumph to its dregs did he address our group with exaggerated politeness.

"I'm very sorry—but I don't see any check. Do any of you gentlemen see how my king is in check?"

We looked at the board and then, discomfited, at Dr B. Czentovic's king was indeed—a child could have seen it—completely covered by a pawn against the bishop's attack, making check impossible. We became uneasy. Had our friend mismoved a piece in his agitation, pushed it a square too far or too short? His attention drawn by our silence, Dr B now, too, stared at the board and began to stammer badly:

"But the king is supposed to be on F7... he's in the wrong place entirely. You've made an illegal move! Everything's wrong on this board... that pawn's supposed to be on G5 and not G4... this is a whole other match... this is..."

He broke off. I had grabbed him by the arm or, rather, pinched his underarm so hard he felt it even in his feverish confusion. He turned and stared at me like a sleepwalker.

"What... what do you want?"

I said nothing but "Remember!" and ran my finger along the scar on his hand. He followed my movement and his eyes stared glassily at the blood-red streak. He began to shiver and a shudder ran through his body.

"For God's sake," he whispered through pale lips. "Have I done or said something insane... have I?..."

"No," I whispered quietly. "But you have to stop this match at once, it's gone on more than long enough. Remember what your doctor said to you!"

Dr B jerked to his feet. "I beg your pardon for my stupid mistake," he said in his usual, courteous tone and bowed to Czentovic. "What I said was of course pure nonsense. It is naturally your match." Then he turned to us. "I must also offer my apologies to you gentlemen. But I did warn you in advance not to expect too much of me. Please forgive the debacle—it was the last time I try my hand at chess."

He bowed and left in the same humble and secretive way he

had first appeared. Only I knew why this man would never again touch a chessboard, while the others were left a little bewildered and with the vague feeling of having narrowly avoided something dangerous and distressing. "Damned fool!" growled the disappointed McConnor. Czentovic was the last to rise from his seat and cast a final glance at the half-finished match.

"Shame," he said magnanimously. "The attack wasn't at all badly set up. For a dilettante, that gentleman is actually extraordinarily gifted."

FEAR

As IRENE CAME DOWN the stairs from her lover's apartment, again that pointless fear suddenly overwhelmed her. All at once there was a shape like a black spinning top circling before her eyes, her knees froze in dreadful rigidity, and she had to catch hold of the banister rail in haste to keep herself from falling abruptly forwards. It was not the first time she had taken the risk of visiting him here, and this sudden fit of terror was by no means new to her. However much she steeled herself against it, every time she set off for home she was always subject, for no reason at all, to such attacks of senseless, ridiculous fear. The way to her rendezvous was infinitely easier. Then she told the cab driver to stop at the corner of the street, swiftly and without looking up she walked the few steps to the front door of the building where he lived, and hurried upstairs. After all, she knew he was waiting for her in the apartment, he would be quick to open the door, and her initial alarm, which had been mingled with ardent impatience, dissolved in the heat of their embrace as they met. But then, when she left to go home, that mysterious shuddering fit came over her, vaguely mingled with a sense of guilt, and the stupid delusion that every stranger in the street could tell from her face where she had been, and might add to her confusion by giving her a bold smile. Even the last few minutes that she spent with her lover were poisoned by rising uneasiness as she anticipated that sensation, and when she prepared to leave her hands were trembling with nervous haste, her mind was distracted as she heard his parting words to her, and she was quick to fend off the last lingering signs of his passion. Everything in her was anxious to be gone, to get away from his apartment building, away from her adventure and back to her placid, bourgeois world. She scarcely dared to look in the mirror for fear of the distrust in her own eyes, yet it was necessary to check that no disorder in her clothing betrayed the passion of the hour they had just passed together. Then came his last words of reassurance, but in vain, for she hardly heard them in her agitation, and she spent the final moment listening behind the safety of his door to make sure no one was going either up or downstairs. Once she was outside the door, however, her fear was waiting, impatient to take her in its grasp, and so imperiously disturbing her heartbeat that she was already breathless as she went down the first few steps, feeling the strength she had nervously summoned up fail her.

She stood there for a moment with her eyes closed, avidly breathing in the cool air in the dimly lit stairwell. Then a door slammed on an upper floor of the building, and she pulled herself together in alarm and hurried on downstairs, while her hands instinctively drew the thick veil she was wearing even closer. And now she faced the threat of that last, most dreadful moment, the terror of stepping out of the door of a building where she did not live into the street, perhaps meeting some acquaintance who happened to be passing and who might ask what she was doing here, thus forcing her, confused as she was, into the dangerous necessity of telling a lie. She lowered her head, like an athlete about to take off for a great leap, and walked fast and with sudden determination towards the half-open front door.

There she collided with a woman who was obviously on her way in. "I'm so sorry," she said, trying to get past quickly. But the woman barred her way, staring at her angrily and at the same time with unconcealed scorn.

"Oh, so I catch you here for once, do I?" she said in a coarse voice, not at all discomposed. "That's right, oh yes, what they call a real lady, ever so respectable! Not satisfied with her husband and all his money and that, no, not her, she has to go stealing a poor girl's fellow too!"

"For God's sake... what do you... You're mistaken..." stammered Irene, making a clumsy attempt to get past. But the sturdy figure of the woman stood four-square in the doorway, and she went on abusing Irene in penetrating tones.

"Not me, no, I ain't mistaken, I know your sort! You been with my beau, my Eduard! Caught you at last, didn't I? Now I know why he's got so little time for me lately... all on account of you, you nasty, horrid..."

"For God's sake!" Irene interrupted her in a fading voice. "Don't shout so loud!" And she instinctively retreated into the front hall of the building. The woman looked at her with derision. She somehow seemed to be enjoying Irene's fear and trembling, her obvious helplessness, for she now examined her victim with a confident smile of scornful satisfaction. Her voice took on a louder and almost weighty tone of malicious relish.

"So that's what them married ladies look like, them fine ladies as go stealing other girls' fellows! Veiled, of course, ho yes, so they can carry on acting all respectable arterwards..."

"What... what do you want from me? I don't know you at all... I have to go..."

"Yes, that's right, go back to your fine husband, acting the lady, nice warm room to sit in, maid to undress you and all. It don't bother your sort what the likes of us do. We could die of hunger for all you care, ain't that a fact? The likes of you respectable ladies—you'd take every last thing we got!"

Pulling herself together and obeying a sudden if vague inspiration, Irene put her hand into her purse and took out whatever she found in the way of banknotes. "Here… here you are, take this, but now let me go. I'll never come back here again… I swear it."

With an unpleasant expression on her face, the woman took the money, muttering, "Bitch!" Irene flinched at the word, but she saw that the woman was standing aside to let her through the doorway, and she hurried out, a sombre, breathless figure running like a suicide about to jump off a tower. She saw faces like distorted masks passing her as she hurried on, making her way with difficulty, her vision clouded, towards a cab, a motor car standing at the street corner. She flung herself down on its upholstery, and then everything in her seemed to freeze rigid and motionless. When the driver finally, and in some surprise, asked his strangely-behaved fare where she wanted to go, she simply stared blankly at him for a moment until her confused mind finally succeeded in understanding what he meant. "Oh, to the railway station, the Südbahnhof," she uttered hastily, and then, as it suddenly occurred to her that the woman might follow, she added, "Quick, quick, please drive fast!"

Only during the drive did she realise how badly the encounter with the woman had shaken her. She felt her hands hanging at her sides, cold and stiff like dead things, and suddenly began trembling so hard that she shook all over. A bitter taste rose in her throat, she felt nausea and at the same time a dull, unfocused fury trying to break convulsively out of her. She would have liked to scream, or lash out with her fists, free herself from the horror of the memory, which was firmly fixed in her mind like a fish hook—that coarse face and scornful laughter, the unpleasant odour of the vulgar woman's bad breath, the coarse mouth spitting hatred and vile abuse at her, the raised red fist that the creature had shaken menacingly. Her nausea grew stronger and stronger, her gorge rose more and more. In addition, the rapid movement of the car was throwing her back and forth, and she was about to ask the driver to slow down when it occurred to her, just in time, that after giving all her banknotes to her tormentor she might not have enough money left to pay him. She quickly signed to him to stop and suddenly, to the driver's further surprise, got out. Fortunately she had just enough money to pay what she owed. But now she found herself in a part of town that was strange to her, full of busy people pushing past, their every word and glance physically hurting her. Her knees were weak with fear, her legs unwilling to carry her on, but she had to get home, and summoning up all her energy she made a superhuman effort to walk on from street to street. It was like wading through a swamp, or walking up to the knees in snow. At last she reached her own building, and with nervous haste— although she immediately moderated it so that her uneasiness would not attract attention—she hurried upstairs.

Only now, as the maidservant took her coat, as she heard her little boy playing with his younger sister in the next room, and her glance, reassured, saw her own things all around her, her property and her security, did she recover an outward appearance of calm, although under the surface a wave of agitation was still painfully rolling through her tense breast. She took off her veil, made a strong effort of will and composed her face into a carefree expression, and then went into the dining room, where her husband was sitting at the table laid for supper and reading the newspaper.

"You're late, my dear Irene, you're late," he greeted her in a tone of gentle reproof, and he stood up and kissed her cheek, arousing an instinctive and painful sense of shame in her. They sat down at the table, and as soon as he had put his newspaper aside he asked casually, "Where have you been all this time?"

"Oh... oh, I went to see Amélie... she had some shopping to do, and I went with her," she told him, angry with her own thoughtlessness for telling her lie so badly. Usually she prepared herself in advance with a carefully invented story that could not be disproved, but in her fear today she had forgotten to devise one, and was forced into this clumsy improvisation. Suppose, she thought, her husband telephoned her friend—there had been a situation like that in the play they had seen at the theatre recently—and asked Amélie whether…

"What's the matter? You seem so nervous… and why haven't you taken your hat off?" her husband asked. She jumped with alarm, feeling caught out yet again in her embarrassment, stood up quickly and went to her room to take her hat off. As she did so, she stared at her restless eyes in the mirror until her glance seemed to be steady again. Then she went back to the dining room.

The maid brought in supper, and it turned into an evening like any other, perhaps rather more silent and less companionable than usual, an evening when their conversation was sporadic, listless, often stumbling. Her thoughts kept going back, and always, with a jolt of horror, came up against that moment when she was so terribly close to the woman who had threatened her. Whenever she reached that point she looked up so that she could feel safe, tenderly touching things close to her—a pleasant proximity, this time—each with its own place in the room determined by memory and significance, and she began to feel a little calmer again. And the clock on the wall, its steely pace proceeding in a leisurely manner through the silence, imperceptibly restored to her heart something of its own regular, carefree and secure rhythm.

Next morning, when her husband had gone to his chambers and the children were out for a walk, leaving her alone at last, that dreadful encounter lost much of its terror when seen in retrospect and in the cold light of day. Irene reminded herself, first, that her veil had been very thick, so that the woman could not possibly have seen her features in detail, and would never be able to recognise her again. She reflected calmly on all the measures she could take to safeguard herself. She would not on any account visit her lover in his apartment again—which surely meant that there was no imminent possibility of another such attack. There remained only the danger of meeting that woman again by chance, but that too was unlikely, for since she had made her escape in a car her assailant could not have followed her. The woman could not know Irene's name, or where she lived, and as she would have gained only an indistinct idea of her features Irene need not fear any other kind of reliable identification. But she was armed even against such an extremely improbable case. Freed from the grip of fear, she decided at once that she would simply keep calm, deny everything, coolly claim that there was some mistake and, as no evidence of her visit to her lover could be produced except on the spot, if necessary charge the woman with blackmail. Not for nothing was Irene the wife of one of the best-known defence lawyers in the capital city; she knew enough from his conversations with professional colleagues to be aware that attempted blackmail had to be nipped in the bud immediately and in the most ruthless way, because any hesitation on the part of the intended victim, any appearance of being ill at ease, would only increase the blackmailer's sense of superiority.

Her first precaution was to write her lover a brief letter telling him that she could not come at the agreed time tomorrow, or indeed for the next few days. On reading through her note, in which she disguised her handwriting for the first time, it struck her as rather frosty in tone, and she was about to replace the offending terms with something more intimate when the memory of yesterday's encounter suddenly showed her that the coolness expressed in her lines was the unconscious result of lively if subliminal animosity. Her pride was injured by the embarrassing discovery that she had replaced such a base, unworthy predecessor in her lover's affections, and reading her letter again in a more resentful mood, she felt vengeful satisfaction in the cold clarity with which it showed that her visits to him depended, so to speak, on her own good humour.

She had met the young man, a pianist of some renown in what was admittedly still a small circle, at an evening entertainment, and soon, without really meaning to and almost without realising it, she had become his lover. Nothing in her blood had really responded to him, nothing sensual, let alone intellectual, had brought her body together with his; she had given herself to him without needing or really even desiring him very much, out of a certain apathetic lack of resistance to his will, and a kind of restless curiosity. Nothing in her had made taking a lover a necessity to her—neither her desires, which were perfectly well satisfied by marital life, nor the feeling so frequently found in women that their intellectual interests are withering away. She was perfectly happy with a prosperous husband whose intellect was superior to hers, two children, contentedly and even lazily at ease in her comfortable, calm, middle-class existence. But a kind of languor in the air may arouse sensuality just as sultry or stormy weather can, a sense of temperate happiness can be more provocative than outright unhappiness, and for many women their contentment itself proves more disastrous than enduring dissatisfaction in a hopeless situation. Satiety can be as much of an incitement as hunger, and it was the very safety and security of Irene's existence that made her feel curious and ready for an adventure. There was no opposition anywhere in her life. She met with soft acceptance in all quarters, concern for her well-being, affection, mild love and domestic respect, and without understanding that such moderation of feeling did not arise from anything outside her, but reflected an absence of deeply felt relationships, in some vague way she felt cheated of real life by her own comfort.

Her first girlish dreams of ecstasy and a great love, lulled by the calm friendship of her first years of marriage and the playful delights of becoming a young mother, were beginning to revive now that she was approaching the age of thirty. And like any woman she believed herself capable of great passion, although her desire for experience did not go hand-in-hand with the courage to pay the true price of an adventure, which is danger. When, at this time of a contented serenity that she could not enhance for herself, the young man approached her with ardent and obvious desire, entering her bourgeois world with all the romantic aura of his art around him—while other men merely paid respectful court to her, praising her as a 'beautiful lady', and indulged in mild flirtations without really desiring her as a woman—she felt deeply intrigued for the first time since her girlhood days. Perhaps all that really attracted her to him was a touch of grief lying like a shadow on his rather too interestingly arranged features. She was not to know that in fact it was something he had learnt, like the technical aspects of his art and the sad, thoughtful melancholy with which he would play an impromptu that he had composed in his head well in advance. To Irene, who in the usual way felt that she was entirely surrounded by the complacent bourgeoisie, this melancholy suggested the idea of a more rarefied world, one that she had glimpsed graphically depicted in books and that moved her romantically at the theatre, and she instinctively leant out past the confines of her everyday feelings to observe it. Spellbound, she paid him a compliment on the spur of the moment, perhaps expressing it more warmly than was proper. It made him look up from the keyboard at the speaker, and that first glance reached out to her. She was alarmed, and at the same time felt the pleasures of alarm. A conversation in which everything appeared to be illuminated and stoked by fires only just under the surface occupied her mind, intriguing her already lively curiosity so much that she did not avoid another meeting at a public recital. After that they saw each other quite often, and before long it was not by chance. A few weeks later, the delightful idea that she, who had never before thought highly of her musical judgement, correctly judging her appreciation of art to be minimal, meant so much to a real artist like him—for he kept assuring her that she was the one who really understood him and could advise him—caused her to agree rather too quickly when he said he would like to play his latest composition to her and her alone. The intentions behind this proposition had perhaps been half-genuine, but they were lost amidst kisses, and it ended with her surprised surrender to him. Her first feeling was one of alarm at this unexpected turn taken by their relationship, moving it into the sensual sphere. The mysterious thrill that had surrounded it was abruptly dispelled, and when her conscience pricked her for committing this unplanned act of adultery, it was only partly assuaged by the tingling sense of vanity in having for the first time defied the bourgeois world in which she lived and as she thought by her own decision. Her horror at her own wickedness, which alarmed her for the first few days, became a source of heightened pride. But these mysterious emotions too were felt at their full strength only at first. Beneath the surface, her instincts resisted this man, and most of all what was new in him, the difference that had in fact aroused her curiosity. The extravagance of his clothing, the gypsy way in which he lived, the irregularity of his financial situation, always swinging between extravagance and embarrassment, were alien to her bourgeois mind. Like most women, she wanted to see an artist as very romantic from a distance, and very well conducted in personal relationships, a fascinating beast of prey, but kept safely behind the iron bars of morality. The passion that intoxicated her in his playing of the piano made her uneasy when they were physically close; she did not really like his sudden, masterful embraces, and instinctively compared their self-willed ruthlessness with the milder ardour of her husband, who was still reticent and respectfully considerate of her even after their years together. But now that she had been unfaithful for the first time she returned to her lover again and again, without being either gratified or disappointed, out of a certain sense of duty and the apathy of habit. She was one of those women, quite often found even among the more reckless and flirtatious, whose bourgeois nature is so strong that it imposes a sense of order even on adultery; they bring an aura of domesticity into their departure from the straight and narrow path, trying in the guise of patience to transform the most unusual feelings into everyday custom. After a few weeks she had fitted her young lover neatly into her life, setting aside one day a week for him, just as she did for her parents-in-law, but in entering into this new relationship she did not give up any of the orderliness of her life, she merely, so to speak, added something to it. Soon her lover made no difference at all to the comfortable mechanism of her existence, he became, as it were, an additional source of temperate happiness, like the idea of a third child or a motor car, and her adventure soon seemed to her as ordinary as her lawful pleasures.

And now that she was called upon, for the first time, to pay the real price of danger for that adventure, she began to calculate its value in meticulous detail. Spoilt by fate, cosseted by her family, and with almost nothing left to wish for in her financially easy circumstances, she found the very first moment of discomfort too much to bear. She immediately resolved that she was not going to give up any part of her freedom from anxiety, and in fact without further ado she was ready to sacrifice her lover to her peace of mind.

His answer, a nervously disjointed letter expressing his dismay, was brought by a messenger that same afternoon. The letter, full of distraught pleading, complaints and accusations, shook her determination to end the relationship because his desire flattered her vanity. Indeed, she was delighted by his frenzied desperation. Her lover begged her, pled urgently with her, at least to grant him a brief meeting, an opportunity of explaining his offence if he had unwittingly injured her in any way. Now she was intrigued by this new game of showing that she was in a sulky mood, and making herself even more desirable to him by refusing her favours without giving any reason. She felt that she was in the midst of excitement, and like all naturally cool people she found it pleasant to be surrounded by surging waves of passion while she herself did not burn with true ardour. She arranged to meet him at a café where, she suddenly remembered, she had once had a rendezvous with an actor when she was a young girl—an episode that admittedly now seemed to her childish in its carefree propriety. How strange, she thought, smiling to herself, that romance, stunted by all these years of marriage, was beginning to blossom in her life again. By now she was almost glad of yesterday's abrupt encounter with that woman—for the first time in a long while, it had made her feel truly strong, stimulating emotions which still left her nervous system secretly tingling, in contrast to its usual state of mild relaxation.

This time she wore a dark, plain dress and a different hat, which would lead the woman's memory astray if they did by any chance meet again. She had a veil ready to disguise herself further, but with sudden defiance she left it at home. Was she, a respected, highly regarded woman, to be afraid to venture out into the street for fear of some female whom she didn't know at all? There was already something curiously tempting mingled with her fear of the danger—an alarmingly pleasurable readiness to do battle, rather like caressing the cold blade of a dagger with her bare fingers, or looking down the black muzzle of a revolver where death in compressed form lurked in waiting. This thrill of adventure was not what her sheltered life was used to, and she toyed with the enticing idea of coming close to it again. The sensation exerted delightful tension on her nerves, sending electrical sparks flying through her bloodstream.

A momentary sense of fear overwhelmed her only in the first moment when she stepped out into the street. It passed through her like the nervous chill when you dip your toes into the water, before entrusting yourself entirely to the waves. But that chill lasted for only a split second, and then, all of a sudden, she felt a strange delight in life rushing through her veins. She relished the pleasure of walking along with more of a light, strong, springy step than she ever known herself to adopt before. She was almost sorry that the café was so close, for some kind of impulse was now urging her to go rhythmically on, attracted by the mysterious magnetism of adventure. But the time she had set aside for this meeting was short, and she felt in her heart, with a pleasing certainty, that her lover was already there waiting for her. Sure enough, he was sitting in a corner when she came in, and leapt to his feet in a state of agitation that she found both pleasant and painful. Such a whirlwind of heated questions and reproaches poured out of him in his mental turmoil that she had to remind him to keep his voice down. Without giving him any idea of the real reason for her failure to visit him, she played with hints so vaguely phrased that they inflamed his passions even more. She could not and would not comply with his wishes this time, she told him, and she even hesitated to make any promises, sensing how much her sudden withdrawal and refusal to give herself excited him. And when, after half-an-hour of heated conversation, she left without giving him the slightest sign of affection, or even holding out the prospect of any in the future, she was glowing with a very strange feeling that she had known before only as a girl. She felt as if a small, tingling fire were burning deep inside her, just waiting for the wind to fan it into flames that would rise and unite above her head. She was quick to notice, in passing, all the glances cast at her in the street, and her unusual ability to attract so much masculine attention made her so curious to see her own face that she suddenly stopped in front of the mirror in the window of a flower shop, to see her own beauty framed in red roses and violets gleaming with dew. She was looking back at herself with sparkling eyes, young and light at heart. A sensuous mouth, half-open, smiled at her with satisfaction, and when she walked on she felt the rhythmical movement of her limbs as if her feet had wings. A need for some physical release, a need to dance or run wildly, took over from the usual sedate pace of her footsteps, and now she was sorry to hear the clock on St Michael's Church, as she hurried past, calling her home to her small, neat, tidy world. Not since girlhood had she felt so light at heart, with all her senses so animated. Nothing like it had sent sparks flying through her body, not in the first days of her marriage or in her lover's embrace, and the idea of wasting this strange lightness, this sweet frenzy of the blood, on well-regulated hours seemed unendurable. Wearily now, she went on. She stopped outside the building where she lived, hesitating once again, wishing to expand her breast and breathe in the fiery air and confusion of the last hour once more, feeling the last, ebbing wave of her adventure deep in her heart.

Then someone touched on her shoulder. She turned around. "What… what do you want this time?" she stammered, frightened to death at the sudden sight of that hated face, and even more frightened to hear herself speak those fateful words. Hadn't she made up her mind not to show that she recognised the woman if she ever met her again, to deny everything, to stand up to the blackmailer? And now it was too late.

"I been waiting here for you this last half-hour, Frau Wagner."

Irene started when she heard her name. So the woman knew it, knew where she lived. All was lost now, she was helpless, at this creature's mercy. She had words on the tip of her tongue, all those carefully prepared and calculated words, but her tongue was paralysed and could not utter a sound.

"Half-an-hour I been waiting, Frau Wagner." The woman repeated her words menacingly. It was like an accusation.

"What do you want… what do you want from me?"

"Why, don't you know that already, Frau Wagner?" Her own name made Irene jump with fright again. "You know what I'm here for right enough."

"I haven't seen him again… let me go! I never will see him again… never."

The woman waited, composed, until the agitated Irene could say no more. Then she replied harshly, as if speaking to an inferior.

"Don't you tell me no lies! I followed you to that caffy, didn't I?" And seeing Irene flinch, she added in tones of derision, "Me, I got no job, see? They fired me from the shop on account of no work coming in, that's what they say, and then there's the hard times and all. Well, we got to spend our time somehow, so us poor girls go walking about a bit, just like you fine, respectable ladies."

The woman spoke with a cold ill will that struck Irene to the heart. She felt defenceless against the naked brutality of such malice, and increasingly dizzy in the grip of the fearful idea that the woman might begin shouting, or her husband might happen to come by, and then all would be lost. She quickly felt in her muff, brought out her silver-mesh purse, and took from it all the money that her fingers could hold. With revulsion, she thrust it into the hand now slowly reaching out in certain expectation of its plunder.

But this time the strange hand did not withdraw humbly as soon as it had the money in its clasp, but stayed outstretched in the air, open like a claw.

"And let's have that nice little silver purse too, for to keep my money safe in!" said the scornfully smiling mouth, with a soft chuckle of a laugh.

Irene looked her in the eye, but only for a second. The creature's insolent, malicious scorn was past bearing. She felt revulsion run through her whole body like a burning pain. She had to get away, well away from the sight of that woman's face! Turning aside, she quickly held out the purse, a valuable item in itself, to the woman, and then ran up the steps with horror on her heels.

Her husband was not home yet, so she was able to fling herself down on the sofa. She lay there as if felled by a hammer-blow, motionless apart from a frantic twitching that ran through her fingers and then up her arm, making it tremble all the way to her shoulder. But nothing in her whole body could put up any defence against the storming violence of the horror that had now been let loose. Only when she heard her husband's voice outside did she pull herself together, making an enormous effort, and force herself to go into the next room, her movements automatic and her senses numbed.

The horror had now moved into her home and would not stir from its rooms. In the many empty hours that kept bringing the images of that terrible meeting back to her mind, wave upon wave of them, her hopeless situation became perfectly clear to her. How it could have happened she had no idea, but the woman knew her name, knew where she lived, and now that her first attempts at blackmail had been so conspicuously successful she certainly would not shun any means of making use of her knowledge to continue her campaign of extortion. She would be a burden on her victim's life year after year, like a nightmare that no effort, however desperate, could dislodge, for although Irene was well-to-do and the wife of a prosperous man, she could not possibly raise a large enough sum to free herself of the woman once and for all without confiding in her husband. In addition, as she knew from hearing occasional stories of his about trials in which he had appeared, all agreements with base, unscrupulous persons, and any promises made to them were entirely null and void. She calculated that she could fend off the moment of doom for a month, maybe two, and then the entire artificial structure of her domestic bliss would collapse. There was little satisfaction in the certain knowledge that the blackmailer would also be brought down in her own fall. What were six months in prison for a woman who undoubtedly led a dissolute life and probably had a criminal record already, by comparison with the life she herself would lose? And she felt, in horror, that it was the only possible life for her. To begin a new one, dishonoured and with a stain on her reputation, seemed unimaginable to Irene, a woman who had received everything in her existence up to now as a gift, who had never been responsible for constructing any part of her own destiny. And then her children were here, her husband, her home, all the things that she realised only now, when she was about to lose them, were so much a part of her life, indeed were the essence of it. Everything that she had merely taken for granted in the past, touching it only with the hem of her garment, she now suddenly felt was dreadfully necessary to her, and the idea that a strange vagrant of a woman lurking somewhere in the streets might have the power to destroy its warm, coherent entity with a single word seemed more than she could grasp, and indeed as improbable as a dream.

She could not avert the disaster—she felt that now with terrible certainty; she had no way of escape. But what... what exactly would happen? She fretted over that question from morning to night. One day a letter to her husband would arrive. She could see him now, coming into the room, pale, with a sombre expression on his face, taking hold of her arm, asking questions... but then... what would happen then? What would he do? Here the pictures in her mind's eye were suddenly extinguished in the darkness of a confused and cruel fear. She had no idea what would happen then, and her speculations plunged to dizzy, endless depths. In this brooding frame of mind, however, she saw how little she really knew her husband, how unable she was to work out in advance what his decision would be. She had married him at the urging of her parents, although with no reluctance, indeed with a pleasant sense of liking for him which was not disappointed later. She had spent eight years of comfortable, quiet contentment at his side, she had borne his children, she shared his home and had spent countless hours physically close to him, but only now that she wondered about his possible behaviour did she realise what a stranger he still was to her. Looking back feverishly at her recollections of the last few years, and feeling as if she were turning ghostly floodlights on them, she discovered that she had never wondered what his nature was really like, and now, after all these years, did not even know whether he should be described as harsh or forbearing, stern or affectionate. Stricken disastrously late by a guilty conscience which itself was engendered by her mortal fear, she had to admit to herself that she had known him only superficially, on the social level, never in that deeper part of his nature where his decision would surely be made at this tragic moment. Instinctively she began keeping an eye open for small traits of character in him, for indications, trying to remember what he had said in conversation about such cases, and she was unpleasantly surprised to realise that he had hardly ever expressed any views of his own to her. Then again, she herself had never turned to him with questions that went very deep. Now, at last, she put her mind to his life as a whole, looking for individual features that might tell her more about his character. Her fear began hammering reluctantly away at every little memory, trying to find a way into the secret chambers of his heart.

She turned her watchful attention to the slightest thing he said, and waited with feverish impatience for the times when he came home. She hardly noticed his greeting, but in his gestures—the way he kissed her hand or stroked her hair there seemed to be an affection that might indicate a deep love of her, although it avoided any stormy demonstrations. He always spoke to her in measured tones, never impatiently or in any agitation, and his general attitude to her was one of kindly composure, yet as she uneasily began to suspect it was not very different from his manner to the servants, and certainly was less warm than his feeling for the children, which always took lively form—sometimes he joked with them cheerfully, sometimes he was passionately affectionate. Today, as usual, he civilly asked about any domestic matters, as if to give her a chance of expressing her interests to him while he said nothing about his own, and for the first time she discovered herself noticing the care with which he treated her, his reserved approach to their daily conversations—which, as she was suddenly horrified to realise, were flat and banal.

He gave nothing of himself away, and her curiosity, longing for something to calm her mind, remained unsatisfied.

As he said nothing to give her a clue, she searched his face. He was sitting in his armchair now, reading a book, his features clearly illuminated by the electric light. She scanned his face as if it were a stranger's, trying to deduce from those well-known yet suddenly unfamiliar features the character that eight years of living together had kept hidden from her indifference. His brow was smooth and well shaped, as if formed by strong intellectual effort; his mouth, however, looked stern and unyielding. Everything about his very masculine features was firm, full of energy and power. Surprised to find beauty in it, she considered that restrained gravity with a certain admiration, seeing the evident austerity of his nature which so far, in her simple-minded way, she had merely thought was not very entertaining, wishing it could have been exchanged for a sociable loquacity. His eyes, however, where the real secret must after all lie, were bent on his book, so that she was unable to consider what they told her. She could only look inquiringly at his profile, as if its curving line meant a single word portending mercy or damnation—a profile now unfamiliar, so harsh that it alarmed her, yet making her aware for the first time, in its determined expression, of its remarkable beauty. All at once she felt that she liked looking at him, and did so with pleasure and pride. Something stirred painfully in her breast as that sensation was aroused in her, a vague and sombre feeling, regret for something neglected, an almost sensuous tension that she could not remember ever having experienced so strongly in his physical presence. Then he looked up from his book. She quickly retreated further into the shadows, so that the burning question in her own eyes would not arouse his suspicion.

*

She had not left the house for three days. And she realised, uneasily, that the rest of the household had noticed the fact that she was suddenly spending so much time at home, for in general it was very unusual for her to stay indoors in her own apartment for many hours on end, let alone whole days. Taking little interest in domestic matters, freed from petty economic anxieties by material independence, bored by her own company, she saw the apartment as little more than a place where she briefly rested. For preference she resorted to the streets, the theatre, the lively company at social gatherings, where something new was coming in from outside all the time. You could enjoy yourself without making any great effort there; you could find much to stimulate the slumbering senses. Irene's cast of mind made her one of that elegant set of the Viennese bourgeoisie whose entire daily timetable seemed to consist, by some tacit agreement, in the constant meeting of all members of the same secret league at the same times of day to discuss their common interests, while it gradually elevated that meeting in order to observe others, that eternal drawing of comparisons, to the entire meaning of its existence. Once isolated and thrown on its own resources, a life so used to casual social intercourse loses any fixed point, the senses rebel without their usual diet of very mild but indispensable stimulation, and solitude degenerates into a kind of nervous self-animosity. Irene felt time weighing endlessly down on her, and without her usual occupations the passing hours lost all their point. She paced up and down the rooms of her apartment as if she were in a dungeon, both idle and agitated. The street and the society world that were her real life were barred to her. The blackmailer stood there with her threat, like the angel with the fiery sword.

Her children were the first to notice this change in her, particularly the elder child, her little boy, who expressed his surprise that Mama was at home so often with embarrassing clarity, while the servants whispered to each other and exchanged surmises with the governess. Irene tried in vain to devise all kinds of necessary reasons, some of them very ingenious, for her conspicuous presence, but in itself the artificial nature of her explanations showed her how years of indifference had made her unnecessary in her own family circle. Whenever she tried to do something actively useful she came up against the interests of others, who resisted her sudden attempts as an intrusion on their own customary rights. There was no place left for her; for lack of contact with it she herself had become a foreign body in the organism of her own household. She did not know what to do with herself and her time, and even her approaches to the children failed, for they suspected that her sudden lively interest in them meant the introduction of a new kind of discipline, and she felt herself blush in shame when, during one of her attempts to look after them, her seven-year-old son asked outright why she wasn't going for so many walks these days. Wherever she tried to lend a helping hand she was disrupting an established order, and when she showed an interest she merely aroused suspicion. And she lacked the skill to make her constant presence less obtrusive by cleverly keeping in the background and staying quietly in a single room, with a single book or performing a single task. Her private fear, turning as all her strong feelings did to nervous strain, hunted her from one room to another. She jumped every time the telephone or the doorbell rang, and kept catching herself looking out into the street from behind net curtains, hungry for other people, or at least the sight of them, longing for freedom, and yet full of fear that suddenly, among all the passing faces, she might see the one face that followed her into her dreams staring up at her. She felt that her quiet existence was suddenly disintegrating, melting away, and this sense of helplessness was giving rise to a presentiment that her life was entirely ruined. These three days in the dungeon of her rooms at home seemed longer to her than all her eight years of marriage.

However, she and her husband had accepted an invitation for the evening of the third day weeks ago, and it was impossible for her to back out suddenly now without giving very good reasons. What was more, the invisible bars of horror that had built up around her life must be broken down some time if she was not to be utterly destroyed. She needed people around her, a couple of hours' rest from her own company, from the suicidal loneliness of fear. Then again, where would she be better protected than in a strange house and surrounded by friends, where would she be safer from the invisible persecution dogging her footsteps? She shuddered just for a second, the brief second when she actually stepped out of the house, venturing into the street for the first time since that second encounter. The woman might be lying in wait anywhere out there. Instinctively, she took her husband's arm, closed her eyes, and quickly walked the few steps from the pavement to the waiting motor car, but then, as she sat beside her husband while the car raced through the empty nocturnal streets, the weight fell from her mind, and as she climbed the steps up to the house they were visiting she knew she was safe. For a few hours she could be the woman she had been for many long years—carefree and happy. Indeed, she felt the intensified, conscious joy of a prisoner leaving the walls of the dungeon and returning to the light of day. There was a rampart against all persecution here, hatred could not come in, everyone here loved, respected and honoured her. She saw her friends, well-dressed people who spoke to her without any ulterior motive, who were bathed in the sparkling glow of the fires of cheerfulness, performing a round dance of enjoyment that, at long last, included her again. For now, as she came in, she felt from the glances turned on her by the other guests that she was beautiful, and she became yet more beautiful through being aware of their admiration after being deprived of it. How good it felt after all those days of silence, when she had felt the sharp ploughshare of that one idea cutting fruitlessly and repeatedly through her brain, while everything in her seemed to be sore and injured—oh, how good it was to hear flattering words again! They revived her like electric sparks crackling beneath her skin, rousing her blood. She stood and stared, something was vibrating restlessly inside her, trying to get out. And all of a sudden she knew it was her imprisoned laughter that wanted to be free. It popped out like a champagne cork, pealing in musical little coloraturas, she laughed and laughed, now and then feeling ashamed of her bacchanalian high spirits, but laughing again next moment. Electricity flashed from her relaxed nerves, all her senses were strong, healthy, stimulated. For the first time in days she ate with real appetite again, and she drank like a woman dying of thirst.

Her desiccated soul, yearning for human company, was absorbing all the life and enjoyment that it could. Music in the next room tempted her, moving far into her beneath her burning skin. The dancing began, and without knowing how she found herself in the middle of the milling throng. She danced as she had never danced in her life before. The circling eddies of the dance cast all her melancholy out of her, the rhythm infected her limbs, breathing ardent movement into her body. If the music stopped she felt that the silence was painful, the snake of restlessness darted its tongue at her quivering limbs, and she flung herself back into the eddies as if into a bath of cool, soothing water that bore her up. She had never been more than an average dancer before, she was too measured, too thoughtful, too cautious and firm in her movements, but this frenzy of liberated delight did away with all physical inhibitions. A steely band of bashful circumspection that usually held her wildest passions in check now broke apart, and she was out of control, restless, her mind blissfully melting away. She felt arms and hands around her, touching and disappearing again, she sensed the breath of spoken words, the tingling of laughter, music flickering in her blood, her whole body was tense, so tense that the clothes on her back were burning, and she would have liked to tear them all off spontaneously, so that she could dance naked and sense this intoxicating frenzy even deeper inside her.

"Irene, what's the matter?" She turned around, swaying, laughter in her eyes, still heated from the embrace of her dancing partner. Her husband's cold, hard look of astonishment struck her to the heart. She was alarmed. Had she danced too wildly? Had her frenzy given anything away?

"What... what do you mean, Fritz?" she stammered, surprised by his suddenly piercing gaze, It seemed to be forcing its way further and further into her, and now she felt it deep inside, close to her heart. She could have cried out aloud beneath that searching, determined gaze.

"How very strange," he murmured at last. There was a note of sombre amazement in his voice. She dared not ask what he meant. But a shudder ran through her when, as he turned away without another word, she saw his shoulders, broad, wide, strong, vigorous, attracting her gaze to the nape of his neck, which was hard as iron. *Like a murderer's*, the thought flashed through her mind, a crazy thought, instantly dismissed. Only now, as if she were seeing her own husband for the first time, did she feel with horror that he was powerful and dangerous.

The music began to play again. A gentleman came up to her, and automatically she took his arm. But now everything about her seemed weighty, and the bright melody no longer brought movement into her stiff limbs. A dull heaviness moved down from her heart towards her feet, every step she took hurt. She had to ask her partner to excuse her. As she stepped back she instinctively looked to see if her husband was near, and jumped in alarm. He was standing directly behind her, as if waiting for her, and once again his penetrating eyes met hers. What did he want? What did he know? She instinctively clutched her dress together at the neck, as if her breasts were bare and she must shield them from him. His silence was as persistent as his gaze.

"Shall we leave now?" she asked anxiously.

"Yes." His voice sounded harsh and unfriendly. He went ahead. Once again she was looking at the broad, menacing back of his neck. Someone put her fur around her shoulders, but she still felt freezing cold. They drove home in silence, sitting side-by-side.

That night she had an oppressive dream. Some kind of strange, loud music was playing, she saw a brightly lit, high-ceilinged hall, she went in. A crowd of people and many bright colours were mingled in movement. Then a young man whose identity she thought she knew, although she could not entirely place him, made his way to her. He took her arm, and she danced with him. She felt well, she was soft and yielding. A great wave of music bore her up, so that she no longer felt the floor beneath her feet, and they danced through many halls with golden chandeliers high up in the roof, radiating little flames like stars, while mirrors on wall after wall reflected her own smile again and again to infinity. The dancing grew wilder and wilder, the music more and more urgent. She realised that the young man was pressing closer to her, his hand digging into her bare arm, making her groan with painful pleasure, and now, as her eyes plunged deep into his, she did think she knew him. She thought he was an actor whom she had adored from afar when she was a little girl. Delighted, she was just about to speak his name, but he silenced her soft cry with an ardent kiss. And so, their lips merged together, the two of them burning like a single body in each other's embrace, they flew through the halls as if borne up on a blissful wind. The walls streamed past, she was no longer conscious of the hovering vault of the ceiling or of the hour, she felt amazingly weightless, all her limbs relaxed. And then, suddenly, someone touched her on the shoulder. She stopped, and the music stopped at the same time, the lights went out, the dark walls moved in on her, and her dancing partner had disappeared. "Give him back, you thief!" shouted that terrible woman, for it was she, making the walls ring with the sound, and she closed ice-cold fingers around Irene's wrist. She resisted, hearing herself cry out with a mad shriek of horror, and the two of them wrestled, but the other woman was stronger. She tore off Irene's pearl necklace, and half her dress with it, leaving her breasts bare and her arms exposed beneath the rags now hanging off her. All of a sudden there were other people around them again, streaming in from all the other halls on a rising tide of noise, staring with derision at her as she stood there half-naked, while the woman screeched: "She stole my beau, she did, that floozie, that adulteress!"

She didn't know where to hide or which way to look, for the people were crowding in closer and closer, women looking at her with inquisitive eyes, hissing at her, grasping at her naked body, and now that her reeling gaze looked around for help she suddenly saw her husband standing motionless in the dark frame of the doorway, his right hand concealed behind his back. She screamed and ran away from him, ran through room after room, and the crowd, greedy for sensation, raced along after her. She felt more and more of her dress slip off, she could hardly clutch at it now. Then a door swung open ahead of her, eagerly she rushed down the stairs to save herself, but the terrible woman was waiting at the bottom of the staircase in her woollen skirt, with her claw-like hands outstretched. Irene swerved aside and ran out into the open air, but the other woman came after her, and so they both chased through the night down long, silent streets, and the street lights, grinning, bent down to greet them. She could hear the woman's wooden clogs clattering along behind her, but whenever she reached a street corner the woman was there already, leaping out at her, and it was the same again at the next corner, she lay in wait beyond all the houses both to right and to left, always there, terrifyingly multiplied. There was no overtaking her, she always went on ahead and was there first, reaching out for Irene, who felt her knees begin to fail her. At last she saw the house where she lived and raced up to it, but as she wrenched the door open there stood her husband with a knife in his hand, his piercing gaze bent on her. "Where have you been?" he asked in sombre tones. "Nowhere," she heard herself say, and already she heard the woman's shrill laughter at her side. "I seen it! I seen it all!" screeched the grinning woman, who was suddenly there with her, laughing like a lunatic. And her husband raised the knife.

"Help!" she cried out. "Help!"

She was staring up, and her horrified eyes met her husband's. What... what was all this? She was in her own room, and the ceiling lamp was on, casting a pale light. She was at home in her bed, she had only been dreaming. But why was her husband sitting on the edge of the bed, looking at her as if she were an invalid? Who had put the light on, why was he sitting there so rigid and motionless, staring at her so gravely? A shiver of horror ran through her once, and then again. Instinctively, she looked at his hand. No, there was no knife in it. Slowly, the drowsiness of sleep wore off, and so did the images it had brought like glaring flashes of lightning. She must have been dreaming, she must have called out in her dream and woken him. But why was he looking at her with such a serious, penetrating, implacably grave expression?

She tried to smile. "What… what is it? Why are you looking at me like that? I think I've been having a nightmare."

"Yes, you called out in a loud voice. I could hear it in the other room."

What did I call out, what did I give away, she thought, trembling, what does he know? She hardly dared to look up at him again. But he was gazing gravely down at her with a strange composure.

"What is it, Irene? There's something the matter with you. You've been so different for the last few days, as if you had a fever, nervous, distracted, and now you cry out for help in your sleep."

She tried to smile again. "No," he persisted. "You mustn't keep anything from me. Is there something on your mind, is anything troubling you? The whole household has noticed how you've changed. You ought to trust me, Irene."

He moved a little closer to her, and she felt his fingers on her bare arm, caressing it. There was a strange light in his eyes. She was overcome by a longing to cast herself on his firm body, cling to him, confess everything and never let him go until he had forgiven her now, this very moment, now that he had seen her suffering.

But the pale light was shining down from the ceiling, illuminating her face, and she was ashamed. She felt afraid to say anything.

"Don't worry, Fritz." She tried to smile again, although she was still shivering all the way down to her bare toes. "I'm only feeling a little nervous strain. It will pass off."

The hand holding hers was quickly withdrawn. She felt afraid, now that she looked at him, pale in the glassy light, his forehead clouded by the shadow of dark thoughts. Slowly, he stood up.

"I don't know why, but these last few days I've felt as if you had something to tell me. Something that concerns only you and me. We are alone now, Irene."

She lay there motionless, as if hypnotised by that grave, veiled glance. How good, she felt, everything could be now, she had only to say two words, two little words—forgive me. And he wouldn't ask what for. But why was the light on, that forthright, bold, light listening to them? She felt she could have said it in the dark, but in the light her strength failed her.

"So there's nothing, really nothing that you want to tell me?"

It was a terrible temptation! How soft his voice was! She had never heard him speak like that before. But the light hanging from the ceiling, that yellow, avid light!

She shook herself. "What can you be thinking of?" she laughed, and was seized by alarm again at hearing her own shrill tone of voice. "If I'm not sleeping well, does that mean I'm keeping secrets from you? Maybe even having some kind of adventure?"

Once more she shivered. How false, how insincere those words sounded. She was horrified by herself, right to the marrow of her bones, and instinctively she looked away from him.

"Well—good night, then." He spoke curtly now, in an entirely different, sharp voice. It sounded like a threat, or black and dangerous mockery.

Then he put out the light. She saw his pale shape disappear through the doorway, soundless, wan, a nocturnal ghost, and when the door closed she felt as if the lid of a coffin were coming down. The whole world, she felt, was dead and hollow except for her own heart, beating loud and frantically against her breast in her rigid body, bringing her pain and more pain every time it beat.

*

Next day, when they were sitting at lunch together—the children had just been quarrelling, and it was quite difficult to make them calm down—the maid brought in a letter. For Madam, she said, and the messenger was waiting for an answer. Surprised, she saw unfamiliar handwriting on the envelope, and quickly opened it, only to suddenly turn pale when she read the first words. All at once she jumped up from the table. She was even more alarmed when she saw, from the evident surprise of the rest of the family, how thoughtlessly revealing her impetuous movement had been.

The letter was short. Just three brief lines: '*Kindly give the bearer of this letter a hundred crowns at once.*' No signature, no date in the obviously disguised handwriting, only that cruelly urgent command! Irene hurried to her room to get the money, but she had mislaid the key to her money box. Frantically, she flung open all her drawers, rattling the contents about until at last she found it. She put the banknotes into an envelope with trembling fingers, and herself gave them to the messenger waiting at the door. She did it all mindlessly, as if under hypnosis, without even considering the possibility of hesitating. And then—hardly two minutes after leaving the dining room—she was back with her family again.

There was silence. She sat down with a shrinking sense of uneasiness, and was just trying to think of some excuse in a hurry when—and her hand shook so much that although she had picked up her glass she had to put it down again in haste—she realised, to her horror, that she had left the letter lying open beside her plate. Just one small movement, and her husband could have picked it up. Maybe a glance would have been enough to read the large, unformed characters in which those few lines were written. Words failed her. Surreptitiously, she crumpled up the note, but now, as she put it in her pocket and looked up, she met her husband's eyes bent severely on her. It was a penetrating, stern and painful glance. She had never known him to look like that before. Only now, during these last few days, had he suddenly made her feel distrustful with such an expression on his face. It shook her to the core, and she was unable to parry it. A glance like that had paralysed her in the middle of dancing, and he had watched over her sleep last night with the same look, his eyes gleaming like the blade of a knife.

Did he know something, or did he want to know it, was that what sharpened his glance, made it so bright, so steely, so painful? And as she was still searching for something to say, a long-forgotten memory came back to her. Her husband had once told her how, as a lawyer, he had faced an investigating judge whose trick it was to look through his files during the examination as if short-sighted, but when the really important question came he would suddenly raise his eyes and turn their piercing gaze, like a dagger, on the suddenly alarmed defendant, who would then be discomposed by this bright lightning flash of concentrated attention, and the lie he had been carefully trying to maintain would lose its force. Could her husband be employing dangerous methods of that kind himself, and was she the victim? She shuddered, particularly because she knew what a great intellectual passion he felt for his chosen profession, far beyond that necessary for a legal career. He could track down the reasons for a crime, its development, the moment it turned to extortion, as intently as others might devote themselves to eroticism or gambling, and on a day when he was engaged in this psychological hunt he seemed to be inwardly radiant. The keen nervous energy that often made him recollect forgotten verdicts in the middle of the night expressed itself outwardly then in a steely inscrutability; he ate and drank little, but smoked the whole time, and he seemed to be saving his words for the coming hour in court. She had once gone to hear him make a plea, and never went again, she was so shaken by the dark passion and almost malevolent fire of his delivery and the sombre, austere expression on his face. Now she suddenly thought she detected the same look again in his fixed gaze under those menacingly frowning brows.

All these lost memories came crowding in on her in that single second, and kept her lips from uttering the words that they were trying to form. She said nothing, and became increasingly confused the more she realised how dangerous her silence was—she was losing her last plausible chance of explaining herself. She dared not raise her eyes, yet now, looking down, she was even more alarmed to see his hands, usually so still and steady, moving up and down on the table like little wild animals. Luckily lunch was soon over, and the children jumped up and ran into the next room, chattering in their clear, cheerful voices, while the governess tried in vain to moderate their high spirits. Her husband also got to his feet, went out of the dining room, treading heavily, and did not look back.

As soon as she was alone she took out the fateful letter again. She read the lines once more: *'Kindly give the bearer of this letter a hundred crowns at once.'* Then she tore it into small pieces in her rage, and was crumpling them up into a ball to throw them in the waste-paper basket when she thought better of it, stopped, leant over the stove on the hearth and threw the paper into the hissing fire. The white flame that sprang up, greedily devouring the threat, soothed her.

At that moment she heard her husband's returning footsteps. He was already at the door. She quickly straightened up, her face flushed from the warmth of the fire and from knowing that she was caught in the act. The door of the stove was still open, giving her away, and she awkwardly tried to hide it by standing in front of the fireplace. He went up to the table, struck a match to light his cigar, and as the flame came close to his face she thought she saw the quivering of his nostrils that always showed he was angry. But he looked at her quite calmly. "I would just like to point out that you are not obliged to show me your correspondence. If you want to keep secrets from me, you are entirely at liberty to do so." She did not reply, she dared not look at him. He waited for a moment, then breathed out the smoke of his cigar as if it came from deep inside him and left the room, again with that heavy tread.

She didn't want to think of anything, she wished only to live in a numb state, filling her heart with empty, pointless occupation. She could not bear to be in the apartment any more, she felt that if she was not to go mad with horror she had to be out in the street among other people. Those hundred crowns had at least, she hoped, bought her a brief respite, a few days of freedom from the blackmailer, and she decided that she would venture to go for a walk. There were several items that she needed to buy, but above all, if she went out walking that would cover up for the noticeable change in her habits in staying at home so much. She had developed a certain way of making her escape. On reaching the front door she rushed out into the busy life of the street with her eyes closed, as if jumping off a springboard. Once she felt the hard paving stones under her feet and knew that the warm torrent of humanity was around her, she went on in nervous haste, or as much haste as a lady could show without attracting attention, walking straight ahead with her eyes fixed on the ground, in the very natural fear of meeting that dangerous gaze again. If the woman was lying in wait, then at least she didn't want to know it. And yet she realised that she was thinking of nothing else, and she jumped in alarm when someone touched her by chance in brushing past. Her nerves reacted painfully to every sound, every footstep behind her, every moving shadow. Only in a vehicle or in a building that she did not know could she breathe freely again.

A gentleman said good afternoon to her. Looking up, she recognised a family friend from the days of her youth, a friendly, talkative man with a grey beard. She usually tried to avoid him because of his way of talking for hours on end about his ailments, which were very likely imaginary. Today, however, she was sorry that she had merely returned his greeting instead of seeking his company. Walking with an acquaintance would have been good protection against another unexpected attack from her blackmailer. She hesitated, and was considering turning back, when she felt as if someone were coming up fast behind her, and instinctively, without stopping to think, she hurried on again. But still, with a sense of foreboding cruelly enhanced by fear, she felt that someone was rapidly approaching behind her back, and she herself walked faster and faster, although she knew that she could not escape pursuit in the end. Her shoulders were beginning to shrink in anticipation of the hand that now—for the steps were coming closer and closer—she felt sure would touch her next moment, and the more she tried to quicken her pace the heavier her knees felt. She sensed that the pursuer was very close.

"Irene!" called a voice behind her urgently, yet speaking in a soft tone, and coming to her senses, she realised that it was not, after all, the voice she feared, the terrible messenger of doom. Breathing a sigh of relief, she turned. It was her lover, and when she stopped so suddenly he almost collided with her. His face was pale, bearing all the signs of agitation, and now, under her uncomprehending gaze, he also looked ashamed. Uncertainly, he raised his hand in greeting and let it sink again when she did not offer him hers. The sight of him was so unexpected that she just stared at him for one or two seconds. In these days of fear, she had forgotten all about him. But now that she saw his pale, inquiring face at close quarters, with that expression of vacant perplexity, a hot wave of rage suddenly surged up in her. Her lips trembled, attempting to form words, and the distress in her face showed so clearly that he could only stammer her name in alarm. "Irene, what's the matter?" And when he saw her impatient gesture, he added meekly, "What harm have I done you?"

She stared at him with barely repressed anger. "What harm have you done me?" she said, with a laugh of derision. "Oh, none! None at all! You've done only good! Only what's right and proper."

His expression was baffled, and his mouth dropped half-open, increasing the ridiculously simple-minded effect of his appearance. "But Irene... Irene!"

"Please don't attract attention here!" she snapped at him brusquely. "And don't trouble to put on an act for me! Your delightful lady friend is sure to be lurking somewhere near, ready to attack me again!"

"Who... who do you mean?"

She could have slapped his foolishly baffled, distorted face. She already felt her hand clutching her umbrella. She had never despised and hated anyone so much.

"But Irene... Irene," he kept stammering in confusion. "What on earth have I done? All of a sudden you stay away... I've been waiting for you day and night. I've been standing outside your apartment block today, waiting for a chance to speak to you for a minute."

"Waiting for... oh, I see! You too." She felt that her anger was driving her mad. It would feel so good to strike him! However, she controlled herself, cast him one more glance of burning revulsion, as if considering whether to spit all her accumulated rage out into his face in a torrent of abuse, and then, instead, she suddenly turned and made her way into the busy crowd without looking back. He stood there with his pleading hand still outstretched, bewildered and shaken, until the movement of the crowd in the street took hold of him and swept him away with it like a leaf sinking in the current, rocking and circling, and finally carried away by no will of its own.

The idea that such a man had ever been her lover suddenly struck her as absolutely unreal and senseless. She could remember nothing about him, not the colour of his eyes or the shape of his face. She had no physical memory of his caresses, and none of his words echoed in her mind apart from that pitiful, childish, dog-like "But, Irene!" stammered out in desperation. Although he was the cause of all misfortune, she had not once thought of him in all these days, even in her dreams. He meant nothing in her life, he was no temptation now, hardly even a memory. She didn't understand how her lips could ever have touched his, and she felt strong enough to have sworn that she had never really listened to him. What had driven her into his arms, what terrible madness had led her to embark on an adventure that her own heart no longer understood, and hardly even her mind? She knew nothing more about it, everything in what had passed was strange to her, she was a stranger to herself.

But then again, hadn't everything else changed in these few days, this single week of horror? Corrosive fear had eaten into her life like nitric acid, separating its elements. The weight of everything was suddenly different, all values were reversed, all relationships confused. She felt as if until this moment she had merely been groping her way vaguely through life with her eyes half closed, and now everything was illuminated with terrible clarity. Before her, as close as her own breath, were considerations that she had never touched but which, she suddenly realised, made up her real life, and others again that had once seemed important to her had dispersed like smoke. Up to this point she had mingled with lively society in the noisy, loquacious company of people who moved in well-to-do circles, and in essence she had lived only for herself, but now, after a week immured in her own household, she felt she did not miss that society. Instead, she was repelled by the pointless hurry and bustle of those who had nothing to do, and instinctively she judged the shallowness of her old inclinations, her constant neglect of love in action, in the light of this first truly strong feeling to come to her. She looked at her past as if looking into an abyss. Married for eight years, and deluding herself that she enjoyed too modest a happiness, she had never tried to come closer to her husband, she had remained a stranger to his real nature and no less to her own children. Paid domestic staff stood between them and her, governesses and servants who relieved her of all those little anxieties which, she only now began to sense—now that she had looked more closely at her children's lives—were more alluring than the ardent glances of men, more delightful than a lover's embrace. Slowly, her life was acquiring new meaning. Everything had affinities, all at once turning a gravely significant face to her. Now that she had known danger, and with that danger a genuine emotion, everything, however strange, suddenly began to have something in common with her. She felt herself in everything, and the world, once as transparent to her as glass, had come to mirror the dark shape of her own shadow. Wherever she looked, whatever she heard, was suddenly real.

She went to sit with the children. Their governess was reading aloud to them, a fairy tale about a princess who was allowed into all the rooms in her palace except the one with a door that was locked with a silver key. She opened the door all the same, and unlocking it sealed her fate. Wasn't that her own story? She too had been intrigued by forbidden fruit, simply because it was forbidden, and it had brought her misfortune. Only a week ago, the simplicity of the little story would have made her smile, but now she felt that there was deep wisdom in it. There was a story in the newspaper about an army officer who had been blackmailed into turning traitor. She shuddered, and understood him. Wouldn't she herself make impossible efforts to get money in order to buy a few days of peace, a semblance of happiness? Every line she read about suicide, every reported crime, every act of desperation suddenly became very real to her. She could identify with all of them—the man tired of life, the desperate man, the seduced maidservant, the abandoned child. Her own story had the ring of theirs. All at once she understood the full richness of life, and knew that no hour of her own existence could seem poor to her any more. Now that it was all coming to an end, she felt for the first time that life was just beginning. And was a vicious female to have the power to take this wonderful sense of being attuned to the whole world, and tear it apart with her coarse hands? Was Irene's one guilty act to bring everything great and fine of which, for the first time, she felt capable, down into ruin?

And why, she thought, blindly resisting a disaster that she unconsciously knew made sense, why such a terrible punishment for a small peccadillo? She knew so many women, vain, bold, sensual, who kept lovers, spending money on them and mocking their husbands in those other men's arms, women who lived a lie and were very much at home there, who became more beautiful in dissembling, stronger as the chase went on, cleverer in danger, while she herself collapsed, powerless, at the first touch of fear, at her first real transgression.

But was she really guilty at all? She felt in her heart that the man who had been her lover was a stranger to her, that she had never given him any part of her real life. She had received nothing from him, he had given her nothing. All of that, now past and forgotten, was not really her offence, it was the misdemeanour of another woman whom she herself did not understand, whom she did not even like to remember. Could you be punished for an offence when time had atoned for it?

Suddenly she felt alarm. She had an idea that she had not thought that herself. Who had said it? Someone close to her, only recently, only a few days ago. She thought about it, and her alarm was no less when she realised that it was her own husband who had put the idea into her mind. He had come home from a trial looking pale and upset, and suddenly, taciturn as he usually was, he had told her and some friends who happened to be present: "Sentence was passed on an innocent man today." Asked what he meant, he told them, still much distressed by the incident, that a thief had been condemned for a crime committed three years before. He himself felt that the offender was innocent, because three years after the crime he was no longer the same man. So another man was being punished, even punished twice over, for he had spent those three years imprisoned in his own fear and the constant anxiety of being found out and convicted.

And she remembered, with horror, how she had contradicted him at the time. Remote from real life as her feelings were, she had seen the criminal only as a pest, a parasite on comfortable bourgeois society, a man who must at all costs be removed from circulation. Only now did she feel how pitiful her arguments had been, how just and kindly his. But would he be able to understand that it was not really another man she had loved, only the idea of adventure? That he himself was also guilty of showing her too much kindness, making her life so enervatingly comfortable? Would he be able to show justice in judging his own case?

But she was not to be allowed to indulge in hope. Another note arrived the very next day, another whiplash reviving her exhausted fear. This time the blackmailer was demanding two hundred crowns, and she handed them over meekly. The sudden steep rise in the sum of blackmail extorted was terrible. Nor did she now feel financially capable of satisfying it, for although her own family was prosperous she was not in any situation to get her hands on large sums without attracting attention. And then, what use would it be? She knew that tomorrow the demand would be for four hundred crowns, soon it would be a thousand, the more she gave the more would be asked, and finally, as soon as her money ran out, the anonymous letter would arrive and it would all be over. What she was buying was only time, a breathing space, two days of rest, or three, maybe a week, but time that was worthless in itself, full of torment and suspense. She had been sleeping poorly for weeks now, and her dreams were worse than waking; she felt the lack of fresh air, exercise, rest, occupation. She could not read any more, could not do anything, hunted as she was by the demons of her own fear. She did not feel well. Sometimes she had to sit down suddenly when her heart palpitated too vigorously, and a restless heaviness filled her limbs with almost painful weariness, like some viscous liquid, but that weariness still fought against sleep. Her whole life was undermined by her devouring fear, her body was poisoned, and in her heart she really longed for her sickness to break out in visible pain, some kind of obvious, perceptible clinical condition, something that those around her would understand and pity. In these hours of secret torment, she envied the sick. How good it must be to lie in a sanatorium, in a white bed between white walls, surrounded by sympathy and flowers. Visitors would come, everyone would be kind to her, and behind the clouds of suffering the great, kindly sun of restoration to health would already be dawning in the distance. If you were in physical pain at least you could groan out loud, but she had to keep acting the tragi-comic part of a woman in good health and good spirits. Every day, almost every hour, faced her with new and terrible situations. She had to smile and look happy while all her nerves were on edge, and no one could even guess at the constant strain of this assumed cheerfulness, the heroic strength that she exerted in the daily yet useless violence she did herself.

Only one of all the people around her seemed, she vaguely felt, to guess something of the terrors she was suffering, and he did so only because he was watching her. She felt sure, and that certainty forced her to be doubly careful, that her husband was thinking about her all the time, just as she was thinking about him. They manoeuvred day and night as if circling around one another, each trying to guess the other's secret while keeping their own safe. He too had changed recently. His menacing severity in those first few days of inquisition had given way to his own manner of showing kindness and concern, and she was instinctively reminded of the days when they had first been engaged. He was treating her like an invalid, with a care and anxiety on her behalf that bewildered her, because such undeserved love made her feel ashamed. On the other hand she also feared it, because it could be just a trick to get her secret out of her at some sudden, unexpected moment. Since the night when he had heard her call out in her sleep, and the day when he had seen the letter in her hands, his distrust had seemed to turn to sympathy. He was trying to win her confidence with a tenderness that sometimes reassured her and made her feel like yielding to him, only to return to her suspicions of him the next moment. Was it just a trick, the tempting trap set by an investigating judge for the defendant, a snare to catch her confidence? If she confessed, would it be like setting out along a drawbridge which was then suddenly raised, leaving her defenceless in his power. Or did he too feel that this state of heightened watchfulness, waiting and listening, was unendurable, was his sympathy strong enough for him to suffer secretly because of her own suffering, which must be getting more visible daily? She felt, with a strange tremor, that at times he was almost offering her the words that would bring release, making it enticingly easy for her to confess. She understood his intentions, and was grateful for his kindness. But she also felt that with her stronger liking for him, her sense of shame was also growing, and it kept a sterner guard on her tongue than his distrust had done before.

Just once at this time he spoke to her very clearly, looking her in the eye. She had come home to hear loud voices as she entered the front hall—her husband's, firm and energetic, and the scolding, loquacious voice of the governess, as well as tears and sobbing from the children. Her first feeling was one of alarm. She was always apprehensive when she heard voices raised, or there was some kind of domestic upset in the household. Fear was her reaction to everything out of the ordinary, and this time it was fear that the letter had already arrived and her secret was out. Whenever she opened the door and came in these days, she looked round at the faces she saw and wondered whether something had happened in her absence; had the catastrophe come down on her while she was out? This time, as she soon realised, much to her relief, it was only a quarrel between the children, and a small improvised trial was in progress. A few days ago an aunt had brought the boy a toy, a brightly painted little horse. His envious younger sister didn't like her own present so much, and was incensed. She had tried in vain to stake a claim to the little horse, behaving so wilfully that the boy had said she wasn't even to touch his toy. That had led first to loud protests from the child and then to a cowed, sullen, obstinate silence. Next morning, however, the little horse had disappeared without trace, and all the boy's efforts to find it were in vain, until by chance the lost toy was finally discovered in pieces in the stove, its wooden parts broken, its skin ripped off and its stuffing removed. Suspicion naturally fell on the little girl—the boy had run to his father in tears to complain of his naughty sister, who couldn't help trying to justify herself, and so the interrogation began.

Irene felt a pang of envy. Why did the children always take their troubles to her husband, never to her? They had always confided their quarrels and complaints to him, and until now she had been happy to be free of these petty squabbles, but suddenly she wanted to be told about them, because she sensed that there was love and trust in such confidences.

The little trial was soon over. The girl denied the charge at first, although with her eyes timidly lowered, and the way her shoulders were shaking gave her away. The governess gave evidence against her—she had heard the child threatening angrily to throw the horse out of the window, and it was useless for the girl to try denying it any further. There was a small outburst of tears and despair. Irene looked at her husband. It was as if he were sitting in judgement not on the child but on herself and her own fate. She might be facing him like that tomorrow, her own shoulders shaking with sobs, the same break in her voice. Her husband looked stern as long as the child stuck to her lie, and then broke her resistance down word by word, without ever letting one of her denials anger him. But once denial had given way to a fit of the sulks he spoke kindly to her, showing but at the same time to some extent excusing the inevitability of her actions, pointing out that she had done her shocking deed in her first, unreasoning anger, never stopping to think that it would really hurt her brother. Then he explained to the child, who was getting less and less sure of herself, that he could understand what she had done, but it was reprehensible all the same, and he spoke so warmly yet so forcefully that in the end she burst into tears and began crying frantically. And finally, through her torrent of tears, she stammered out her confession.

Irene hurried over to embrace the weeping child, but the little girl angrily pushed her away. Her husband, too, shook his head, a warning to her not to show pity too soon, for he did not want the offence to go unpunished, and the punishment he decreed, which was slight in itself but went to the child's heart, was that she could not go to a children's party next day, after she had been looking forward to it for weeks. The child was still in tears as she heard sentence passed, and her brother began crowing over her, but his premature show of malice instantly brought retribution down on his own head. The upshot was that he too was refused permission to go to the party because of the malice he had shown his sister. Sadly, comforted only by the fact that they were both being punished, the two of them finally went away, and Irene was left alone with her husband.

Here at last, she suddenly felt, was an opportunity for them to stop conversing through insinuations, a chance for her make her own confession under cover of a discussion of the little girl's guilt and her admission of it. A sense of relief came over her at the idea of being able to confess and ask for compassion, at least in veiled form. If he looked kindly on her plea for the child, it would be like a sign and an omen, and she knew that then she might be able to summon up the courage to speak on her own behalf.

"Oh, Fritz," she began, "Are you really going to stop the children going to their party tomorrow? They'll be very unhappy, especially Helene. After all, what she did wasn't so very bad. Why are you so hard on her? Don't you feel sorry for the poor child?"

He looked at her. Then he sat down at his leisure. Yes, he obviously seemed willing to discuss the subject at greater length, and a foreboding, both pleasant and unnerving, made her suspect that he was prepared to argue it point-by-point with her. Everything in her was waiting for his long pause to end. But perhaps intentionally, perhaps because he was deep in thought, he let it go on for a long time before continuing.

"Don't I feel sorry for her, you ask? Well, I won't say any more about that today. She feels better now that she's been punished, although her punishment seems bitter too. She was unhappy yesterday when she put the broken bits of the poor little horse in the stove. Everyone in the house was looking for it, and she was afraid all day that it was sure to be found. That fear was worse than the punishment, which after all is something definite, and whether it's hard on her or not, it's still better than the terrible uncertainty and cruel suspense she was feeling earlier. As soon as she knew her punishment she felt all right. Don't let her tears lead you astray; yes, they came pouring out, but they'd been dammed up inside her before, and they hurt worse there than on the surface. If she weren't a child, or if we could somehow see right into her mind, I think we'd discover that she is really glad to have been found out, in spite of her punishment and her tears. She's certainly happier than she was yesterday, when she appeared not to have a care in the world, and no one suspected her."

Irene looked up. She felt as if every word were directed at her. But he seemed to take no notice of her, perhaps misinterpreting her movement, and only went on in a firm voice:

"It really is so, you can believe me. I've seen this kind of thing in court and from legal investigations. Defendants in court suffer most from the secrecy, the threat of discovery, the cruel pressure on them to maintain a lie against thousands of little surreptitious attacks. It's terrible to see a case where the judge already has everything in his hands—the defendant's guilt, the proof of it, perhaps he even has his verdict ready, only there's no confession yet, it's still locked inside the defendant, and however he tries he can't get it out. I hate to see a defendant writhing and squirming while his 'Yes, I did it' has to be torn out of his resisting flesh as if it were on a fish hook. Sometimes it gets stuck high in his throat, and still there's an irresistible force inside him trying to bring it to the light of day. Defendants retch on it, the words are almost spoken, and then the evil power comes over them, that extraordinary sense of mingled defiance and fear, and they swallow it down again. And the struggle begins all over again. Sometimes the judges are suffering more than the prisoner in the dock. The criminal always sees the judge as his enemy, whereas in fact he is trying to help. As a defending lawyer I'm really supposed to warn my clients against confessing, I'm expected to shore up their lies, consolidate them, but in my heart I often can't bring myself to do it, because not confessing makes them suffer worse than confessing to their crime and paying the penalty. I still don't really understand how someone can commit a crime, in full knowledge of the danger, and then not find the courage to confess. It seems to me that their petty fear of a few little words is more pitiful than any crime."

"Do you think it's… it's always just fear that… that keeps people from speaking out? Couldn't it be… well, couldn't it be shame? Suppose they're ashamed to talk about it and expose themselves in front of so many people?"

He looked up in surprise. He was not used to getting answers from her. But the word she had used evidently fascinated him.

"Shame, you say... well, shame is only a kind of fear, but a better one, a fear not of the punishment but... yes. Yes, I see what you mean."

He had risen to his feet, strangely agitated, and was walking up and down. The idea seemed to have struck a chord, bringing something in him to vigorous life. He suddenly stopped.

"I'll admit, yes, shame in front of other people, strangers... the hoi polloi who devour other people's troubles in newspaper stories like a sandwich... but for that very reason they could at least tell those who are close to them. Do you remember that arsonist, the one I was defending last year? The one who took such a curious liking to me? He told me everything, little stories about his childhood, incidents even more intimate than that. You see, he had certainly committed the crime, and he was found guilty, but he wouldn't confess it even to me. That was because he was afraid I might give him away. It wasn't shame, because he trusted me... I think I was the only person for whom he'd ever felt anything like friendship in his life. So it wasn't a sense of shame in front of strangers... what would that mean when he knew he could trust me?"

"Perhaps—" She had to turn away because he was looking at her so intently, and she heard a tremor in his voice. "Perhaps you'd feel most ashamed with... with those you're closest to."

He stopped suddenly, as if a powerful idea had seized on him.

"Then you think... you think..." And suddenly his voice changed, became soft and low. "You think little Helene might have confessed more easily to someone else? The governess, perhaps. You think she..."

"I'm sure of it. She put up such resistance to you only because... well, what you think matters more than anything to her. Because... because she loves you best."

He stopped again.

"You… you may be right. Yes, I'm sure you are. How strange that I never thought of that before… yet it's so simple. Yes, I may have been too hard on her. You know me—I don't mean it like that. But I'll go in and see her now… and of course she can go to the party, I only wanted to punish her for her defiance, her resistance and… well, I suppose for not trusting me. But you're quite right, I don't want you to think I can't forgive… Irene, I wouldn't like you, of all people, to think such a thing."

He was looking at her, and she felt herself blushing under his gaze. Was he saying these things on purpose, or was it coincidence, a dangerous, insidious coincidence? She still felt so dreadfully undecided.

"Well, the sentence is quashed." A certain cheerfulness seemed to come back into his voice. "Helene is free to go to the party, and I'll tell her so myself. Are you satisfied with me now? Or is there anything else you want? You… you see… you see I'm in a magnanimous mood today… maybe because I'm glad to have seen an injustice in time. That always brings relief, Irene, always…"

She thought she understood what the emphasis in his words meant. Instinctively she moved closer to him, she already felt the words rising in her, and he too stepped forwards as if he was in haste to take from her whatever so obviously troubled her. Then she met his eyes, and saw in them an eager desire for her confession, for some part of herself, a burning impatience, and all at once everything she had been feeling collapsed. Her hand fell wearily to her side, and she turned away. It was useless, she felt, she would never be able to say the one thing that would set her free, the one thing that was burning inside her and consuming her peace of mind. She sensed a warning in the air, like thunder coming closer, but she knew she could not escape. And in the secret depths of her heart she longed, now, for what she had feared so long, the lightning flash of discovery that would come as a release.

Her wish was to be granted sooner than she guessed. The struggle had been going on for fourteen days now, and Irene felt she had exhausted her strength. It was four days since she had heard from the woman, and fear had lodged so deep in her body, was so much at one with her blood, that she started up abruptly whenever the doorbell rang so that she would be in time to intercept the next blackmail letter herself. There was impatience, almost even longing in her avid expectation, for with every payment she bought an evening of peace, a few hours with the children, a walk. For an evening, for a day she could breathe easily, go out into the street, visit friends. Although to be sure sleep, in its wisdom, would not let such a poor sort of comfort blind her deceitfully to certain knowledge of the danger always close at hand. Her sleep brought dreams of fear to consume her by night.

Once again, she had run to answer the door when the bell rang, even though she realised that her restless desire to get there ahead of the servants was bound to be noticed, and could easily arouse hostile suspicions. But while sober circumspection might put up little acts of resistance, it weakened when, at the sound of the telephone ringing, a step in the street behind her, or the summons of the doorbell her whole body was on the alert, as if it had felt the lash of a whip. And now the sound of the bell had brought her out of her room and running to the door again. She opened it only to find herself looking in surprise, for a moment, at a strange lady. Then, retreating in alarm, she recognised the hated face of the blackmailer, who was wearing a new outfit and an elegant hat.

"Why, if it ain't you in person, Frau Wagner. I'm ever so glad. I got something important to say to you." And without waiting for any answer from the terrified Irene, who was supporting herself with one trembling hand on the door handle, she marched in, put down her sunshade—a sunshade of a glaring, bright-red hue, obviously bought with the fruits of her blackmailing raids. She was moving with great assurance, as if she were in her own home, looking around with pleasure, as if with a sense of reas-surance, at the handsome furnishings. She walked on, uninvited, to the door of the drawing room, which was half-open. "This way, right?" she asked with some derision, and when the alarmed Irene, still incapable of saying anything, tried to deter her, she added reassuringly: "We can get this settled good and quick if you'd like to see me out of here."

Irene followed her without protest. The mere idea that her blackmailer was here, in her own apartment, paralysed her. It was an audacity going beyond her worst expectations. She felt as if she must be dreaming the whole thing.

"Ooh, nice place you got here, very nice," said the woman, admiring her surroundings with obvious satisfaction as she low-ered herself into a chair. "Ever so cosy, this is. Look at all them pictures, too. Well, you can see what a poor way the likes of us live. Now you got a nice life here, Frau Wagner, a real nice life."

And now at last, as she saw the criminal female so much at ease in her own drawing room, the tormented Irene's fury burst out.

"What do you think you're doing, you blackmailer? Following me into my own home! But I'm not letting you torture me to death. I'm going to!…"

"Now, now, I wouldn't speak so loud, not if I was you," the other woman answered, with insulting familiarity. "That door's not closed, the servants can hear. Well, that's no skin off of my nose. I'm not denying nothing, Lord save us, no, after all, I can't be no worse off in jail than now, not with the sort of miserable life I lead. But you, Frau Wagner, you want to go a bit more careful-like. I'll close that door right now if you really want to let off steam. Tell you what, though, might as well tell you straight out, shouting all them bad words won't get you nowhere with me."

Irene's resolve, steeled for a moment by anger, collapsed helplessly again in the face of the woman's implacability. Like a child waiting to hear what it must do, she stood there uneasily, almost humbly.

"Well then, Frau Wagner, I won't beat about the bush. I'm in a bad way, like I told you before, you know that by now. So I need cash down. I been in debt a long time, and there's other stuff as well. That's why I come here to get you to help me out with—well, let's say four hundred crowns."

"But I can't," Irene stammered, horrified by the sum of money, which indeed she did not have in the apartment in ready cash. "I really don't have that much any more. I've already given you three hundred crowns this month. Where do you think I'd get the money?"

"Oh, you'll do it and no mistake, just you think how. A rich lady like you, why, you can get all the money you want. But you got to do it, see? So think it over, Frau Wagner, why don't you? You'll do it all right."

"I really don't have it. I'd be happy to give it to you, but I truly can't get hold of such a large sum of money. I could give you something... maybe a hundred crowns..."

"Like I said, four hundred, that's what I need." She spoke brusquely, as if insulted by the suggestion.

"But I just don't have it!" cried the desperate Irene. Suppose her husband were to come in now, she thought fleetingly, he could come home at any moment. "I swear I don't have it."

"Then you better make sure you do."

"I can't."

The woman looked her up and down as if assessing her value.

"Well, let's see… f'rinstance, that ring there. Suppose you was to pawn that, it'd fetch a tidy sum. Not that I know that much about joolery, never had none meself… but I reckon you'd get four hundred crowns for it."

"My ring!" cried Irene. It was her engagement ring, the only one that she never took off, a setting of a beautiful precious stone that made it very valuable.

"Go on, why not? I'll send you the pawnshop ticket, you can get it back any time you like. I'm not planning to redeem it and keep it, not me. What'd a poor girl like me do with a posh ring like that?"

"Why are you persecuting me? Why do you torment me? I can't… I can't. Surely you must understand that. I've done all I could, you can see I have. Oh, surely you must understand! Take pity on me!"

"Nobody never took no pity on me. I could've starved to death for all anyone cared. Why'd I have pity on a rich lady like you?"

Irene was about to return a forceful answer, but then—and her blood ran cold—she heard the latch of the front door fall into place. It must be her husband coming home from his chambers. Without stopping to think, she snatched the ring from her finger and handed it to the woman waiting there, who swiftly pocketed it.

"Don't you worry, I'll be off now," nodded the woman, perceiving the unspeakable fear in her face and the close attention she was paying to the front hall, where a man's footsteps were clearly audible. She opened the drawing-room door, and in passing wished good day to Irene's husband as he came in. He glanced at her for a moment, but did not seem to pay her much attention as she left.

"A lady coming to ask about something," explained Irene, with the last of her strength, as soon as the door had closed behind the woman. The worst moment was over. Her husband did not reply, but calmly went into the dining room, where the table was already laid for lunch.

Irene could almost feel the air burning the place on her finger that was usually enclosed by the cool circle of her ring. It was as if the bare skin were the mark of a brand that would inevitably attract all eyes. She hid her hand again and again during the meal, and as she did so she was plagued by a curious feeling, the result of nervous strain, that her husband's glance kept going to that hand, following it in all its wanderings. With all her might, she tried to distract his attention and keep a conversation going by asking constant questions. She talked and talked, to him, to the children, to the governess, again and again she rekindled the conversation with the little flames of her inquiries, but her breath kept running out, it was stifled, it failed her. She did her best to seem in high spirits and persuade the others to be cheerful, she teased the children, egging them on to argue with each other, but they neither argued nor laughed. Even she felt that her cheerfulness must be striking a false note, and it subconsciously alienated them. The harder she tried, the less successful her efforts were. Finally she fell silent, exhausted.

The others were silent too. All she heard was the faint clatter of plates, and inside her the rising voices of her fear. Then, all of a sudden, her husband said: "Where's your ring today, Irene?"

She started nervously. Deep inside her something said a single phrase. All over! But still she instinctively put up a defence. Summon up all your strength, she told herself. Just for one more sentence, one more word. Find one more lie, a final lie.

"I... I took it to be cleaned."

And as if the lie itself had strengthened her, she added firmly: "I'm getting it back the day after tomorrow." The day after tomorrow. Now she was bound to her word. The lie would surely collapse, and she with it, if she did not succeed in redeeming the ring. She had set the time limit herself, and all of a sudden a new feeling was added to her confused fears, a kind of happiness to know that the moment of decision was so close. The day after tomorrow. Now she knew how much time she had left, and she felt a curious calm born of that certainty mingling with her fear. Something rose in her, a new strength. The power to live and the power to die.

The knowledge that, at last, her decision was certainly so close began to bring unexpected clarity to her mind. As if miraculously, her nervous stress gave way to logical thought, her fear to a crystal-clear calm suddenly enabling her to see everything in her life as if it were transparent, and to value it at its true worth. She weighed up her life as a whole and felt that it was still a heavy weight, but that if she could only hold on to it in the new, intensified, more elevated frame of mind that these days of fear had shown her, if she could begin it again from the beginning, pure and sure and straightforward, she was ready to do so. But to live the life of a divorced woman, an adulteress, stained by scandal—no, she was too tired for that, and too tired to continue the dangerous game of buying respite for a limited period. Resistance, she felt, was unthinkable now. The end was near; she might be given away by her husband, her children, by everything around her, and indeed by herself. Flight from an apparently omnipresent adversary was impossible. And confession, the one thing that could surely help her, was out of the question; she knew that by now. There was only one path still open to her, but it was a path from which there was no return.

Life was still alluring. Today was one of those typical spring days that sometimes break vigorously out of the bonds of winter, a day with a blue sky so high and wide that it made you feel you were breathing easily again after many dismal, wintry hours.

The children came running in, wearing clothes in pale colours for the first time this year, and she had to force herself not to shed tears in response to their happy jubilation. As soon as the sound of their laughter and its painful echo in her mind had died away, she set about carrying out her own decisions with determination. First she was going to try to recover the ring, for whatever happened to her now, she did not want any suspicion to fall on her memory. No one must have visible evidence of her guilt. No one, least of all her children, was ever to guess at the terrible secret that had torn her away from them. It must appear to be pure chance, and no one's responsibility.

First she went to a pawnbroker's to pledge an inherited piece of jewellery that she almost never wore, thus providing herself with enough money, if need be, to buy back the ring that could betray her from the woman who had taken it. Then, as soon as she had the cash in her bag, she went walking at random, earnestly hoping for what, until yesterday, she had most feared—to meet the blackmailer. The air was mild, the sun shone above the rooftops. Something in the wild wind chasing white clouds swiftly over the sky seemed to have infected the people walking in the street, all of them at a lighter, livelier pace than in the bleak days of winter gloom. And she herself thought she felt something of it. The idea of dying, the idea she had caught in flight yesterday and clasped firmly in her trembling hand, became a monstrosity, eluded her senses. Was it possible that a word from some dreadful woman could destroy all this, the buildings with their bright façades, the surging of her own blood? Could a word extinguish the never-ending flame with which the whole world blazed in her fast-breathing heart?

She walked and walked, but her head was not bowed now. Her eyes searched almost eagerly for the woman she expected to see. Now the prey was in search of the hunter, and just as a weakened, hunted animal, feeling that escape is no longer possible, will turn suddenly with the defiance of despair to face its pursuer, ready to fight back, she too wanted to see her tormentor face to face and fight back with the very last of the strength that the will to live gives desperate creatures. She stayed close to her home on purpose, because it was the neighbourhood where the blackmailer had usually lain in wait for her, and once she even hurried across the road when the clothes worn by another woman reminded her of the person she was after. The ring itself was not her chief anxiety—recovering it would mean only postponement, not release—but she did long for the meeting as a kind of sign from fate, sealing a life and death decision that had been made by some higher power but depended on her own determination. However, she could not see the woman anywhere. She had disappeared into the endless hurry and bustle of the great city like a rat going down its hole. Disappointed, but not yet hopeless, she went home in the middle of the day and continued her vain search immediately after lunch. She patrolled the streets again, and when she could not find the woman anywhere she felt a revival of the horror that she had almost managed to stifle. It was not the woman herself who troubled her now, nor the ring, but the mysterious aspect of all those meetings. Her reasoning mind could no longer entirely comprehend it. The woman had discovered her name and address as if by magic, she knew all about the hours she kept, she knew about her domestic life, she had always turned up at the worst, most dangerous moments, and now all of a sudden she had disappeared just when she was actually wanted. She must be somewhere in the hurry and bustle of the city, close when she wanted to be close, yet out of reach as soon as Irene wanted to find her. And the amorphous nature of the threat, the elusive proximity of the blackmailer, close to her own life and yet beyond contact, left the already exhausted Irene a helpless prey to her ever more mystifying fears. Nervously now, with a feverish step, she kept walking up and down the same streets. Walking the streets like a prostitute, she thought. But the woman was nowhere to be seen. Now darkness came down like a menace, the early spring evening cast shadows over the clear colour of the sky, and night was falling fast. Lights came on along the streets, the stream of humanity was making its way home at a faster pace, all life seemed to be swallowed up in its dark current. She went up and down a few more times, scrutinising the street once more with all that remained of her hope, and then she turned home. She was freezing cold.

Wearily, she went up to the apartment. She heard the children being put to bed, but she avoided going in to say goodnight to them, wishing them well for that one night while she herself thought of the eternal night ahead of her. Why go in to them now? To sense the unclouded happiness of their exuberant kisses, see the love in their bright faces? Why torment herself still further with a joy that was already lost? She gritted her teeth—no, she didn't want the sensations of life any more, the kindness and laughter that linked her to so many memories, when all those links must be violently broken tomorrow. She would think only of unpleasant things, ugly and vile, her own undoing, the blackmailer, the scandal, everything that was driving her to the edge of the abyss.

Her husband's return interrupted her dismal, lonely reflections. He was in a good mood and struck up a lively conversation, trying to come close to her, at least in words, and asking a great many questions. She thought she detected a certain nervousness in the sudden concern he showed for her, but remembering yesterday's conversation she was not going to involve herself in another like it. Her fears kept her from letting love bind her or affection hold her back. He seemed to feel her reluctance, and be rather troubled by it. For her part, she was afraid that his concern would lead to another approach to her, and she said goodnight early. "I'll see you tomorrow, then," he replied. Then she left him.

Tomorrow—how close that was, and how endlessly far away! She passed a sleepless night, monstrously long and dark. Gradually the noises of the street died away, and from the reflections falling into her room she saw that the lights there were going out. Sometimes she thought she could sense the breathing of her family in the other rooms of the apartment, the lives of her children, of her husband, of the whole world, so close and yet so far away, almost lost to her now. But at the same time she was aware of an indescribable silence that seemed to proceed not from anything natural, anything around her, but from within, from some mysteriously rushing source. She felt coffined in endless silence, and the darkness of the invisible sky weighed down on her breast. Now and then the hours chimed a number in the darkness, and then the night was black and lifeless, but for the first time she thought she could understand the meaning of that endless, empty darkness. She was not thinking about farewells or her death any longer, only of how she could go to meet it, while sparing her children and herself, as far as possible, the shame of creating any sensation. She thought of all the ways she knew that led to death, all the possible methods of doing away with herself, until with a kind of happy surprise she suddenly remembered that the doctor had prescribed morphine for her when she was suffering from insomnia during a painful illness. She had taken the bitter-sweet poison in small drops out of a little bottle, and had been told at the time that its contents were enough to induce a gentle slumber. Oh, not to be hunted any more, to be able to rest, rest for ever, not to feel the hammer blows of fear on her heart any longer! The thought of that gentle slumber seemed immensely desirable to the sleepless Irene. She already thought she could taste the bitter flavour on her lips while her senses softly faded away. Quickly, she pulled herself together and put on the light. She soon found the little bottle, still half-full, but she was afraid that it might not be enough. Feverishly, she searched her chest of drawers until she finally found the prescription that would allow her to have a larger quantity made up for her. She folded the prescription, smiling, as if it were a banknote of a high denomination. Now she held death in her hands. Shivering slightly with cold, yet reassured, she was going back to bed when, as she passed the illuminated mirror, she suddenly saw herself approaching in the dark frame, ghostly, pale, hollow-eyed, and wrapped in her white nightdress as if in a shroud. Horror came over her. She put out the light, fled freezing to the bed she had left, and lay awake until day began to dawn.

In the morning she burnt her letters and put all kinds of small matters in order, but as far as she could she avoided seeing the children and everything else that was dear to her. She wanted to hold life at arm's length now, not clutch it to her with desire and feel its enticements. It would make her decision harder to put into practice if she hesitated, and hesitation could only be in vain. Then she went out into the street once more to try her luck for the last time, hoping to see the blackmailer. Once again she walked restlessly up and down the streets, but no longer with that sense of heightened tension. Something in her was worn out, and she could not go on with the struggle. She walked and walked for two hours as if it were a duty. The woman was nowhere to be seen. That did not hurt her now. She almost stopped wishing for the encounter, she felt so powerless. She looked at the faces of people in the street, and they all seemed strange to her, all of them dead and gone. Everything was somehow far away, lost, and did not belong to her any more.

Only once did she start. She felt as if, looking around, she had suddenly met her husband's eyes on the other side of the street, gazing at her with that strange, hard, piercing expression that she had only recently seen in them. Apprehensively, she looked again, but the figure had disappeared behind a passing vehicle, and she reassured herself by remembering that he was always in court at this time of day. Her agitation and her search were making her lose all sense of time, and she was late for lunch. But as usual he was not home yet himself, and did not arrive until a couple of minutes later. She thought that he seemed a little upset about something.

Now she was counting the hours until evening, and was alarmed to find how many there still were. How odd that was— you needed so little time to say goodbye, everything seemed worthless when you knew you couldn't take it with you. A kind of drowsiness came over her. She mechanically went up and down the street again, at random now, without thinking or looking. The driver of a carriage pulled back his horses at a crossing; she had only just seen the pole of the carriage in front of her in time. The driver swore at her; she hardly turned. An accident would have meant safety, or postponement. Well, chance had spared her the decision. Wearily, she went on. It was good to think of nothing at all, just feel a confused, vague sense of the approaching end, a mist gently rising and enveloping everything.

When she happened to look up and saw the name of the street, she shuddered. In her confused wanderings, chance had brought her almost to the building where her former lover lived. Was that a sign? Perhaps he might yet be able to help her. He must know the woman's address. She was trembling almost joyfully. Why hadn't she thought of that before? It was the simplest solution! All at once her limbs felt stronger, hope gave new vigour to the sad, bewildered ideas in her head. He must go to that person with her and put an end to it once and for all. He must threaten the woman, force her to stop her blackmailing. Perhaps a good sum of money might even get her out of the city entirely. She suddenly felt sorry to have spoken as she did to the poor creature recently, but he would help her, she was sure of that. How strange that this hope of rescue came only now, at the last minute.

She hurried up the steps and rang the bell. No one came to the door. She listened; she felt as if she had heard cautious footsteps on the other side. She rang the bell once more. Silence again. And again a faint noise inside. Then her patience was exhausted—she rang and rang the bell without stopping. No less than her life was at stake.

At last there was movement behind the door, the lock clicked, and it was opened just a crack. "It's me," she quickly said.

Now he did open the door, looking as if her visit was a shock. "You... ah, so it's you, dear lady," he stammered, switching to a more formal tone and visibly embarrassed. "I was just... forgive me... I wasn't expecting... wasn't expecting to see you. Do please forgive my outfit." He indicated his shirtsleeves. His shirt was open at the neck, and he wore no collar.

"I have to speak to you. It's urgent. You must help me," she said—uneasily, because he was keeping her standing in the hall like a beggar. "Won't you let me come in and listen to me for a moment?" she added, her nerves on edge.

"Well," he murmured awkwardly, with a surreptitious glance behind him, "it's just that at this minute... I can't really..."

"You must, must listen to me. It's your fault, after all, it's your duty to help me... you must get back the ring for me, you must! Or at least tell me her address. She's been persecuting me, and now she's disappeared... you must help me, listen, you must."

He was staring at her. Only now did she realise that she was gasping out her words disjointedly.

"But of course, you don't know... Well, she, I mean your mistress, the other one, the woman saw me leave you that last time, and since then she's been pursuing me, blackmailing me... torturing me to death. Now she has my ring, and I must, I must get it back. I must have it by this evening, I said that today I'd... oh, will you help me?"

"But... but I..."

"Will you or won't you?"

"But I don't know any such person. I don't know who you're talking about. I've never had anything to do with any such woman." He sounded almost angry.

"So... so you don't know her? She just said so, she plucked it out of thin air? And she knows your name, too, and where I live. So perhaps it's not true that she's been blackmailing me? Perhaps I've simply been dreaming the whole thing?"

She burst into shrill laughter. He was clearly uncomfortable. For a moment it passed through his mind, as he saw her sparkling eyes, that she might be mad. Her behaviour was disturbed, her words made no sense. Anxiously, he looked around.

"Please calm down, dear lady... I assure you, there's some mistake. It's quite out of the question, it must... no, I can't understand it myself. I don't know any women like that. The couple of relationships I've had here since my... well, as you know, I haven't been here long, and they weren't that kind of... I don't want to name names, but this is ridiculous. I assure you there must be some mistake."

"So you won't help me?"

"But of course... if I can."

"Then... then come with me. We'll visit her together."

"Visit her? Who do you mean?" Again, as she seized his arm, he had a terrible feeling that she was deranged.

"*Her*... Will you come or not?"

"Of course, of course." His suspicions were reinforced by the strength of her urgings. "Of course I will."

"Then come along... this is life or death to me."

He had to make a great effort to prevent himself from smiling. Then he suddenly became formal in his manner.

"Please forgive me, dear lady, but it's out of the question at the moment. I'm giving a piano lesson... I can't leave now..."

"I see... I see." Her shrill laughter rang out in his face. "So this is how you give piano lessons, in your shirtsleeves... You liar!" And suddenly, as an idea came to her, she lunged forwards. He tried to hold her back. "So she's here, that blackmailer, here with you, is she? Perhaps you're both playing this game. Perhaps the two of you share everything you've extorted from me. But I'm going to get my hands on her. I'm not afraid of anything now." She was shouting at the top of her voice. He held her firmly, but she fought with him, tore herself away and ran to the bedroom door.

A figure quickly retreated. Someone who had obviously been listening behind the door. The horrified Irene found herself staring at a lady who was a total stranger to her. Her dress was rather disarranged, and she hastily turned her face away. Irene's lover, thinking her mad, had followed to restrain her and prevent any misfortune, but she was already on her way out of the bedroom again. "Excuse me," she murmured. She felt utterly confused. She understood none of it, she felt nothing but endless revulsion and a great weariness.

"Excuse me," she said again, seeing him look uneasily at her. "Tomorrow... tomorrow you'll understand it all... that's to say, I... oh, I don't understand any of it myself any more." She spoke to him as if he were a stranger. Nothing in this man reminded her that she had ever listened to a word he said, and she scarcely felt her own body. Now everything was even more confused than it had been. All she knew was that there must be a lie somewhere. But she was too tired to think any more, too tired to go on looking. With her eyes almost closed, she went down the steps like a condemned criminal going to the gallows.

The street was dark when she went out into it. Perhaps, the thought crossed her mind, she's waiting outside now; perhaps all will be well at the last minute. She felt as if she ought to fold her hands and pray to her forgotten God. Oh, if she could just buy herself a few months, the few months between now and summer, and then spend the summer holiday peacefully in the country, where the blackmailer couldn't get at her, living among the fields and meadows. Just one summer, but it would be so full, so complete that it would count as more than a whole human lifetime. She looked longingly down the now-dark street. She thought she saw someone standing in the entrance of a building, but as she came closer the figure retreated into the entrance hall. For a moment she thought she saw some similarity to her husband. It was the second time today that she had feared meeting him suddenly in the street with his eyes bent on her. She hesitated, hoping to make sure, but the figure had disappeared into the shadows. Uneasily, she went on with a curiously tense sensation at the nape of her neck, as if transfixed by a burning glance behind her. She turned around once, but there was no one in sight.

It was not far to the pharmacy. She went in, shivering slightly. The pharmacist took her prescription and went to make it up. In that one minute she absorbed the sight of everything in the shop—the shining scales, the delicate little weights, the small labels, and up on the shelves the rows of essences with their strange Latin names. Unconsciously, she looked along them all, spelling them out. She heard the clock ticking, breathed in the characteristic aroma of the place, that sweetish, greasy aroma of medicaments, and suddenly remembered that as a child she had always asked her mother to let her go and fetch anything from the pharmacy, because she liked the smell and the strange look of all the shiny little pots. At the same time she realised, horrified, that she had forgotten to say goodbye to her mother, and she felt dreadfully sorry for the poor woman. What a shock it would be to her, thought Irene in alarm, but the pharmacist was already counting out the colourless drops from a big-bellied vessel into a little blue bottle. She watched, spellbound, as the death that would soon be streaming through her veins moved from that larger vessel into the smaller one, and a chill ran though her. Mindlessly, in a kind of hypnotic trance, she watched his fingers as he put the stopper into the full bottle and stuck the label over its curving sides. All her senses were paralysed, numbed by the terrible idea.

"That'll be two crowns, please," said the pharmacist. She woke from her rigid calm, and looked around her strangely. Then she automatically put her hand in her bag to take out the money. Everything was still like a dream. She looked at the coins without recognising them at once, and involuntarily took her time about counting the money out.

At that moment she felt her arm pushed vigorously aside, and heard coins clinking as they were dropped into the glass dish on the counter. Beside her, a hand reached out and picked up the little bottle.

Instinctively, she turned, and her glance froze. It was her husband standing there, his lips tightly compressed. His face was pale, and damp beads of perspiration shone on his forehead.

She felt close to fainting, and had to hold on to the counter for support. All at once she realised that she had indeed seen him in the street earlier, and he had been waiting in the entrance to that building just now. Something in her had guessed that he was there. For a split second she wildly recollected the day's events.

"Come along," he said in a low, choked voice. She looked fixedly at him, and marvelled inside herself, at a very deep and dark level of her mind, for obeying him. And for the way her steps matched themselves to his without her knowing it.

They crossed the road side by side. Neither looked at the other. He was still carrying the little bottle. Once he stopped, and wiped his damp brow. She slackened her own pace too, not meaning to and unaware of it. But she dared not look at him. Neither spoke a word. The noise of traffic in the street surged between them.

On the steps outside their building, he let her go ahead of him. And as soon as he was no longer beside her, she began swaying as she walked. She stopped, and did not move on. Then he was supporting her arm. At the touch she started, and hurried up the last steps more quickly.

She went into the drawing room, and he followed her. The walls shone with a dark glow, the pieces of furniture could hardly be told apart. They still had not said a word. He tore the paper off the wrapping, opened the little bottle, and poured its contents away. Then he flung it violently into a corner. She shrank at the clattering sound as it fell.

Still they were silent. She felt him controlling himself, felt it without looking at him. At last he came over to her. Came close, and then very close. She could feel his heavy breathing, and with her fixed and clouded gaze she saw the glitter of his eyes standing out in the darkness of the room. She waited for his outburst of anger, shivering in spite of the firm grasp of his hand holding her. Irene's heart stood still, only her nerves vibrated like the strings of a musical instrument at high tension. Everything in her was expecting chastisement, and she almost wanted to hear his fury. But he still said nothing, and with endless surprise she felt that his approach to her was gentle. "Irene," he said, and his voice was strangely soft, "how much longer are we going to torment each other?"

Then it all broke out of her suddenly, convulsively and with overpowering force, like one great, mindless, animal scream. At last it burst out, all the sobbing she had suppressed and fought down in these last weeks. An angry hand seemed to grasp her from inside, shaking her hard, she was staggering as if she were drunk, and would have fallen to the floor if he had not supported her.

"Irene," he soothed her, "Irene, Irene." He spoke her name more and more softly, reassuringly, as if he could calm the desperate turbulence of her overstrained nerves by uttering it with increasing tenderness. But only sobs answered him, wild gasps and choking sounds of pain that passed through her whole body. He led, or rather carried, her convulsed form to the sofa and laid it down. But the sobbing would not stop. A fit of weeping shook her limbs like electric shocks, waves of shivering and cold seemed to run through her tortured body. Her nerves, which had been expecting the worst for weeks now, were torn apart, and the torment raged through her numbed body unchecked.

Greatly dismayed, he held her shuddering form, clasped her cold hands, kissed her dress and the back of her neck first soothingly, then wildly, in fear and passion, but the tremors still kept passing through her hunched figure as if something were tearing her apart. And the tumultuous wave of her sobbing, liberated at last, rose from inside her. He felt her face—cool, bathed in tears—and the throbbing veins at her temples. Unspeakable fear came over him. He knelt down so that he could speak closer to her face.

"Irene." He kept touching her. "Why are you crying like that? It's all over... all over now... why are you still tormenting yourself? You mustn't be afraid any more. She'll never come back, never again..."

Her body reared up again, but he held her firmly with both hands. He was afraid when he sensed the desperation tearing at her tormented body. It was as if he had murdered her. He kissed her again and again, stammering out words of apology.

"Never again... never. I swear it. How could I have known you'd take it so badly? I only wanted to... to bring you back to your duties here... get you to leave him... for ever, and come back to us. When I found out by chance, what else could I do? I couldn't tell you myself... I thought, I kept thinking you'd come back... that's why I sent that poor creature to hunt you down... and she really is a poor creature, an out-of-work actress. She was reluctant to agree, but I wanted... now I see it was wrong, but I did want you back. I've always shown you I was ready to... that I only wanted to forgive, but you didn't understand. But I never... never meant to drive you so far... I've suffered so much seeing all this. I was watching every step you took... if only because of the children, you understand, I had to make you... it was because of the children... But it's all over now, everything will be all right again now..."

Faintly, from an endless distance away, she heard words spoken close to her, but did not understand them. There was a roaring sound inside her that rose above everything else, a tumult of the senses in which all feeling was lost. She sensed touches on her skin, kisses, caresses, and her own tears, now cooling down, but the blood inside her was full of sound, full of a sombre, droning note that swelled powerfully and was now pealing like a thunderous chime of bells. And then everything distinct was lost. Coming round from her faint, still confused, she felt that she was being undressed, saw her husband's face, kind and anxious, as if through dense clouds. Then she fell down into the dark, down into the long, black, dreamless sleep that she had needed for so long.

When she opened her eyes next morning, it was light and bright in her room. And she felt light and bright herself, the clouds had lifted, and her own blood felt cleansed as if by a thunderstorm. She tried to think what had happened to her, but it all still seemed like a dream. The throbbing inside her seemed improbable, light, liberated, like floating through spaces in sleep, and to make sure that she was not dreaming she tentatively felt her own hands.

Suddenly she came to herself with a start; her ring was back, sparkling on her finger. All at once she was wide awake. The confused words, heard and yet not heard while she was half-fainting, a sombre presentiment she had felt even earlier, but had never allowed to become real thought and suspicion, suddenly came together, showing a clear connection. All at once she understood everything—her husband's questions, her lover's baffled astonishment, the whole mesh was unravelled, and she saw the terrible net in which she had been entangled. Bitterness and shame overwhelmed her, once more her nerves began to quiver, and she was almost sorry to have woken from that calm and dreamless sleep.

Then she heard laughter in the next room. The children were up and about, noisily greeting the new day like birds waking up. She distinctly heard her son's voice, and for the first time, surprised, realised how like his father he sounded. A quiet smile came to her lips, and rested there. She lay with her eyes closed to relish, at a deeper level, her real life or what it was, and it was now her happiness too. Something still hurt her, deep inside, but it was a promising pain, burning but mild, just as wounds burn when scar tissue is about to close over them for ever.

CONFUSION

THEY MEANT WELL, my students and colleagues in the Faculty: there it lies, solemnly presented and expensively bound, the first copy of the Festschrift dedicated to me by the members of the Department of Languages and Literature on the occasion of my sixtieth birthday and to mark my thirty years of academic teaching. It is nothing short of a complete biographical record: no minor essay of mine has been overlooked, no ceremonial address, no trifling review in the annual volume of some learned journal or other has failed to be exhumed from its papery grave by bibliographical industry—my entire career up to the present day is set out with impeccable clarity, step by step like a well-swept staircase—it would be truly ungrateful of me to take no pleasure in this touching diligence. What I myself had thought lost, spent and gone, returns to me united and well-ordered in the form presented here: no, I cannot deny that as an old man I now scan these pages with the same pride as did the schoolboy whose report from his teachers first indicated that he had the requisite ability and strength of mind for an academic career.

And yet: when I had leafed through the two hundred industrious pages and looked my intellectual reflection in the eye, I couldn't help smiling. Was that really my life, did it truly trace as purposeful a course with such ease, from the first to the present day, as the biographer describes, sorting the paper records into order? I felt exactly as I did when I first heard my own voice on a recording: initially I did not recognize it at all, for it was indeed my voice but only as others hear it, not as I hear it myself through my blood and within my very being, so to speak. And so I, who have spent a lifetime depicting human beings in the light of their work, portraying the intrinsic intellectual structure of their worlds, was made aware again from my own experience of the impenetrability in every human life of the true core of its being, the malleable cell from which all growth proceeds. We live through myriads of seconds, yet it is always one, just one, that casts our entire inner world into turmoil, the second when (as Stendhal has described it) the internal inflorescence, already steeped in every kind of fluid, condenses and crystallizes—a magical second, like the moment of generation, and like that moment concealed in the warm interior of the individual life, invisible, untouchable, beyond the reach of feeling, a secret experienced alone. No algebra of the mind can calculate it, no alchemy of premonition divine it, and it can seldom perceive itself.

The book says not a word about this most secret factor in my mental development: that was why I couldn't help smiling. Everything it says is true—only what genuinely matters is missing. It merely describes me, it says nothing real about me. It speaks of me, but does not reveal what I am. The carefully compiled index comprises two hundred names—and the only one missing is the name of the man from whom all my creativity derived, who determined the course my life would take, and now calls me back to my youth with redoubled force. The book covers everything else, but not the man who gave me the gift of language and with whose tongue I speak: and suddenly I feel to blame for this craven silence. I have spent my life painting portraits of human beings, interpreting figures from past centuries for the benefit of today's sensibilities, and never thought of turning to the picture of the one most present to my mind. As in Homeric days, then, I will give that beloved shade my own blood to drink, so that he may speak to me again, and although he grew old and died long ago, be with me now that I too am growing old. I will add a page not previously written to those on open display, a confession of feelings to be set beside that scholarly book, and for his sake I will tell myself the true story of my youth.

B EFORE BEGINNING, I leaf once again through the book which claims to depict my life. And once again I cannot help smiling. How did they think they could reach the true core of my being when they chose to approach it in the wrong way? Even their very first step is wide of the mark! A former schoolmate, well disposed towards me and also a bearer of the honorary title of Privy Councillor, claims that even at grammar school my passion for the humanities distinguished me from all the other pupils. Your memory is at fault, my dear Privy Councillor! As far as I was concerned, anything in the way of humanist studies represented coercion which I could barely endure; I ground my teeth and fumed at it. For the very reason that, as the son of a headmaster in our small North German town, I was familiar at home with education as a means of earning a living, I hated everything to do with languages and literature from child-hood: Nature, true to her mystic task of preserving the creative instinct, always impels the child to reject and despise its father's inclinations. Nature does not want weak, conformist progeny, merely continuing from where the previous generation left off: she always sets those of a kind at loggerheads, allowing the later-born to return to the ways of their forefathers only after making a laborious but fruitful detour. My father had only to venerate scholarship for my self-assertive instinct to regard it as mere intellectual sophistry; he praised the classics as a model to be followed, so they seemed to me didactic and I hated them. Surrounded by books, I despised them; with my father constantly pressing intellectual pursuits on me, I felt furious dislike for every kind of knowledge passed on by written tradition; it was not surprising, therefore, that I barely scraped through my school-leaving examinations and then vigorously resisted any idea of continuing my studies. I wanted to be an army officer, or join the navy, or be an engineer, although I had no really compelling inclination for any of those professions. Only my distaste for the papery didacticism of scholarship made me wish for a practical and active rather than an academic career. But my father, with his fanatical veneration for universities and everything to do with them, insisted on my following a course of academic studies, and the only concession I could win was permission to choose English as my subject rather than classics (a compromise which I finally accepted with the private reservation that a knowledge of English, the language of the sea, would make it easier for me later to adopt the naval career I so fervently desired).

Nothing could be further from the truth in that curriculum vitae of mine, then, than the well-meant statement that thanks to the guidance of meritorious professors I grasped the basic principles of the study of the arts in my first term—what did my passion for liberty, now impetuously breaking out, care then for lectures and lecturers? On my first brief visit to the lecture hall its stuffy atmosphere and the lecture itself, delivered in a monotonously clerical and self-important drone, so overcame me with weariness that it was an effort not to put my head down on the desk and doze off. Here I was back at the school I had thought myself so happy to escape, complete with classroom, teacher's lectern in an excessively elevated position, and quibbling pedantry—I could not help feeling as if sand were running out of the thin-lipped open mouth of the Privy Councillor addressing us, so steadily did the words of the worn lecture notebook drop into the thick air. The suspicion I had entertained even as a schoolboy that I had entered a morgue of the spirit, where uncaring hands anatomized the dead, was revived to an alarming degree in this factory churning out second-hand Alexandrian philosophy—and how intensely did I feel that instinct of rejection the moment the lecture I had sat through with such difficulty was over, and I stepped out into the streets of the city, the Berlin of those days which, surprised by its own growth, was bursting with a virility too suddenly attained, sparks flying from all its stones and all its streets, while the feverishly vibrant pace of life forced itself irresistibly on everyone, and in its avid greed greatly resembled the intoxication of my own only recently recognized sense of virility. Both the city and I had suddenly emerged from a repressive petit bourgeois atmosphere of Protestant orderliness, and were plunged too rapidly into a new delirium of power and opportunity—both of us, the city and I, a young fellow starting out in life, vibrated like a dynamo with restlessness and impatience. I never understood and loved Berlin as much as I did then, for every cell in my being was crying out for sudden expansion, just like every part of that overflowing, warm human honeycomb—and where could the impatience of my forceful youth have released itself but in the throbbing womb of that heated giantess, that restless city radiating power? It grasped me and took me to itself, I flung myself into it, went down into its very veins, my curiosity rapidly orbiting its entire stony yet warm body—I walked its streets from morning to night, went out to the lakes, discovered its secret places: I was truly a man possessed as, instead of paying attention to my studies, I flung myself into the lively and adventurous business of exploration. In these excesses, however, I was simply obeying an idiosyncrasy of my own—incapable from childhood of doing two things at once, I immediately became emotionally blind to any other occupation; everywhere and at all times I have felt the same impulse to press forward along a single line, and even in my work today I tend to sink my teeth so doggedly into a problem that I will not let go until I feel I have entirely drained it of substance.

At that time in Berlin my sense of liberation was so powerfully intoxicating that I could not endure even the brief seclusion of the lecture hall or the constraint of my own lodgings; everything that did not bring adventure my way seemed a waste of time. Still wet behind the ears, only just out of leading strings, the provincial youth that I was forced himself to appear a grown man—I joined a fraternity, sought to give my intrinsically rather shy nature a touch of boldness, jauntiness, heartiness; I had not been in the place a week before I was playing the part of cosmopolitan man about town, and I learned, with remarkable speed, to lounge and loll at my ease in coffee-houses, a true *miles gloriosus*. This chapter of manhood of course included women—or rather '*girls*', as we called them in our student arrogance—and it was much to my advantage that I was a strikingly good-looking young man. Tall, slim, the bronzed hue of the sea coast still fresh on my cheeks, my every movement athletically supple, I had a clear advantage over the pasty-faced shop-boys, dried like herrings by the indoor air, who like us students went out every Sunday in search of prey in the dance-floor cafés of Halensee and Hundekehle (then still well outside the city). I would take back to my lodgings now a flaxen-haired, milky-skinned servant girl from Mecklenburg, heated by the dancing, before she went home from her day off, now a timid, nervous little Jewish girl from Posen who sold stockings in Tietz's—most of them easy pickings, to be had for the taking and passed on quickly to my friends. The anxious schoolboy I had been only yesterday, however, found the unsuspected ease of his conquests a heady surprise—my successes, so cheaply won, increased my daring, and gradually I came to regard the street merely as the hunting

233

ground for these entirely undiscriminating exploits, which were a kind of sport to me. Once, as I was stalking a pretty girl along Unter den Linden and—by pure coincidence—I came to the university, I could not help smiling to think how long it was since I had crossed that august threshold. Out of sheer high spirits I and a like-minded friend went in; we just opened the door a crack, saw (and an incredibly ridiculous sight it seemed) a hundred and fifty backs bent over their desks and scribbling, as if joining in the litany recited by a white-bearded psalmodist. Then I closed the door again, let the stream of that dull eloquence continue to flow over the shoulders of the industrious listeners, and strode jauntily out with my friend into the sunny avenue. It sometimes seems to me that a young man never wasted his time more stupidly than I did in those months. I never read a book, I am sure I never spoke a sensible word or entertained a thought worth the name—instinctively I avoided all cultivated society, merely in order to let my recently aroused body savour all the better the piquancy of the new and hitherto forbidden. This self-intoxication, this waste of time in wreaking havoc on oneself, may come naturally to every strong young man suddenly let off the leash—yet my peculiar sense of being possessed by it made this kind of dissolute conduct dangerous, and nothing was more likely than that I would have frittered away my life entirely, or at least have fallen victim to a dullness of feeling, had not chance suddenly halted my precipitous mental decline.

That chance—and today I gratefully call it a lucky one— consisted in my father's being unexpectedly summoned to the Ministry in Berlin for the day, for a headmasters' conference. As a professional educationalist, he seized his chance to get a random sample of my conduct without previous notice, taking me unawares and by surprise. His tactics succeeded perfectly. As usual in the evening, I was entertaining a girl in my cheap student lodgings in the north of the city—access was through my landlady's kitchen, divided off from my room by a curtain—and entertaining her very intimately too when I heard a knock on the door, loud and clear. Supposing it was another student, I growled crossly: "Sorry, not at home." After a short pause, however, the knocking came again, once, twice, and then, with obvious impatience, a third time. Angrily, I got into my trousers to send the importunate visitor packing, and so, shirt half-open, braces dangling, barefoot, I flung the door open, and immediately, as if I had been struck in the face by a fist, I recognized my father's shape in the darkness outside. I could make out little more of his face in the shadows than the lenses of his glasses, shining in the reflected light. However, that shadowy outline was enough for the bold words I had already prepared to stick in my throat, like a sharp fishbone choking me; for a minute or so I stood there, stunned. Then—and a terrible moment it was!—I had to ask him humbly to wait in the kitchen for a few minutes while I tidied my room. As I have said, I didn't see his face, but I sensed that he knew what was going on. I sensed it from his silence, from the restrained manner in which, without giving me his hand, he stepped behind the curtain in the kitchen with a gesture of distaste. And there, in front of an iron stove smelling of warmed-up coffee and turnips, the old man had to stand waiting for ten minutes, ten minutes equally humiliating to both of us, while I bundled the girl out of bed and into her clothes, past my father, who was listening against his will, and so out of the house. He could not help noticing her footsteps, and the way the folds of the curtain swung in the draught of air as she hurried off, and still I could not bring the old man in from his demeaning place of concealment: first I had to remedy the disorder of the bed, which was all too obvious. Only then—and I had never in my life felt more ashamed—only then did I face him.

My father retained his composure in this difficult situation, and I still privately thank him for it. Whenever I wish to remember him—and he died long ago—I refuse to see him from the viewpoint of the schoolboy who liked to despise him as no more than a correcting machine, constantly carping, a schoolmaster bent on precision; instead, I always conjure up his picture at this most human of moments, when deeply repelled, yet restraining himself, the old man followed me without a word into the oppressive atmosphere of my room. He was carrying his hat and gloves and was about to put them down automatically, but then made a gesture of revulsion, as if reluctant to let any part of himself touch such filth. I offered him an armchair; he did not reply, merely warded off all contact with the objects in this room with a movement of rejection.

After standing there, turned away from me, for a few icy moments, he finally took off his glasses and cleaned them with deliberation, a habit of his which, I knew, was a sign of embarrassment; nor did it escape me that when he put them on again the old man passed the back of his hand over his eyes. He felt ashamed in my presence, and I felt ashamed in his; neither of us could think of anything to say. Secretly I feared that he would launch into a sermon, an eloquent address delivered in that guttural tone I had hated and derided ever since my schooldays. But—and I still thank him for it today—the old man remained silent and avoided looking at me. At last he went over to the rickety shelf where my textbooks stood and opened them—one glance must have told him they were untouched, most of their pages still uncut. "Your lecture notes!" This request was the first thing he had said. Trembling, I handed them to him, well knowing that the shorthand notes I had made covered only a single lecture. He looked rapidly through the two pages, and placed the lecture notes on the table without the slightest sign of agitation. Then he pulled up a chair, sat down, looked at me gravely but without any reproach in his eyes, and asked: "Well, what do you think about all this? What now?"

This calm question floored me. Everything in me had been strung up—if he had spoken in anger, I would have let fly arrogantly in return, if he had admonished me emotionally I would have mocked him. But this matter-of-fact question broke the back of my defiance: its gravity called for gravity in return, its forced calm demanded respect and a readiness to respond. What I said I scarcely dare remember, just as the whole conversation that followed is something I cannot write down to this day—there are moments of emotional shock, a kind of swelling tide within, which when retold would probably sound sentimental, certain words which carry conviction only once, in private conversation and arising from an unforeseen turmoil of the feelings. It was the only real conversation I ever had with my father, and I had no qualms about voluntarily humbling myself; I left all the decisions to him. However, he merely suggested that I might like to leave Berlin and spend the next semester studying at a small university elsewhere; he was sure, he said almost comfortingly, that from now on I would work hard to make up for my omissions. His confidence shook me; in that one second I felt all the injustice I had done the old man throughout my youth, enclosed as he was in cold formality. I had to bite my lip hard to keep the hot tears in my eyes from flowing. And he may have felt something similar himself, for he suddenly offered me his hand, which shook as it held mine for a moment, and then made haste to leave. I dared not follow him, but stood there agitated and confused, and wiped the blood from my lip with my handkerchief, so hard had I dug my teeth into it in order to control my feelings.

This was the first real shock that, at the age of nineteen, I experienced—without a word spoken in anger, it overthrew the whole grandiose house of cards I had built during the last three months, a house constructed out of masculinity, student debauchery and bragging. I felt strong enough to give up all lesser pleasures for the act of will demanded of me, I was impatient to turn my wasted abilities to intellectual pursuits, I felt an avid wish for gravity, sobriety, discipline and severity. It was now that I vowed myself entirely to study, as if to a monastic ritual of sacrifice, although unaware of the transports of delight awaiting me in scholarship, and never guessing that adventures and perils lie ready for the impetuous in that rarefied world of the intellect as well.

The small provincial town where, with my father's approval, I had chosen to spend the next semester was in central Germany. Its far-flung academic renown was in stark contrast to the sparse collection of houses surrounding the university building. I did not have much difficulty in finding my way to my alma mater from the railway station, where I left my luggage for the time being, and as soon as I was inside the university, a spacious building in the old style, I felt how much more quickly the inner circle closed here than in the bustling city of Berlin. Within two hours I had enrolled and visited most of the professors; the only one not immediately available was my professor of English language and literature, but I was told he could be found taking his class at around four in the afternoon.

Driven by impatience, reluctant to waste an hour, as eager now to embark on the pursuit of knowledge as I had once been to avoid it, and after a rapid tour of the little town—which was sunk in narcotic slumber by comparison with Berlin—I turned up at the appointed place punctually at four o'clock. The caretaker directed me to the door of the seminar room. I knocked. And thinking a voice inside had answered, I went in.

However, I had misheard. No one had told me to come in, and the indistinct sound I had caught was only the professor's voice raised in energetic speech, delivering an obviously impromptu address to a close-packed circle of about two dozen students who had gathered around him. Feeling awkward at entering without permission because of my mistake, I was going to withdraw quietly again, but feared to attract attention by that very course of action, since so far none of the hearers had noticed me. Accordingly I stayed near the door, and could not help listening too.

The lecture had obviously arisen spontaneously out of a colloquium or discussion, or at least that was what the informal and entirely random grouping of teacher and students suggested—the professor was not sitting in a chair which distanced him from his audience as he addressed them, but was perched almost casually on a desk, one leg dangling slightly, and the young people clustered around him in informal positions, perhaps fixed in statuesque immobility only by the interest they felt in hearing him. I could see that they must have been standing around talking when the professor suddenly swung himself up on the desk, and from this more elevated position drew them to him with words as if with a lasso, holding them spellbound where they were. It was only a few minutes before I myself, forgetting that I had not been invited to attend, felt the fascinating power of his delivery working on me like a magnet; involuntarily I came closer, not just to hear him but also to see the remarkably graceful, all-embracing movements of his hands which, when he uttered a word with commanding emphasis, sometimes spread like wings, rising and fluttering in the air, and then gradually sank again harmoniously, with the gesture of an orchestral conductor muting the sound. The lecture became ever more heated as the professor, in his animated discourse, rose rhythmically from the hard surface of desk as if from the back of a galloping horse, his tempestuous train of thought, shot through with lightning images, racing breathlessly on. I had never heard anyone speak with such enthusiasm, so genuinely carrying the listeners away—for the first time I experienced what Latin scholars call a *raptus*, when one is taken right out of oneself; the words uttered by his quick tongue were spoken not for himself, nor for the others present, but poured out of his mouth like fire from a man inflamed by internal combustion.

I had never before known language as ecstasy, the passion of discourse as an elemental act, and the unexpected shock of it drew me closer. Without knowing that I was moving, hypnotically attracted by a force stronger than curiosity, and with the dragging footsteps of a sleepwalker I made my way as if by magic into that charmed circle—suddenly, without being aware of it, I was there, only a few inches from him and among all the others, who themselves were too spellbound to notice me or anything else. I immersed myself in the discourse, swept away by its strong current without knowing anything about its origin: obviously one of the students had made some comment on Shakespeare, describing him as a meteoric phenomenon, which had made the man perched on the desk eager to explain that Shakespeare was merely the strongest manifestation, the psychic message of a whole generation, expressing, through the senses, a time turned passionately enthusiastic. In a single outline he traced the course of that great hour in England's history, that single moment of ecstasy which can come unexpectedly in the life of every nation, as in the life of every human being, a moment when all forces work together to forge a way strongly forward into eternity. Suddenly the earth has broadened out, a new continent is discovered, while the oldest power of all, the Papacy, threatens to collapse; beyond the seas, now belonging to the English since the Spanish Armada foundered in the wind and waves, new opportunities arise, the world has opened up, and the spirit automatically expands with it—it too desires breadth, it too desires extremes of good and evil; it wishes to make discoveries and conquests like the conquistadors of old, it needs a new language, new force. And overnight come those who speak that language, the poets, fifty or a hundred in a single decade, wild, boisterous fellows who do not, like the court poetasters before them, cultivate their little Arcadian gardens and versify on elegant mythological themes—no, they storm the theatre, they set up their standard in the wooden buildings that were once merely the scene of animal shows and bloodthirsty sports, and the hot odour of blood still lingers in their plays, their drama itself is a *Circus Maximus* where the wild beats of emotion fall ravenously on one another. These unruly and passionate hearts rage like lions, each trying to outdo the others in wild exuberance; all is permitted, all is allowed on stage: incest, murder, evildoing, crimes, the boundless tumult of human nature indulges in a heated orgy; as the hungry beasts once emerged from their cages, so do the inebriated passions now race into the wooden-walled arena, roaring and dangerous. It is a single outburst exploding like a petard, and it lasts for fifty years: a rush of blood, an ejaculation, a uniquely wild phenomenon prowling the world, seizing on it as its prey—in this orgy of power you can hardly hear individual voices or make out individual figures. Each strikes sparks off his neighbour, they learn and they steal from each other, they strive to outdo one another, to surpass each other's achievement, yet they are all only intellectual gladiators in the same festive games, slaves unchained and urged on by the genius of the hour. It recruits them from dark, crooked rooms on the outskirts of the city, and from palaces too: Ben Jonson, the mason's grandson; Marlowe, the son of a cobbler; Massinger, the offspring of an upper servant; Philip Sidney, the rich and scholarly statesman—but the seething whirlpool flings them all together; today they are famous, tomorrow they die, Kyd and Heywood in dire poverty, starving like Spenser in King Street, none of them living respectable lives, ruffians, whore-masters, actors, swindlers, but poets, poets, poets every one. Shakespeare is only at their centre, "the very age and body of the time", but no one has the time to mark him out, so stormy is the turmoil, so vigorously does work spring up beside work, so strongly does passion exceed passion. And as suddenly as it vibrantly arose that magnificent eruption of mankind collapses again, twitching; the drama is over, England exhausted, and for another hundred years the damp and foggy grey of the Thames lies dull upon the spirit again. A whole race has scaled the heights and depths of passion in a single onslaught, feverishly spewing the overflowing, frenzied soul from its breast—and there the land lies now, weary, worn out; pettifogging Puritanism closes the theatres and thus silences the impassioned language, the Bible alone is heard again, the word of God, where the most human word of all had made the most fiery confessions of all time, and a single ardent race lived for thousands in its own unique way.

And now, with a sudden change of direction, the dazzling discourse is turned on us: "So now do you see why I don't begin my course of lectures in chronological order, with King Arthur and Chaucer, but with the Elizabethans, in defiance of all the rules? And do you see that what I most want is for you to be familiar with them, get a sense of that liveliest of periods? One can't have literary comprehension without real experience, mere grammatical knowledge of the words is useless without recognition of their values, and when you young people want to understand a country and its language you should start by seeing it at its most beautiful, in the strength of its youth, at its most passionate. You should begin by hearing the language in the mouths of the poets who create and perfect it, you must have felt poetry warm and alive in your hearts before we start anatomizing it. That's why I always begin with the gods, for England is Elizabeth, is Shakespeare and the Shakespeareans, all that comes earlier is preparation, all that comes afterwards pale imitation of that true bold leap into infinity—but here, and you must feel it for yourselves, young people, here is the most truly alive youthfulness in the world. All phenomena, all humanity is to be recognized only in its fiery form, only in passion. For the intellect arises from the blood, thought from passion, passion from enthusiasm—so look at Shakespeare and his kind first, for they alone will make you young people genuinely young! Enthusiasm first, then diligence—enthusiasm giving you the finest, most extreme and greatest tutorial in the world, before you turn to studying the words.

"Well, that's enough for today—goodbye to you!" With an abrupt concluding gesture his hand rose in the air and imperiously descended again with an unexpected movement, and he jumped down from the desk at the same time. As if shaken apart, the dense crowd of students dispersed, seats creaked and banged, desks were pushed back, twenty hitherto silent throats suddenly began to speak, to clear themselves, to take a deep breath—only now did I realize how magnetic had been the spell closing all those living lips. The tumultuous discussion in that small space was all the more heated and uninhibited now; several students approached the lecturer with thanks, or some other comment, while the others exchanged impressions, their faces flushed, but no one stood by calmly, no one was left untouched by the electric tension, its contact now suddenly broken, yet its aura and its fire still seeming to crackle in the close air of the room.

I myself could not move—I felt I had been pierced to the heart. Of an emotional nature myself, unable to grasp anything except in terms of passion, my senses racing headlong on, I had felt carried away for the first time by another human being, a teacher; I had felt a superior force before which it was both a duty and a pleasure to bow. I felt the blood hot in my veins, my breath came faster, that racing rhythm throbbed through my body, seizing impatiently on every joint in it. Finally I gave way to instinct and slowly made my way to the front to see the man's face, for strange to say, as he spoke I had not perceived his features at all, so indistinct had they seemed, so immersed in what he was saying. Even now I could at first see only the indistinct outline of a shadowy profile; he was standing in the dim light by the window, half turning towards one of the students, hand laid in a friendly manner on his shoulder. Yet even that fleeting movement had an intimacy and grace about it which I would never have thought possible in an academic.

Meanwhile some of the students had noticed me, and to avoid appearing too much of an unwanted intruder I took a few more steps towards the professor and waited until he had finished his conversation. Only then did I see his face clearly: a Roman head, with a brow like domed marble, and a wave of hair cascading back, a shining white shock, bushy at the sides, the upper part of the face of an impressively bold and intellectual cast—but below the deeply shadowed eyes it was immediately made softer, almost feminine, by the smooth curve of the chin, the mobile lips with the nerves fluttering around the restless line of the sporadic smile. The attractive masculinity of the forehead was resolved by the more pliant lines of the flesh in the rather slack cheeks and mobile mouth; seen at close quarters his countenance, at first imposing and masterful, appeared to make up a whole only with some difficulty. His bearing told a similarly ambiguous story. His left hand rested casually on the desk, or at least seemed to rest there, for little tremors constantly passed over the knuckles, and the slender fingers, slightly too delicate and soft for a man's hand, impatiently traced invisible figures on the bare wooden surface, while his eyes, covered by heavy lids, were lowered in interest as he talked. Whether he was simply restless, or whether the excitement was still quivering in his agitated nerves, the fidgety movement of his hand contrasted with the quiet expectancy of his face as he listened; he seemed immersed in his conversation with the student, weary yet attentive.

At last my turn came. I approached him, gave him my name and said what I wanted, and at once his bright eyes turned on me, the pupils almost shining with blue light. For two or three full seconds of inquiry that glance traversed my face from chin to hairline; I may well have flushed under this mildly inquisitorial observation, for he answered my confusion with a quick smile. "So you want to enrol with me? Well, we must have a longer talk. Please forgive me, but I can't see to it at once; I have something else I must do, but perhaps you'll wait for me down by the entrance and walk home with me." So saying, he gave me his hand, a slender and delicate hand that touched my fingers more lightly than a glove, and then turned in a friendly manner to the next student.

I waited outside the entrance for ten minutes, my heart beating fast. What was I to say if he asked after my studies, how could I confess that I had never thought about poetry much in either my work or my hours of leisure? Would he not despise me, even exclude me without more ado from that ardent circle which had so magically surrounded me today? But no sooner did he appear, rapidly striding closer with a smile, than his presence dispelled all my awkwardness, and I confessed unasked (unable to conceal anything about myself from him) to the way in which I had wasted my first term. Yet again that warm and sympathetic glance dwelt on me. "Well, music has rests as well as notes," he said with an encouraging smile, and obviously intent on not shaming my ignorance further he turned to humdrum personal questions—where was my home, where was I going to lodge here? When I told him that I had not yet found a room he offered his help, suggesting that I might like to enquire first in the building where he himself lived; a half-deaf old lady had a nice little room to rent, and any of his students who took it had always been happy there. He'd see to everything else himself, he said; if I really showed that I meant what I said about taking my studies seriously, he would consider it a pleasant duty to help me in every way. On reaching his rooms he once again offered me his hand and invited me to visit him at home next evening, so that we could work out a programme of study for me together. So great was my gratitude for this man's unhoped-for kindness that I merely shook his hand respectfully, raised my hat in some confusion, and forgot to say even a word of thanks.

O F COURSE I immediately rented the little room in the same building. I would have taken it even if it had not appealed to me at all, solely for the naively grateful notion of being physically closer to this captivating man, who had taught me more in an hour than anyone else I had ever heard. But the room was charming anyway: on the attic floor above my professor's own lodgings, it was a little dark because of the overhanging wooden gables, and its window offered a panoramic view of the nearby rooftops and the church tower. There was a green square in the distance, and the clouds I loved at home sailed overhead. The landlady, a little old lady who was deaf as a post, looked after her lodgers with a touchingly maternal concern, I had come to an agreement with her within a couple of minutes, and an hour later I was hauling my suitcase up the creaking wooden stairs.

I did not go out that evening; I even forgot to eat or smoke. The first thing I did was to take the Shakespeare I happened to have packed out of my case and read it impatiently, for the first time in years. That lecture had aroused my passionate curiosity, and I read the poet's words as never before. Can one account for such transformations? A new world suddenly opened up on the printed page before me, the words moved vigorously towards me as if they had been seeking me for centuries; the verse coursed through my veins in a fiery torrent, carrying me away, inducing the same strange sense of relaxation behind the brow as one feels in a dream of flight. I shook, I trembled, I felt the hot surge of my blood like a fever—I had never had such an experience before, yet I had done nothing but listen to an impassioned lecture. However, the exhilaration of that lecture must have lingered on within me, and when I read a line aloud I heard my voice unconsciously imitating his, the sentences raced on in the same headlong rhythm, my hands felt impelled to move, arching in the air like his own—as if by magic, in a single hour, I had broken through the wall which previously stood between me and the world of the intellect, and passionate as I was by nature, I had discovered a new passion, one which has remained with me to the present day: a desire to share my enjoyment of all earthly delights in the inspired poetic word. By chance I had come upon Coriolanus, and as if reeling in a frenzy I discovered in myself all the characteristics of that strangest of the Romans: pride, arrogance, wrath, contempt, mockery, all the salty, leaden, golden, metallic elements of the emotions. What a new delight it was to divine and understand all this at once, as if by magic! I read on and on until my eyes were burning, and when I looked at the time it was three-thirty in the morning. Almost alarmed by this new force which had both stirred and numbed my senses for six hours on end, I put out the light. But the images still glowed and quivered within me; I could hardly sleep with longing for the next day and looking forward to it, a day which was to expand the world so enchantingly opened up to me yet further and make it entirely my own.

N EXT DAY, however, brought disappointment. My impatience had made me one of the first to arrive at the
lecture hall, where my teacher (as I will call him from now
on) was to speak on English phonetics. Even as he came in I
received a shock—was this the same man as yesterday, or was
it only my excited mood and my memory that had made him a
Coriolanus, wielding words in the Forum like lightning, heroically bold, crushing, compelling? The figure who entered the
room, footsteps dragging slightly, was a tired old man. As if a
shining but opaque film had been lifted from his countenance I
now saw, from where I was sitting in the front row of desks, his
almost unhealthily pallid features, furrowed by deep wrinkles
and broad crevices, with blue shadows wearing channels away in
the dull grey of his cheeks. Lids too heavy for his eyes shadowed
them as he read his lecture, and the mouth, its lips too pale,
too thin, delivered the words with no resonance: where was his
merriment, where were the high spirits rejoicing in themselves?
Even the voice sounded strange, moving stiffly through grey,
crunching sand at a monotonous and tiring pace, as if sobered
by the grammatical subject.

I was overcome by restlessness. This was not the man I had been
waiting for since the early hours of the morning—where was the
astrally radiant countenance he had shown me yesterday? This
was a worn-out professor droning his way objectively through
his subject; I listened with growing anxiety, wondering whether
yesterday's tone might return after all, the warmly vibrant note
that had struck my feelings like a hand playing music, moving

them to passion. Increasingly restless, I raised my eyes to him, full of disappointment as I scanned that now alien face: yes, this was undeniably the same countenance, but as if emptied, drained of all its creative forces, tired and old, the parchment mask of an elderly man. Were such things possible? Could a man be so youthful one minute and have aged so much the next? Did such sudden surges of the spirit occur that they could change the countenance as well as the spoken word, making it decades younger?

The question tormented me. I burned within, as if with thirst, to know more about the dual aspect of this man, and as soon as he had left the rostrum and walked past us without a glance, I hurried off to the library, following a sudden impulse, and asked for his works. Perhaps he had just been tired today, his energy muted by some physical discomfort, but here, in words set down to endure, I would find the key to his nature, which I found so curiously challenging, and the way to approach it. The library assistant brought the books; I was surprised to find how few there were. So in twenty years the ageing man had published only this sparse collection of unbound pamphlets, prefaces, introductions, a study of whether or not Pericles was genuinely by Shakespeare, a comparison between Hölderlin and Shelley (this admittedly at a time when neither poet was regarded as a genius by his own people)—and apart from that mere odds and ends of literary criticism? It was true that all these works announced a forthcoming two-volume publication: *The Globe Theatre: History, Productions, Poets*—but the first mention of it was dated two decades ago, and when I asked again the librarian confirmed that it had never appeared. Rather hesitantly, with only half my mind on them, I leafed through these writings, longing for them to revive that powerful voice, that surging rhythm. But these works moved at a consistently measured pace;

nowhere did I catch the ardently musical rhythm of his headlong discourse, leaping over itself as wave breaks over wave. What a pity, something sighed within me. I could have kicked myself, I felt so angry and so suspicious of the feelings I had too quickly and credulously entertained for him.

But I recognized him again in that afternoon's class. This time he did not begin by speaking himself. Following the custom of English college debates the students, a couple of dozen of them, were divided into those supporting the motion and those opposing it. The subject itself was from his beloved Shakespeare, namely, whether Troilus and Cressida (from his favourite work) were to be understood as figures of burlesque: was the work itself a satyr play, or did its mockery conceal tragedy? Soon what began as mere intellectual conversation became electrical excitement and took fire, with his skilful hand fanning the flames—forceful argument countered claims made casually, sharp and keen interjections heated the discussion until the students were almost at loggerheads with each other. Only once the sparks were really flying did he intervene, calming the overexcited atmosphere and cleverly bringing the debate back to its subject, but at the same time giving it stronger intellectual stimulus by moving it surreptitiously into a timeless dimension—and there he suddenly stood amidst the play of these dialectical flames, in a state of high excitement himself, both urging on and holding back the clashing opinions, master of a stormy wave of youthful enthusiasm which broke over him too. Leaning against the desk, arms crossed, he looked from one to another, smiling at one student, making a small gesture encouraging another to contradict, and his eyes shone with as much excitement as yesterday. I felt he had to make an effort not to take the words out of their mouths. But he restrained himself—by main force, as I could tell from the way his hands were pressed more and more firmly over his breast like the stave of a barrel, as I guessed from the mobile corners of his mouth, which had difficulty in suppressing the words rising to his lips. And suddenly he could do it no longer, he flung himself into the debate like a swimmer into the flood—raising his hand in an imperious gesture he halted the tumult as if with a conductor's baton; everyone immediately fell silent, and now he summed up all the arguments in his own vaulting fashion. And as he spoke the countenance he had worn yesterday re-emerged, wrinkles disappeared behind the flickering play of nerves, his throat arched, his whole bearing was bold and masterful, and abandoning his quiet, attentive attitude he flung himself into the talk as if into a torrent. Improvisation carried him away—now I began to guess that, sober-minded in himself, when he was teaching a factual subject or was alone in his study he lacked that spark of dynamite which here, in our intense and breathlessly spellbound company, broke down his inner walls; he needed—oh yes, I felt it—he needed our enthusiasm to kindle his own, our receptive attitude for his own extravagance, our youth for his own rejuvenated fervour. As a player of the cymbals is intoxicated by the increasingly wild rhythm of his own eager hands, his discourse became ever grander, ever more ardent, ever more colourful as his words grew more fervent, and the deeper our silence (I could not help feeling that we were all holding our breath in that room) the more elevated, the more intense was his performance, the more did it sound like an anthem. In those moments we were all entirely his, all ears, immersed in his exuberance.

Yet again, when he suddenly ended with a quotation from Goethe on Shakespeare, our excitement impetuously broke out. Yet again he leaned against the desk exhausted, as he had leaned there yesterday, his face pale but with little runs and trills of the nerves twitching over it, and oddly enough the afterglow of the sensuality of release gleamed in his eyes, as if in a woman who has just left an overpowering embrace. I felt too shy to speak to him now, but by chance his glance fell on me. And obviously he sensed my enthusiastic gratitude, for he smiled at me in a friendly manner, and leaning slightly towards me, hand on my shoulder, reminded me to go to see him that evening as we had agreed.

I was at his door at seven o'clock precisely, and with what trepidation did I, a mere boy as I was, cross that threshold for the first time! Nothing is more passionate than a young man's veneration, nothing more timid, more feminine than its uneasy sense of modesty. I was shown into his study, a semi-twilit room in which the first things I saw, looking through the glass panes over them, were the coloured spines of a large number of books. Over the desk hung Raphael's *School of Athens*, a picture which (as he told me later) he particularly loved, because all kinds of teaching, all forms of the intellect are symbolically united here in perfect synthesis. I was seeing it for the first time, and instinctively I thought I traced a similarity to his own brow in the highly individual face of Socrates. A figure in white marble gleamed behind me, an attractively scaled-down bust of the Paris *Ganymede*, and beside it there was a *St Sebastian* by an old German master, tragic beauty set, probably not by chance, beside its equivalent enjoying life to the full. I waited with my heart beating fast, as breathless as all the nobly silent artistic figures around me; they spoke to me of a new kind of intellectual beauty, a beauty that I had never suspected and that still was not clear to me, although I already felt prepared to turn to it with fraternal emotion. But I had no time to look around me, for at this point the man I was waiting for came in and approached me, once again showing me that softly enveloping gaze, smouldering like a hidden fire, and to my own surprise thawing out the most secret part of me. I immediately spoke as freely to him as to a friend, and when he asked about my studies in Berlin the tale of my father's visit suddenly sprang to my lips—I took fright even as I spoke of it—and I assured this stranger of my secret vow to devote myself to my studies with the utmost application. He looked at me, as if moved. Then he said: "Not just with application, my boy, but above all with passion. If you do not feel impassioned you'll be a schoolmaster at best—one must approach these things from within and always, always with passion." His voice grew warmer and warmer, the room darker and darker. He told me a great deal about his own youth, how he too had begun foolishly and only later discovered his own inclinations—I must just have courage, he said, and he would help me as far as lay within him; I must not scruple to turn to him with any questions, ask anything I wanted to know. No one had ever before spoken to me with such sympathy, with such deep understanding; I trembled with gratitude, and was glad of the darkness that hid my wet eyes.

I could have spent hours there with him, taking no notice of the time, but there was a soft knock on the door. It opened, and a slender, shadowy figure came in. He rose and introduced the newcomer. "My wife." The slender shadow came closer in the gloom, placed a delicate hand in mine, and then said, turning to him: "Supper's ready." "Yes, yes, I know," he replied hastily and (or so at least it seemed to me) with a touch of irritation. A chilly note suddenly seemed to have entered his voice, and when the electric light came on he was once again the ageing man of that sober lecture hall, bidding me good night with a casual gesture.

I SPENT THE NEXT two weeks in a passionate frenzy of reading and learning. I scarcely left my room, I ate my meals standing up so as not to waste time, I studied unceasingly, without a break, almost without sleep. I was like that prince in the Oriental fairy tale who, removing seal after seal from the doors of locked chambers, finds more and more jewels and precious stones piled in each room and makes his way with increasing avidity through them all, eager to reach the last. In just the same way I left one book to plunge into another, intoxicated by each of them, never sated by any; my impetuosity had moved on to intellectual concerns. I had a first glimmering of the trackless expanses of the world of the mind, which I found as seductive as the adventure of city life had been, but at the same time I felt a boyish fear that I would not be up to it, so I economized on sleep, on pleasures, on conversation and any form of diversion merely so that I could make full use of my time, which I had never felt so valuable before. But what most inflamed my diligence was vanity, a wish to come up to my teacher's expectations, not to disappoint his confidence, to win a smile of approval, I wanted him to be conscious of me as I was conscious of him. Every fleeting occasion was a test; I was constantly spurring my clumsy but now curiously inspired mind on to impress and surprise him; if he mentioned an author with whom I was unfamiliar during a lecture, I would go in search of the writer's works that very afternoon, so that next day I could show off by parading my knowledge in the class discussion. A wish uttered in passing which the others scarcely noticed was transformed in my mind into an order; in this way a casual condemnation of the way students were always smoking was enough for me to throw away my lighted cigarette at once, and give up the habit he deplored immediately and for ever. His words, like an evangelist's, bestowed grace and were binding on me too; I was always on the qui vive, attentive and intent upon greedily snapping up every chance remark he happened to drop. I seized on every word, every gesture, and when I came home I bent my mind entirely to the passionate recapitulation and memorizing of what I had heard; my impatient ardour felt that he alone was my guide, and all the other students merely enemies whom my aspiring will urged itself daily to outstrip and outperform.

Either because he sensed how much he meant to me, or because my impetuosity appealed to him, my teacher soon distinguished me by showing his favour publicly. He gave me advice on what to read, although I was a newcomer to the class he brought me to the fore in general debate in an almost unseemly manner, and I was often permitted to visit him for a confidential talk in the evening. On these occasions he would usually take a book down from the shelf and read aloud in his sonorous voice, which always rose an octave and grew more resonant when he was excited. He read from poems and tragedies, or he explained controversial cruxes; in those first two weeks of exhilaration I learned more of the nature of art than in all my previous nineteen years. We were always alone during this evening hour. Then, about eight o'clock, there would be a soft knock on the door: his wife letting him know that supper was ready. But she never again entered the room, obviously obeying instructions not to interrupt our conversation.

S o FOURTEEN DAYS had gone by, days crammed to the full, hot days of early summer, when one morning, like a steel spring stretched too taut, my ability to work deserted me. My teacher had already warned me not to overdo my industry, advising me to set a day aside now and then to go out and about in the open air—and now his prophecy was suddenly fulfilled: I awoke from a stupefied sleep feeling dazed, and when I tried to read I found that the characters on the page flickered and blurred like pinheads. Slavishly obeying every least word my teacher uttered, I immediately decided to follow his advice and take a break from the many days avidly devoted to my education in order to amuse myself. I set out that very morning, for the first time made a thorough exploration of the town, parts of which were very old, climbed the hundreds of steps to the church tower in the cause of physical exercise, and looking out from the viewing platform at the top discovered a little lake in the green spaces just outside town. As a coast-dwelling northerner, I loved to swim, and there on the tower, from which even the dappled meadows looked like shimmering pools of green water, an irresistible longing to throw myself into that beloved element again suddenly overcame me like a gust of wind blowing from my home. No sooner had I made my way to the swimming pool after lunch and begun splashing about in the water than my body began to feel at ease again, the muscles in my arms stretched flexibly and powerfully for the first time in weeks, and within half-an-hour the sun and wind on my bare skin had turned me back into the impetuous lad of the old days who would scuffle vigorously with his friends and venture his life in daredevil exploits. Striking out strongly, exercising my body, I forgot all about books and scholarship. Returning to the passion of which I had been deprived so long, in the obsessive way characteristic of me, I had spent two hours in my rediscovered element, I had dived from the board some ten times to release my strength of feeling as I soared through the air, I had swum right across the lake twice, and my vigour was still not exhausted. Spluttering, with all my tense muscles stretched, I looked around for some new test, impatient to do something notable, bold, high-spirited.

Then I heard the creak of the diving board from the nearby ladies' pool and felt the wood quivering as someone took off with strong impetus. Curving as it dived to form a steely crescent like a Turkish sword, the body of a slender woman rose in the air and came down again head first. For a moment the dive drove a splashing, foaming white whirlpool into the water, and then the taut figure reappeared, striking out vigorously for the island in the middle of the lake. "Chase her! Catch up with her!" An urge for athletic pleasure came over my muscles, and with a sudden movement I dived into the water and followed her trail, stubbornly maintaining my tempo, shoulders forging their way forward. But obviously noticing my pursuit, and ready for a sporting challenge herself, my quarry made good use of her start, and skilfully passed the island at a diagonal angle so that she could make her way straight back. Quickly seeing what she meant to do, I turned as well, swimming so vigorously that my hand, reaching forward, was already in her wake and only a short distance separated us—whereupon my quarry cunningly dived right down all of a sudden, to emerge again a little later close to the barrier marking off the ladies' pool, which prevented further pursuit. Dripping and triumphant, she climbed the steps and had to stop for a moment, one hand to her breast, her breath obviously coming short, but then she turned, and on seeing me with the barrier keeping me away gave a victorious smile, her white teeth gleaming. I could not really see her face against the bright sunlight and underneath her swimming cap, only the bright and mocking smile she flashed at me as her defeated opponent.

I was both annoyed and pleased: this was the first time I had felt a woman's appreciative glance on me since Berlin—perhaps an adventure beckoned. With three strokes I swam back into the men's pool and quickly flung my clothes on, my skin still wet, just so that I could be in time to catch her coming out at the exit. I had to wait ten minutes, and then my high-spirited adversary—there could be no mistaking her boyishly slender form—emerged, stepping lightly and quickening her pace as soon as she saw me waiting there, obviously meaning to deprive me of the chance of speaking to her. She walked with the same muscular agility she had shown in swimming, with a sinewy strength in all her joints as they obeyed that slender, perhaps too slender body, a body like that of an ephebe; I was actually gasping for breath and had difficulty in catching up with her escaping figure as she strode out, without making myself conspicuous. At last I succeeded, swiftly crossed the path ahead of her at a point where the road turned, airily raising my hat in the student manner, and before I had really looked her in the face I asked if I could accompany her. She cast me a mocking sideways glance, and without slowing her rapid pace replied, with almost provocative irony: "Why not, if I don't walk too fast for you? I'm in a great hurry." Encouraged by her ease of manner, I became more pressing, asked a dozen inquisitive and on the whole rather silly questions, which she none the less answered willingly, and with such surprising freedom that my intentions were confused rather than challenged. For my code of conduct when approaching a woman in my Berlin days was adjusted to expect resistance and mockery rather than frank remarks such as my interlocutor made while she walked rapidly along, and once again I felt I had shown clumsiness in dealing with a superior opponent.

But worse was to come. For when, more indiscreetly importunate than ever, I asked where she lived, two bright and lively hazel eyes were suddenly turned on me, and she shot back, no longer concealing her amusement: "Oh, very close to you indeed." I stared in surprise. She glanced sideways at me again to see if her Parthian shot had gone home. Sure enough, it had struck me full in the throat. All of a sudden my bold Berlin tone of voice was gone; very uncertainly, indeed humbly, I asked, stammering, whether my company was a nuisance to her. "No, why?" she smiled again. "We have only two more streets to go, we can walk them together." At that moment my blood was in turmoil, I could scarcely go any further, but what alternative did I have? To walk away would have been even more of an insult, so I had to accompany her to the building where I lodged. Here she suddenly stopped, offered me her hand, and said casually: "Thank you for your company! You'll be seeing my husband at six this evening, I expect."

I must have turned scarlet with shame. But before I could apologize she had run nimbly upstairs, and there I stood, thinking with horror of the artless remarks I had so foolishly and audaciously made. Boastful idiot that I was, I had invited her to go on a Sunday outing as if she were some little seamstress, I had paid indirect compliments to her physical charm, then launched into sentimental complaints of the life of a lonely student—my self-disgust nauseated me so much that I was retching with shame. And now she was going off to her husband, full of high spirits, to tell him about my foolishness—a man whose opinion meant more to me than anyone's. I felt it would be more painful to appear ridiculous to him than to be whipped round the market square naked in public.

I passed dreadful hours until evening came: I imagined, a thousand times over, how he would receive me with his subtle, ironic smile—oh, I knew he was master of the art of making a sardonic comment, and could sharpen a jest to such keen effect that it drew blood. A condemned man could not have climbed the scaffold with a worse sensation of choking than mine as I climbed the stairs, and no sooner did I enter his room, swallowing a large lump in my throat with difficulty, than my confusion became worse than ever, for I thought I had heard the whispering rustle of a woman's dress in the next room. My high-spirited acquaintance must be in there listening, ready to relish my embarrassment and enjoy the discomfiture of a loud-mouthed young man. At last my teacher arrived. "What on earth's the matter with you?" he asked, sounding concerned. "You look so pale today." I made some non-committal remark, privately waiting for the blow to fall. But the execution I feared never came; he talked of scholarly subjects, just the same as usual: not a word contained any ironic allusion, anxiously as I listened for one. And first amazed, then delighted, I realized that she had said nothing.

At eight o'clock the usual knock on the door came. I said goodnight with my heart in my throat again. As I went out of the doorway she passed me: I greeted her, and her eyes smiled slightly at me. My blood flowing fast, I took this forgiveness on her part as a promise that she would keep silent in the future too.

F ROM THEN ON I became attentive in a new way; hitherto, my boyish veneration of the teacher whom I idolized had seen him so much as a genius from another world that I had entirely omitted to think of his private, down-to-earth life. With the exaggeration inherent in any true enthusiasm, I had imagined his existence as remote from all the daily concerns of our methodically ordered world. And just as, for instance, a man in love for the first time dares not undress the girl he adores in his thoughts, dares not think of her as a natural being like the thousands of others who wear skirts, I was disinclined to venture on any prying into his private life: I knew him only in sublimated form, remote from all that is subjective and ordinary. I saw him as the bearer of the word, the embodiment of the creative spirit. Now that my tragicomic adventure had suddenly brought his wife across my path, I could not help observing his domestic and family life more closely; indeed, although against my will, a restless, spying curiosity was aroused within me. And no sooner did this curiosity awaken than it became confused, for on his own ground his was a strange, an almost alarmingly enigmatic existence. The first time I was invited to a family meal, not long after this encounter, and saw him not alone but with his wife, I began to suspect that they had a strange and unusual relationship, and the further I subsequently made my way into the inner circle of his home, the more confusing did this feeling become. Not that any tension or sense that they were at odds made itself felt in word or gesture: on the contrary, it was the absence of any such thing, the lack of any tension at all between them that enveloped them both so strangely and made their relationship opaque, a heavy silence of the feelings, like the heaviness of the *föhn* wind when it falls still, which made the atmosphere more oppressive than a stormy quarrel or lightning flashes of hidden rancour. Outwardly, there was nothing to betray any irritation or tension, but their personal distance from each other could be felt all the more strongly. In their odd form of conversation, question and answer touched only briefly, as it were, with swift fingertips, and never went wholeheartedly along together hand in hand. Even their remarks to me were hesitant and constrained at mealtimes. And sometimes, until we returned to the subject of work, the conversation froze entirely into a great block of silence which in the end no one dared to break. Its cold weight would lie oppressively on my spirit for hours.

His total isolation horrified me more than anything. This man, with his open, very expansive disposition, had no friends of any kind; his students alone provided him with company and comfort. No relationship but correct civility linked him to his university colleagues, he never attended social occasions; often he did not leave home for days on end to go anywhere but the twenty steps or so it took him to reach the university. He buried everything silently within him, entrusting his thoughts neither to any other human being nor to writing. And now, too, I understood the volcanic, fanatically exuberant nature of his discourse in his circle of students—after being dammed up for days his urge to communicate would break out, all the ideas he carried silently within him rushed forth, with the uncontrollable force known to horsemen when a mount is fresh from the stable, breaking out of the confines of silence into this headlong race of words.

At home he spoke very seldom, least of all to his wife. It was with anxious, almost ashamed surprise that even I, an inexperienced young man, realized that there was some shadow between these two people, in the air and ever present, the shadow of something intangible that none the less cut them off completely from one another, and for the first time I guessed how many secrets a marriage hides from the outside world. As if a pentagram were traced on the threshold, his wife never ventured to enter his study without an explicit invitation, a fact which clearly signalled her complete exclusion from his intellectual world. Nor would my teacher ever allow any discussion of his plans and his work in front of her; indeed, I found it positively embarrassing to hear him abruptly break off his passionate, soaring discourse the moment she came in. There was even something almost insulting and manifestly contemptuous, devoid of civility, in his brusque and open rejection of any interest she showed—but she appeared not to be insulted, or perhaps she was used to it. With her lively, boyish face, light and agile in her movements, supple and lithe, she flew upstairs and downstairs, was always busy yet always had time for herself, went to the theatre, enjoyed all kinds of athletic sports—but this woman aged about thirty-five took no pleasure in books, in the domestic life of the household, in anything abstruse, quiet, thoughtful. She seemed at ease only when—always warbling away, laughing easily, ready for bantering conversation—she could move her limbs in dancing, swimming, running, in some vigorous activity; she never spoke to me seriously, but always teased me as if I were an adolescent boy; at the most, she would accept me as a partner in our high-spirited trials of strength. And this swift and light-hearted manner of hers was in such confusingly stark contrast to my teacher's dark and entirely withdrawn way of life, which could be lightened only by some intellectual stimulus, that I kept wondering in amazement what on earth could have brought these two utterly different natures together. It was true that this striking contrast did me personally nothing but good; if I fell into conversation with her after a strenuous session of work, it was as if a helmet pressing down on my brow had been removed; the ecstatic ardour was gone, life returned to the earthly realm of clear, daylight colours, cheerfulness playfully demanded its dues, and laughter, which I had almost forgotten in my teacher's austere presence, did me good by relieving the overwhelming pressure of my intellectual pursuits. A kind of youthful camaraderie grew up between her and me; and for the very reason that we always spoke casually of unimportant matters, or went to the theatre together, there was no tension at all in our relationship. Only one thing—awkwardly, and always confusing me—interrupted the easy tenor of our conversations, and that was any mention of his name. Here my probing curiosity inevitably met with an edgy silence on her part, or when I talked myself into a frenzy of enthusiasm with a strangely enigmatic smile. But her lips remained closed on the subject: she shut her husband out of her life as he shut her out of his, in a different way but equally firmly. Yet the two of them had lived together for fifteen years under the same secluded roof.

The more impenetrable this mystery, the more it appealed to my passionate and impatient nature. Here was a shadow, a veil, and I felt its touch strangely close in every draught of air; sometimes I thought myself close to catching it, but its baffling fabric would elude me, only to waft past me again next moment, never becoming perceptible in words or taking tangible form. Nothing, however, is more arousing and intriguing to a young man than a teasing set of vague suspicions; the imagination, usually wandering idly, finds its quarry suddenly revealed to it, and is immediately agog with the newly discovered pleasure of the chase. Dull-minded youth that I had been, I developed entirely new senses at this time—a thin-skinned membrane of the auditory system that caught every give-away tone, a spying, avid glance full of keen distrust, a curiosity that groped around

265

in the dark—and my nerves stretched elastically, almost painfully, constantly excited as they apprehended a suspicion which never subsided into a clear feeling.

But I must not be too hard on my breathlessly intent curiosity, for it was pure in nature. What raised all my senses to such a pitch of agitation was the result not of that lustful desire to pry which loves to track down base human instincts in someone superior—on the contrary, that agitation was tinged with secret fear, a puzzled and hesitant sympathy which guessed, with uncertain anxiety, at the suffering of this silent man. For the closer I came to his life the more strongly was I oppressed by the almost three-dimensional deep shadows on my teacher's much-loved face, by that noble melancholy—noble because nobly controlled—which never lowered itself to abrupt sullenness or unthinking anger; if he had attracted me, a stranger, on that first occasion by the volcanic brilliance of his discourse, now that I knew him better I was all the more distressed by his silence and the cloud of sadness resting on his brow. Nothing has such a powerful effect on a youthful mind as a sublime and virile despondency: Michelangelo's *Thinker* staring down into his own abyss, Beethoven's mouth bitterly drawn in, those tragic masks of suffering move the unformed mind more than Mozart's silver melody and the radiant light around Leonardo's figures. Being beautiful in itself, youth needs no transfiguration: in its abundance of strong life it is drawn to the tragic, and is happy to allow melancholy to suck sweetly from its still inexperienced bloom, and the same phenomenon accounts for the eternal readiness of young people to face danger and reach out a fraternal hand to all spiritual suffering.

And it was here that I became acquainted with the face of a man genuinely suffering in such a way. The son of ordinary folk, growing up in safety and bourgeois comfort, I knew sorrow only in its ridiculous everyday forms, disguised as anger, clad in the yellow garment of envy, clinking with trivial financial concerns—but the desolation of that face, I felt at once, derived from a more sacred element. This darkness was truly of the dark; a pitiless pencil, working from within, had traced folds and rifts in cheeks grown old before their time. Sometimes when I entered his study (always with the timidity of a child approaching a house haunted by demons) and found him so deep in thought that he failed to hear my knock, when suddenly, ashamed and dismayed, I stood before his self-forgetful figure, I felt as if it were only Wagner sitting there, a physical shell in Faust's garment, while the spirit roamed mysterious chasms, visiting sinister ceremonies on Walpurgis Night. At such moments his senses were entirely sealed away; he heard neither an approaching footstep nor a timid greeting. Then, suddenly recollecting himself, he would start up and try to cover the awkwardness: he would walk up and down and try to divert my observant glance away from him by asking questions. But the darkness still shadowed his brow for a long time, and only his ardent discourse could disperse those clouds gathering from within.

He must sometimes have felt how much the sight of him moved me, perhaps he saw it in my eyes, my restless hands, perhaps he suspected that a request for his confidence hovered unseen on my lips, or recognized in my tentative attitude a secret longing to take his pain into myself. Yes, surely he must feel it, for he would suddenly interrupt his lively conversation and look at me intently, and indeed the curious warmth of his gaze, darkened by its own depth, would pour over me. Then he would often grasp my hand, holding it restlessly for some time—and I always expected: now, now, now he is going to talk to me. But instead there was usually a brusque gesture, sometimes even a cold, intentionally deflating or ironic remark. He, who was enthusiasm itself, who nourished and aroused it in me, would suddenly strike it away from me as if marking a mistake in a poorly written essay, and the more he saw how receptive to him I was, yearning for his confidence, the more curtly would he make such icy comments as: "You don't see the point," or: "Don't exaggerate like that," remarks which angered me and made me despair. How I suffered from this man who moved from hot to cold like a bright flash of lightning, who unknowingly inflamed me, only to pour frosty water over me all of a sudden, whose exuberant mind spurred on my own, only to lash me with irony—I had a terrible feeling that the closer I tried to come to him, the more harshly, even fearfully he repelled me. Nothing could, nothing must approach him and his secret.

For I realized more and more acutely that secrecy strangely, eerily haunted his magically attractive depths. I guessed at something unspoken in his curiously fleeting glance, which would show ardour and then shrink away when I gratefully opened my mind to him; I sensed it from his wife's bitterly compressed lips, from the oddly cold, reserved attitude of the townspeople, who looked almost offended to hear praise of him—I sensed it from a hundred oddities and sudden moments of distress. And what torment it was to believe myself in the inner circle of such a life, and yet to be wandering, lost as if in a labyrinth, unable to find the way to its centre and its heart!

However, it was his sudden absences that I found most inexplicable and agitating of all. One day, when I was going to his lecture, I found a notice hanging up to say that there would be no classes for the next two days. The students did not seem surprised, but having been with him only the day before I hurried home, afraid he might be ill. His wife merely smiled dryly when my impetuous entrance betrayed my agitation. "Oh, this happens quite often," she said, in a noticeably cold tone. "You just don't know about it yet." And indeed the other students told me that he did indeed disappear overnight like this quite often, sometimes simply telegraphing an apology; one of them had once met him at four in the morning in a Berlin street, another had seen him in a bar in a strange city. He would rush off all at once like a cork popping out of a bottle, and on his return no one knew where he had been. His abrupt departure upset me like an illness; I went around absent-mindedly, restlessly, nervously for those two days. Suddenly my studies seemed pointlessly empty without his familiar presence, I was consumed by vague and jealous suspicions, indeed I felt something like hatred and anger for his reserve, the way he excluded me so utterly from his real life, leaving me out in the cold like a beggar when I so ardently wished to be close to him. In vain did I tell myself that as a boy, a mere student, I had no right to demand explanations and ask him to account for himself, when he was already kind enough to give me a hundred times more of his confidence than his duty as a university teacher required. But reason had no power over my ardent passion ten times a day, foolish boy that I was, I asked whether he was back yet, until I began to sense bitterness in his wife's increasingly brusque negatives. I lay awake half the night and listened for his homecoming step, and in the morning I lurked restlessly close to his door, no longer daring to ask. And when at last and unexpectedly he entered my room on the third day I gasped—my surprise must have been excessive, or so at least I saw from its reflection in the embarrassed displeasure with which he asked a few hasty, trivial questions. His glance avoided mine. For the first time our conversation went awkwardly, one comment stumbling over another, and while we both carefully avoided any reference to his absence, the very fact that we were ignoring it prevented any open discussion. When he left me my curiosity flared up like a fire—it came to devour my sleeping and waking hours.

M Y EFFORTS TO FIND elucidation and deeper understanding lasted for weeks—I kept obstinately making my way
towards the fiery core I thought I felt volcanically active beneath
that rocky silence. At last, in a fortunate hour, I succeeded in
making my first incursion into his inner world. I had been sitting in his study once again until twilight fell, as he took several
Shakespearean sonnets out of a locked drawer and read those
brief verses, lines that might have been cast in bronze, first in
his own translation, then casting such a magical light on their
apparently impenetrable cipher that amidst my own delight I felt
regret that everything this ardent spirit could give was to be lost
in the transience of the spoken word. And suddenly—where I got
it from I do not know—I found the courage to ask why he had
never finished his great work on *The History of the Globe Theatre.*
But no sooner had I ventured on the question than I realized,
with horror, that I had inadvertently and roughly touched upon
a secret, obviously painful wound. He rose, turned away, and said
nothing for some time. The room seemed suddenly too full of
twilight and silence. At last he came towards me, looked at me
gravely, his lips quivering several times before they opened slightly,
and then painfully made his admission: "I can't tackle a major
work. That's over now—only the young make such bold plans. I
have no stamina these days. Oh, why hide it? I've become capable
only of brief pieces; I can't see anything longer through. Once
I had more strength, but now it's gone. I can only talk—then it
sometimes carries me away, something takes me out of myself.
But I can't work sitting still, always alone, always alone."

His resignation shattered me. And in my fervent conviction I urged him to reconsider, to record in writing all that he so generously scattered before us daily, not just giving it all away but putting his own thoughts into constructive form. "I can't write now," he repeated wearily, "I can't concentrate enough." "Then dictate it!" I cried, and carried away by this idea I urged, almost begged him: "Dictate it to me. Just try! Perhaps only the beginning—and then you may find you can't help going on. Oh, do try dictating, I wish you would—for my sake!"

He looked up, first surprised, then more thoughtful. The idea seemed to give him food for thought. "For your sake?" he repeated. "You really think it could give anyone pleasure for an old man like me to undertake such a thing?" I felt him hesitantly beginning to yield, I felt it from his glance, a moment ago turned sadly inward, but now, softened by warm hope, gradually looking out and brightening. "You really think so?" he repeated; I already felt a readiness streaming into his mind, and then came an abrupt: "Then let's try! The young are always right, and is wise to do as they wish." My wild expressions of delight and triumph seemed to animate him: he paced rapidly up and down, almost youthfully excited, and we agreed that we would set to work every evening at nine, immediately after supper—for an hour a day at first. We began on the dictation next evening.

How can I describe those hours? I waited for them all day long. By afternoon a heavy, unnerving restlessness was weighing electrically on my impatient mind; I could scarcely endure the hours until evening at last came. Once supper was over we would go straight to his study, I sat at the desk with my back turned to him while he paced restlessly up and down the room until he had got into his rhythm, so to speak, until he raised his voice and launched into the prelude. For this remarkable man constructed it all out of his musicality of feeling: he always needed some vibrant note to set his ideas flowing. Usually it was an image, a bold metaphor, a situation visualized in three dimensions which he extended into a dramatic scene, involuntarily working himself up as he went rapidly along. Something of all that is grandly natural in creativity would often flash from the swift radiance of these improvisations: I remember lines that seemed to be from a poem in iambic metre, others that poured out like cataracts in magnificently compressed enumerations like Homer's catalogue of ships or the barbaric hymns of Walt Whitman. For the first time it was granted to me, young and new to the world as I was, to glimpse something of the mystery of the creative process—I saw how the idea, still colourless, nothing but pure and flowing heat, streamed from the furnace of his impulsive excitement like the molten metal to make a bell, then gradually, as it cooled, took shape, I saw how that shape rounded out powerfully and revealed itself, until at last the words rang from it and gave human language to poetic feeling, just as the clapper gives the bell its sound. And in the same way as every single sentence rose from the rhythm, every description from a picturesquely visualized image, so the whole grandly constructed work arose, not at all in the academic manner, from a hymn, a hymn to the sea as infinity made visible and perceptible in earthly terms, its waves reaching from horizon to horizon, looking up to heights, concealing depths—and among them, with crazily sensuous earthly skill, ply the tossing vessels of mankind. Using this maritime simile in a grandly constructed comparison, he presented tragedy as an elemental force, intoxicating and destructively overpowering the blood. Now the wave of imagery rolls towards a single land— England arises, an island eternally surrounded by the breakers of that restless element which perilously encloses all the ends of the earth, every zone and latitude of the globe. There, in England, it sets up its state—there the cold, clear gaze of the sea penetrates the glassy housing of the eye, eyes grey and blue; every man is both a man of the sea and an island, like his own country, and strong, stormy passions, represented by the storms and danger of the sea, are present in a race that had constantly tried its own strength in centuries of Viking voyaging. But now peace lies like a haze over this land surrounded by surging breakers; accustomed to storms as they are, however, its people would like to go to sea again, they want headlong, raw events attended by daily danger, and so they re-create that rising, lashing tension for themselves in bloody and tragic spectacles. The wooden trestles are constructed for baiting animals and staging fights between them. Bears bleed to death, cockfights arouse a bestial lust for horror; but soon more elevated minds wish to draw a pure and thrilling tension from heroic human conflicts. Then, building on the foundations of religious spectacle and ecclesiastical mystery plays, there arises that other great and surging drama of humanity, all those adventures and voyages return, but now to sail the seas of the heart, a new infinity, another ocean with its spring tides of passion and swell of the spirit to be navigated with excitement, and to be ocean-tossed in it is the new pleasure of this later but still strong Anglo-Saxon race: the national drama of England emerges, Elizabethan drama.

And the formative word rang out, full-toned, as he launched himself with enthusiasm into the description of that barbarically primeval beginning. His voice, which at first raced along fast in a whisper, stretching muscles and ligaments of sound, became a metallically gleaming airborne craft pressing on ever more freely, ever further aloft—the room, the walls pressed close in answer, became too small for it, it needed so much space. I felt a storm surging over me, the breaking surf of the ocean's lip powerfully uttered its echoing word; bending over the desk, I felt as if I were standing among the dunes of my home again, with the great surge of a thousand waves coming up and sea spray flying in the wind. All the sense of awe that surrounds both the birth of a man and the birth of a work of literature broke for the first time over my amazed and delighted mind at this time.

If my teacher ended his dictation at the point where the strength of his inspiration tore the words magnificently away from their scholarly purpose, where thought became poetry, I was left reeling. A fiery weariness streamed through me, strong and heavy, not at all like his own weariness, which was a sense of exhaustion or relief, while I, over whom the storm had broken, was still trembling with all that had flowed into me. Both of us, however, always needed a little conversation afterwards to help us find sleep or rest. I would usually read over what I had taken down in shorthand, and curiously enough, no sooner did my writing become spoken words than another voice breathed through my own and rose from it, as if something had transformed the language in my mouth. And then I realized that, in repeating his own words, I was scanning and forming his intonations with such faithful devotion that he might have been speaking out of me, not I myself—so entirely had I come to echo his own nature. I was the resonance of his words. All this is forty years ago, yet still today, when I am in the middle of a lecture and what I am saying breaks free from me and spreads its wings, I am suddenly, self-consciously aware that it is not I myself speaking, but someone else, as it were, out of my mouth. Then I recognize the voice of the beloved dead, who now has breath only on my lips; when enthusiasm comes over me, he and I are one. And I know that those hours formed me.

T HE WORK GREW, it grew around me like a forest, its shade
gradually excluding any view of the outside world. I lived
only in that darkness, in the work that spread wider and further,
among the rustling branches that roared ever more loudly, in
the man's warm and ambient presence.

Apart from my few hours of university lectures and classes,
my whole day was devoted to him. I ate at their table, day and
night messages passed upstairs and downstairs to and from
their lodgings—I had their door key, and he had mine so that
he could find me at any time of day without having to shout
for our half-deaf old landlady. However, the more I became
one with this new community, the more totally did I turn away
from the outside world: I shared not only the warmth of this
inner sphere but its frosty isolation. My fellow students, without
exception, showed me a certain coldness and contempt—who
knew whether some secret verdict had been passed on me, or
just jealousy provoked by our teacher's obvious preference for
me? In any case, they excluded me from their society, and in
class discussions it seemed that they had agreed not to speak to
me or offer any greeting. Even the other professors did not hide
their hostility; once, when I asked the professor of Romance
languages for some trivial piece of information, he fobbed me off
ironically by saying: "Well, intimate as you are with Professor...
you should know that." I sought in vain to account to myself for
such undeserved ostracism. But the words and looks I received
eluded all explanation. Ever since I had been living on such close
terms with that lonely couple, I myself had been entirely isolated.

This exclusion would have given me no further cause for concern, since my mind, after all, was entirely bent on intellectual pursuits, except that in the end the constant strain was more than my nerves could stand. You do not live for weeks in a permanent state of intellectual excess with impunity, and moreover in switching too wildly from one extreme to the other I had probably turned my whole life upside down far too suddenly to avoid endangering the equilibrium secretly built into us by Nature. For while my dissolute behaviour in Berlin had relaxed my body pleasantly, and my adventures with women gave playful release to dammed-up instincts, here an oppressively heavy atmosphere weighed so constantly on my irritated senses that they would only churn around in electrical peaks within me. I forgot how to enjoy deep, healthy sleep, although—or perhaps because—I was always up until the early hours of the morning copying out the evening's dictation for my own pleasure (and burning with puffed-up impatience to hand the written sheets to my beloved mentor at the earliest opportunity). Then my university studies and the reading through which I raced called for further preparation, and my condition was aggravated, not least, by my conversations with my teacher, since I strained every nerve in Spartan fashion so as never to appear to him in a poor light. My abused body did not hesitate to take revenge for these excesses. I suffered several brief fainting fits, warning signs that I was putting an insane strain on Nature—but my hypnotic sense of exhaustion increased, all my feelings were vehemently expressed, and my exacerbated nerves turned inward, disturbing my sleep and arousing confused ideas of a kind I had previously restrained.

The first to notice an obvious risk to my health was my teacher's wife. I had already seen her concerned glance dwelling on me, and she made admonitory remarks during our conversations with increasing frequency, saying, for instance, that I must not try to conquer the world in a single semester. Finally she spoke her mind. "Now that's enough," she said sharply one Sunday when I was working away at my grammar, while it was beautiful sunny weather outside, and she took the book away from me. "How can a lively young man be such a slave to ambition? Don't take my husband as your example all the time; he's old and you are young, you need a different kind of life." That undertone of contempt flashed out whenever she spoke of him, and devoted to him as I was it always roused me to indignation. I felt that she was intentionally, perhaps in a kind of misplaced jealousy, trying to keep me further away from him, countering my extreme enthusiasm with ironic comments. If we sat too long over our dictation in the evening she would knock energetically on the door, and force us to stop work in spite of his angry reaction. "He'll wear your nerves out, he'll destroy you completely," she once said bitterly on finding me in a state of exhaustion. "Look what he's reduced you to in just a few weeks! I can't stand by and watch you harming yourself any longer. And what's more…" She stopped, and did not finish her sentence. But her lip was quivering, pale with suppressed anger.

Indeed, my teacher did not make it easy for me: the more passionately I served him, the more indifferent he seemed to my eagerly helpful devotion. He rarely gave me a word of thanks; in the morning, when I took him the work on which I had laboured until late at night, he would say, dryly: "Tomorrow would have done." If my ambitious zeal outdid itself in offering unasked-for assistance, his lips would suddenly narrow in mid-conversation, and an ironic remark would repel me. It is true that if he then saw me flinch, humiliated and confused, that warmly enveloping gaze would be turned on me again, comforting me in my despair, but how seldom, how very seldom that was! And the way he blew hot and cold, sometimes coming so close as to cast me into turmoil, sometimes fending me off in annoyance, utterly confused my unruly feelings which longed—but I was never able to say clearly what it was I really longed for, what I wanted, what I required and aspired to, what sign of his regard I hoped for in my enthusiastic devotion. For if one feels reverent passion even of a pure nature for a woman, it unconsciously strives for physical fulfilment; nature has created an image of ultimate union for it in the possession of the body—but how can a passion of the mind, offered by one man to another and impossible to fulfil, ever find complete satisfaction? It roams restlessly around the revered figure, always flaring up to new heights of ecstasy, yet never assuaged by any final act of devotion. It is always in flux but can never flow entirely away; like the spirit, it is eternally insatiable. So when he came close it was never close enough for me, his nature was never entirely revealed, never really satisfied me in our long conversations; even when he cast aside all his aloofness I knew that the next moment some sharp word or action could cut through our intimacy. Changeable as he was, he kept confusing my feelings, and I do not exaggerate when I say that in my overexcited state I often came close to committing some thoughtless act just because his indifferent hand pushed away a book to which I had drawn his attention, or because suddenly, when we were deep in conversation in the evening and I was absorbing his ideas, breathing them all in, he would suddenly rise—having only just laid an affectionate hand on my shoulder—and say brusquely: "Off you go, now! It's late. Good night." Such trivialities were enough to upset me for hours, indeed for days. Perhaps my exacerbated feelings, constantly overstretched, saw insults where none were intended—although what use are explanations thought up to soothe oneself when the mind is so disturbed? But it went on day after day—I suffered ardently when he was close, and froze when he kept his distance, I was always disappointed by his reserve, he gave no sign to mollify my feelings, I was cast into confusion by every chance occurrence.

And oddly enough, whenever he had injured my sensitive feelings it was with his wife that I took refuge. Perhaps it was an unconscious urge to find another human being who suffered similarly from his silent reserve, perhaps just a need to talk to someone and find, if not help, at least understanding—at any rate, I resorted to her as if to a secret ally. Usually she mocked my sense of injury away, or said, with a cold shrug of her shoulders, that I should be used to his hurtful idiosyncrasies by now. Sometimes, however, when sudden desperation reduced me all at once to a quivering mass of reproaches, incoherent tears and stammered words, she would look at me with a curious gravity, with a glance of positive amazement, but she said nothing, although I could see movement like stormy weather around her lips, and I felt it was as much as she could do not to come out with something angry or thoughtless. She too, no doubt, would have something to tell me, she too had a secret, perhaps the same as his; but while he would repel me brusquely as soon as I said something that came too close, she generally avoided further comment with a joke or an improvised prank of some kind.

Only once did I come close to extracting some comment from her. That morning, when I took my teacher the passage he had dictated, I could not help saying enthusiastically how much this particular account (dealing with Marlowe) had moved me. Still burning with exuberance, I added admiringly that no one would ever pen so masterly a portrait again; hereupon, turning abruptly away, he bit his lip, threw the sheets of paper down and growled scornfully: "Don't talk such nonsense! Masterly? What would you know about it?" This brusque remark (probably just a shield hastily assumed to hide his impatient modesty) was enough to ruin my day. And in the afternoon, when I was alone with his wife, I suddenly fell into a kind of fit of hysteria, grasped her hands and said: "Tell me, why does he hate me so? Why does he despise me so much? What have I done to him, why does everything I say irritate him? Help me—tell me what to do! Why can't he bear me—tell me, please tell me!"

At this, assailed by my wild outburst, she turned a bright eye on me. "Not bear you?" And a laugh broke from her mouth, a laugh rising to such shrill heights of malice that I involuntarily flinched. "Not bear you?" she repeated, looking angrily into my startled eyes. But then she bent closer—her gaze gradually softened and then became even softer, almost sympathetic—and suddenly, for the first time, she stroked my hair. "Oh, you really are a child, a stupid child who notices nothing, sees nothing, knows nothing. But it's better that way—or you would be even more confused."

And with a sudden movement she turned away.

I SOUGHT CALM IN VAIN—as if tied up in a black sack in an anxious dream from which there was no awakening, I struggled to understand, to rouse myself from the mysterious confusion of these conflicting feelings.

Four months had passed in this way—weeks of self-improvement and transformation such as I had never imagined. The term was fast approaching an end, and I faced the imminent vacation with a sense of dread, for I loved my purgatory, and the soberly non-intellectual atmosphere of my home threatened me like exile and deprivation. I was already hatching secret plans to pretend to my parents that important work kept me here, weaving a skilful tissue of lies and excuses to prolong my present existence, although it was devouring me. But the day and the hour had long ago been ordained for me elsewhere. That hour hung invisibly over me, just as the sound of the bell striking midday lies latent in the metal, ready to chime suddenly and gravely, urging laggards to work or to departure.

How well that fateful evening began, how deceptively well! I had been sitting at table with the two of them—the windows were open, and a twilit sky with white clouds was slowly filling their darkened frames: there was something mild and clear in their majestically hovering glow; one could not help feeling it deep within. His wife and I had been talking more casually, more easily, with more animation than usual. My teacher sat in silence, ignoring our conversation, but his silence presided over it with folded wings, so to speak. Looking sideways, I glanced surreptitiously at him—there was something curiously radiant about him today, a restlessness devoid of anything nervous, like the movement of those summer clouds. Sometimes he took his wine glass and held it up to the light to appreciate the colour, and when my happy glance followed that gesture he smiled slightly and raised the glass to me. I had seldom seen his face so untroubled, his movements so smooth and composed; he sat there in almost solemn cheerfulness, as if he heard music in the street outside, or were listening to some unseen conversation. His lips, around which tiny movements usually played, were still and soft as a peeled fruit, and his forehead when he turned it gently to the window took on the refraction of the mild light and seemed to me nobler than ever. It was wonderful to see him at peace like that: I did not know whether it was the reflection of the pure summer evening, whether the mild, soft air did him good, or whether some pleasant thought were illuminating him from within. But used as I was to reading his countenance like a book, I felt that today a kinder God had smoothed out the folds and crevices of his heart.

And it was with curious solemnity, too, that he rose and with his usual movement of the head invited me to follow him to his study: for a man who normally moved fast, he trod with strange gravity. Then he turned back, took an unopened bottle of wine from the sideboard—this too was unusual—and carried it thoughtfully into the study with him. His wife, like me, seemed to notice something strange in his behaviour; she looked up from her needlework with surprise in her eyes and, silent and intent, observed his unusually measured step as we went to the study to work.

The familiar dimness of the darkened room awaited us as usual; there was only a golden circle of light cast by the lamp on the piled white sheets of paper lying ready. I sat in my usual place and repeated the last few sentences of the manuscript;

he always needed to hear the rhythm, which acted as a tuning fork, to get himself in the right mood and let the words stream on. But while he usually started immediately once that rhythm was established, this time no words came. Silence spread in the room, a tense silence already pressing in on us from the walls. He still seemed not quite to have collected himself, for I heard him pacing nervously behind my back. "Read it over again!" Odd how restlessly his voice suddenly vibrated. I repeated the last few paragraphs: now he started, going straight on from what I had said, dictating more abruptly but faster and with more consistency than usual. Five sentences set the scene; until now he had been describing the cultural prerequisites of the drama, painting a fresco of the period, an outline of its history. Now he turned to the drama itself, a genre finally settling down after all its vagabond wanderings, its rides across country in carts, building itself a home licensed by right and privilege, first the Rose Theatre and the Fortuna, wooden houses for plays that were wooden themselves, but then the workmen build a new wooden structure to match the broader breast of the new poetic genre, grown to virility; it rises on the banks of the Thames, on piles thrust into the damp and otherwise unprofitable muddy ground, a massive wooden building with an ungainly hexagonal tower, the Globe Theatre, where Shakespeare, the great master, will strut the stage. As if cast up by the sea like a strange ship, with a piratical red flag on the topmost mast, it stands there firmly anchored in the mud. The groundlings push and shove noisily on the floor of the theatre, as if in harbour, the finer folk smile down and chat idly with the players. Impatiently, they call for the play to begin. They stamp and shout, bang the hilts of their daggers on the boards, until at last a few flickering candles are brought out to illuminate the stage below, and casually costumed figures step forward to perform what appears to be an improvised comedy. And then—I remember his words to this day—"a storm of words suddenly blows up, the sea, the endless sea of passion, sends its bloody waves surging out from these wooden walls to reach all times, all parts of the human heart, inexhaustible, unfathomable, merry and tragic, full of diversity, a unique image of mankind—the theatre of England, the drama of Shakespeare."

With these words, uttered in an elevated tone, he suddenly ceased. A long, heavy silence followed. Alarmed, I turned round: my teacher, one hand clutching the table, stood there with the look of exhaustion I knew well. But this time there was something alarming in his rigidity. I jumped up, fearing that something had happened to him, and asked anxiously whether I should stop. He just looked at me, breathless, his gaze fixed, and remained there immobile for a while. But then his starry eye shone bright blue again, his lips relaxed, he stepped towards me. "Well—haven't you noticed anything?" He looked hard at me. "Noticed what?" I stammered uncertainly. Then he took a deep breath and smiled slightly; after long months, I felt that enveloping, soft and tender gaze again. "The first part is finished." I had difficulty in suppressing a cry of joy, so warmly did my surprise surge through me. How could I have missed seeing it? Yes, there was the whole structure, magnificently built on foundations of the distant past, now on the threshold of its grand design: now they could enter, Marlowe, Ben Jonson, Shakespeare, striding the stage victorious. The great work was celebrating its first anniversary. I made haste to count the pages. This first part amounted to a hundred and seventy close-written sheets, and was the most difficult, for what came next could be freely drawn, while hitherto the account had been closely bound to the historical facts. There was no doubt of it, he would complete his work—our work!

Did I shout aloud, did I dance around with joy, with pride, with delight? I don't know. But my enthusiasm must have taken unforeseen forms of exuberance, since his smiling gaze moved to me as I quickly read over the last few words, eagerly counted the pages, put them together, weighed them in my hand, felt them lovingly, and already, with my calculations running on ahead, I was imagining what it might be like when we had finished the whole book. He saw his own hidden pride, deeply concealed and dammed up as it was, reflected in my joy; touched, he looked at me with a smile. Then he slowly came very, very close to me, put out both hands and took mine; unmovingly, he looked at me. Gradually his pupils, which usually held only a quivering and sporadic play of colour, filled with that clear and radiant blue which, of all the elements, only the depths of water and of human feeling can represent. And this brilliant blue shone from his eyes, blazed out, penetrating me; I felt its surge of warmth moving softly to my inmost being, spreading there, extending into a sense of strange delight; my whole breast suddenly broadened with that vaulting, swelling power, and I felt an Italian noonday sun rising within me. "I know," said his voice, echoing above this brilliance, "that I would never have begun this work without you. I shall never forget what you have done. You gave my tired mind the spur it needed, and what remains of my lost, wasted life you and you alone have salvaged! No one has ever done more for me, no one has helped me so faithfully. And so it is you," he concluded, changing from the formal *Sie* to the familiar *du* pronoun—"it is you whom I must thank. Come! Let us sit together like brothers for a while!"

He drew me gently to the table and picked up the bottle standing ready. There were two glasses there as well—he had intended this symbolic sharing of the wine as a visible sign of his gratitude to me. I was trembling with joy, for nothing more violently confuses one's inner sense than the sudden granting of an ardent wish. The sign of his confidence, the open sign for which I had unconsciously been longing, had found the best possible means of expression in his thanks: the fraternal use of *du*, offered despite the gulf of years between us, was made seven times more precious by the obstacle that gulf represented. The bottle was about to strike its note, the still silent celebratory bottle which would soothe my anxieties for ever, replacing them with faith, and already my inner mind was ringing out as clearly as that quivering, bright note—when one small obstacle halted the festive moment: the bottle was still corked, and we had no corkscrew. He was about to go and fetch one, but guessing his intention I ran impatiently ahead of him to the dining-room—for I burned to experience that moment, the final pacification of my heart, the public statement of his regard for me.

As I ran impetuously through the doorway into the lighted corridor, I collided in the dark with something soft which hastily gave way—it was my teacher's wife, who had obviously been listening at the door. But strange to say, violently as I had collided with her she uttered not a sound, only stepped back in silence, and I myself, incapable of any movement, was so surprised that I said nothing either. This lasted for a moment—we both stood there in silence, feeling ashamed, she caught eavesdropping, I frozen to the spot by this unexpected discovery. But then there was a quiet footstep in the dark, a light came on, and I saw her, pale and defiant, standing with her back to the cupboard; her gaze studied me gravely, and there was something dark, admonitory and threatening in her immobile bearing. However, she said not a word.

My hands were shaking when, after groping around nervously for some time, half-blinded, I finally found the corkscrew; I had to pass her twice, and when I looked up I met that fixed gaze, gleaming hard and dark as polished wood. Nothing about her betrayed any shame at having been found secretly eavesdropping; on the contrary, her eyes, sharp and determined, were now darting threats which I could not understand, and her defiant attitude showed that she was not minded to move from this unseemly position, but intended to go on keeping watch and listening. Her superior strength of will confused me; unconsciously, I avoided the steady glance bent on me like a warning. And when finally, with uncertain step, I crept back into the room where my teacher was impatiently holding the bottle, the boundless joy I had just felt had frozen into a strange anxiety.

But how unconcernedly he was waiting, how cheerfully his gaze moved to me—I had always dreamed of seeing him like that some day, with the cloud of melancholy removed from his brow! Yet now that it was at peace for the first time, ardently turned to me, every word failed me; all my secret joy seeped away as if through hidden pores. Confused, indeed ashamed, I heard him thanking me again, still using the familiar *du*, and our glasses touched with a silvery sound. Putting his arm around me in friendly fashion, he led me over to the armchairs, where we sat opposite each other, his hand placed loosely in mine; for the first time I felt that he was entirely open and at ease. But words failed me; my glance involuntarily kept going to the door, where I feared she might still be standing and listening. She can hear us, I kept thinking, she can hear every word he says to me, every word I say to him—why today, why today of all days? And when, with that warm gaze enveloping me, he suddenly said: "There's something I would like to tell you about my own youth today," I put out a hand to stop him, showing such alarm that he looked up in surprise. "Not today," I stammered, "not today... please forgive me." The idea of his giving himself away to an eavesdropper whose presence I must conceal from him was too terrible.

Uncertainly, my teacher looked at me. "What's the matter?" he asked, sounding slightly displeased.

"I'm tired... forgive me... somehow it's been too much for me... I think," and here I rose to my feet, trembling, "I think I'd better go." Involuntarily my glance went past him to the door, where I could not help feeling that hostile curiosity must still be jealously on watch behind the wood.

Moving slowly, he too rose from his chair. A shadow moved over his suddenly tired face. "Are you really going already... today, of all days?" He held my hand; imperceptible pressure made it heavy. But suddenly he dropped it abruptly, like a stone. "A pity," he said, disappointed, "I was so much looking forward to speaking freely to you for once. A pity!" For a moment a profound sigh hovered like a dark butterfly in the room. I was deeply ashamed, and I felt a curiously inexplicable fear; uncertainly, I stepped back and closed the door of the room behind me.

I GROPED MY WAY laboriously up to my room and threw myself on the bed. But I could not sleep. Never before had I felt so strongly that my living quarters were separated from theirs only by thin floorboards, that there was only the impermeable dark wood between us. And now, with my sharpened senses and as if by magic, I sensed them both awake below me. Without seeing or hearing, I saw and heard him pacing restlessly up and down his study, while she sat silently or wandered around listening elsewhere. But I felt that both of them had their eyes open, and their wakefulness was horribly imparted to me—it was a nightmare, the whole heavy, silent house with its shadows and darkness suddenly weighing down on me.

I threw the covers off. My hands were sweating. What place had I reached? I had sensed the secret quite close, its hot breath already on my face, and now it had retreated again, but its shadow, its silent, opaque shadow still murmured in the air, I felt it as a dangerous presence in the house, stalking on quiet paws like a cat, always there, leaping back and forth, always touching and confusing me with its electrically charged fur, warm yet ghostly. And in the dark I kept feeling his encompassing gaze, soft as his proffered hand, and that other glance, the keen, threatening, alarmed look in his wife's eyes. What business did I have in their secret, why did the pair of them bring me into the midst of their passion with my eyes blindfolded, why were they chasing me into the preserves of their own unintelligible strife, each forcing a blazing accumulation of anger and hatred into my mind?

My brow was still burning. I sat up and opened the window. Outside, the town lay peaceful under the summer clouds; windows were still lamplit, but the people sitting in them were united by calm conversation, cheered by a book or by domestic music-making. And surely calm sleep reigned where darkness already showed behind the white window frames. Above all these resting rooftops, mild peace hovered like the moon in silvery mists, a relaxed and gentle silence, and the eleven strokes of the clock striking from the tower fell lightly on all their ears, whether they chanced to be listening or were dreaming. Only I still felt wide awake, balefully beset by strange thoughts. Some inner sense was feverishly trying to make out that confused murmuring.

Suddenly I started. Wasn't that a footstep on the stairs? I sat up, listening. Sure enough, something was making its way blindly up them, something in the nature of cautious, hesitant, uncertain footsteps—I knew the creak and groan of the worn wood. Those footsteps could only be coming towards me, only to me, since no one else lived up here on the top floor except for the deaf old lady, and she would have been asleep long ago and never had visitors. Was it my teacher? No, that was not his rapid, restless tread; these footsteps hesitated and waited cravenly—there it was again!—on every step: an intruder, a criminal might approach like this, not a friend. I strained my ears so intently that there was a roaring in them. And suddenly a frosty sensation crept up my bare legs.

Then the latch clicked quietly—my sinister visitor must already be on the threshold. A faint draught of air on my bare toes told me that the outer door had been opened, yet no one else, apart from my teacher, had the key. But if it were he—why so hesitant, so strange? Was he anxious about me, did he want to see if I was all right? And why did my sinister visitor hesitate now, just outside the door? For his furtively creeping step had suddenly stopped. I was equally immobile as I faced the horror. I felt as if I ought to scream, but my throat was closed with mucus. I wanted to open the door; my feet refused to move. Only a thin partition now divided me and my mysterious visitor, but neither of us took a step forward to face the other.

Then the bell in the tower struck—only once, a quarter-to-twelve. But it broke the spell. I flung the door open.

And indeed there stood my teacher, candle in hand. The draught from the door as it suddenly swung open made the flame leap with a blue light, and behind it, gigantic and separated from him as he stood there motionless, his quivering shadow flickered drunkenly over the wall behind him. But he too moved when he saw me; he pulled himself together like a man woken from sleep by a sudden breath of keen air, shivering and involuntarily pulling the covers around him. Only then did he step back, the dripping candle swaying in his hand.

I trembled, scared to death. "What's the matter?" was all I could stammer. He looked at me without speaking; words failed him too. At last he put the candle down on the chest of drawers, and immediately the bat-like fluttering of shadows around the room was calmed. Finally he stammered: "I wanted... I wanted..."

Again his voice failed. He stood looking at the floor like a thief caught in the act. This anxiety was unbearable as we stood there, I in my nightshirt, trembling with cold, he with his back bowed, confused with shame.

Suddenly the frail figure moved. He came towards me—at first a smile, malevolent, faun-like, a dangerous, glinting smile that showed only in his eyes (for his lips were compressed) grinned rigidly at me for a moment like a strange mask—and then the voice spoke, sharp as a snake's forked tongue: "I only wanted to say... we'd better not. You... It isn't right, not a young student and his teacher, do you understand?" He had changed back to the formal *Sie* pronoun. "One must keep one's distance... distance... distance..."

And he looked at me with such hatred, such insulting and vehement ill-will that his hand involuntarily clenched. I stumbled back. Was he mad? Was he drunk? There he stood, fist clenched, as if he were about to fling himself on me or strike me in the face.

But the horror lasted only a second; and then that penetrating glance was lowered and turned in on itself. He turned, muttered something that sounded like an apology, and picked up the candle. His shadow, an obedient black devil which had fallen to the floor, rose again and swirled to the door ahead of him. And then he himself was gone, before I had summoned up the strength to think of anything to say. The latch of the door clicked shut; the stairs creaked heavily, painfully, under what seemed his hasty footsteps.

I SHALL NOT FORGET that night; cold rage alternated wildly with a baffled, incandescent despair. Thoughts flashed through my mind like flaring rockets. Why does he torment me, my anguished and tortured mind asked a hundred times, why does he hate me so much that he will creep upstairs at night on purpose to hurl such hostile insults in my face? What have I done to him, what was I supposed to do instead? How am I to make my peace without knowing what I've done to hurt him? I flung myself on the bed in a fever, got up, buried myself under the covers again, but that ghostly picture was always in my mind's eye: my teacher slinking up here, confused by my presence, and behind him, mysterious and strange, that monstrous shadow tumbling over the wall.

When I woke in the morning, after a short period of brief and shallow slumber, I told myself at first that I must have been dreaming. But there were still round, yellow, congealed drops of candle wax on the chest of drawers. And in the middle of the bright, sunlit room my dreadful memory of last night's furtive visitor returned again and again.

I stayed in my room all morning. The thought of meeting him sapped my strength. I tried to write, to read; nothing was any use. My nerves were undermined and might fall into shattering convulsions at any moment, I might begin sobbing and howling—for I could see my own fingers trembling like leaves on a strange tree, I was unable to still them, and my knees felt as weak as if the sinews had been cut. What was I to do? What was I to do? I asked myself that question over and over again until I was exhausted; the blood was already pounding in my temples, there were blue shadows under my eyes. But I could not go out, could not go downstairs, could not suddenly face him without being certain of myself, without having some strength in my nerves again. Once again I flung myself on the bed, hungry, confused, unwashed, distressed, and once again my senses tried to penetrate the thin floorboards: where was he now, what was he doing, was he awake like me, was he as desperate as I myself?

Midday came, and I still lay on the fiery rack of my confusion, when I heard a step on the stairs at last. All my nerves jangled with alarm, but it was a light, carefree step running upstairs two at a time—and now a hand was knocking at the door. I jumped up without opening it. "Who's there?" I asked. "Why don't you come downstairs to eat?" replied his wife's voice, in some annoyance. "Aren't you well?" "No, no," I stammered in confusion. "Just coming, just coming." And now there was nothing I could do but get my clothes on and go downstairs. But my limbs were so unsteady that I had to cling to the banister.

I went into the dining-room. My teacher's wife was waiting in front of one of the two places that had been laid, and greeted me with a mild reproach for having to be reminded. His own place was empty. I felt the blood rise to my face. What did his unexpected absence mean? Did he fear our meeting even more than I did? Was he ashamed, or didn't he want to share a table with me any more? Finally I made up my mind to ask whether the Professor wasn't coming in to lunch.

She looked up in surprise. "Don't you know he went away this morning, then?" "Went away?" I stammered. "Where to?" Her face immediately tensed. "My husband did not see fit to tell me, but probably—well another of his usual excursions." Then she turned towards me with a sudden sharp, questioning look. "You mean that you don't know? He went up to see you on purpose last night—I thought it was to say goodbye... how strange, how very strange that he didn't tell you either."

"Me!" I could utter only a scream. And to my shame and disgrace, that scream swept away everything that had been so dangerously dammed up in me during the last few hours. Suddenly it all burst out in a sobbing, howling, raging convulsion—I vomited a gurgling torrent of words and screams tumbling over one another, a great swirling mass of confused desperation, I wept—no, I shook, my trembling mouth brought up all the torment that had accumulated inside me. Fists drumming frantically on the table like a child throwing a tantrum, face covered with tears, I let out what had been hanging over me for weeks like a thunderstorm. And while I found relief in that wild outbreak, I also felt boundless shame in giving so much of myself away to her.

"What on earth is the matter? For God's sake!" She had risen to her feet, astonished. But then she hurried up to me and led me from the table to the sofa. "Lie here and calm down." She stroked my hands, she passed her own hands over my hair, while the aftermath of my spasms still shook my trembling body. "Don't distress yourself, Roland—please don't distress yourself. I know all about it, I could feel it coming." She was still stroking my hair, but suddenly her voice grew hard. "I know just how he can confuse one, nobody knows better. But please believe me, I always wanted to warn you when I saw you leaning on him so much, on a man who can't even support himself. You don't know him, you're blind. You are a child—you don't know anything, or not yet, not today. Or perhaps today you have begun to understand something for the first time—in which case all the better for him and for you."

She remained bending over me in warm concern, and as if from vitreous depths I felt her words and the soothing touch of calming hands. It did me good to feel a breath of sympathy again at long, long last, and then to sense a woman's tender, almost maternal hand so close once more. Perhaps I had gone without that too long as well, and now that I felt, through the veils of my distress, a tenderly concerned woman's sympathy, some comfort came over me in the midst of my pain. But oh, how ashamed I was, how ashamed of that treacherous fit in which I had let out my despair! And it was against my will that, sitting up with difficulty, I brought it all out again in a rushing, stammering flood of words, all he had done to me—how he had rejected and persecuted me, then shown me kindness again, how he was harsh to me for no reason, no cause—a torturer, but one to whom ties of affection bound me, whom I hated even as I loved him and loved even as I hated him. Once more I began to work myself up to such a pitch that she had to soothe me again. Once more soft hands gently pressed me back on the ottoman from which I had jumped up in my agitation. At last I calmed down. She preserved a curiously thoughtful silence; I felt that she understood everything, perhaps even more than I did myself.

For a few minutes this silence linked us. Then she stood up. "There—now you've been a child long enough; you must be a man again. Sit down at the table and have something to eat. Nothing tragic has happened—it was just a misunderstanding that will soon be cleared up." And when I made some kind of protest, she added firmly, "It will soon be cleared up, because I'm not letting him play with you and confuse you like that any more. There must be an end to all this; he must finally learn to control himself. You're too good for his dangerous games. I shall speak to him, trust me. But now come and have something to eat."

Ashamed and without any volition of my own, I let her lead me back to the table. She talked of unimportant matters with a certain rapid eagerness, and I was inwardly grateful to her for seeming to ignore my wild outburst and forgetting it again.

Tomorrow, she said, was Sunday, and she was going for an outing on a nearby lake with a lecturer called W and his fiancée, I ought to come too, cheer myself up, take a rest from my books. All the malaise I felt, she said, just showed that I was overworking and my nerves were overstretched; once I was in the water swimming, or out on a walk, my body would soon regain its equilibrium.

I said I would go. Anything but solitude now, anything but my room, anything but my thoughts circling in the dark. "And don't stay in this afternoon either! Go for a stroll, take some exercise, amuse yourself!" she urged me. Strange, I thought, how she guesses at my most intimate feelings, how even though she's a stranger to me she knows what I need and what hurts me, while I, who ought to know, fail to see it and torment myself. I told her I would do as she suggested. And looking up gratefully, I saw a new expression on her face: the mocking, lively face that sometimes gave her the look of a pert, easy-going boy had softened to a sympathetic gaze; I had never seen her so grave before. Why does he never look at me so kindly, asked something confused and yearning in me, why does he never seem to know when he is hurting me? Why has he never laid such helpful, tender hands on my hair, on my own hands? And gratefully I kissed hers, which she abruptly, almost violently withdrew. "Don't torment yourself," she repeated, and her voice seemed close to me.

But then her lips pressed together in a hard line again, and suddenly straightening her back she said, quietly: "Believe me, he doesn't deserve it."

And that almost inaudibly whispered remark struck pain into my almost pacified heart once more.

W HAT I SET OUT to do that afternoon and evening seems so ridiculous and childish that for years I have blushed to think of it—indeed, internal censorship was quick to blot out its memory. Well, today I am no longer ashamed of my clumsy foolishness—on the contrary, how well do I understand the impulsive, muddled ideas of the passionate youth who wanted to vault over his own confused feelings by main force.

I see myself as if at the end of a hugely long corridor, viewed through a telescope: the desperate, desolate boy climbing up to his room, not knowing what to do with himself. And then putting on another coat, bracing himself to adopt a different gait, making wild and determined gestures, and suddenly marching out into the street with a vigorously energetic tread. Yes, there I go, I recognize myself, I know every thought in the head of the poor silly, tormented boy I was then; suddenly, in front of the mirror in fact, I pulled myself together and said: "Who cares for him! To hell with him! Why should I torment myself over that old fool! She's right—I ought to have some fun, I ought to amuse myself for once! Here goes!"

And that, indeed, was how I walked out into the street. At first it was an effort to liberate myself—then a race, a mere cowardly flight from the realization that my cheerful fun wasn't so cheerful after all, and that block of ice still weighed as heavily on my heart as before. I still remember how I walked along, my heavy stick clasped firmly in my hand, looking keenly at every student, with a dangerous desire to pick a quarrel with someone raging in me, a wish to take out my anger, which had no outlet, on the first man I came across. But fortunately no one troubled to pay me any attention. So I made my way to the café usually frequented by my fellow students at the university, ready to sit down at their table unasked and take the slightest gibe as provocation. Once again, however, my readiness to quarrel found no object—the fine day had tempted most of them to go out of town, and the two or three sitting together greeted me civilly and gave my fevered, touchy mood not the slightest excuse to take offence. I soon rose from the table, feeling irritated, and went off to what is now no longer a dubious inn in the suburbs, where the riff-raff of the town, out for a good time, crowded close together among beer fumes and smoke to the loud music of a ladies' wind band. I tipped two or three glasses of liquor hastily down my throat, invited a lady of easy virtue to my table along with her friend, also a hard-bitten and much painted demi-mondaine, and took a perverted pleasure in drawing attention to myself. Everyone in the little town knew me, everyone knew I was the Professor's student, and as for the women, their bold dress and conduct made it obvious what they were—so I relished the false, silly pleasure of compromising my reputation and with it (so I foolishly thought) his too; let them all see that I don't care for him, I thought, let them see I don't mind what he thinks—and I paid court to my bosomy female companion in front of everyone in the most shameless and unseemly manner. I was intoxicated by my angry ill-will, and we were soon literally intoxicated too, for we drank everything indiscriminately—wine, spirits, beer—and carried on so boisterously that chairs toppled over and our neighbours prudently moved away. But I was not ashamed, on the contrary; let him hear about this, I raged foolishly, let him see how little I care for him, I'm not upset, I don't feel injured, far from it: "Wine, more wine!" I shouted, banging my fist down on the table so that the glasses shook. Finally I left with the two women, one on my right arm, the other on my left, marching straight down the high street where the usual nine o'clock promenade brought students and their girls, citizens and military men together for a pleasant stroll—like a soiled and unsteady clover leaf, the three of us rampaged along the road making so much noise that in the end a policeman, looking annoyed, approached us and firmly told us to pipe down. I cannot describe what happened next in detail—a blue haze of strong liquor blurs my memory, I know only that, disgusted by the two intoxicated women and scarcely in control of my senses any more, I bought myself free of them, drank more coffee and cognac somewhere, and then, outside the university building, delivered myself of a tirade against all professors, for the delectation of the young fellows who gathered around me. Then, out of a vague wish to soil myself yet further and do him an injury—oh, the delusions of passionate and confused anger!—I meant to go into a house of ill repute, but I couldn't find the way, and finally staggered sullenly home. My unsteady hand had some trouble in opening the front door of the building, and it was with difficulty that I dragged myself up the first few steps of the stairs.

But then, outside his door, all my oppressive sense of intoxication vanished as if my head had suddenly been doused in icy water. Instantly sobered, I was staring into the distorted face of my own helplessly raging foolishness. I cringed with shame. And very quietly, grovelling like a beaten dog, hoping that no one would hear me, I slunk up to my room.

I SLEPT LIKE THE DEAD; when I woke, sunlight was flooding the floor and rising slowly to the edge of my bed. I got out of it with a sudden movement. Memories of the previous evening gradually came into my aching head, but I repressed the shame, I wasn't going to feel ashamed any more. It was his fault, after all, I insisted to myself, it was all his fault that I'd been so dissolute. I calmed myself by thinking that yesterday's events were nothing but a normal student prank, perfectly permissible in a man who had done nothing but work and work for weeks on end; but I did not feel happy with my own self-justification, and rather apprehensively I timidly went down to my teacher's wife, remembering that I had agreed yesterday to go on her outing with her.

It was odd—no sooner did I touch the handle of his door than he was present in me again, but so too was that burning, unreasonable, churning pain, that raging despair. I knocked softly, and his wife came to let me in with a strangely soft expression. "What nonsense have you been up to, Roland?" she said, but sympathetically rather than reproachfully. "Why do you give yourself such a bad time?" I was taken aback: so she had already heard of my foolish conduct. But she immediately helped me to get over my embarrassment. "We're going to be sensible today, though. Dr W and his fiancée will be here at ten, and then we'll go out to the lake and row and swim and forget all that stupid stuff." With great trepidation I ventured to ask, unnecessarily, whether the Professor was back yet. She looked at me without answering, and I knew for myself that it was a pointless question.

At ten sharp the lecturer arrived, a young physicist who, rather isolated himself as a Jew among the other academics, was really the only one of them who mixed with our reclusive little society; he was accompanied by his fiancée, or more likely his mistress, a young girl who was always laughing artlessly in a slightly silly way, but that made her just the right company for such an improvised excursion. First we travelled by train—eating, talking and laughing all the way—to a tiny lake nearby, and after my weeks of strenuous gravity I was so unused to any light-hearted conversation that even this one hour of it went to my head like slightly sparkling wine. Their childish high spirits succeeded entirely in diverting my thoughts from the subject that they usually circled, like bees buzzing around a darkly oozing honeycomb, and no sooner did I step into the open air and feel my muscles stretched to the full again in an improvised race with the young woman than I was the fit, carefree boy of the past once more.

Down at the lake we hired two rowing boats; my teacher's wife steered mine, and the lecturer and his girlfriend shared the rowing between them in the other. No sooner had we pushed off than a spirit of competitive sport made us try to overtake each other. I was at a clear disadvantage, since there were two people rowing the other boat and I had to contend with them on my own, but throwing off my coat I plied the oars so vigorously, being a trained oarsman myself, that my strong strokes kept drawing us ahead. We spurred ourselves on with mocking remarks called from boat to boat, and careless of the burning July sun, indifferent to the sweat inelegantly drenching us, we laboured to outstrip one another, irrepressible galley slaves labouring in the heat of athletic pleasure. At last our goal was near, a little tree-grown tongue of land projecting into the lake, we rowed harder than ever, and to the triumph of my companion in the boat, herself in the grip of the spirit of competition, our keel was the first to ground on the beach. I climbed out, hot, perspiring, intoxicated by the unfamiliar sun, the roar of my excited blood in my veins and by the pleasure of victory—my heart was hammering away and my sweaty clothes clung close to my body. The lecturer was in no better state, and instead of earning praise for our determination in the struggle we were the object of much high-spirited mockery from the women for our breathlessness and rather pitiful appearance. At last they allowed us a respite to cool off; amidst jokes and laughter, a ladies' changing room and a gentlemen's changing room were improvised to the right and left of a bush. We quickly put our swimming costumes on; pale underclothes and naked arms flashed into view on the other side of the bush, and the two women were already splashing happily in the water as we men got ready too. The lecturer, less exhausted than I was myself after defeating the two of them, immediately jumped in after the ladies, but as I had rowed a little too hard and could still feel my heart thudding against my ribs I lay comfortably in the shade for a while first, enjoying the sensation of the clouds moving over me and the pleasantly sweet droning sensation of weariness surging through the circulation of my blood.

But after a few minutes I heard loud shouts from the water: "Come on, Roland! We're having a swimming race! A swimming competition! A diving competition!" I stayed put; I felt as if I could lie like this for a thousand years, my skin gently warmed as the sun fell on it and at the same time cooled by the tenderly caressing breeze. But again I heard laughter, and the lecturer's voice: "He's on strike! We've really worn him out! You go and fetch the lazy fellow." And sure enough, I could hear someone splashing towards me, and then, from very close, her voice: "Come on, Roland! It's a swimming race! Let's show those two!" I didn't answer, I enjoyed making her look for me. "Where are you, then?" The gravel crunched, I heard bare feet running along the beach in search of me, and suddenly there she was, her wet swimming costume clinging to her boyishly slender body. "Oh, there you are, you lazy thing! Come along, lazybones, the others have almost reached the island." But I lay at ease on my back, stretching idly. "It's much nicer here. I'll follow later."

"He won't come in," she laughed, calling through her cupped hand in the direction of the water. "Then push the show-off in!" shouted the lecturer's voice back from afar. "Oh, do come on," she urged me impatiently, "don't let me down!" But I just yawned lazily. Then, in mingled jest and annoyance, she broke a twig off the bush as a switch. "Come on!" she repeated energetically, striking me a playful blow on the arm to encourage me. I started—she had hit too hard, and a thin red mark like blood ran over my arm. "Well, I'm certainly not coming now," I said, both joking and slightly angry myself. But at this, sounding really cross, she commanded: "Come on, will you! This minute!" And when, defiantly, I did not move, she struck another blow, harder this time, a sharp and burning stroke. All at once I jumped up angrily to snatch the switch away from her, she retreated, but I seized her arm. Involuntarily, as we wrestled for possession of the switch, our half-naked bodies came close. And when I seized her arm and twisted the wrist to make her drop it, and she bent far back trying to evade me, there was a sudden snapping sound—the buckle holding the shoulder strap of her swimming costume had come apart, the left cup fell from her bare breast, and its erect red nipple met my eye. I could not help looking, just for a second, but I was cast into a state of confusion—trembling and ashamed, I let go of the hand I had been clutching. She turned away, blushing, to perform a makeshift repair on the broken buckle with a hairpin. I stood there at a loss for words. She was silent too. And from that moment on there was an awkward, suppressed uneasiness between the two of us.

"HALLO... HALLO... where are you both?" the voices came echoing over from the little island. "Just coming," I replied quickly, and glad to escape more embarrassment I threw myself vigorously into the water. A couple of diving strokes, the inspiring pleasure of driving myself forward through the water, the clarity and cold of the unfeeling element, and already that dangerous murmuring and hissing in my blood receded, as if washed away by a stronger, purer pleasure. I soon caught up with the other two, challenged the lecturer, who was not a very strong athlete, to a series of competitions in which I emerged the victor, and then we swam back to the little tongue of land where my teacher's wife, who had stayed behind and was already dressed again, was waiting to organize a cheerful picnic unpacked from the baskets we had brought along. But exuberant as the light-hearted conversation was between the four of us, we two involuntarily avoided speaking to each other directly—we talked and laughed as if ignoring one another. And when our glances did meet we hastily looked away again, in an unspoken complicity of feeling: the embarrassment of the little incident had not yet ebbed away, and each of us sensed, ashamed and uneasy, that the other was remembering it too.

The rest of the afternoon passed quickly, with more rowing on the lake, but the heat of our enthusiasm for sport increasingly gave way to a pleasant weariness: the wine, the warmth, the sun we had soaked up gradually seeped further into our blood, making it flow redder than before. The lecturer and his girlfriend were already allowing themselves little familiarities which the

305

two of us were obliged to watch with a certain embarrassment; they moved closer and closer to each other while we kept our distance all the more scrupulously; but the fact that we were two couples was particularly evident when the pair of them lagged behind on the woodland path, obviously to kiss undisturbed, and when we two were left alone awkwardness inhibited our conversation. In the end all four of us were glad to be back in the train, the engaged couple looking forward to an evening together, we happy to escape an embarrassing situation.

The lecturer and his girlfriend accompanied us home. We all went upstairs together, and no soon were we inside than I once more felt the tormenting premonition of his presence, the presence for which I confusedly yearned. "Oh, if only he were back!" I thought impatiently. And just as if she had divined the sigh which did not quite rise from my lips, she said: "Let's see if he's back yet."

We went in. The place was quiet. Everything in his study was still abandoned; unconsciously, my agitated feelings imagined his oppressed, tragic figure in the empty chair. But the sheets of paper lay untouched, waiting as I was waiting myself. Then bitterness returned: why had he fled, why had he left me alone? Jealous rage rose more and more grimly within me, once again I dully felt my foolishly confused desire to do something to harm him, something hateful.

His wife had followed me. "You'll stay to supper, I hope? You ought not to be alone today." How did she know I was afraid of my empty room, of the creaking of the stairs, of brooding over my memories? She always did guess everything going on in me, every unspoken thought, every ignoble desire.

A kind of fear came over me, a fear of myself and the vague turmoil of hatred within me, and I wanted to refuse. But cravenly, I did not venture to say no.

I HAVE ALWAYS had a horror of adultery, but not for any self-righteous moral reasons, not out of prudery and convention, not so much because taking possession of a strange body is theft committed in the dark, but because almost every woman will give away her husband's most intimate secrets at such moments—every one of them is a Delilah stealing his most human secret from the man she is deceiving and casting it before a stranger, the secret of his strength or of his weakness. The betrayal, it seems to me, is not that a woman gives herself of her own free will but that then, to justify herself, she will uncover her husband's loins and expose him unknown to himself, as if in his sleep, to the curiosity of another man, and to scornfully relished laughter.

It is not, therefore, that when confused by blind and angry desperation I took refuge in his wife's first sympathetic and only then tender embrace—ah, how fatefully swift is the move from one feeling to the other—it is not what I still feel today was the worst thing I ever did in my life (for it happened in spite of ourselves, we both plunged unconsciously, unknowingly, into those burning depths), but the fact that among the tumbled pillows I let her tell me intimate details of him, that I allowed her, all on edge as she was herself, to give away the innermost secrets of her marriage. Why did I suffer her, without repelling her, to tell me that he had not touched her physically for years, and to indulge in dark hints: why did I not command her to keep silent over this most intimate core of his being? But I was so eager to know his secret myself, so anxious to feel that he had injured me, her, everyone, that I dizzily accepted her angry confession of his neglect of her—after all, it was so like the sense of rejection I had felt myself! And so it was that the two of us, out of a shared and confused hatred, performed an act that looked like love, but while our bodies sought each other and came together we were both thinking and speaking of him all the time, of nothing but him. Sometimes what she said hurt me, and I was ashamed to be involved with what I disliked. But my body no longer obeyed my will, and instead wildly sought its own pleasure. Shuddering, I kissed the lips which were betraying the person I most loved.

Next morning I crept up to my room, the bitter flavour of disgust and shame in my mouth. Now that the warmth of her body no longer troubled my senses I felt the glaring reality, the repulsive nature of my betrayal. I knew at once that I would never again be able to look him in the face, never again take his hand—I had robbed myself, not him, of what meant most to me.

There was only one solution now: flight. Feverishly I packed all my things, piled my books into a stack, paid my landlady—he must not find me again, I must disappear from his life, mysteriously and for no apparent reason, just as he had disappeared from mine.

But amidst all this activity my hand suddenly froze. I had heard the creaking of the wooden stairs, footsteps coming rapidly up the steps—his footsteps.

I must have turned white as a sheet, for as soon as he entered he reacted with horror. "What's the matter with you, my boy? Are you unwell?"

I retreated. I flinched away from him as he was about to come closer and offer me a helping hand.

"What on earth is the matter?" he asked in alarm. "Has something happened to you? Or... or are you still angry with me?"

I clung convulsively to the window frame. I could not look at him. His sympathetic, warm voice tore something like a wound open in me—close to fainting, I felt it well up in me, hot, very hot, burning and consuming, a glowing flood of shame.

He too stood there in surprise and confusion. And suddenly, with his voice very faint, hesitant and low, he whispered an odd question: "Has... has someone... been telling you something about me?"

Without turning to him, I made a gesture of denial. But some anxious idea seemed to be uppermost in his mind, and he repeated doggedly: "Tell me—admit it... has anyone been telling you something about me? Anyone—I'm not asking who."

I denied it again. He stood there at a loss. But suddenly he seemed to have noticed that my bags were packed, my books stacked together, and saw that his arrival had just interrupted my preparations to leave. Agitated, he came up to me. "You mean to go away, Roland, I can see you do... tell me the truth."

Then I pulled myself together. "I must go away... forgive me, I can't talk about it... I'll write to you." My constricted throat could utter no more, and my heart thudded with every word.

He stood quite still. Then, suddenly, that familiar weariness of his came over him. "It may be better this way, Roland... yes, of course, it is... for you, for everyone. But before you leave I would like to talk to you once more. Come at seven, at our usual time, and we'll say goodbye man to man. No flight from ourselves, though, no letters... that would be childish and unworthy... and what I would like to tell you is not for pen and paper. You will come, won't you?"

I only nodded. My gaze still dared not move from the window. But I saw none of the brightness of the morning any more; a dense, dark veil had dropped between me and the world.

At seven I entered that beloved room for the last time: early dusk filtered dimly through the portières, the smooth stone of the marble statues scarcely gleamed from the back of the room, and the books slumbered, black behind the mother-of-pearl shimmer of the glass doors over the bookcase. Ah, secret place of my memories, where the word became magical to me and I knew the intoxication and enchantment of the intellect as nowhere else—I always see you as you were at that hour of farewell, and I still see the venerated figure slowly, slowly rising from his chair and approaching me, a shadowy form, only the curved brow gleaming like an alabaster lamp in the dim light, and the white hair of an old man waving above it like drifting smoke. Now a hand, raised with difficulty, was proffered and sought mine, now I saw the eyes turned gravely towards me, and felt my arm gently taken as he led me back to the place where he was sitting.

"Sit down, Roland, and let us talk frankly. We are men and must be honest. I won't press you—but would it not be better for this last hour to bring full clarity between us? So tell me, why do you want to leave? Are you angry with me for that thoughtless insult?"

I made a gesture of denial. How terrible to think that he, the man betrayed, the man deceived, was still trying to take the blame on himself!

"Have I done you some other injury, consciously or unconsciously? I know I am sometimes rather strange. And I have irritated and tormented you against my own will. I have never thanked you enough for all your support—I know it, I know it, I have always known it, even in those moments when I hurt you. Is that the reason—tell me, Roland, for I would like us to part from one another with honesty."

Once again I shook my head: I could not speak. His voice had been firm; now it became a little unsteady.

"Or… let me ask you again… has anyone told you anything about me, anything that you think base… repulsive… anything that… that makes you despise me?"

"No! No, no!" The protest burst from me like a sob: did he think I could despise him? I despise him!

His voice now grew impatient. "Then what is it? What else can it be? Are you tired of the work? Or does something else make you want to go? A woman… is it a woman?"

I said nothing. And that silence was probably so different in nature that he felt in it the positive answer to his question. He leaned closer and whispered very softly, but without agitation, without any agitation or anger at all:

"Is it a woman? Is it… my wife?"

I was still silent, and he understood. A tremor ran through my body: now, now, now he would burst out, attack me, strike me, chastise me… and I almost wanted him to whip me, the thief, the deceiver, whip me like a mangy dog from his desecrated home. But strangely, he remained entirely still… and he sounded almost relieved when he murmured as if to himself: "I might have known it." He paced up and down the room a couple of times. Then he stopped in front of me and said, as it seemed to me, almost dismissively:

"And that… that is what you take so hard? Didn't she tell you that she is free to do as she likes, take what she likes, that I have no rights over her? No right to forbid her anything, nor the least desire to do so… And why, for whose sake, should she have controlled herself, and for you of all people… you are young, you are bright, beautiful… you were close to us, how could she not love you, such a beautiful young man, how could she help but love you? For I…" Suddenly his voice began to falter, and he leaned close, so close that I felt his breath. Again I sensed the warm embrace of his gaze, again I saw that strange light in his eyes, just as it had been before in those rare and strange moments between us. He came ever closer.

And then he whispered softly, his lips hardly moving: "For I love you too."

D ID I START? Did I show involuntary alarm? My body must have made some movement of surprise or evasion, for he flinched back like a man rejected. A shadow fell over his face. "Do you despise me now?" he asked very quietly. "Am I repulsive to you?"

Why could I find nothing to say? Why did I simply sit there in silence, unlovingly, embarrassed, numbed, instead of going to the man who loved me and disabusing him of his mistaken fear? But all the memories were in wild turmoil within me; as if a cipher had suddenly solved the coded language of those incomprehensible messages, I now understood it all with terrible clarity: his tender approaches and his brusque defensiveness—shattered, I understood that visit in the night and his grimly determined flight from the passion I so enthusiastically pressed on him. Yes, I had always felt the love in him, tender and timid, now surging out, now forcibly inhibited again, I had loved and enjoyed it in the radiance fleetingly falling on me—yet as the word love now came from his bearded mouth, a sensuously tender sound, horror both sweet and terrible entered my mind. And much as I burned in humility and in pity for him, confused, trembling, shattered boy that I was, I could find nothing to say in answer to his unexpected revelation of his passion.

He sat there crushed, staring at my silence. "It seems to you so terrible, then, so terrible," he murmured. "You too... you will not forgive me either, you to whom I have kept my mouth so firmly closed that I almost choked—from whom I have hidden myself as from no one else... but it's better for you to know it

313

now, and then it will no longer weigh on my mind. It was too much for me anyway... oh, far too much... an end is better, better than such silence and concealment."

How sadly he spoke, his voice full of tenderness and shame; the trembling note in it went to my heart. I was ashamed of myself for preserving so cold, so unfeelingly frosty a silence before this man who had given me more than anyone alive, and who now so pointlessly humbled himself before me. My soul burned to say something comforting to him, but my trembling lips would not obey me. And so I sat awkwardly there, wretchedly shifting in my chair until, almost angrily, he tried to cheer me. "Don't sit there like that, Roland, in such dreadful silence... pull yourself together. Is it really so terrible? Are you so ashamed of me? It's all over now, you see, I have told you everything... let us at least say goodbye properly as two men, two friends should."

But I still had no power over myself. He touched my arm. "Come, Roland, sit down beside me. I feel easier now that you know, now that there's honesty between us at last... At first I kept fearing you might guess how dear you are to me... then I hoped you would feel it for yourself, so that I would be spared this confession... but now it has happened, now I am free, and now I can speak to you as I have never spoken to another living soul. For you have been closer to me than anyone else in all these years, I have loved you as I loved no one before you... Like no one else, my child, you have awakened the last spark in me. So as we part you should also know more of me than anyone else does. In all our time together I have felt your silent questioning so clearly... you alone shall know my full story. Do you want me to tell it to you?"

He saw my assent in my glance, in my confused and shattered expression.

"Come close then… come close to me. I cannot say such things out loud." I leaned forward—devoutly, I can only say. But no sooner was I sitting opposite him waiting, listening, than he rose again. "No, this won't do… you mustn't look at me or… or I can't talk about it." And he put out his hand to turn off the light.

Darkness fell over us. I sensed him near me, knew it from his breathing which somewhere passed into the unseen heavily, almost stertorously. And suddenly a voice rose in the air between us and told me the whole story of his life.

S INCE THAT EVENING when the man I so venerated opened up like a shell that had been tightly closed and told me his story, since that evening forty years ago, everything our writers and poets present as extraordinary in books, everything shown on stage as tragic drama, has seemed to me trivial and unimportant. Is it through complacency, cowardice, or because they take too short a view that they speak of nothing but the superficial, brightly lit plane of life where the senses openly and lawfully have room to play, while below in the vaults, in the deep caves and sewers of the heart, the true dangerous beasts of passion roam, glowing with phosphorescent light, coupling unseen and tearing each other apart in every fantastic form of convolution? Does the breath of those beasts alarm them, the hot and tearing breath of demonic urges, the exhalations of the burning blood, do they fear to dirty their dainty hands on the ulcers of humanity, or does their gaze, used to a more muted light, not find its way down the slippery, dangerous steps that drip with decay? And yet to those who truly know, no lust is like the lust for the hidden, no horror so primevally forceful as that which quivers around danger, no suffering more sacred than that which cannot express itself for shame.

But here a man was disclosing himself to me exactly as he was, opening up his inmost thoughts, eager to bare his battered, poisoned, burnt and festering heart. A wild delight like that of a flagellant tormented itself in the confession he had kept back for so many years. Only a man who had been ashamed all his life, cowering and hiding, could launch with such intoxication and so overwhelmed into so pitiless a confession. He was tearing the life from his breast piecemeal, and in that hour the boy I then was looked down for the first time into the unimaginable depths of human emotion.

At first his voice hovered in the room as if disembodied, an indistinct haze of agitation, uncertainly hinting at secret events, yet this laborious control of passion in itself made me divine the force it was to show, just as when you hear certain markedly decelerating bars of music, foreshadowing a rapid rhythm, you feel the furioso in your nerves in advance. But then images began to flicker up, raised trembling by the inner storm of passion and gradually showing in the light. I saw a boy at first, a shy and introverted boy who dared not speak to his comrades, but who felt a confused, a physically demanding longing for the best-looking boys at the school. However, when he approached one too affectionately he was firmly repelled, a second mocked him with cruel clarity, and worse still, the two of them revealed his outlandish desires to the other boys. At once a unanimous kangaroo court ostracized the confused boy with scorn and humiliation from their cheerful company, as if he were a leper. His way to school became a daily penance, and his nights were disturbed by the self-disgust of one marked out early as a pariah, feeling that his perverse desires, although so far they featured only in his dreams, denoted insanity and were a shameful vice.

His voice trembled uncertainly as he told the tale—for a moment it seemed about to fade away in the darkness. But a sigh raised it again, and new images rose from the gloomy haze, ranged one by one, shadowy and ghostly. The boy became a student in Berlin, and for the first time the underworld of the city offered him a chance to satisfy the inclinations he had so long controlled—but how soiled their satisfaction was by disgust, how poisoned by fear!—those surreptitious encounters on dark street corners, in the shadows of railway stations and bridges, how poor a thing was their twitching lust, how dreadful did the danger make them, most of them ending wretchedly in blackmail and always leaving a slimy snail-trail of cold fear behind for weeks! The way to hell lay between darkness and light—while the crystal element of the intellect cleansed the scholar in the bright light of the industrious day, the evening always impelled the passionate man towards the dregs of the outskirts of town, the community of questionable companions avoiding any policeman's spiked helmet, and took him into gloomy beer cellars whose dubious doors opened only to a certain kind of smile. And he had to steel his will to hide this double life with care, to conceal his Medusa-like secret from any strange gaze, to preserve the impeccably grave and dignified demeanour of a junior lecturer by day, only to wander incognito by night in the underworld of shameful adventures pursued by the light of flickering lamps. Again and again the tormented man strained to master a passion which diverged from the accustomed track by applying the lash of self-control, again and again his instincts impelled him towards the dark and dangerous. Ten, twelve, fifteen years of nerve-racking struggles with the invisibly magnetic power of his incurable inclination were like a single convulsion. He felt satisfaction without enjoyment, he felt choking shame, and came to be aware of the dark aspect, timidly concealed in itself, of his fear of his own passions.

At last, quite late, after his thirtieth year, he made a violent attempt to force his life round to the right track. At the home of a relative he met his future wife, a young girl who, vaguely attracted by the mystery clinging about him, offered him genuine affection. And for once her boyish body and youthfully spirited bearing managed, briefly, to deceive his passion. Their fleeting relationship conquered his resistance to all things feminine, he overcame it for the first time, and hoping that thanks to this attraction he would be able to master his misdirected inclinations, impatient to chain himself fast when for once he had found a prop against his inner propensity for the dangerous, and having made a full admission of it to her first, he quickly married the girl. Now he thought the way back to those terrible zones would be barred to him. For a few brief weeks he was carefree, but soon the new stimulus proved ineffective and his original longings became insistent and overpowering. From then on the girl whom he had disappointed and who disappointed him served only as a façade to conceal his revived inclinations. Once again he walked his perilous way on the edge of the law and society, looking down into the dark dangers below.

And a particular torment was added to his inner confusion: he was offered a position where such inclinations as his are a curse. A junior lecturer, who soon became a full professor, he was professionally obliged to be constantly involved with young men, and temptation kept placing new blooms of youth in front of him, ephebes of an invisible *gymnasion* within the world of Prussian conventionality. And all of them—another curse, another danger!—loved him passionately without seeing the face of Eros behind their teacher's mask, they were happy when his comradely but secretly trembling hand touched them, they lavished enthusiasm on a man who had to keep strict control over himself. His were the torments of Tantalus: to be harsh to those who pressed their admiration on him, to fight a never-ending battle with his own weakness! And when he felt that he had almost succumbed to temptation he always suddenly took flight. Those were the escapades whose lightning advent and recurrence had so confused me: now I saw that the terrible way he took was a means of flight from himself, a flight into the horrors of chasms and crooked alleys. He always went to some large metropolis where he would find intimates haunting the wrong side of the tracks, men of the lower classes whose encounters besmirched him, whorish youths instead of young men of elevated and upright minds, but this disgust, this mire, this vileness, this poisonously mordant disappointment was necessary if he were to be sure of resisting the lure of his senses at home, in the close, trusting circle of his students. Ah, what encounters—what ghostly yet malodorously earthly figures his confession conjured up before my eyes! For this distinguished intellectual, in whom a sense of the beauty of form was as natural and necessary as breath, this master of all emotions was fated to encounter ultimate humiliation in low dives, smoky and smouldering, which admitted only initiates; he knew the impudent demands of rent boys with made-up faces, the sugary familiarity of perfumed barbers' assistants, the excited giggling of transvestites in women's skirts, the rabid greed of itinerant actors, the coarse affection of tobacco-chewing sailors—all these crooked, intimidated, perverse, fantastic forms in which the sexual instinct, wandering from the usual way, seeks and knows itself in the meaner areas of big cities. He had encountered all kinds of humiliation, ignominy and vileness on these slippery paths; several times he had been robbed of everything on him (being too weak and too high-minded to scuffle with a coarse groom), he had been left without his watch, without his coat, and in addition was spurned by his drunken comrade when he returned to their shady hotel on the city outskirts. Blackmailers had got their claws into him, one of them had dogged his footsteps at the university for months, sitting boldly in the front row of the audience and glancing up with a sly smile at the professor known all over town who, trembling to see the man's knowing winks, could deliver his lecture only with a great effort. Once—my heart stood still when he confessed this too—once he had been picked up by the police in a disreputable bar in Berlin at midnight with a whole gang of such fellows; a stout, red-cheeked sergeant took down the trembling man's name and position with the scornful, superior smile of a subaltern suddenly able to put on airs in front of an intellectual, graciously indicating at last that this time he was being let off with a caution, but henceforward his name would be on a certain list. And as a man who has sat too long in bars that smell of liquor finds its odour clinging at last to his clothes, so rumours and gossip gradually went round here in his own town, beginning in some place that could not be traced; it was the same as in his class at school—in the company of his colleagues their conversation and greetings to him became ostentatiously more and more frosty, until here too a glazed and transparent area of alienation cut the isolated man off from all of them. And even in the safety of his home, behind many locked doors, he still felt he was being spied on and known for what he was.

But this tormented, fearful heart was never offered the grace of pure friendship by a nobly minded man, the worthy return of a virile and powerful affection: he always had to divide his feelings into below and above, his tender longings for his young and intellectual students at the university, and those companions hired in the dark of whom he would think with revulsion next morning. Never, as he began to age, did he experience a pure inclination, a youth's wholehearted affection for him, and weary of disappointment, his nerves worn out by struggling through this thorny thicket, he had resigned himself to the idea that he was done for, when suddenly a young man came into his life who showed a passionate liking for him, ageing as he was, who willingly offered up his words, his whole being, who felt ardently for him—and he, unsuspectingly overwhelmed, now faced in alarm the miracle for which he had no longer hoped, feeling himself unworthy now of such a pure, spontaneously offered gift. Once again a messenger of youth had appeared, a handsome form and a passionate mind burning for him with intellectual fire, affectionately bound to him by a link of sympathy, thirsting for his liking, and with no idea of its own danger. With the torch of Eros in his guileless soul, bold and innocent as Parsifal the holy fool, this youth bent close to the poisoned wound, unaware of his magic or that even his arrival brought healing—it was the boy for whom he had waited so long, for all his life, and who came into it too late, at the last sunset hour.

And as he described this figure his voice rose from the darkness. A lightness seemed to come into it, a deep sound of affection lent it music as that eloquent mouth spoke of the young man, his late-come love. I trembled with excitement and sympathy, but suddenly—my heart was struck as if by a hammer. For that ardent young man of whom my teacher spoke was... was... shame sprang to my cheeks... was I myself: I saw myself step forward as if out of a burning mirror, enveloped in such a radiance of undivined love that its reflection singed me. Yes, I was the young man—more and more closely I recognized myself, my urgent enthusiasm, my fanatical desire to be close to him, the ecstasy of yearning for which the intellect was not enough, I was the foolish, wild boy who, unaware of his power, had roused the burgeoning seeds of creativity once again in the withdrawn scholar, had once again inflamed the torch of Eros in his soul as its weary flame burned low. In amazement I now realized what I, who had felt so timid, meant to him, it was my headlong impetuosity that he loved as the most sacrosanct surprise of his old age—and with a shudder I also saw how powerfully his will had fought with me: for from me of all people, whom he loved purely, he did not want to experience rejection and contempt, the horror of insulted physicality, or see this last grace granted by cruel Fortune made a lustful plaything for the senses. That was why he resisted my persistence so firmly, poured sudden cold water ironically over my overflowing emotions, sharply added a note of conventional rigour to soft and friendly conversations, restrained the hand reaching tenderly out—for my sake alone he forced himself to all the brusque behaviour meant to sober me up and preserve him, conduct which had distressed my mind for weeks. The confused devastation of the night when, in the dream world of his overpowered senses, he had climbed the creaking stair to save himself and our friendship with those hurtful remarks was cruelly clear to me now. And shuddering, gripped, moved as if in a fever, overflowing with pity, I understood how he had suffered for my sake, how heroically he had controlled himself for me.

That voice in the darkness, ah, that voice in the darkness, how I felt it penetrate my inmost breast! There was a note in it such as I had never heard before and have never heard since, a note drawn from depths that the average life never plumbs. A man speaks thus only once in his life to another, to fall silent then for ever, as in the legend of the swan which is said to be capable of raising its hoarse voice in song only once, when it is dying. And I received that fervent, ardently urgent voice pressing on with its tale into me with a shuddering and painful sensation, as a woman takes a man into herself.

Then, suddenly, the voice fell silent, and there was nothing but darkness between us. I knew he was close to me. I had only to lift my hand and reach out to touch him. And I felt a powerful urge to comfort the suffering man.

But then he made a movement. The light came on. Tired, old and tormented, a figure rose from his chair—an exhausted old man slowly approached me. "Goodbye, Roland—not another word between us now! I am glad you came—and we must both be glad that you are going... goodbye. And—let me kiss you as we say farewell."

As if impelled by some magic power I stumbled towards him. That smouldering light, usually hidden as if by drifting mists, was now glowing openly in his eyes; burning flames rose from them. He drew me close, his lips pressed mine thirstily, nervously, and with a trembling convulsion he held my body close to his.

It was a kiss such as I have never received from a woman, a kiss as wild and desperate as a deathly cry. The trembling of his body passed into me. I shuddered, in the strange grip of a terrible sensation—responding with my soul, yet deeply alarmed by the defensive reaction of my body when touched by a man—I responded with an eerie confusion of feeling which stretched those few seconds out into a dizzying length of time.

Then he let go of me—with a sudden movement as if a body were being violently torn apart—turned with difficulty and threw himself into his chair, his back to me. Perfectly rigid, he leaned forward into the empty air for a few moments. But gradually his head became too heavy, he bent it first more wearily, more dully, and then his brow, like something too weighty swaying for a while and then suddenly falling, dropped to the desktop with a hollow, dry sound.

Infinite waves of pity surged through me. Involuntarily I stepped closer. But then, suddenly, he straightened his bent spine, and as he turned back his hoarse voice, dull and admonitory, groaned from the cup of his clenched hands: "Go away! Go away! Don't... don't come near me... for God's sake, for both our sakes, go now, go!"

I understood. And I retreated, shuddering; I left that beloved room like a man in flight.

I NEVER SAW HIM AGAIN. I never received any letter or message. His work was never published, his name is forgotten; no one else knows anything about him, only I alone. But even today, as once I did when I was a boy still unsure of myself, I feel that I have more to thank him for than my mother and father before him or my wife and children after him. I have never loved anyone more.

JOURNEY
INTO THE PAST

"THERE YOU ARE!" He went to meet her with arms outstretched, almost flung wide. "There you are," he repeated, his voice climbing the scale from surprise to delight ever more clearly, while his tender glance lingered on her beloved form. "I was almost afraid you wouldn't come!"

"Do you really have so little faith in me?" But only her lips playfully uttered this mild reproach, smiling. Her blue eyes lit up, shining with confidence.

"No, not that, I never doubted that—what in this world can be relied on more than your word? But think how foolish I was—suddenly this afternoon, entirely unexpectedly, I can't think why, I felt a spasm of senseless fear. I was afraid something could have happened to you. I wanted to send you a telegram, I wanted to go to you, and just now, when the hands of the clock moved on and still I didn't see you, I was horribly afraid we might miss each other yet again. But thank God, you're here now—"

"Yes, I'm here," she smiled, and once more a star shone brightly from the depths of those blue eyes. "I'm here and I'm ready. Shall we go?"

"Yes, let's go," his lips automatically echoed her. But his motionless body did not move a step, again and again his loving gaze lingered on her incredible presence. Above them, to right and left, the railway tracks of Frankfurt Central Station clanged and clanked with the noise of iron and glass, shrill whistling cut through the tumult in the smoky concourse, twenty boards imperiously displayed different departure and arrival times, complete with the hours and the minutes, while in the maelstrom of the busy crowd he felt that she was the only person really present, removed from time and space in a strange trance of passionate bemusement. In the end she had to remind him, "It's high time we left, Ludwig, we haven't bought tickets yet." Only then did his fixed gaze move away from her, and he took her arm with tender reverence.

The evening express to Heidelberg was unusually full. Disappointed in their expectation that first-class tickets would get them a compartment to themselves, after looking around in vain they finally chose one occupied only by a single grey-haired gentleman leaning back in a corner, half asleep. They were already pleasurably looking forward to an intimate conversation when, shortly before the whistle blew for the train to leave, three more gentlemen strode into the compartment, out of breath and carrying bulging briefcases. The three newcomers were obviously lawyers, in such a state of animation over a trial which had just ended that their lively discussion entirely ruled out the chance of any further conversation, so the couple resigned themselves to sitting opposite one another without saying a word. Only when one of them looked up did he or she see, in the uncertain shade cast like a dark cloud by the lamp, the other's tender glance lovingly looking that way.

With a slight jolt, the train began to move. The rattling of the wheels drowned out the legal conversation, muting it to mere noise. But then, gradually, the jolting and rattling turned to a rhythmic swaying, like a steel cradle rocking the couple into dreams. And while the rattling wheels invisible below them rolled onward, into a future that each of them imagined differently, the thoughts of both returned in reverie to the past.

They had recently met again after an interval of more than nine years. Separated all that time by unimaginable distance, they now felt this first silent intimacy with redoubled force. Dear God, how long and how far apart they had been—nine years and four thousand days had passed between then and this day, this night! How much time, how much lost time, and yet in the space of a second a single thought took him back to the very beginning. What had it been like? He remembered every detail; he had first entered her house as a young man of twenty-three, the curve of his lips covered by the soft down of a young beard. Struggling free early from a childhood of humiliating poverty, growing up as the recipient of free meals provided by charity, he had made his way by giving private tuition, and was embittered before his time by deprivation and the meagre living that was all he earned. Scraping together pennies during his day's work to buy books, studying by night with weary, over-strained nerves, he had completed his studies of chemistry with distinction and, equipped with his professor's special recommendation, he had gone to see the famous industrialist G, distinguished by the honorary title of Privy Councillor and director of the big factory in Frankfurt-am-Main. There he was initially given menial tasks to perform in the laboratory, but soon the Councillor became aware of the serious tenacity of this young man, who immersed himself in his work with all the pent-up force of single-minded determination, and he began taking a particular interest in him. By way of testing his new assistant he gave him increasingly responsible work, and the young man, seeing the possibility of escaping from the dismal prison of poverty, eagerly seized his chance. The more work he was given, the more energetically he tackled it, so that in a very short time he rose from being one of dozens of assistants to becoming his employer's right-hand man, trusted to conduct secret experiments, his "young friend", as the Councillor benevolently liked to call him. For although the young man did not know it, a probing mind inside the private door of the director's office was assessing his suitability for higher things, and while the ambitious assistant thought he was merely mastering his daily work in a mood of furious energy, his almost invisible employer had him marked out for a great future. For some years now the ageing Councillor, who was often kept at home and sometimes even in bed by his very painful sciatica, had been looking for a totally reliable and intellectually well-qualified private secretary, a man to whom he could turn for discussion of the firm's most confidential patents, as well as those experiments that had to be made with all the requisite discretion. And at last he seemed to have found him. One day he put an unexpected proposition to the startled young man: how would he like to give up the furnished room he rented in the suburbs, and take up residence in Councillor G's spacious villa, where he would be closer to hand for his employer? The young man was surprised by this proposition, coming as it did out of the blue, but the Councillor was even more surprised when, after a day spent thinking it over, the young man firmly declined the honour of his employer's offer, rather clumsily hiding his outright refusal behind thin excuses. Eminent scientist as the Councillor was in his own field, he did not have enough psychological experience to guess the true reason for this refusal, and the defiant young man may not even have acknowledged it to himself. It was, in fact, a kind of perverted pride, the painful sense of shame left by a childhood spent in dire poverty. Coming to adulthood as a private tutor in the distastefully ostentatious houses of the *nouveaux riches*, feeling that he was a nameless hybrid being somewhere between a servant and a companion, part and yet not part of the household, an ornamental item like the magnolias on the table, placed there and then cleared away again as required, he found himself brimming over with hatred for his employers and the sphere in which they lived, the heavy, ponderous furniture, the lavishly decorated rooms, the over-rich meals, all the wealth that he shared only on sufferance. He had gone through much in those houses: the hurtful remarks of impertinent children; the even more hurtful pity of the lady of the house when she handed him a few banknotes at the end of the month; the ironic, mocking looks of the maids, who were always ready to be cruel to the upper servants, when he moved into a new house with his plain wooden trunk and had to hang his only suit and put away his grey, darned underwear, that infallible sign of poverty, in a wardrobe that was not his own. No, never again, he had sworn to himself, he would never live in a strange house again, never go back to riches until they belonged to him, never again let his neediness show, or allow presents tactlessly given to hurt his feelings. Never, never again. Outwardly his title of *Doctor*, cheap but impenetrable armour, made up for his low social status, and at the office his fine achievements disguised the still sore and festering wounds of his youth, when he had felt ashamed of his poverty and of taking charity. So no, he was not going to sell the handful of freedom he now had, his jealously guarded privacy, not for any sum of money. And he declined the flattering invitation, even at the risk of wrecking his career, with excuses and evasions.

Soon, however, unforeseen circumstances left him no choice. The Councillor's state of health deteriorated so much that he had to spend a long time bedridden, and could not even keep in touch with his office by telephone. The presence of a private secretary now became an urgent necessity and finally, if the young man did not want to lose his job, he could no longer resist his employer's repeated and pressing requests. God knows, he thought, the move to the villa had been difficult for him; he still clearly remembered the day when he first rang the bell of the grand house, which was rather in the old Franconian style, in the Bockenheimer Landstrasse The evening before, so that his poverty would not be too obvious, he had hastily bought new underwear, a reasonably good black suit and new shoes, spending his savings on them—and those savings were meagre, for on his salary, which was not high, he was also keeping an old mother and two sisters in a remote provincial town. And this time a hired man delivered the ugly trunk containing his earthly goods ahead of him—the trunk that he hated because of all the memories it brought back. All the same, discomfort rose like some thick obstruction in his throat when a white-gloved servant formally opened the door to him, and even in the front hall he met with the satiated, self-satisfied atmosphere of wealth. Deep-piled carpets that softly swallowed up his footsteps were waiting, tapestries hung on the walls even in the hall, demanding solemn study, there were carved wooden doors with heavy bronze handles, clearly not intended to be touched by a visitor's own hand but opened by a respectfully bowing servant. In his defiantly bitter mood, he found all this oppressive. It was both heady and unwelcome. And when the servant showed him into the guest-room with its three windows, the place intended as his permanent residence, his sense of being an intruder who was out of place here gained the upper hand. Yesterday he had been living in a draughty little fourth-floor back room, with a wooden bedstead and a tin basin to wash in, and now he was supposed to make himself at home here, where every item of the furnishings seemed boldly opulent, aware of its monetary value, and looked back at him with scorn as a man who was merely tolerated here. All he had brought with him, even he himself in his own clothes, shrank to miserable proportions in this spacious, well-lit room. His one coat, ridiculously occupying the big, wide wardrobe, looked like a hanged man; his few washing things and his shabby shaving kit lay on the roomy, marble-tiled wash-stand like something he had coughed up or a tool carelessly left there by a workman; and instinctively he threw a shawl over the hard, ugly wooden trunk, envying it for its ability to lie in hiding here, while he himself stood inside these four walls like a burglar caught in the act. In vain he tried to counter his ashamed, angry sense of being nothing by reminding himself that he had been specifically asked for, pressingly invited to come. But the comfortable solidity of the items around him kept demolishing his arguments. He felt small again, insignificant, of no account in the face of this ostentatious, magnificent world of money, servants, flunkeys and other hangers-on, human furniture that had been bought and could be lent out. It was as if his own nature had been stolen from him. And now, when the servant tapped lightly at the door and appeared, his face frozen and his bearing stiff, to announce that the lady of the house had sent to ask if the doctor would call on her, he felt, as he hesitantly followed the man through the suite of rooms, that for the first time in years his stature was shrinking, his shoulders already stooping into an obsequious bow, and after a gap of years the uncertainty and confusion he had known as a boy revived in him.

However, no sooner had he approached her for the first time than he felt an agreeable sensation as his inner tension relaxed, and even before, as he straightened his back after bowing to her, his eyes took in the face and figure of the woman speaking to him, her words had come irresistibly to his ears. Those first words were "Thank you", spoken in so frank and natural a tone that they dispersed the dark clouds of ill humour hanging over him and went to his heart as he heard them. "Thank you very much, doctor," she said, cordially offering him her hand, "for accepting my husband's invitation in the end. I hope I shall soon be able to show you how extremely grateful to you I myself am. It may not have been easy for you; a man doesn't readily give up his freedom, but perhaps it will reassure you to know that you have placed two people deeply in your debt. For my part, I will do all I can to make you feel that this house is your home."

Something inside him pricked up its ears. How did she know that he had been unwilling to give up his freedom, how was it that her first words went straight to the festering, scarred, sensitive part of his nature, straight to the seat of his nervous terror of losing his independence to become only a hired servant, living here on sufferance? How had she managed to brush all such thoughts of his aside with that first gesture of her hand? Instinctively he looked up at her, and only now was he aware of a warm, sympathetic glance confidently waiting for him to return it.

There was something serenely gentle, reassuring, cheerfully confident about that face. Her pure brow, still youthfully smooth, radiated clarity, and above it the demurely matronly style in which she parted her hair seemed almost too old for her. Her hair itself was a dark mass falling in deep waves, while the dress around her shapely shoulders and coming up to her throat was also dark, making the calm light in her face seem all the brighter. She resembled a bourgeois Madonna, a little like a nun in her high-necked dress, and there was a maternal kindness in all her movements. Now she gracefully came a step closer, her smile anticipating the thanks on his own faltering lips. "Just one request, my first, and at our first meeting, too. I know that when people who haven't been acquainted for very long are living in the same house, that's always a problem, and there's only one way of dealing with it—honesty. So please, if you feel ill at ease here in any way, if any kind of situation or arrangement troubles you, do tell me about it freely. You are my husband's private secretary, I am his wife, we are linked by that double duty, so please let us be honest with one another."

He took her hand, and the pact was sealed. From that first moment he felt at home in the house. The magnificence of the rooms was no longer a hostile threat to him, indeed on the contrary, he immediately saw it as the essential setting for the elegant distinction that, in this house, muted and made harmonious all that seemed inimical, confused and contradictory outside it. But only gradually did he come to realize how exquisite artistic taste made mere financial value subject to a higher order here, and how that muted rhythm of existence was instinctively becoming part of his own life and his own conversation. He felt curiously reassured—all keen, vehement, passionate emotions became devoid of malice and edginess. It was as if the deep carpets, the tapestries on the walls, the coloured shutters absorbed the brightness and noise of the street, and at the same time he felt that this sense of order did not arise spontaneously, but derived from the presence of the quietly spoken woman whose smile was always so kindly. And the following weeks and months made him pleasantly aware of what he had felt, as if by magic, in those first minutes. With a fine sense of tact, she gradually and without making him feel any compulsion drew him into the inner life of this house. Sheltered but not guarded, he sensed attentive sympathy bent on him as if at a distance; any little wishes of his were granted almost as soon as he had expressed them, and granted so discreetly, as if by household elves, that they made explicit thanks impossible. When he had been leafing through a portfolio of valuable engravings one evening and particularly admired one of them—it happened to be Rembrandt's *Faust*—he found a framed reproduction hanging over his desk two days later. If he mentioned that a friend had recommended a certain book, there would be a copy on his bookshelves next day. His room was adapting, as if unconsciously, to his wishes and habits; often he did not notice exactly what details had changed at first, but just felt that the place was more comfortable, warmer, brighter, until he realized, say, that the embroidered Oriental coverlet he had admired in a shop window was covering the ottoman, or the light now shone through a raspberry-coloured silk shade. He liked the atmosphere here better and better for its own sake, and was quite unwilling to leave the house, where he had also become a close friend of a boy of eleven, and greatly enjoyed accompanying him and his mother to the theatre or to concerts. Without his realizing it, all that he did outside his working hours was bathed in the mild moonlight of her calm presence.

From that first meeting he had loved this woman, but passionately as his feelings surged over him, following him even into his dreams, the crucial factor that would shake him to the core was still lacking—his conscious realization that what, denying his true feelings, he still called admiration, respect and devotion was in fact love—a burning, unbounded, absolute and passionate love. Some kind of servile instinct in him forcibly suppressed that realization; she seemed so distant, too far away, too high above him, a radiant woman surrounded by a circle of stars, armoured by her wealth and by all that he had ever known of women before. It would have seemed blasphemous to think of her as a sexual being, subject to the same laws of the blood as the few other women who had come his way during his youth spent in servitude: the maidservant at the manor house who, just once, had opened her bedroom door to the tutor, curious to see if a man who had studied at university did it the same way as the coachman and the farm labourer; the seamstress he had met in the dim light of the street lamps on his way home. No, this was different. She shone down from another sphere, beyond desire, pure and inviolable, and even in his most passionate dreams he did not venture so far as to undress her. In boyish confusion, he loved the fragrance of her presence, appreciating all her movements as if they were music, glad of her confidence in him and always fearing to show her any of the overwhelming emotion that stirred within him, an emotion still without a name, but long since fully formed and glowing in its place of concealment.

But love truly becomes love only when, no longer an embryo developing painfully in the darkness of the body, it ventures to confess itself with lips and breath. However hard it tries to remain a chrysalis, a time comes when the intricate tissue of the cocoon tears, and out it falls, dropping from the heights to the farthest depths, falling with redoubled force into the startled heart. That happened quite late, in the second year of his life as one of the household.

One Sunday the Councillor had asked him to come into his study, and the fact that, unusually for him, he closed the door behind them after a quick greeting, then calling through on the house telephone to say they were not to be disturbed, in itself strongly suggested that something special was about to be communicated. The old man offered him a cigar and lit it with ceremony, as if to gain time before launching into a speech that he had obviously thought out carefully in advance. He began by thanking his assistant at length for his services. In every way, said the Councillor, he had even exceeded his own confident expectations and borne out his personal liking for him; he, the Councillor, had never had cause to regret entrusting even his most intimate business affairs to a man he had known for so short a time. Well, he went on, yesterday important news from overseas had reached the company, and he did not hesitate to tell his assistant at once—the new chemical process, with which he was familiar, called for considerable amounts of certain ores, and the Councillor had just been informed by telegram that large deposits of the metals concerned had been found in Mexico. Swift action was vital if they were to be acquired for the company, and their mining and exploitation must be organized on the spot before any American companies seized this great opportunity. That in turn called for a reliable but young and energetic man. To him personally, said the Councillor, it was a painful blow to deprive himself of his trusted and reliable assistant, but when the board of directors met he had thought it his duty to suggest him as the best and indeed the only suitable man for the job. He would feel himself compensated by knowing that he could guarantee him a brilliant future. In the two years it would take to set up the business in Mexico, the young man could not only build up a small fortune for himself, thanks to the large remuneration he would receive, he could also look forward to holding a senior position in the company on his return. "Indeed," concluded the Councillor, spreading his hands in a congratulatory gesture, "I feel as if I saw you sitting here in my place some day, carrying through to its end the work on which, old as I now am, I embarked three decades ago."

Such a proposition, coming suddenly out of a clear sky—how could it not go to an ambitious man's head? There at last was the door, flung wide as if by the blast of an explosion, showing him the way out of the prison of poverty, the lightless world of service and obedience, away from the constantly obsequious attitude of a man forced to act and think with humility. He gazed avidly at the papers and telegrams before him, seeing hieroglyphics gradually formed into the imposing if still vague contours of this mighty plan. Numbers suddenly came cascading down on him, thousands, hundreds of thousands, millions to be managed, accounted for, acquired, the fiery atmosphere of commanding power in which, dazed and with his heart beating fast, he suddenly rose from his dull, subservient sphere of life as if in a dreamlike balloon. And over and above all this, it was not just money on offer, not just business deals and ventures, a game played for high stakes, responsibility—no, something much more alluring tempted him. Here was the chance to fashion events, to be a pioneer. A great task lay ahead, the creative occupation of bringing ore out of the mountains where it had been slumbering for thousands of years in the mindless sleep of stone, of driving galleries into that stone, building towns, seeing houses rise up, roads spread out, putting mechanical diggers to work, and cranes circling in the air. Behind the mere framework of calculations a wealth of fantastic yet vivid images began to form—farmsteads, farmhouses, factories, warehouses, a new part of the world of men where as yet there was nothing, and it would be for him to set it up, directing and regulating operations. Sea air, spiced by the intoxication of all that is far distant, suddenly entered the small, comfortably upholstered study; figures stacked up into a fantastic sum. And in an ever more heated frenzy of exhilaration that gave wings to every decision, he had it all summarized in broad outline, and the purely practical details were agreed. A cheque for a sum he could never have expected was suddenly crackling crisply in his hand, and after the agreement had been reiterated, it was decided that he would leave on the next Southern Line steamer in ten days' time. Then he had left the Councillor's study, still heated by the swirl of figures, reeling at the idea of the possibilities that had been conjured up, and once outside the door he stood staring wildly around him for a moment, wondering if the entire conversation could have been a phantasmagoria conjured up by wishful thinking. The space of a wing-beat had raised him from the depths into the sparkling sphere of fulfilment; his blood was still in such turmoil after so stormy an ascent that he had to shut his eyes for a moment. He closed them as one might take a deep breath, simply to be in control again, sensing his inner being more powerfully and as if separated from himself. This state of mind lasted for a minute, but then, as he looked up again refreshed, and his eyes wandered around the familiar room outside the study, they fell as if by chance on a picture hanging over the large chest, and lingered there. It was her portrait. Her picture looked back at him with lips gently closed, curving in a calm smile that also seemed to have a deeper meaning, as if it had understood every word of what was going on inside him. And then, in that second, an idea that he had entirely overlooked until now flashed through his mind—if he took up the position offered to him, it meant leaving this house. My God, he said to himself, leaving *her*. Like a knife, the thought cut through the proudly swelling sail of his delight. And in that one second of uncontrolled surprise the whole artificially piled edifice of his imaginings collapsed, crushing his heart, and with a sudden painful jolt of the heart muscle he felt how painful, how almost deadly the idea of doing without her was to him. Leaving her, oh God, leaving her—how could he ever have contemplated it, how could he have made that decision as if he still belonged to himself, as if he were not held here, in her presence, by all the bonds of his emotions, their deepest roots? The idea broke out violently, it was elemental, a quivering physical pain, a blow struck through his whole body from the top of his skull to the bottom of his heart, a lightning bolt tearing across the night sky and illuminating everything. And now, in that blinding light, it was impossible not to realize that every nerve and fibre of his being was flowering with love for her, his dear one. No sooner had he silently uttered the magical word *love* than countless little associations and memories shot sparkling through his mind, with the extraordinary speed that only the utmost alarm can conjure up. Every one of them cast bright light on his feelings, on all the little details that he had never before ventured to admit to himself or understand. And only at this point did he realize how utterly he had been in thrall to her, and for how long—many months now.

Hadn't it been during Easter week this year, when she went to stay with her family for three days, that he had paced restlessly from room to room as if lost, unable to read a book, his mind in turmoil, although he could not say why? And on the night when she was to return, hadn't he stayed up until one in the morning to hear her footsteps? Hadn't his nervous impatience kept sending him downstairs too soon, to see if the car wasn't coming yet? He remembered how, when his hand accidentally brushed hers at the theatre, a frisson ran from the touch of their fingers to the back of his neck. Now a hundred such little flashes of memory, trifles of which he had hardly been aware, raced stormily into his mind, into his blood, as if every dam had been breached, and they all made straight for his heart and came together there. Instinctively, he pressed his hand to his chest, where that heart was beating so violently, and now there was no help for it, he could no longer keep from admitting what his diffident and respectful instinct had so carefully managed to obscure for so long—he could not live now away from her presence. To be without that mild light shining on his way for two years, two months, even just two weeks, to enjoy no more of their pleasant conversations in the evenings—no, it was impossible to bear such a thought. And what had filled him with pride only ten minutes earlier, the mission to Mexico, the thought of his rise to have command of creative power, had shrunk within a second, had burst like a sparkling soap bubble. All that it meant now was distance, absence, a dungeon, banishment and exile, annihilation, a deprivation that he could not survive. No, it was impossible—his hand was already moving to the door handle again, he was on the point of going back into the study to tell the Councillor that he wouldn't do it, to say he felt unworthy of the mission, he would rather stay here. But anxiety spoke up, warning him: not now! He must not prematurely betray a secret that was only just revealing itself to him. And he wearily withdrew his fevered hand from the cool metal.

Once again he looked at her picture—the glance of her eyes seemed to be gazing ever deeper into him, but he could not see the smile around her mouth any more. Instead, he thought, she looked gravely, almost sadly out of the picture, as if to say, "You wanted to forget me." He couldn't bear that painted yet living gaze. He stumbled to his room, sinking on the bed with a strange sensation of horror almost like fainting, but curiously pervaded by a mysterious sweetness. Feverishly, he thought back to all that had happened to him in this house since he first arrived, and everything, even the most insignificant detail, now had a different meaning and appeared in a different light; it was all irradiated by the inner light of understanding, its weight was light as it soared up in the heated air of passion. He remembered all the kindness she had shown him. He was still surrounded by it; his eyes looked for the signs of it, he felt the things that her hand had touched, and they all had something of the joy of her presence in them. She was there in those inanimate objects; he sensed her friendly thoughts in them. And that certainty of her goodwill to him overwhelmed him with passion, yet deep below its current something in his nature still resisted, like a stone—there was something left unthought, something not yet cleared out of the way, and it had to be cleared out of the way before his emotions could flow freely. Very cautiously, he made his way towards that dark place in the depths of his emotion, he knew already what it meant, yet he dared not touch it. But the current kept driving him back to that one place, that one question. And it was this: was there not—he dared not say love, but at least liking for him on her part, shown in all those small attentive acts, a mild affection, if without passion, in the way she listened for his presence and showed concern for him? That sombre question went through him, heavy, black waves rose in his blood, breaking again and again, but they could not roll it away. If only I could think clearly, he said to himself, but his thoughts were in too much passionate turmoil, mingling with confused dreams and wishes, and pain was churned up again and again from the uttermost depths of his being. So he lay there on his bed for perhaps an hour or two hours, entirely outside himself, sensations dulled by his numbing mixture of emotions, until suddenly a gentle tapping at his door brought him back to himself. The cautious tapping of slender knuckles; he thought he recognized their touch. He jumped up and ran to the door.

There she stood before him, smiling. "Oh, doctor, why don't you come down? The bell has rung for dinner twice."

She spoke almost in high spirits, as if she took a little pleasure in catching him out in a small act of negligence. But as soon as she saw his face, with his hair clinging around it in damp strands, his dazed eyes shyly avoiding hers, she herself turned pale.

"For God's sake, what has happened to you?" she faltered, and the tone of horror in her breaking voice went through him like desire. "Nothing, nothing," he said, quickly pulling himself together. "I was deep in thought, that's all. The whole thing was too much for me, too sudden."

"What? What whole thing? Tell me!"

"Don't you know? Didn't the Councillor tell you anything about it?"

"No, nothing!" she urged him impatiently, almost driven mad by the nervous, burning, evasive expression in his eyes. "What's happened? Tell me, please tell me!"

Then he summoned up all the strength in him to look at her clearly and without blushing. "The Councillor has been kind enough to give me an important and responsible mission, and I have accepted it. In ten days' time I'm sailing for Mexico, to stay there for two years."

"Two years! Dear God!" It was a cry rather than words, as her own horror shot up from deep within her. And she put out her hands in instinctive denial. It was useless for her to try, next moment, denying the feeling that had burst out of her, for already (and just how had that happened?) he had taken the hands she so passionately reached out to fend off her fear in his own, and before they knew it their trembling bodies were both aflame. Countless hours and days of unconscious longing and thirst were quenched in an endless kiss.

He had not drawn her to him, she had not drawn him to her. they had met as if driven together by a storm, falling clasped together into a bottomless abyss of the unconscious, and sinking into it was like a sweet yet burning trance—emotions too long pent up poured out in a single second, inflamed by the magnetism of chance. Only slowly, as the lips that had clung together parted, as they were still shaken by the unreality of it all, did he look into her eyes and saw a strange light behind their tender darkness. And only then was he overwhelmed by the realization that this woman, the woman he loved, must have loved him in return for a long time, for weeks, months, years, keeping tenderly silent, glowing with maternal feeling, until a moment such as this struck through her soul. The incredible nature of the realization was intoxicating. To think that he was loved, loved by the woman he had thought beyond his reach—heaven opened up, endless and flooded with light. This was the radiant noon of his life. But at the same time it all collapsed next moment, splintering sharply. For the realization that she loved him was also a farewell.

The two of them spent the ten days until his departure in a constant state of wild, ecstatic frenzy. The sudden explosive force of the feelings they had now confessed had broken down all dams and barriers, all morality and pride. They fell on one another like animals, hot and greedy, whenever they met to snatch two stolen minutes in a dark corridor, behind a door, in a corner. Hand made its way to hand, lips to lips, the restless blood of one met its kindred blood in the other, each longed feverishly for the other, every nerve burned for the sensuous touch of foot, hand, dress, some living part of the yearning body. At the same time they had to exert self-control in the house, she to hide the love that kept blazing up in her from her husband, her son, the servants, he to remain intellectually capable of the calculations, meetings and deliberations for which he was now responsible. They could never snatch more than seconds, quivering, furtive seconds when danger lay in wait, they could fleetingly approach each other only with their hands, their lips, their eyes, a greedily stolen kiss, and each, already intoxicated, was further intoxicated by the other's hazy, sultry, smouldering presence. But it was never enough, they both felt that, never enough. So they wrote each other burning love letters, slipping ardent notes into one another's hands like schoolchildren. He found hers in the evening, under the pillow on which he could get no sleep; she in turn found his in her coat pockets, and all these notes ended in a desperate cry asking the unhappy question: how could they bear it, a sea, a world, uncounted months, uncounted weeks, two years between blood and blood, glance and glance? They thought of nothing else, they dreamed of nothing else, and neither of them had an answer to the question, only their hands, eyes and lips, the unconscious servants of their passion, moved back and forth, longing to come together, pledging inner constancy. And then those stolen moments of touching, embracing fervently behind doors drawn nearly closed, those fearful moments would overflow with lust and fear at once, in Bacchanalian frenzy.

However, although he longed for it he was never granted full possession of the beloved body that he sensed, through her unfeeling, obstructive dress, passionately moving, feeling it pressing as if hot and naked against his—he never came really close to her in that too brightly lit house, always awake and full of ears to hear them. Only on the last day, when she came to his room, already cleared, on the pretext of helping him to pack but really to say a last goodbye, and stumbled and fell against the ottoman as she swayed under the onslaught of his embrace—then, when his kisses were already burning on the curve of her breasts under the dress he had pulled up, and were greedily travelling over the hot, white skin to the place where her heart beat in response to his own as she gasped for breath, when in that moment of surrender the gift of her body was almost his, then in her passion she stammered out a last plea. "Not now! Not here! I beg you!"

And even his heated blood was still so obedient, so much in thrall to her, so respectful of the woman he had loved as a sacred being for so long, that once again he controlled his ardour and moved away as she rose, swaying, and hid her face from him. He himself turned away too and stood there, trembling and fighting with his instincts, so visibly affected by the grief of his disappointment that she knew how much his love, denied fulfilment, was suffering because of her. Then, back in command of her own feelings again, she came close and quietly comforted him. "I couldn't do it here, in my own house, in his own house. But when you come back, yes, whenever you like."

*

The train stopped with a clatter, screeching in the vice-like hold of the brake applied to it. Like a dog waking under the touch of the whip, his eyes woke from reverie, and—what a happy moment of recognition—look, there she was, his beloved who had been so far away for so long. Now she sat there, close enough for him to feel her breathing. The brim of her hat cast a little shadow on her face as she leaned back. But as if, unconsciously, she had understood that he wanted to see her face she sat up straight, and looked at him with a mild smile. "Darmstadt," she said, glancing out of the window. "One more station to go." He did not reply. He just sat looking at her. Time is helpless, he thought to himself, helpless in the face of our feelings. Nine years have passed, and not a note in her voice is different, not a nerve in my body hears her in any other way. Nothing is lost, nothing is past and over, her presence is as much of a tender delight now as it was then.

He looked with passion at her quietly smiling mouth, which he could hardly remember kissing in the past, and then down at the white hands lying relaxed and at rest on her lap; he longed to bend and touch them with his lips, or take those quietly folded hands in his, just for a second, one second! But the talkative gentlemen sharing the compartment were already beginning to look at him curiously, and for the sake of his secret he leaned back again in silence. Once more they sat opposite one another without a sign or a word, and only their eyes met and kissed.

Outside a whistle blew, the train began to roll out of the station once more, and the swinging, swaying monotony of that steel cradle rocked him back into his memories. Ah, the dark, endless years between then and now, a grey sea between shore and shore, between heart and heart! What had it been like? There was a memory that he did not want to touch, he did not wish to recollect the moment of their last goodbye, the moment on the station platform in the city where, today, he had been waiting for her with his heart wide open. No, away with it, it was over and not to be thought of any more, it was too terrible. His thoughts flew back, back again; another landscape, another time opened up in his dreams, conjured up by the rapid rhythm of the rattling wheels. He had gone to Mexico with a heart torn in two, and he managed to endure the first months there, the first terrible weeks that passed before any message from her arrived, only by cramming his head full of figures and drafted designs, by exhausting himself physically with long rides and expeditions out into the country, and what seemed endless negotiations and enquiries, but he carried them through with determination. From morning to night, he locked himself into the engine-house of the company, constantly at work hammering out numbers, talking, writing all the time, only to hear his inner voice desperately crying out one name, hers. He numbed himself with work as another man might with alcohol or drugs, merely to deaden the strength of his emotions. But every evening, however tired he was, he sat down to describe on sheet after sheet of paper, writing for hour after hour, everything that he had done in the day, and by every post he sent whole bundles of these feverishly written pages to a cover address on which they had agreed, so that his distant beloved could follow his life hourly as she used to at home, and he felt her mild gaze resting on his daily work, sharing it in her mind over a thousand sea miles, over hills and horizons. The letters he received from her were his reward. Her handwriting was upright, her words calm, betraying passion but in disciplined form. They told him first, without complaint, about her daily life, and it was as if he felt her steady blue gaze bent on him, although without her smile, the faint, reassuring smile which removed all that was severe from any gravity. These letters had been food and drink to the lonely man. In his own passionate emotion, he took them with him on journeys through the plains and the mountains, he had pockets specially sewn to his saddle to protect them from sudden cloudbursts and the rivers that they had to ford on surveying expeditions. He had read those letters so often that he knew them by heart, word for word, he had unfolded them so often that the creases in the paper were wearing transparent, and certain words were blurred by kisses and tears. Sometimes, when he was alone and knew that no one was near him, he began reading them aloud in her own tone of voice, magically conjuring up the presence of his distant love. Sometimes he suddenly rose in the night when he had thought of a particular word, a sentence, a closing salutation, put on the light to find it again and to dream of the image of her hand in the written characters, moving on up from that hand to her arm, her shoulder, her head, her whole physical presence transported over land and sea. And like a man chopping trees down in the jungle, he chopped into the wild and still impenetrably menacing time ahead of him with berserk strength and frenzy, impatient to see it thinning out, to have his return in sight, his journey home, the prospect that he had imagined a thousand times of the moment when they would first embrace again. He had hung a calendar over the bed roughly knocked together for him in his quickly constructed wooden house with its corrugated iron roof in the new workers' colony, and every evening he would cross off the day he had just worked his way through—though he often impatiently crossed it off as early as midday—and he counted and re-counted the ever-diminishing black and red series of days still to be endured: four hundred and twenty, four hundred and nineteen, four hundred and eighteen days to go before they met again. For he was not counting, as other people have done since the birth of Christ, from a beginning but only up to a certain time, the time of his return. And whenever that span of time reached a round number, four hundred or three hundred and fifty or three hundred, or when it was her birthday or name-day, the day when he first saw her or the day when she first revealed her own feelings for him—on such days he always gave a kind of party for those around him, who wondered why, and in their ignorance asked questions. He gave money to the *mestizos*' dirty children and brandy to the workers, who shouted and capered around like wild brown foals, he put on his own Sunday best and had wine brought, and the finest of the canned food. A flag flew, a flame of joy, from a specially erected flagpole, and if neighbours or his assistants, feeling curious, asked what saint's day or other strange occasion he was celebrating, he only smiled and said, "Never mind that, just celebrate it with me!"

So it went on for weeks and months, a year worked its way to death and then another half a year, then there were only seven small, wretched, poor little weeks left until the day appointed for his return. In his boundless impatience he had long ago worked out how long the voyage would take, and to the astonishment of the clerks in the shipping office had booked and paid for his passage on the *Arkansas* a hundred days before she was due to leave.

Then came the disastrous day that pitilessly tore up not only his calendar but, with total indifference, the lives and thoughts of millions, leaving them in shreds. A day of disaster indeed—early in the morning, in his capacity as a surveyor, he had ridden across the sulphur-yellow plain and up into the mountains with horses and mules, taking two foremen and a party of labourers, to investigate a new drilling site where it was thought there might be magnesite. The *mestizos* hammered, dug, pounded and generally investigated the site under a pitiless sun that blazed down from overhead, and was reflected back again at a right angle from the bare rock. But like a man possessed he drove the workers on, would not allow his thirsty tongue the hundred paces it would take him to go to the quickly dug trench for water—he wanted to get back to the post office and see her letter, her words. And when they had not reached the full depth of the site on the third day, and the trial borehole was still being drilled, he was overcome by a senseless longing for her message, a thirst for her words, which deranged him so far that he decided to ride back alone all night, just to collect the letter that must surely have come in the post yesterday. He simply left the others in their tent and, accompanied only by one servant, rode along a dangerously dark bridle path all night to the railway station. But when in the morning, freezing from the icy cold of the mountain range, they finally rode their steaming horses into the little town, an unusual sight met their eyes. The few white settlers had left their work and were standing around the station in the midst of a shouting, questioning, stupidly gaping throng of *mestizos* and native Indians. It was difficult to make a way through this agitated crowd, but once they had reached the post office they found unexpected news waiting. Telegrams had come from the coast—Europe was at war, Germany against France, Austria against Russia. He refused to believe it, dug his spurs into the flanks of his stumbling horse so hard that the frightened animal reared, whinnying, and raced away to the government building, where he heard even more shattering news. It was all true, and even worse, Britain had also declared war. The seven seas were closed to Germans. An iron curtain had come down between the two continents, cutting them off from each other for an incalculable length of time.

It was useless for him to pound the table with his clenched fist in his first fury, as if to strike out at an invisible foe; millions of helpless people were now raging in the same way as the dungeon walls of their destiny closed in on them. He immediately weighed up all the possibilities of smuggling himself across to Europe by some bold and cunning means, thus checkmating Fate, but the British consul, a friend of his who happened to be present, indicated with a cautious note of warning in his voice that he personally was obliged to keep an eye on all his movements from now on. So he could comfort himself only with the hope, soon to be disappointed, as it was for millions of others, that such madness could not last long, and within a few weeks or a few months this foolish prank played by diplomats and generals left to their own devices would be over. Before long, something else was added to that thin fibre of hope, a stronger power and better able to numb his feelings—work. In cables sent by way of Sweden, his company commissioned him to prevent possible sequestration by registering his Mexican branch of it independently and running it, with a few figureheads appointed to the board, as a Mexican firm. This task called for the utmost managerial energy. Since the war itself, that imperious entrepreneur, also wanted ore from the mines, production must be speeded up and the company's work was redoubled. It required all his powers, and drowned out even the echo of any thoughts of his own. He worked with fanatical intensity for twelve or fourteen hours a day, sinking into bed in the evening worn down by the crushing weight of numbers, to sleep dreamlessly,

Yet all the same, while he thought his feelings were unchanged, his passionate inner tension gradually relaxed. It is not in human nature to live entirely on memories, and just as the plants and every living structure need nourishment from the soil and new light from the sky, if their colours are not to fade and their petals to drop, even such apparently unearthly things as dreams need a certain amount of nourishment from the senses, some tender pictorial aid, or their blood will run thin and their radiance be dimmed. And so it was with this passionate man before he even noticed it. When weeks, months, and finally a year and then a second year brought not a single message from her, not a written word, no sign, her picture gradually began to fade. Every day consumed in work made another grain or so of ash settle over her memory; it still showed through, like the red glow under the ashes in the grate, but finally the grey layer grew thicker and thicker. He still sometimes took out her letters, but the ink had faded, the words no longer went straight to his heart, and once he was shocked, looking at her photograph, to find that he could no longer remember the colour of her eyes. And it was less and less often that he picked up those once precious proofs of love, the letters that had magically given him new life, without realizing that he was tired of her eternal silence, tired of talking senselessly to a shadow that never answered. In addition the mining business, which was soon doing very well, threw him together with other people, other partners; he sought out company, friends, women. And when a trip in the third year of the war took him to the house of a prosperous German businessman in Vera Cruz, and he met the man's daughter, a quiet, blonde, home-loving girl, fear of being always alone in the middle of a world rushing headlong into hatred, war and madness overcame him. He quickly made up his mind and proposed marriage. Then came a child, a second followed, living flowers flourishing on the forgotten grave of his love. Now the circle was closed; all was busy activity outside it, inside there was domestic calm, and after four or five years he would not have known the man he once was.

But then there came a day full of stormy emotions and the sound of bells, when the telegraph wires hummed, and loud voices were raised all the streets, proclaiming in large letters the news that peace had finally been made, when the British and Americans in town celebrated the destruction of his native land with loud and inconsiderate rejoicing. On that day, revived by memories of his country, which he loved again in its time of misfortune, her figure too came back into his mind, forcing its way into his emotions. How had she lived through those years of misery and deprivation on which the newspapers here dwelt at length, and with relish, with much busy activity on the part of journalists? Had her house, his house, been spared the upheavals and looting, were her husband and her son still alive? In the middle of the night he rose from the side of his peacefully sleeping wife, put on a light, and spent five hours until dawn writing a letter that seemed as if it would never end, a letter in which he told her, soliloquizing to himself, all about his life in the last five years. After two months, when he had almost forgotten writing his own letter, the answer came—undecidedly, he weighed the large envelope in his hands. Even the familiar handwriting suggested subversion. He dared not break the seal at once, as if, like Pandora's box, this sealed letter contained something forbidden. He carried it around with him for two days in his breast pocket, and sometimes he felt his heart beating against it. But the letter, once it was opened at last, was neither obtrusively over-familiar nor cold and formal. Its calm handwriting conveyed the tender affection that he had always liked so much in her. Her husband had died at the very beginning of the war, she wrote; she hardly liked to mourn him too much, for it meant that he had been spared a great deal. He did not live to see the danger to his company, the occupation of their city, the misery of his own nation, which had become drunk on the idea of victory far too soon. She herself and her son were in good health, and she was so glad to hear good news of him, better than she could give of herself. She congratulated him on his marriage in honest and unequivocal terms; instinctively he assessed them warily, but no concealed undertone marred their clear meaning. It was all said frankly, without any ostentatious sentimental pathos, all the past seemed to be resolved in the purity of her continued sympathy, passion was transfigured as bright, crystalline friendship. He had never expected any less of her distinction of mind, yet sensing her clear, sure nature (he thought he was suddenly looking into her eyes again, grave and yet smiling in reflected kindness), sensing all that, a kind of grateful emotion overcame him. He sat down at once and wrote to her at length, and their exchange of confidences, something that he had long missed, was resumed on both sides. In this instance, the cataclysm affecting a whole world had been unable to wreak destruction.

He was now deeply grateful for the straightforward form his life had assumed. He was professionally successful, the business was prospering, at home his children were slowly growing from delicate, flower-like infancy to playful, talkative little creatures who regarded him with affection and kept him amused in the evening. And all that was left of the past, of the fiery blaze of his youth which had painfully consumed his days and nights, was a certain glow, the good, quiet light of friendship, making no demands and in no way dangerous. So two years later, when an American firm asked him to negotiate on its behalf for chemical patents in Berlin, it was a perfectly natural idea for him to think of greeting his lover of the past, now his friend, in person. As soon as he arrived in Berlin, his first request in his hotel was to be connected by telephone to her address in Frankfurt; it seemed to him symbolic that nine years later the number was still the same. A good omen, he thought, nothing has changed. Then the telephone on the table rang boldly, and suddenly he was trembling with anticipation at the idea of hearing her voice again after so many years, a voice conjured up by that ringing, reaching this place across fields and meadows, above buildings and factory chimneys, close in spite of the many miles of years and water and earth between them. And no sooner had he given his name than he suddenly heard her cry out, in amazed astonishment, "Ludwig, is that really you?" It made its way to his ears first and then, dropping lower, to his heart, which was suddenly throbbing and full of blood. All at once something had set him alight. He had difficulty in speaking, and the light weight of the receiver dangled from his hand. The clear, startled note of surprise in her voice, her cry of joy ringing out, must have touched some hidden nerve in him, for he felt the blood humming in his temples and found it hard to make out what she was saying. And without consciously intending to do so, or knowing that he would, for it was as if someone were prompting him, he promised what he had never meant to say at all—he would be coming to Frankfurt the day after tomorrow. With that, his calm was destroyed. He feverishly did what he had come to do in Berlin, travelling swiftly around by motor car to get all the negotiations successfully completed at high speed. And when, on waking next morning, he remembered his dreams of the night just past, he knew that for the first time in years—the first time for four years—he had dreamed of her again.

Two days later, as he approached her house in the morning after a freezing night, having sent a telegram to announce his arrival, he suddenly thought, looking down at his own feet: this is not the way I walk, not the way I walk back across the ocean, going straight ahead with a confident, determined stride. Why am I walking like the shy, diffident twenty-three-year-old of the old days, anxiously dusting down his shabby coat again and again with shaking fingers, putting on his new gloves before ringing the doorbell? Why is my heart suddenly beating so fast, why do I feel self-conscious? In the old days I had secret presentiments of whatever was waiting to pounce on me beyond that copper-embossed door, and whether it would be good or bad. But why do I bow my head now, why does my rising uneasiness do away with all my firmness and certainty? He tried to remember who he was now, but in vain; he thought of his wife, his children, his house, his company, the foreign land where he lived. But all of that had faded, as if carried away by a ghostly mist; he felt alone, a petitioner once more, like the clumsy boy of the past in her presence. And the shaking hand that he now placed on the metal door handle was hot.

But as soon as he was inside the house that sense of being a stranger was gone, for the old manservant, now thin and desiccated, almost had tears in his eyes. "Doctor, it's you!" he kept faltering, with a sob in his voice. He was much moved. Odysseus, he thought, the household dogs recognize you, will the mistress of the house know you again too? But she was already opening the inner door, and came towards him with her hands held out. For a moment, as their hands joined, they looked at each other. It was a brief yet magically satisfying moment of comparison, examination, assessment, ardent memory and diffident delight, a moment when they happily exchanged covert glances again. Only then was the question resolved in a smile, and their glances became a familiar greeting. Yes, she was still the same, a little older, to be sure, on the left-hand side of her head silver threads ran through her hair, which she still wore parted in the middle, that glint of silver made her mild, friendly expression a little graver and more composed than before, and he felt the thirst of endless years quenched as he drank in the voice that now spoke to him, so intimate with its soft touch of regional accent. "Oh," she said, "how nice of you to come."

The sound was as pure and free as a tuning fork striking exactly the right note, and it set the tone for their entire conversation. Questions and anecdotes passed back and forth, like a pianist's right and left hands moving over the keyboard, clear and musical as they responded to one another. All the pent-up, smouldering awkwardness was dispersed by her presence and her first words. As long as she spoke, every thought obeyed her. But as soon as she fell silent, her eyelids lowered in thought, veiling her eyes, a question shot through his mind as swiftly as a shadow: "Aren't those the lips I kissed?" And when she was called away to the telephone, leaving him alone in the room for a moment, the past came pressing stormily in on him from all sides. As long as her lucid presence ruled, that uncertain voice inside him had been subdued, but now every chair, every picture spoke to him, almost inaudibly whispering quiet words heard by him alone. I lived in this house, he could not help thinking, something of me lingers here, something of those years, the whole of me is not yet at home across the ocean, and I still do not live entirely in my own world. Then she came back into the room, cheerful as ever, and once again such ideas retreated into the background. "You will stay to lunch, won't you, Ludwig?" she said, taking it for granted. And he did stay, he stayed all day, and in conversation they looked back together at the past years. Only now that he was speaking of them did they truly seem real to him. And when he finally left, kissing her gentle maternal hand, and the door had closed behind him, he felt as if he had never been away.

That night, however, alone in the strange hotel room, with only the ticking of the clock beside him and his heart beating even harder in his breast, that sense of peace and calm was gone. He couldn't sleep, he rose, put on the light, switched it off again and lay there awake. He kept thinking of her lips, and how he had known them in a way very different from today's gently conversing familiarity. And suddenly he knew that all the casual talk between them had been pretence, that there was something still unrelieved and unresolved in their relationship, and the friendliness was merely an artificial mask over a nervous face, fitfully working in the throes of restless passion. He had imagined another kind of reunion with her for too long, on too many nights by the camp fire in his hut beyond the seas, for too many years and too many days—he had envisaged the two of them falling into each other's arms in a burning embrace, the final surrender, a dress slipping to the ground—he had imagined it too long for this friendliness, this courteous talk as they sounded each other out to ring entirely true. Actor and actress, he said to himself, we are both putting on a performance but neither of us is deceived. She is surely sleeping as little as I am tonight, he thought.

And when he went to see her next morning, she must have seen his loss of self-control and noticed his agitation and the evasive expression on his face at once, for the first thing she herself said was confused, and even later she could not find her way back to yesterday's easy, composed tone. Today their conversation was a matter of fits and starts, with pauses and awkward moments that had to be overcome with a forceful effort. Something or other stood between them, and questions and answers, invisibly coming up against it, ran into a dead end like bats flying into a wall. They both felt that they were skirting some other subject as they talked, and finally the conversation died down, reeling from this cautious circling of their words. He realized it in time and, when she invited him to stay for lunch again, invented an urgent appointment in the city.

She said she was very sorry, and indeed the shy warmth of her heart did now venture back into her voice. But she did not seriously try to keep him there. As she accompanied him out, their eyes nervously avoided each other. Something was crackling along their nerves, again and again conversation stumbled over the invisible obstacle that went with them from room to room, from word to word, and that now, growing stronger, took their breath away. So it was a relief when he was at the door, his coat already on. But all of a sudden, making up his mind, he turned back. "In fact there *is* something else I wanted to ask you before I go."

"You want to ask me something? By all means!" she smiled, radiant once again with the joy of being able to fulfil a wish of his.

"It may be foolish," he said, his glance diffident, "but I know that you'll understand. I would very much like to see my room again, the room where I lived for two years. All this time I've been down in the reception rooms that you keep for visitors, and if I leave like this, you see, I wouldn't feel I had been in my former home. As a man grows older he goes in search of his own youth, taking silly pleasure in little memories."

"You, grow older, Ludwig?" she replied almost light-heartedly. "I never thought you were so vain! Look at me, look at this grey streak in my hair. You're only a boy by comparison with me, and you talk of growing older already. You must allow me to take precedence there! But how forgetful of me not to have taken you straight to your room, for that's what it still is. You will find nothing changed; nothing ever changes in this house."

"I hope that includes you," he said, trying to make a joke of it, but when she looked at him his expression instinctively changed to one of tender warmth.

She blushed slightly. "People may grow old, but they remain the same."

They went up to his old room. Even as they entered it there was a slight awkwardness, for she stood aside after opening the door to let him in, and as each of them courteously drew back at the same time to make way for the other, their shoulders briefly collided in the doorway. Both instinctively retreated, but even this fleeting physical contact was enough to embarrass them. She said nothing, but was overcome by a paralysing self-consciousness which was doubly perceptible in the silent, empty room. Nervously, she hurried over to the cords at the windows and pulled up the curtains, to let more light fall on the dark furnishings that seemed to be crouching there. But no sooner had bright light come suddenly rushing in than it was as if all those items of furniture suddenly had eyes and were stirring restlessly in alarm. Everything stood out in a significant way, speaking urgently of some memory. Here was the wardrobe that her attentive hand had always secretly kept in order for him, there were the bookshelves to which an addition was made when he had uttered a fleeting wish, there—speaking in yet sultrier tones—was the bed, where countless dreams of her, he knew, lay hidden under the bedspread. There in the corner—and this memory was burning hot as it came back to his mind—there was the ottoman where she had freed herself from him that last time. Inflamed by the passion now rekindled and blazing up, he saw signs and messages everywhere, left there by the woman now standing beside him, quietly breathing, compellingly strange, her eyes turned away and inscrutable. And the dense silence of the years, lying heavily as if slumped in the room, took alarm at their human presence and now assumed powerful proportions, settling on their lungs and troubled hearts like the blast of an explosion. Something had to be said, something must overcome that silence to keep it from overwhelming them—they both felt it. It was she, suddenly turning, who broke the silence.

"Everything is just as it used to be, don't you think?" she began, determined to say something innocent and casual, although her voice was husky and shook a little. However he did not echo her friendly, conversational tone, but gritted his teeth.

"Oh yes, everything." Sudden inner rage forced the words abruptly and bitterly out of his mouth. "Everything is as it used to be except for us, except for us!"

The words cut into her. Alarmed, she turned again.

"What do you mean, Ludwig?" But she did not meet his gaze, for his eyes were not seeking hers now but staring, silent and blazing, at her lips, the lips he had not touched for so many years, although once, moist on the inside like a fruit, they had burned against his own burning lips. In her embarrassment she understood the sensuality of his gaze, and a blush covered her face, mysteriously rejuvenating her, so that she looked to him just as she had looked in this same room when he was about to leave. Once again she tried to fend off that dangerous gaze drawing her in, intentionally misunderstanding what could not be mistaken.

"What do you mean, Ludwig?" she repeated, but it was more of a plea for him not to tell her than a question requiring an answer.

Then, with a firm, determined look, he fixed his eyes on hers with masculine strength. "You pretend not to understand me, but I know you do. Do you remember this room—and do you remember what you promised me here… when I came back?"

Her shoulders were shaking as she still tried to fend him off. "No, don't say it, Ludwig… this is all old history, let's not touch on it. Where are those times now?"

"In us," he replied firmly, "in what we want. I have waited nine years, keeping grimly silent, but I haven't forgotten. And I am asking you, do you still remember?"

"Yes." She looked at him more steadily now. "I have not forgotten either."

"And will you—" he had to take a deep breath, to give force to what he as about to say—"will you keep your promise?"

The colour came to her face again, surging up to her hairline. She moved towards him, as if to placate him. "Ludwig, do think! You said you haven't forgotten anything—so don't forget, I am almost an old woman now. When a woman's hair turns grey she has no more to wish for, no more to give. I beg you, let the past rest."

But a great desire now came over him to be hard and determined. "You are trying to avoid me," he said inexorably, "but I have waited too long. I ask you, do you remember your promise?"

Her voice faltered with every word she spoke. "Why do you ask me? There's no point in my saying this to you now, now that it's all too late. But if you insist, I will answer you. I could never have denied you anything, I was always yours from the day when I first met you."

He looked at her—how honest she was even in her confusion, how truthful and straightforward, showing no cowardice, making no excuses, his steadfast beloved, always the same, preserving her dignity so wonderfully at every moment, both reserved and candid. Instinctively he stepped towards her, but as soon as she saw his impetuous movement she warded him off.

"Come along now, Ludwig, come   let's not stay here, let's go downstairs. It is midday, the maid could come looking for me at any moment. We mustn't stay here any longer."

And so irresistibly did her own strength dominate his will that, just as in the past, he obeyed her without a word. They went down to the reception rooms, through the front hall and to the door without another word, without exchanging a glance. At the door, he suddenly turned to her.

"I can't say any more to you now, forgive me. I will write to you."

She smiled at him gratefully. "Yes, do write to me, Ludwig, that will be better."

And no sooner was he back in his hotel room than he sat down at the desk and wrote her a long letter, compulsively carried along by his suddenly thwarted passion from word to word, from page to page. This was his last day in Germany for months, he wrote, for years, perhaps for ever, and he would not, could not leave her like this, pretending to make cool conversation, forced into the mendacity of correct social behaviour. He wanted to, he must talk to her once more, away from the house, away from fears and memories and the oppressive, inhibiting, watchful atmosphere of its rooms. So he was asking whether she would take the evening train with him to Heidelberg, where they had both once been for a brief visit a decade ago when they were still strangers to one another, yet already feeling a presentiment of intimacy. Today, however, it would be to say goodbye, a last goodbye, it was what he still most profoundly desired. He was asking her to give him this one evening, this night. He hastily sealed the letter and sent it over to her house by messenger. In quarter-of-an-hour the messenger was back, bringing a small envelope sealed with yellow wax. His hand trembled as he tore it open. There was only a note inside it, a few words in her firm, determined handwriting, set down on the paper in haste, yet in her forceful handwriting:

"What you ask is folly, but I never could, I never will deny you anything. I will come."

The train slowed down as they passed the flickering lights of a station. Instinctively the dreamer's gaze moved away from introspection to look outside himself, again seeking tenderly for the figure of his dream in the alternating light and shade. Yes, there she was, ever faithful, always silently loving, she had come with him, to him—again and again he savoured her physical presence. And as if something in her had sensed his questing glance, feeling that shyly caressing touch from afar, she sat up straight now and looked out of the window beyond which the vague outlines of the landscape, wet in the spring darkness, slipped past like glittering water.

"We should be arriving soon," she said as if to herself.

"Yes," he said, sighing deeply, "it has taken so long."

He himself did not know whether, by those words impatiently uttered, he meant the train journey or all the long years leading up to this hour—a confused sense of mingled dream and reality surged through him. He felt only that beneath him the rattling wheels were rolling on towards something, towards some moment that, now in a strangely muted mood, he could not clarify in his mind. No, he would not think of that, he would let an invisible power carry him on as it willed, with his limbs relaxed, towards something mysterious. He felt a kind of bridal expectation, sweet and sensuous yet vaguely mingled with anticipatory fear of its own fulfilment, with the mysterious shiver felt when something endlessly desired suddenly comes physically close to the aston- ished heart. But he must not think that out to the end now, he must not want anything, desire anything, he must simply stay like this, carried on into the unknown as if in a dream, carried on by a strange torrent, without physical sensation and yet still feeling, desiring yet achieving nothing, moving on into his fate and back into himself. Oh, to stay like this for hours longer, for an eternity, in this continuous twilight, surrounded by dreams—but already, like a faint fear, the thought came into his mind that this could soon be over.

Here and there, in all directions, electric sparks of light were flickering on in the valley like fireflies, brighter and brighter as they blinked past. Street lamps closed together in straight double rows, the tracks were rattling by, and already a pale dome of brighter vapour was emerging from the darkness.

"Heidelberg," said one of the legal gentlemen to his compan- ions. All three picked up their bulging briefcases and hurried out of the compartment so as to reach the carriage door as soon as possible. The wheels, with brakes applied to them, were now jolting and rattling into the station. There was an abrupt, bone-shaking jerk, the train's speed slackened, and the wheels squealed only once more, like a tortured animal. For a second the two of them sat alone, facing each other, as if startled by the sudden onset of reality.

"Are we there already?" She sounded almost alarmed.

"Yes," he replied, and stood up. "Can I help you?" She refused with a gesture and went quickly ahead. But on the step down from the carriage she hesitated, her foot faltering for a moment as if about to step down into ice-cold water. Then she pulled herself together, and he followed in silence. And then they stood on the platform side by side for a moment, helpless with awkward emotion, like strangers, and the small suitcase weighed heavy as it dangled from his hand. Suddenly the engine beside them, snorting again, let off steam shrilly. She started, and then looked at him, her face pale, her eyes unsure and bewildered.

"What is it?" he asked.

"A pity it's over; it was so pleasant, just riding along like that. I could have gone on for hours and hours."

He said nothing. He had been thinking just the same at that moment. But now it *was* over, and something had to happen.

"Shall we go?" he cautiously asked.

"Yes, let's go," she murmured barely audibly. None the less, they still stood there side by side, as if some spring inside them had broken. Only then—and he forgot to take her arm—did they turn undecidedly away towards the station exit.

They left the station, but no sooner were they out of the door than stormy noise met their ears, drums rattling, the shrill sound of pipes—it was a patriotic demonstration of veterans' associations and students in support of the Fatherland. Like walls on the move, marching in ranks four abreast, flags flying, men in military garb were goose-stepping along, feet thudding heavily on the ground, marching all in time like a single man, necks thrown stiffly back, the very image of powerful determination with mouths open in song, one voice, one step, keeping time. In front marched generals, white-haired dignitaries bedecked with orders and flanked by companies of younger men, marching with athletic firmness, carrying huge banners held vertically erect and bearing death's heads, the swastika, the banners of the Reich waving in the wind, their broad chests thrust out, their heads braced as if to march against an enemy's batteries. They marched in a throng—they might have been propelled forward by a fist keeping time—all in geometrical order, preserving a distance as precise as if it had been drawn by compasses, keeping step, every nerve gravely tensed, a menacing expression on their faces, and every time a new rank—of veterans, of youth groups, of students—passed the raised platform where percussion instruments kept drumming out a steely rhythm on an invisible anvil, the many heads turned with military precision. With one accord they looked left, a movement running along the backs of all those necks, and the banners were raised as if on strings before the army commander who, stony-faced, was taking the salute of these civilians. Beardless boys, youths with the first down on their chins, faces etched with the lines of age, workers, students, soldiers or boys, they all looked exactly the same for that split second, with their harsh, determined, angry expressions, chins defiantly jutting, hands going to the hilts of invisible swords. And again and again, from troop to troop, the drumbeat hammered out, its monotony doubly inflaming feelings, keeping the marchers' backs straight, their eyes hard, forging war and vengeance by their invisible presence here in a peaceful square, under a sky with soft clouds sweetly passing over it.

"Madness," he exclaimed to himself, in astonishment, faltering. "Madness! What do they want? Once again, once again!"

War once again, war that had so recently shattered his whole life? With a strange shudder, he looked at those young faces, staring at the black mass on the move in ranks of four, like a square strip of film running, unrolling out of a narrow alley as if out of a dark box, and every face it showed was instantly rigid with bitter determination, a threat, a weapon. Why was this threat so noisily uttered on a mild June evening, hammered home in a gently dreaming city?

"What do they want? What do they want?" The question still had him by the throat. Only just now he had seen the world in bright, musical clarity, with the light of love and tenderness shining over it, he had been part of a melody of kindness and trust. And suddenly the iron steps of that marching throng were treading everything down, men girding themselves for the fray, men of a thousand different kinds, shouting with a thousand voices, yet expressing only one thing in their eyes and their onward march, hate, hate, hate.

He instinctively took her arm so as to feel something warm, love, passion, kindness, sympathy, a soft, soothing sensation, yet the drums broke through his inner silence, and now that all the thousands of voices were raised in what was unmistakably a war song, now that the ground was shaking with feet marching in time, the air exploding in sudden jubilant hurrahs from the huge mob, he felt as if something tender and sweet-sounding inside him was crushed by the powerful, noisily forceful drone of reality.

A slight movement at his side drew his attention to her hand with its gloved fingers, gently deterring his own from clenching so wildly into a fist. Then he turned his eyes, which had been fixed on the crowd—she was looking at him pleadingly, without words, he merely felt her gently compelling touch on his arm.

"Yes, let's go," he murmured, pulling himself together, hunching his shoulders as if to ward off something invisible, and he began forcing a way through the conveniently close-packed crowd of spectators, all staring as silently as he had been, spellbound, at the never-ending march past of these military legions. He did not know where he was going, he just wanted to get out of this tumultuous crowd, away from this square where all that was gentle in him, all dreams, were being ground down as if in a mortar by this pitiless rhythm. Just to get away, be alone with her, with this one woman, surrounded by the dark, under a roof, feeling her breath, able to look into her eyes at his leisure, unwatched, for the first time in ten years, to enjoy being alone with her. It was something he had promised himself in so many dreams, and now it was almost swept away by that swirling human mass marching and singing, a surging wave constantly breaking over itself. His nervous gaze went to the buildings, all with banners draped over their facades, but many of them had gold lettering proclaiming that they were business premises, and some were restaurants. All at once he felt the little suitcase pulling slightly at his hand, conveying a message—he longed to rest, to be at home somewhere, and alone! To buy a handful of silence and a few square metres of space! And as if in answer, the gleaming golden name of a hotel now leaped to the eye above a tall stone façade, and its glazed porch curved out to meet them. He was walking slowly, taking shallow breaths. Almost dazed, he stopped, and instinctively let go of her arm. "This is supposed to be a good hotel. It was recommended to me," he said untruthfully and awkwardly.

She flinched back in alarm, blood pouring into her pale face. He lips moved, trying to say something—perhaps the same words she had said ten years ago, that distressed, "Not now! Not here."

But then she saw his gaze turning to her, anxious, disturbed, nervous. And she bowed her head in silent consent, and followed him, with small and daunted steps, to the entrance.

In the reception area of the hotel a porter, wearing a brightly coloured cap and with the self-important air of a ship's captain at his lookout post, stood behind the desk that kept them at a distance. He did not move towards them as they hesitantly entered, merely cast a fleeting and disparaging look at them, taking in the small suitcase. He waited, and they had to approach him. He was now apparently busy again with the folio pages of the big register open before him. Only when the prospective guests were right in front of him did he raise cool eyes to inspect them objectively and severely. "Have you booked in with us, sir?" He then responded to the almost guilty negative by leafing through the register again. "I'm afraid we are fully booked. There was a big ceremony here today, the consecration of the flag—but," he added graciously, "I'll see what I can do."

Oh, to punch this sergeant-major with his braided uniform in the face, thought the humiliated man bitterly. A beggar again, a petitioner, an intruder for the first time in a decade. But by now the self-satisfied porter had finished his lengthy study of the register. "Number twenty-seven has just fallen vacant, a double room, if you'd care to take that." What was there to do but to say, with a muted growl, a swift, "Yes, that will do," and his restless fingers took the key handed to him, impatient as he already was to have silent walls between himself and this man. Then, behind him, he heard the stern voice again: "Register here, please," and a rectangular form was place in front of him, with ten or twelve headings to boxes that must be filled in with title, name, age, place of origin, place of residence, all the intrusive questions that officialdom puts to living human beings. The distasteful task was quickly performed, pencil flying—only when he had to enter her surname, untruthfully uniting it in marriage with his (though once that had been his secret wish), did the light weight of the pencil shake clumsily in his hand. "Duration of stay, please," demanded the implacable doorman, running his eye over the completed form and pointing to the one box still empty. "One day," wrote the pencil angrily. In his agitation he felt his moist forehead and had to take off his hat, the air here in this strange place seemed so oppressive.

"First floor on the left," said a courteous waiter, swiftly coming up as the exhausted man turned aside. But he was looking around for her. All through this procedure she had been standing motionless, showing intense interest in a poster announcing a Schubert recital to be given by an unknown singer, but as she stood there, very still, a slight quiver kept passing over her shoulders like the wind blowing over a grassy meadow. He noticed, ashamed, how she was controlling her agitation by main force; why, he thought against his will, did I tear her away from her quiet home to bring her here? But now there was no going back. "Come on," he urged her quietly. Without showing him her face, she moved away from the poster that meant nothing to them and went ahead up the stairs, slowly and treading heavily, with difficulty—like an old woman, he involuntarily reflected.

That thought lasted for a mere second as she made her way up the few steps, with her hand on the banister rail, and he immediately banished the ugly idea. But something cold and hurtful remained in his mind, replacing the thought he had so forcibly dismissed from it.

At last they were upstairs in the corridor—those two silent minutes had been an eternity. A door stood open. It was the door of their room, and the chambermaid was still busy with broom and duster in it. "I'll soon be finished," she excused herself. "The room's only this moment been vacated, but sir and madam can come in, I'll just fetch clean sheets."

They went in. The air in the closed room was musty and sweetish, smelling of olive soap and cold cigarette smoke. Somewhere the unseen trace of other guests still lingered.

Boldly, perhaps still warm from human bodies, the unmade double bed bore visible witness to the point and purpose of this room. He was nauseated by its explicit meaning, and instinctively went to the window and opened it. Soft damp air, mingled with the muted noise of the street, drifted slowly in past the gently fluttering curtains. He stayed there at the open window, looking out intently at the now dark rooftops. How ugly this room was, how shaming their presence here seemed, how disappointing was this moment when they were together, a moment longed for so much over the years—but neither he nor she had wanted it to be so sudden, to show itself in all its shameless nudity! For the space of three, four, five breaths—he counted them—he looked out, too cowardly to speak first, but then he forced himself to do so. No, no, this would not do, he said. And just as he had known and feared in advance, she stood in the middle of the room as if turned to stone in her grey dustcoat, her arms hanging down as if they had snapped, as if she were something that did not belong here and had entered this unpleasant room only by the accident of force and chance. She had taken off her gloves, obviously to put them down, but then she must have felt revulsion against the idea of placing them anywhere here, and so they dangled empty from her fingers, like the husks of her hands. Her gaze was fixed, her eyes veiled, but when he turned they looked at

him with a plea in them. He understood. "Why don't we—"
and his voice stumbled over the breath he was expelling—"why
don't we go for a little walk? It's so gloomy in here."

"Yes, yes!" She uttered the word as if liberating it, letting fear
off the chain. And already her hand was reaching for the door
handle. He followed her more slowly, and saw her shoulders
shaking like the flanks of an animal when it has just escaped
the clutch of deadly claws.

The street was waiting, warm and crowded. In the wake of the
ceremonial rally, the human current was still restless, so they
turned off into quieter streets, finding the path through the woods
that had taken them up to the castle on an excursion ten years
ago. "It was a Sunday, do your remember?" he said, instinctively
speaking in a loud voice, and she, obviously calling the same
memory to mind, replied quietly, "I haven't forgotten anything
I did with you. Otto had his school friend with him, and they
hurried on ahead so fast that we almost lost them in the woods.
I called for him, telling him to come back, and I didn't do it
willingly, because I so much wanted to be alone with you. But
we were still strangers to each other at that time."

"And today too," he said, trying to make a joke of it. But she
did not reply. I ought not to have said that, he felt vaguely; what
makes me keep comparing the past with the present? But why
can't I say anything right to her today? The past always comes
between us, the time that has gone by.

So they climbed the rising slope of the road in silence. The
houses below them were already huddling close together in the
faint light, the curving river showed more clearly in the twilight
of the valley, while here the trees rustled and darkness fell over
them. No one came towards them, only their own shadows

went ahead in silence. And whenever a lamp by the roadside cast its light on them at an angle, the shadows ahead merged as if embracing, stretching, longing for one another, two bodies in one form, parting again only to embrace once more, while they themselves walked on, tired and apart from each other. As if spellbound, he watched this strange game, that escape and recapture and separation again of the soulless figures, shadowy bodies that were only the reflection of their own. With a kind of sick curiosity he saw the flight and merging of those insubstantial figures, and as he watched the black, flowing, fleeting image before him, he almost forgot the living woman at his side. He was not thinking clearly of anything, yet he felt vaguely that this furtive game was a warning of something that lay deep as a well within him, but was now insistently rising, like the bucket dipped into the well menacingly reaching the surface. What was it? He strained every sense. What was the shadow play here in the sleeping woods telling him? There must be words in it, a situation, something he had experienced, heard, felt, something hidden in a melody, a deeply buried memory that he had not touched for many years.

And suddenly it came to him, a lightning flash in the darkness of oblivion—yes, words, a poem that she had once read aloud to him in the drawing room in the evening. A French poem, he still knew the words, and as if blown to him by a hot wind they were suddenly rising to his lips; he heard those forgotten lines from a poem in another language spoken, over a space of ten years, in her voice:

> *Dans le vieux parc solitaire et glacé*
> *Deux spectres cherchent le passé.*

And as soon as those lines lit up in his memory, an image joined them at magical speed—the lamp with its golden light in the darkened drawing room where she had read Verlaine's poem to him one evening. He saw her in the shadow cast by the lamp, sitting both near to him and far away, beloved and out of reach, he suddenly felt his own heart of those days hammering with excitement to hear her voice coming to him on the musical wave of the words, hearing her say the words of the poem—although only in the poem—words that spoke of love and longing, in a foreign language and meant for a stranger, yet it was intoxicating to hear them in that voice, her voice. He wondered how he could have forgotten it all these years, that poem, that evening when they had been on their own in the house, confused because they were alone, taking flight from the dangers of conversation into the easier terrain of books, where a confession of more intimate feelings sometimes showed clearly through the words and the melody, flashing like light in the bushes, sparkling intangibly, yet comforting without any palpable presence. How could he have forgotten it for so long? But how was it that the forgotten poem had suddenly surfaced again? Involuntarily, he spoke the lines aloud, translating them:

> *In the old park, in ice and snow caught fast*
> *Two spectres walk, still searching for the past.*

And no sooner had he said it than she understood, and placed the room-key, heavy and shining, in his hand, so abruptly did that one sharply outlined, bright association plucked from the sleeping depths of memory come to the surface. The shadows there on the path had touched and woken her own words, and more besides. With a shiver running down his spine, he suddenly felt the full truth and sense of them. Had not those spectres searching for their past been muted questions, asked of a time that was no longer real, mere shadows wanting to come back to life but unable to do so now? Neither she nor he was the same any more, yet they were searching for each other in a vain effort, fleeing one another, persisting in disembodied, powerless efforts like those black spectres at their feet.

Unconsciously, he must have groaned aloud, for she turned. "What's the matter, Ludwig? What are you thinking of?"

But he merely dismissed it, saying, "Nothing, nothing!" And he listened yet more intently to what was within him, to the past, to see whether that voice of memory truly foretelling the future would not speak to him again, revealing the present to him as well as the past.